Praise for Susanna Gregory

'A lively and intelligent tale set vividly in turbulent medieval England' *Publishers Weekly* on *An Unholy Alliance*

'A good, serious and satisfying read'
Irish Times on *A Masterly Murder*

'Excellent . . . the historical research is first rate. All in all, great entertainment for cold winter days'
Eurocrime on *To Kill or Cure*

'Once again Susanna Gregory has combined historical accuracy, amusing characterisation and a corking good plot to present a section of British history that is often overlooked: the emergence from the Dark Ages to Renaissance in the field of education and medicine' *Historical Novel Society* on *A Poisonous Plot*

'Carefully researched, imaginative and evocative . . . this is a gritty but humorous period mystery'
Good Book Guide on *The Cheapside Corpse*

'Gregory never fails to impress with her immaculate research, creating an exciting and vivid historical, social and political backdrop and embellishing her stories with authentic detail and thrilling atmosphere'
Lancashire Evening Post on *The Chelsea Strangler*

Also by Susanna Gregory

The Thomas Chaloner series

A Conspiracy of Violence
Blood on the Strand
The Butcher of Smithfield
The Westminster Poisoner
A Murder on London Bridge
The Body in the Thames
The Piccadilly Plot
Death in St James's Park
Murder on High Holborn
The Cheapside Corpse
The Chelsea Strangler

The Matthew Bartholomew series

A Plague on Both Your Houses
An Unholy Alliance
A Bone of Contention
A Deadly Brew
A Wicked Deed
A Masterly Murder
An Order for Death
A Summer of Discontent
A Killer in Winter
The Hand of Justice
The Mark of a Murderer
The Tarnished Chalice
To Kill or Cure
The Devil's Disciples
A Vein of Deceit
The Killer of Pilgrims
Mystery in the Minster
Murder by the Book
The Lost Abbot
Death of a Scholar
A Poisonous Plot
A Grave Concern

SUSANNA GREGORY

A PLAGUE ON BOTH YOUR HOUSES

sphere

SPHERE

First published in Great Britain as a paperback original in 1996 by Warner Books
Published from 2003 by Time Warner Paperbacks
Published from 2007 by Sphere
This edition reissued in 2016 by Sphere

1 3 5 7 9 10 8 6 4 2

A CIP catalogue record for this book is available from the British Library.

ISBN 978-0-7515-6802-8

Printed and bound in Great Britain by Clays Ltd, St Ives plc

Papers used by Sphere are from well-managed forests
and other responsible sources.

MIX
Paper from
responsible sources
FSC® C104740

Sphere
An imprint of
Little, Brown Book Group
Carmelite House
50 Victoria Embankment
London EC4Y 0DZ

An Hachette UK Company
www.hachette.co.uk

www.littlebrown.co.uk

fOREWORD

I well remember meeting Susanna Gregory for the first time. It was at Dead on Deansgate, a popular crime festival run by the Crime Writers' Association and Waterstones in the nineties, and because it was my first visit, I was quite nervous. It was a relief to meet another new writer, although she was not overwhelmed like me. She was much more confident and assured.

Susanna was already known to me. I had read her first novel *A Plague on Both Your Houses*, and from that moment I was hooked. Susanna has an immediacy and clarity of style that is a delight. She can summarise a character with the precision of a Conan Doyle, so that the reader instantly recognises that person even in a book populated with a large cast, and can perfectly depict the motivations of many different men and women so that each is defined and comprehensible and adds to her plots.

For such a delightful woman, I was surprised at the ferocity of her stories, because they are not for the faint-hearted. These are tales of violence and murder that reek of authenticity. That she has a genuine under-standing of crimes and the savagery of men is undoubted. I confess, it surprised me when I met her in the flesh. Her writing didn't seem to match the quiet, amiable author I encountered at Deansgate.

Appearances in the CWA can be deceptive. When I got to know her better I learned that after university Susanna had been a police officer in Leeds with the West Yorkshire Police. That made her understanding of crime more comprehensible. And it must be a great benefit for a crime writer, to have witnessed crime scenes and to have been involved in investigations.

But police work did not suit her. Susanna went to Durham University for post-graduate studies and then went on to Cambridge to take her PhD. She then conducted research on heavy-metal contaminants in the teeth and bones of marine mammals. Indeed, she has participated in more than twenty field trips to the Arctic and Antarctic.

However it was the author whom I grew to know and appreciate. Her creation, Matthew Bartholomew, is first introduced in *A Plague on Both Your Houses*. In this, as in *An Unholy Alliance* and *A Bone of Contention*, he is the investigator of a series of murders set against the back-ground of the Black Death, the plague that cut down perhaps a half of the population of Britain and Europe. These books are set so firmly in their period that the plague is almost a character in its own right. Although it only hits Cambridge one third of the way into the first book, even before that it is well established because of rumours of its passage across the country, and the over-worked physician Matthew must strain to help the peasants and the others in his college, Michaelhouse.

It is this, the college, that is the second strand to her work, and that provides such strength to her stories. Michaelhouse is a college in the university at Cambridge. It is desperate to compete with Oxford and secure its position. For that the senior fellows of Cambridge are prepared to consider all methods to further their colleges. Political intrigues between the two universities, between individual colleges, and still more between those who seek to control the colleges, give life and zest to her tales. Rarely has internal company politics been stripped so bare between the pages of a book.

If Susanna had only written the Matthew Bartholomew series, she would have cause for pride, but of course she has written much more. Her Thomas Chaloner series is enormously popular, as is the collaborative Simon Beaufort series, written with her husband Beau Riffenburgh, and her work with Medieval Murderers. Indeed, she must be one of the nation's most prolific writers, with some forty-five published novels and ten more collaborations to her name. Very few authors ever achieve such a rate.

Susanna Gregory has been my Queen of Crime for many years. I am honoured to have known her for twenty years, and delighted to celebrate her wonderful writing with this collection of the first three books she wrote, all of them favourites of mine. I hope you like them too.

Michael Jecks
August 2016

Michael Jecks is the author of the Templar medieval mysteries set in the West Country as well as the Hundred Years War trilogy, and has just started a new Tudor series. He is also a member of the Medieval Murderers.

To my husband for his encouragement and enthusiasm

Cambridge circa 1348

Castle
All Saints
St. Giles
St. Peters
Chesterton Lane
Barnwell Way

Scale of Yards
100 50 0 100 200 300

Great Bridge
St. Clement
School of Pythagoras
Bridge Street
King's Ditch
St. Radegund's (Benedictine Convent)
Barnwell Causeway
St. John's Hospital
King's Hall
Round Church
All Saints
Franciscan Friary
Michaelhouse
King's Childer Lane
Milne Lane
High Street
Barnwell Field
St. Michael's Lane
Penney Lane
St. Michael
Trinity Hall
Holy Trinity
Barnwell Gate
St. Mary
Clare College
St. Andrew the Great
St. John Zachary
St. Edward
King's Ditch
Milne Street
Dominican Friary
St. Benedict
Carmelites
Trumpington Gate
St. Botolph
Small Bridges
Hall of Valence Marie
Mill
St. Peter Without
Peterhouse
St. Edmund's Priory (Canons of St. Gilbert of Sempringham)

N
W E
S

Michaelhouse circa 1348

1 Students
2 Alcote
3 Medical store
4 Bartholomew and Abigny
5 Kelfrith
6 William
7 Wilson
8 Michael
9 Olivers
10 Swynford
11 Augustus's room
12 Commoners' room

Upper Floor

Servery | 7 | 1 | 1 | 1 | 8

Hall

Stairs

High Table

Hearth

Servants' Quarters

'Conclave'

12 | 11 | 10 | 1 | 9

Ground Floor

Brewery

Store

Fish-ponds

Well

Bakery

Buttery | 1 | 1 | 1 | 2 | 3 | 4

Pantry

Stables

Kitchens

Porter's Lodge

Stairs

Main Gate

Store

Kitchen Gardens

Apple trees

Laundry

Kitchen

Outbuildings

Pantry

Pantry | 1 | 1 | 1 | 5 | 1 | 6

Back Gate

Not to scale

PROLOGUE

Cambridge, 1348

THE SCHOLAR WAITED IN THE BLACK SHADOWS OF the churchyard trees for the Sheriff's night patrol to pass by, trying to control his breathing. Two of the men stopped so close that he could have reached out and touched them. They stood for several minutes, leaning against the wall surrounding the churchyard, looking up and down the deserted road. The scholar held his breath until he thought he would choke. He could not be discovered now: there was so much to lose.

Eventually, the Sheriff's men left, and the scholar took several unsteady breaths, forcing himself to remain in the safety of the shadows until he was certain that they had gone. He jumped violently as a large cat stalked past his hiding place, glancing at him briefly with alert yellow eyes. He watched it sit for a moment in the middle of the road, before it disappeared up a dark alleyway.

The scholar gripped the voluminous folds of his cloak, so that he would not stumble on them, and slipped out of the trees into the road. The moon was almost full, and shed an eerie white light along the main street. He peered carefully both ways, and, satisfied that there was

1

no one to see him, he made his way stealthily down the street towards his home.

The main gates of the College were locked, but the scholar had ensured that the little-used back door was left open. He turned from the High Street into St Michael's Lane. He was almost there.

He froze in horror as he saw someone was already in the lane: another scholar, also disobeying College rules by being out at night, was walking towards him. Heart thumping, he ducked into a patch of tall nettles and weeds at the side of the road, in the hope that his stillness and dark cloak would keep him hidden. He heard the footsteps come closer and closer. Blood pounded in his ears, and he found he was trembling uncontrollably. The footsteps were almost level with him. Now he would be uncovered and dragged from his hiding place!

He almost cried in relief as the footfall passed him by, and faded as his colleague turned the corner into the High Street. He stood shakily, oblivious to the stinging of the nettles on his bare hands, and ran to the back gate. Once inside, he barred it with unsteady hands, and made his way to the kitchens. Faint with relief, he sank down next to the embers of the cooking fire and waited until his trembling had ceased. As he prepared to return to his room to sleep away what little remained of the night, he wondered how many more such trips he might make before he was seen.

Several hours later, the Bishop's Mill miller dragged himself from his bed, tugged on his boots, and set off to his work. The sky was beginning to turn from dark blue to silver in the east, and the miller shivered in the crispness of the early morning. He unlocked the door to the building and then went to feed the fat pony that he kept to carry flour to the town.

A short distance away, he could hear the rhythmic whine and swish of the water-wheel, powered by a fast-running channel diverted from the river. The miller had grown so familiar with its sound that he never noticed it unless there was something wrong. And there was something wrong this morning. There was an additional thump in the rhythm.

The miller sighed irritably. Only the previous week he had been forced to ask the help of his neighbours to free the branch of a tree that had entangled itself in the wheel, and he was loathe to impose on their good graces again so soon. He tossed some oats to the pony, and, wiping his hands on his tunic, he went to investigate. As he drew nearer, he frowned in puzzlement. It did not sound like a branch had been caught, but something soggier and less rigid. He rounded the corner and approached the great wheel, creaking and pounding as the water roared past it.

He felt his knees turn to jelly as he saw the wheel and what was caught in it, and sank onto the grass, unable to tear his eyes away. The body of a man was impaled there, black robes flapping wetly around him as the wheel dragged him under the water again and again. As the wheel lifted the body, one arm flopped loose in a ghostly parody of a wave, which continued until the body dived, feet first, back into the water for another cycle. The horrified miller watched the body salute him three times before he was able to scramble to his feet and race towards the town screaming for help.

1

THE DULL THUD OF HORSES' HOOVES AND THE
gentle patter of rain on the wooden coffin were
the only sounds to disturb the silence of the dawn.
Black-gowned scholars walked slowly in single file along
the High Street, following the funeral cart past the town
gate to the fields beyond, where the body of their Master,
Sir John Babington, would be laid in its final resting place.
Somewhere behind him, Matthew Bartholomew heard
one of the students stifle a giggle. He turned round and
scowled in the general direction of the offending noise.
Nerves, doubtless, he thought, for it was not every day
that the College buried a Master who had taken his own
life in such a bizarre manner.

The small procession was allowed through the gate
by sleepy night-watchmen who came to the door of their
guardroom to look. One of them furtively nudged the
other and both smirked. Bartholomew took a step towards
them, but felt Brother Michael's restraining hand on his
shoulder. Michael was right; it would be wrong to turn
Sir John's funeral into a brawl. Bartholomew brought
his anger under control. Sir John had been one of the
few men in the University who had been liked by the
townspeople, but they had been quick to turn against

him once the manner of his death became known. Had Sir John died a natural death, he would have been buried in the small churchyard of St Michael's, and been given a glorious funeral. Instead, church law decreed that, as a suicide, he should be buried in unconsecrated ground, and be denied any religious ceremony. So, in the first grey light of day, Sir John was escorted out of the city by the scholars of Michaelhouse, to be laid to rest in the waterlogged fields behind the church of St Peter-without-Trumpington Gate.

The horse pulling the cart bearing the coffin stumbled in the mud, causing the cart to lurch precariously. Bartholomew sprang forward to steady it, and was surprised to see Thomas Wilson, the man most likely to be Sir John's successor, do the same. The eyes of the two men met for an instant, and Wilson favoured Bartholomew with one of his small pious smiles. Bartholomew looked away. No love had been lost between the smug, self-satisfied Wilson and Sir John, and it galled Bartholomew to watch Wilson supervise Sir John's meagre funeral arrangements. He took a deep breath, and tried not to think how much he would miss Sir John's gentle humour and sensible rule.

Wilson gave an imperious wave of a flabby white hand, and Bartholomew's book-bearer, Cynric ap Huwydd, hurried forward to help the ostler lead the horse off the road and across the rough land to the grave site. The cart swayed and tipped, and the coffin bounced, landing with a hollow thump. Wilson seized Cynric's shoulder angrily, berating him for being careless in a loud, penetrating whisper.

Bartholomew had had enough. Motioning to the other Fellows, he edged Sir John's coffin from the cart, and together they lifted it onto their shoulders. They began the long walk across the fields to where the grave had been dug in a ring of sturdy oak trees. Bartholomew had chosen the spot because he knew Sir John had liked to read in the shade of the trees in the summer, but he began to doubt his choice as the heavy wood cut into his shoulder and his arms began to ache. After a few minutes, he felt himself being nudged aside, and smiled gratefully as the students came forward to take their turn.

Wilson walked ahead, and stood waiting at the graveside, head bowed and hands folded in his sleeves like a monk. The students lowered their burden to the ground and looked at Bartholomew expectantly. He arranged some ropes, and the coffin was lowered into the ground. He nodded to Cynric and the other book-bearers to start to fill in the grave, and, taking a last look, he turned to go home.

'Friends and colleagues,' began Wilson in his rich, self-important voice, 'we are gathered together to witness the burial of our esteemed Master, Sir John Babington.'

Bartholomew froze in his tracks. The Fellows had agreed the night before that no words would be spoken: it was felt that there were none needed – for what could be said about Sir John's extraordinary suicide? It had been decided that the Fellows and the students should escort Sir John to his resting place in silence, and return to the College still in silence, as a mark of respect. Sir John had done much to bring a relative peace to his College in a city where the scholars waged a constant war with each other and with the townsfolk. A few of his policies had made him unpopular with some University authorities, especially those who regarded learning to be the domain of the rich.

'Sir John,' Wilson intoned, 'was much loved by us all.' At this, Bartholomew gazed at Wilson in disbelief. Wilson had led the opposition to almost anything Sir John had tried to do, and on more than one occasion had left the hall at dinner red-faced with impotent fury because Sir John had easily defeated his arguments with his quiet logic.

'He will be sorely missed,' continued Wilson, looking down mournfully as Cynric shovelled earth.

'Not by you!' muttered Giles Abigny, the College's youthful teacher of philosophy, so that only Bartholomew could hear him. 'Not when you stand to gain so much.'

'May the Lord look upon his soul with mercy,' Wilson continued, 'and forgive him for his iniquitous ways.'

Bartholomew felt the anger boil inside him. He thrust his clenched fists under his scholar's tabard so that they should not betray his fury to the students, and looked to see the reaction of the other Fellows. Abigny was positively glowering at Wilson, while Brother Michael watched with a sardonic smile. The other theologians, Father William and Father Aelfrith, were more difficult to read. Bartholomew knew that Aelfrith did not like Wilson, but was too politic to allow it to show. William, who had backed Wilson on many occasions against Sir John, now stood listening impassively. The last two Fellows, Roger Alcote and Robert Swynford, who taught the subjects of the Quadrivium, nodded at Wilson's words.

The book-bearers had almost finished filling in the grave. A miserable drizzle-laden wind swished through the trees, and somewhere a lone blackbird was singing. Wilson's voice droned on with its platitudes for a man he had neither liked nor respected, and Bartholomew abruptly turned on his heel and strode away. He heard Wilson falter for an instant, but then continue louder than before so that the wind carried his words to Bartholomew as he walked away.

'May the Lord look kindly on the College, and guide her in all things.'

Bartholomew allowed himself a disgusted snort. Presumably, Wilson's idea of the Lord guiding the College was to make him, Wilson, the next Master. He heard footsteps hurrying behind him, and was not surprised that Giles Abigny had followed his lead and left the group.

'We will be in trouble, Matt,' he said with a sidelong grin at Bartholomew. 'Walking out on Master Wilson's carefully prepared speech.'

'Not Master yet,' said Bartholomew, 'although I imagine that will come within the week.'

They arrived back at the road and paused to scrape some of the clinging mud from their boots. It started to rain hard and Bartholomew felt water trickling down his back. He looked back across the field, and saw Wilson leading the procession back to the College. Abigny took his arm.

'I am cold and wet. Shall we see if Hugh Stapleton will give us breakfast at Bene't Hostel? What I need now is a roaring fire and some strong wine.' He leaned a little closer. 'Our lives at Michaelhouse will soon change beyond anything we can imagine – if we have a livelihood there at all. Let us make the best of our freedom while we still have it.'

He tugged at Bartholomew's sleeve, urging him back along the High Street towards Bene't Hostel. Bartholomew thought for a moment before following. Behind them, Wilson's procession filed through the town gate as he led the way back to Michaelhouse. Wilson's lips pursed as he saw Bartholomew and Abigny disappear through the hostel door; he was not a man to forget insults to his pride.

As Bartholomew had predicted, Wilson was installed as the new Master of Michaelhouse within a week of Sir John's funeral. The students, commoners, and servants watched as the eight Fellows filed into the hall to begin the process of electing a new Master. The College statutes ordered that a new Master should be chosen by the Chancellor from two candidates selected by the Fellows. Bartholomew sat at the long table, picking idly at a splinter of wood while his colleagues argued. Wilson had support from Alcote, Swynford and Father William. Bartholomew, Brother Michael and Abigny wanted Father Aelfrith to be the other candidate, but Bartholomew knew which of the two the Chancellor would select, and was reluctant to become too embroiled in a debate he could not win. Eventually, seeing that it would divide the College in a way that neither Wilson nor Aelfrith could heal, Aelfrith declined to allow his name to go forward. Alcote offered to take his place, a solution that met with little enthusiasm from either side.

The Chancellor selected Wilson, who immediately began in the way he intended to continue, by having three students 'sent down' for playing dice on a Sunday, sacking the brewer for drinking, and declaring that everyone –

Fellows, commoners and students – should wear only black on Sundays. Bartholomew had to lend several of his poorer students the money to purchase black leggings or tunics, since they only possessed garments made of cheap brown homespun wool, which were harder-wearing and more practical than the more elegant black.

The day of Wilson's installation dawned clear and blue, although judging from the clatter and raised voices from the kitchen, most of the servants had been up with their duties all night. Bartholomew rose as the sky began to lighten, and donned the ceremonial red gown that marked him as a Doctor of the University. He sat on the bed again and looked morosely through the window across the yard. Term had not yet begun, so there were only fifteen students in residence, but they made up for the deficit with excited shouting and a good deal of running. Through the delicate arched windows opposite, he could see Fathers William and Aelfrith trying to quieten them down. Reluctantly, Bartholomew walked across the dry packed earth of the yard for breakfast in the hall, a rushed affair that was clearly an inconvenience for the harried servants.

The installation itself was grand and sumptuous. Dressed in a splendid gown of deep purple velvet with fur trimmings, and wearing his black tabard over the top, Wilson processed triumphantly through Cambridge, scattering pennies to the townsfolk. A few grubby urchins followed the procession, jeering insults, and several of the citizens spat in disdain. Wilson ignored them all, and throughout the long Latin ceremony at Michaelhouse in which he made his vows to uphold the College statutes and rules, he could scarcely keep the smug satisfaction from his face.

A PLAGUE ON BOTH YOUR HOUSES

Many influential people were present from the University and the town. The Bishop of Ely watched the proceedings with a bored detachment, while the Chancellor and the Sheriff exchanged occasional whispers. Some of the town's officials and merchants had been invited too. They stood together, displaying a magnificent collection of brilliant colours and expensive cloth. Bartholomew saw Thomas Exton, the town's leading physician, dressed in a gown of heavy blue silk, surrounded by his enormous brood of children. Near him was Bartholomew's brother-in-law, Sir Oswald Stanmore, who owned estates to the south of Cambridge, and had made a fortune in the wool trade. He was flanked by his younger brother, Stephen, and Bartholomew's sister Edith.

Giles Abigny had refused to attend, announcing that he had a disputation to organise with Hugh Stapleton, the Principal of Bene't Hostel. Brother Michael made his disapproval of Wilson known by muttering loudly throughout the proceedings, and by coughing, apparently uncontrollably, in those parts that should have been silent. Bartholomew did what was expected of him, but without enthusiasm, his thoughts constantly straying back to Sir John.

Bartholomew looked at Wilson in his finery seated in the huge wooden chair at the head of the high table in Michaelhouse's hall, and suddenly felt a surge of anger against Sir John. He had done so much to bring long-standing disputes between the University and the town to a halt, and, as a brilliant lawyer and stimulating teacher, had attracted many of the best students to the College. His lifelong ambition had been to write a book explaining the complexities of English law for students, a book that still lay unfinished in his rooms.

11

Everything had been going so well for Sir John and for the College under his care, so why had he killed himself?

Bartholomew, Father Aelfrith, and Robert Swynford had dined with Sir John the night before his death, and he had been in fine spirits then, full of enthusiasm for starting a new section of his book, and looking forward to a sermon he had been invited to give at the University Church. Bartholomew and the others had left Sir John around eight o'clock. Cynric had seen Sir John leave the College a short time later, the last to see him alive. The following morning, Sir John's body had been found in the water-wheel.

As a practising physician and the College's Master of Medicine, Bartholomew had been summoned to the river bank, where the white-faced miller stood as far away as he could from the corpse. Bartholomew shuddered as he thought about Sir John's body that morning. He tried to concentrate on Father William's rapid Latin in the ceremony that would install Thomas Wilson as the new Master of Michaelhouse.

Finally, Father William nodded to Cynric, who began to ring the bell to proclaim that the College ceremony was over. Noisily, the students began to clatter out of the hall, followed rather more sedately by the Fellows and commoners, all moving towards St Michael's Church, where the College would ask God's blessing on Wilson's appointment. Bartholomew paused to offer his arm to Augustus of Ely, one of the commoners, who had taught law at the University for almost forty years before old age made his mind begin to ramble, and he had been given permission by Sir John to spend the rest of his days housed and fed by the College. Michaelhouse had ten commoners. Six were old men, like Augustus, who had given a lifetime's service to the University; the others were visiting scholars who were using Michaelhouse's facilities for brief periods of study.

Augustus turned his milky blue eyes on Bartholomew and gave him a toothless grin as he was gently escorted out of the dim hall into the bright August sunshine.

'This is a sad day for the College,' he crowed to Bartholomew, drawing irritable looks from some of the other scholars.

'Hush, Augustus,' said Bartholomew, patting the veined old hand. 'What is done is done, and we must look to the future.'

'But such sin should not go unpunished,' the old man continued. 'Oh, no. It should not be forgotten.'

Bartholomew nodded patiently. Augustus's mind had become even more muddled after the death of Sir John. 'It will not be forgotten,' he said reassuringly. 'Everything will be well.'

'Fool!' Augustus wrenched his arm away from Bartholomew, who stared at him in surprise. 'Evil is afoot, and it will spread and corrupt us all, especially those who are unaware.' He took a step backwards, and tried to straighten his crooked limbs. 'Such sin must not go unpunished,' he repeated firmly. 'Sir John was going to see to that.'

'What do you mean?' asked Bartholomew, bewildered.

'Sir John had begun to guess,' said Augustus, his faded blue eyes boring into Bartholomew. 'And see what happened.'

'The man is senile.' Robert Swynford's booming voice close behind him made Bartholomew jump.

13

Augustus began to sway back and forth, chanting a hymn under his breath. 'See? He does not know what rubbish he speaks.' He put his arm over Augustus's shoulders and waved across for Alexander the Butler to come to take him back to his quarters. Augustus flinched away from his touch.

'I will take him,' said Bartholomew, noting the old man's distress. 'He has had enough for today. I will make a posset that will ease him.'

'Yes, all the pomp and ceremony has shaken his mind even more than usual,' said Swynford, eyeing Augustus with distaste. 'God preserve us from a mindless fool.'

'God preserve us from being one,' snapped Bartholomew, angered by Swynford's intolerance. He was surprised at his retort. He was not usually rude to his colleagues. Reluctantly, he admitted to himself that Wilson's installation and old Augustus's words had unsettled him.

'Come, Matt,' said Swynford, dropping his usual bluff manner. 'It has been a hard time for us all. Let us not allow the ramblings of a drooling old man to spoil our chances of a new beginning. The man's mind has become more unhinged since Sir John died. You said so yourself only yesterday.'

Bartholomew nodded. Two nights before, the entire College had been awakened by Augustus, who had locked himself in his room and was screaming that there were devils trying to burn him alive. He had the window shutters flung open, and was trying to crawl out. It had taken Bartholomew hours to calm him, and then he had had to promise to stay in Augustus's room for the rest of the night to ensure the devils did not return. In the morning, Bartholomew had been prodded awake by an

14

irate Augustus demanding to know what he was doing uninvited in his quarters.

Augustus stopped swaying and looked at Bartholomew, a crafty smile on his face. 'Just remember, John Babington, hide it well.'

Swynford tutted in annoyance. 'Take him to his bed, Alexander, and see that one of the servants stays with him. The poor man has totally lost the few remaining wits he had.'

Alexander solicitously escorted Augustus towards the north wing of the College where the commoners lived. As they went, Bartholomew could hear Augustus telling Alexander that he would not need any supper as he had just eaten a large rat he had seen coming out of the hall.

Swynford put his hand on Bartholomew's shoulder and turned him towards St Michael's. 'Tend to him later, Matt. We should take our places in the church.'

Bartholomew assented, and together they walked up St Michael's Lane to the High Street. Throngs of people milled around outside the church, attracted no doubt by hopes of more scattered pennies.

They elbowed their way through the crowd, earning hostile glances from some people. The last fight between the scholars and the townspeople had been less than a month before, and two young apprentices had been hanged for stabbing a student to death. Feelings still ran high, and Bartholomew was glad when he reached the church doors.

Father William had already begun to celebrate the mass, gabbling through the words at a speed that never failed to impress Bartholomew. The friar glanced across at the late-comers as they took their places at the altar rail, but his face betrayed no sign of annoyance. Brother Michael, for all his mumblings during the College ceremony, had rehearsed his choir well, and even the clamour of the people waiting outside lessened as angelic voices soared through the church.

Bartholomew smiled. Sir John had loved the choir, and often gave the children extra pennies to sing while he dined in College. Bartholomew wondered whether Master Wilson would spare a few pennies for music to brighten the long winter evenings. He stole a glance at Wilson to see if there was any indication that he was appreciating the singing. Wilson's head was bowed as he knelt, but his eyes were open and fixed on his hands. Bartholomew looked closer, and almost laughed aloud. Wilson was calculating something, counting on his fat, bejewelled fingers. His mind was as far from Michael's music or William's mass as Augustus's would have been.

The church became stuffy from the large number of people packed into it, and an overwhelming number of smells began to pervade: strongly scented cloth, sweat, incense, feet, and, as always, the rank stink of the river underlying it all. Occasionally, a cooling breeze would waft in through one of the glassless windows, bringing a moment of relief to those inside. Despite Father William's speedy diction, the ceremonial mass was long, and, for those townspeople who did not know Latin, incomprehensible. Students and citizens alike became bored: first they shuffled, trying to ease legs aching from standing, and then, restlessly, they began to whisper to each other.

Finally, the mass ended, and Wilson led the way out of the church and back to College for the celebratory feast. The sky that had been a brilliant blue for most of the day had started to cloud over. Bartholomew shivered, finding the fresh air chilly after the closeness of the church.

Outside, the crowd of townspeople had grown, drawn by the pomp and splendour. Bartholomew could see that their mood was surly, resentful of the wealth that bespoke itself in the gowns of many of the scholars, and of their assumed superiority. As Wilson's procession filed out of the church, Bartholomew could hear whispered comments about idle scholars draining the town of its affluence, comments that became more than whispers as the crowd grew in confidence.

Aware that such an ostentatious display of Michaelhouse wealth might serve to alienate the townspeople, Wilson had ordered that coins be distributed among the poor to celebrate his new post. Cynric and the other book-bearers, who had been told to give out the small leather bags containing pennies, were almost mobbed as the crowd surged towards them. Immediately, any semblance of order was lost, as handfuls of money were grabbed by those strong enough to push their way to the front. Fists began to fly, and the book-bearers beat a hasty retreat, leaving the crowd to fight over the coins.

Bartholomew saw students begin to group together, some of them holding sticks and small knives. Hastily he ordered them back to their Colleges or hostels. It would take very little to spark off a town brawl. Even the sight of a group of students, armed and spoiling for a fight, could be enough to start a full scale riot.

Most of the students left, many looking disappointed, but Bartholomew saw two of Michaelhouse's students, the Oliver brothers, darting here and there. Within a few minutes they had assembled a group of at least thirty black-gowned scholars, some from Michaelhouse, but most from other Colleges and hostels.

He groaned to himself. He strongly suspected that the Oliver brothers had been involved in starting the last town brawl. And what better time for another than now? The townsfolk were already massed, many angry that they had not managed to grab any of Wilson's money, and resentment still festered regarding the hanging of the two apprentices. It would take only a shouted insult from a student to a townsperson, and all hell would break loose. Some would just use fists, but others, especially the Oliver brothers, would use knives and sharpened sticks, and the injuries, like last time, would be horrific. Why anyone would want to start such a scene was beyond Bartholomew's imagination, but there were the students, already furtively sharing out the illicit weapons they had concealed in their robes.

Cynric stood behind him. 'Cynric! Fetch the Proctor and warn him that there may be trouble,' Bartholomew said urgently.

'As quick as I can,' Cynric whispered, grabbing Bartholomew's sleeve, 'but watch out for yourself. This looks ugly.' When Bartholomew turned to look at him, he had already gone, moving quickly in and out of the lengthening shadows with all the stealth of a cat.

The light was failing quickly now, and it was difficult to distinguish faces. The Oliver brothers, however, could be identified in virtually any light. Well over six feet tall, they both sported long fair hair that fell to their shoulders and were renowned for their flamboyant clothes. Even in the gloom, Bartholomew could see gold thread glittering on the gown of Elias, the elder of the two.

'All Michaelhouse scholars have been invited to attend Master Wilson's feast,' said Bartholomew pleasantly to Elias. 'It should be a night to remember. I am sure you will enjoy it.'

Nephews of the influential Abbess of St Radegund's Convent, Michaelhouse had been enticed to accept the Olivers as students in exchange for a small house on Foul Lane. They were not noted for their dedication to learning: Elias could barely read and write, although his younger brother showed a natural quickness of mind that could have been trained in scholarly matters had he shown the slightest willingness to learn.

'We have promised to visit our aunt tonight.' Henry Oliver had approached unnoticed. The slow-witted Elias gave him a grateful look, and Bartholomew, not for the first time, had to admire young Oliver's cunning. How could a teacher of Michaelhouse forbid a devoted nephew from visiting the venerable Abbess of St Radegund's?

'This is a very special day for our new Master,' said Bartholomew. 'I know he would appreciate both of you being present to share it with him.'

Henry Oliver narrowed his eyes. 'But we have promised our aunt,' he said in a mock-pleading manner. 'I could not bear to have the noble lady disappointed.'

'I am sure she will not be,' insisted Bartholomew, 'when you explain why.' Hiding his irritation at Oliver's ploy – after all, the Abbess of St Radegund's was no frail old crone living solely for visits from her kin, but a healthy, strong-minded woman in early middle age – he took Oliver firmly by the arm and began walking towards St Michael's Lane. Behind them, the students muttered, but, deprived of their leader, reluctantly began to disperse, those from Michaelhouse falling in behind Bartholomew and Henry.

Bartholomew felt, rather than saw, the shower of small stones that followed them. Henry slowed, and tried to turn back, but Bartholomew dragged him round the corner into St Michael's Lane, and increased his speed as much as he could without actually breaking into a run. He stole a glance behind him, and saw that a good part of the crowd from outside the church had followed them, and Bartholomew and his students were outnumbered at least five to one.

'We should all have stayed together,' Henry Oliver hissed, squirming in Bartholomew's grasp. 'Now, what chance do we have!'

'Every chance if we do not retaliate,' Bartholomew returned, nevertheless unnerved by the continuing hail of small stones that rained down upon them.

They neared the College gates, and Bartholomew wondered whether the last of the students would be able to escape the crowd. He let go of Henry, and pushed him towards the College. 'Go quickly!' he said urgently, 'And make sure the gates are ready to be fastened once all the students are inside.'

Henry needed no second bidding; he was no fool and knew when courage in a fight became stupidity. He set off down the lane with his fellow students streaming behind him. Bartholomew saw that a group of four scholars, Elias Oliver included, had been slow to follow him, and were now being jostled and shoved by those at the front of the advancing crowd. A sturdy man in a blacksmith's apron gave Elias a hard push, almost sending him sprawling. Elias bunched his fists, his face a mask of anger. One of the other students pulled him forward as Bartholomew silently urged them not to fight back.

The first of the four broke into a run. He reached the College gates, and was hauled through them by those already safe inside. Bartholomew noticed that Henry had the sturdy oak gates all but closed already, just a crack remaining to allow the stragglers in before they would be slammed shut on the mob outside.

As Elias drew level with Bartholomew, the blacksmith drew a wicked-looking blade from his apron, and jabbed wildly with it. Bartholomew wrenched Elias out of the path of the slicing blade and, abandoning all further pretence of calm, yelled for the last three students to run for their lives. White-faced, they obeyed, only just staying ahead of the mob, which surged after them. Gasping for breath, the three, with Bartholomew at the rear, shot through the gates, which were slammed shut; heavy bars were shot across as the mob crashed into them.

Bartholomew heard screams and yells, and knew that the people in the front were being crushed against the gates and walls by those behind. A student slumped to the ground as a further barrage of stones flew over the high walls. Master Wilson came scurrying out of the hall, flanked by his Fellows and guests, to see what all the commotion was about, and stopped short as he saw the lethal volley of missiles raining over the walls.

'A fitting end to a miserable day.' Bartholomew turned, and saw Giles Abigny helping to hold the gate against the battering from outside. He winced as a particularly heavy thump jarred it. Leaving his post to be filled by the students that came pouring from the dormitories at the sound of the affray, most already in their cleanest gowns in anticipation of the feast to come, he motioned Bartholomew into a doorway where they could not be overheard, his fresh face unusually serious. 'We should pick our scholars more carefully, Matt. Young Henry Oliver was all set to slam the door before you were inside, and would have done had I not been there.'

Bartholomew looked at him in disbelief. 'You must be mistaken, he . . .'

'No mistake, Matt. I heard him say to that spotty student of yours, the one from Fen Ditton who always has a cold . . .'

'Francis Eltham?'

'Indeed. I heard him tell Eltham to make sure that the gate was closed before you reached it. I ensured it remained open, but Oliver was furious. Look at him now.'

Bartholomew easily spotted the Oliver brothers among the milling students – they stood a head taller than the rest. Now that the immediate danger was over, the scholars had regained their confidence, and were shouting taunts to the people outside. Henry Oliver did not join in. He stood glowering, his face distorted with anger. Bartholomew saw him raise a bunched fist, and Eltham shrank back. As if he felt their eyes on him, Oliver turned his head slowly and stared back. Bartholomew felt the hairs on the back of his neck rise as he felt the venom of his stare. Abruptly, Oliver turned away, and stalked off towards his room.

'What have you done to deserve that?' wondered Abigny, disconcerted at such raw hatred.

'Prevented him from starting a riot, I suppose,' said Bartholomew. 'I had no idea he was so dedicated to causing chaos.'

The shouting outside the gates increased, and then

faltered. Bartholomew heard horses' hooves, and knew that the Sheriff and his troops had arrived, and were beginning to disperse the crowd. The battering on the College gates stopped, and the only sounds were the Sheriff's men telling people they could either go home or spend the night in the Castle, and the groans of the people who had been crushed against the gates.

'Michaelhouse!' Bartholomew recognised the voice of the Sheriff, and went to help open the gates.

The Sheriff had been compelled to use his garrison to break up many a fight between the University and the townspeople, and was heartily sick of it. Since he was unlikely to be able to rid himself of the townspeople, he often felt he would like to rid himself of the University and all its bickering and warring factions. Students from Norfolk, Suffolk, and Huntingdonshire fought scholars from Yorkshire and the north, and they all fought the students from Wales and Ireland. Masters and scholars who were priests, friars, or monks were always at odds with those who were not. And there was even dispute between the different religious Orders, the large numbers of Franciscan, Dominican, Augustinian, and Carmelite friars, who begged their livings, at loggerheads with the rich Benedictines and the Austin Canons who ran the Hospital of St John.

As the gates opened, he glowered in at the assembly, making no attempt to enter. The Senior Proctor, the man who kept law and order in the University, stood next to the Sheriff, his beadles – men who were University constables – ranged behind him. Master Wilson hurried forward, his gorgeous purple gown billowing about him.

'My Lord Sheriff, Master Proctor,' he began, 'the townies have attacked us totally unprovoked!'

'I admire a man who takes such care to seek the truth before speaking,' Bartholomew said in an undertone to Abigny. Wilson's was also an imprudent remark, considering many of his guests were townspeople.

Abigny snorted in disgust. 'He should have known better than to try to distribute money today. He must have known what might happen.'

'I suggested he should let the priests give it out at mass on Sunday,' said Bartholomew, watching with distaste as Wilson regaled the Sheriff with claims that the townspeople had attacked the College out of pure malice.

'But that might have entailed some of the credit passing to the priests and not to him,' said Abigny nastily. He gestured outside. 'See to your patients, Physician.'

Bartholomew remembered the groans and shrieks as the crowd had surged against Michaelhouse's wall, chastened that he had not thought to see to the injured sooner. By the gate, a beadle stood by two prostrate forms, while more beadles bent over others further down the lane.

'Dead, Doctor,' said the beadle, recognising Bartholomew. Bartholomew knelt to examine the bodies. Both were young men, one wearing the short coat of an apprentice. He pressed down on the young man's chest, feeling the sogginess that meant his ribs were broken and the vital organs underneath crushed. The neck of the second man was broken, his head twisted at an obscene angle. Death would have come instantly to both of them. Bartholomew crossed himself, and paused at the gate to shout for Brother Michael to do what he could for their unshriven souls.

The other beadles moved aside to allow Bartholomew to examine the injured. Miraculously, there were only four of them, although Bartholomew was sure others had been helped home by friends. None of the four was in mortal danger. One middle-aged man had a superficial head wound that nevertheless bled copiously. Bartholomew gave him a clean piece of linen to stem the bleeding, and moved on to examine the next one. The woman seemed to have no injuries, but was deeply in shock, her eyes wide and dull, and her whole body shaking uncontrollably.

'Her son is over there.' Bartholomew saw that the speaker was the blacksmith, lying against the wall with his leg at an awkward angle. He followed the blacksmith's nod and saw that he meant one of the men who had died. He turned back to the woman and took her cold, clammy hands in his.

'Where is her husband? Can we send for someone to come to take her home?'

'Her husband died last winter of the ague. The lad was all she had. Doubtless she will starve now.'

'What is her name?' Bartholomew asked, feeling helpless.

'Rachel Atkin,' the blacksmith replied. 'What do you care?'

Bartholomew sighed. He saw cases like Rachel's almost every day, old people and women with children deprived of those who could provide for them. Even giving them money, which he did sometimes, did no more than relieve the problem temporarily. Poverty was one of the aspects of being a physician he found most difficult to deal with. Often, he would tend to an injury or an illness, only to find that his patient had died from want of good food or warmth.

He released the woman's hands, and went to

examine the blacksmith's leg. It was a clean break, with no punctured skin. It only needed to be set, and, given time and rest, would heal well enough. As he gently squeezed and probed the break, testing for splinters of bone, the blacksmith leaned towards him. Bartholomew realised that the ale fumes on his breath probably accounted for the fact that he did not scream, as many patients might, when his leg was examined. He should set it as soon as possible for the same reason.

'Why did you interfere?' the blacksmith slurred.

Bartholomew ignored him, and went to look at the last injury, a man complaining of pains in his back.

'It was under control,' the blacksmith continued. 'We knew what we were doing.'

'I am sure you did,' said Bartholomew absently, running his hands down the man's spine. He straightened up. 'Just bruised,' he said to the man, 'go home and rest, and in a few days it will feel better.' He turned to the blacksmith. 'I can set your leg now, or you can go to a surgeon. I do not care which you choose.'

The blacksmith looked dubious, and narrowed his eyes. 'I have heard of you, Physician. You tell the other doctors that they should not use leeches . . .'

There was a muted snigger from the listening beadles, and Bartholomew cut the blacksmith off abruptly by standing and preparing to leave. He had no desire to enter into a medical debate with the man. He knew his medical teaching was regarded with suspicion, even fear, by some people, but no one could deny that fewer patients died under his care than that of his colleagues. His success where they had failed often drove desperate people to him, and those he had healed usually rallied to his defence when others questioned or criticised his methods.

'And how much will it cost me?' sneered the blacksmith, seizing a corner of Bartholomew's gown to prevent him from walking away.

Bartholomew looked down at him. 'A shroud and a gravedigger for the woman's son.'

The blacksmith met his eyes, peering up to see if he could detect any trickery there. After a moment's thought, he nodded, and lifted his arms so that the beadles could help him into Michaelhouse, where Bartholomew had a small surgery.

Bartholomew quickly bandaged the first man's head, and sent him home. The woman still sat on the ground, staring into space. The beadles had lifted the bodies of the young men onto a cart to be taken to St Michael's Church, while Brother Michael had finished his prayers and was walking back into the College. Coming to a decision, Bartholomew reached down and took the woman by the hand, pulling her to her feet. He ignored the surprised looks of the porters at the gate, and made for the kitchens, Rachel Atkin in tow.

All the College servants were furiously busy preparing for Master Wilson's feast. Bartholomew pushed his way through the kitchens to the servants' living quarters beyond. Agatha, the enormous laundress, sat there, folding napkins in readiness for the feast. She looked up as he entered, her bushy grey eyebrows coming together as she saw the woman.

'Now what?' she demanded, struggling to heave her considerable bulk to her feet. 'What troubles have you brought me this time, you young scoundrel?'

Bartholomew smiled. Women were not generally

employed in the Colleges, but Agatha was quite an exception. Sir John had hired her when he first came to Michaelhouse, instantly recognising her abilities for organisation and efficiency. She had gradually established herself as undisputed leader of the College staff, and the College owed its smooth and generally conflict-free running to Agatha.

'You are always saying that you need an assistant,' he said, smiling at her. 'Could you take this one, just for a few days?'

'She is stark staring mad!' Agatha bellowed, peering suspiciously into Rachel Atkin's face.

'No, not mad, just grieving for her son,' said Bartholomew gently. Rachel began to look around her vacantly. 'Will you give her a chance? Not tonight – she should sleep. But maybe for a few days?'

'Are you insane?' Agatha shouted. 'What will Windbag Wilson say when he hears you have brought a woman into the College? He only tolerates me because he knows in his heart that I am twice the man that he will ever be. He will be after your blood, Master Matthew. I have heard that he is going to demand that all the Fellows take major holy orders like Michael and the Franciscans. He will have something to say about women in the College, you can be sure of that!'

'Just for a few days until I can think of something else. Please, Agatha?'

Agatha hid a smile, and put her hands on her ample hips. She had had a soft spot for the dark-haired physician ever since he had arrived at the College to teach medicine four years before and had cured her of a painful swelling on her foot. She had been dubious of accepting his help because he had abandoned the usual implements of his trade – leeches, star-charts, and urine examination – and had even been known to practise surgery, a task normally left to barbers. But Bartholomew's treatment of Agatha's foot had worked, and Agatha was not a woman to question something that improved the quality of her life so dramatically.

She eyed the woman impassively noting her old but clean dress, and the careful darns. 'Out of the question! You will be expecting me to share my own room with her next!'

'No, I . . .' began Bartholomew, but stopped as Agatha elbowed him out of the way, and steered Rachel towards one of the small rooms in which the servants slept. He needed to say no more. Rachel Atkin was in good hands for now, and he was sure he and Agatha could work out something between them later.

He dodged his way back through the frenetic activity of the kitchens and walked across the courtyard towards his room. The Sheriff and Wilson had gone, but students and servants were scurrying back and forth as the bell rang to announce that the feast was about to begin.

The blacksmith lay on the pallet in the tiny chamber Bartholomew used to store his medicines, and where the College's three precious medical books were kept chained to the wall. Engaging the help of two burly porters, Bartholomew pulled and heaved on the leg until he was certain the bones were in correct alignment. The porters exchanged grimaces of disgust as the sound of grating bone filled the room. But the blacksmith had apparently taken several healthy swigs from the jug of wine that stood on the table and was virtually unconscious by the time Bartholomew began: with the exception of one or two grunts, he lay motionless through the entire proceeding. Bartholomew bound the leg tightly between two sticks of wood, and checked his patient for signs of shock or fever.

The porters left, and Bartholomew covered the blacksmith with his cloak and left him to sleep. His family could collect him in the morning. He went into the room that he shared with Abigny, and slumped on his bed, suddenly feeling drained. What a day! He had sat through Wilson's interminable installation, narrowly averted a riot, almost been locked out of the College to face an enraged mob, attended four patients, and set a broken leg.

He leaned back against the wall and closed his eyes, feeling a warm lethargy creep over him. It would be pleasant to drift off to sleep. The courtyard outside was quiet now, and he could just hear the murmur of voices coming from the feast in the hall. His place at the high table would be empty and he would be missed. He should go or Wilson would take his absence as a personal insult, and would try to make life unbearable for him. He sat still for a few minutes, and then forced himself to stand up. He need only stay until the speeches were over. Speeches! He almost sat down again at the thought of listening to Master Wilson pontificate, but he had not eaten since breakfast, and the smells of cooking from the kitchen had been delicious.

He brushed hastily at the dust and mud that clung to his best gown, and straightened the black robe underneath. He walked across the courtyard, stopping on the way to look in on Augustus. The commoners shared a large dormitory on the upper floor of the southern wing, but because Augustus talked to himself and kept the others awake, he had been given a small room of his own, an unusual privilege for any College member, but especially a commoner. The commoners' room and Augustus's chamber were dark, but Bartholomew could make out Augustus lying on the bed, and could hear his slow, rhythmic breathing. In the main dormitory, Brother Paul, another commoner too frail to attend the feast, coughed wetly and muttered in his sleep.

Satisfied, Bartholomew made his way to the hall, and tried to slip as unobtrusively as possible into his seat at the high table at the raised end of the hall. Wilson leaned forward and shot him an unpleasant look. Next to Bartholomew, Giles Abigny had already had far too much to drink, and was regaling Brother Michael with a story of his experiences with a prostitute in London. For a monk, Michael was showing an unseemly interest. On Bartholomew's other side, the two Franciscan friars, Aelfrith and William, were already deep in some debate about the nature of original sin, while Wilson, Alcote and Swynford huddled together plotting God knew what. Bartholomew ate some of the spiced venison slowly, realising that he had grown so used to plain College fare, that the strongly flavoured meats and piquant sauces were too rich for him. He wondered how many scholars would over-indulge and make themselves sick. The ever-growing pile of gnawed bones and the grease-splattered table near Michael indicated that *he* had no such reservations.

A roar of laughter from the students jolted him from his thoughts. Members of the College usually spoke Latin, or occasionally court French, at the few meals where speaking was permitted, and the conversation was generally learned. But tonight, as a gesture of courtesy to his secular guests, Wilson had decreed that the conversation might be in any language. Bartholomew glanced around the hall, noting the brightly coloured tapestries, begged and borrowed from other Colleges for the occasion, that adorned the walls. The walls were normally bare so as not to distract scholars from their studies, and the benches, now draped with rich cloths, were plain wood. The guests from the town added splashes of colour among the students' black gowns. Servants scurried here and there bearing large jugs of wine and platters of food that left trails of spilled grease. In the gallery normally occupied by the Bible scholar, a small group of musicians fought to make their singing heard over the hubbub.

Down the table, Brother Michael chortled with unmonklike delight as he listened with rapt attention to Abigny. Fortunately for him, his imprudent laughter was screened from the austere Franciscan Fellows by another roar of laughter from the students.

The Oliver brothers were the centre of attention, a group of younger students gathering round them admiringly. Bartholomew heard Elias telling them how he had been the last one through the gates to make sure that all the others were safe inside. At that moment, Henry looked up towards the high table, and stared at Bartholomew, his blue eyes blazing with hatred. They held each other's gaze for a moment, before Henry, with a sneer, looked away.

Bartholomew was puzzled. He had had very little to do with the Oliver brothers – they were not his students, and he had never had to deal with them for any disciplinary breaches. He found it hard to believe that all the hatred that Henry had put into that look came from the incident outside the church. The mob had been in an ugly mood, and he had averted what

32

might very easily have turned into a bloodbath. So what had he done to earn such emotions?

He tried to put it out of his mind. He was tired, and was probably reading far too much into Henry Oliver's looks. He sipped at the fine wine from France that Wilson had provided to toast his future success as Master, and leaned his elbows on the table. Abigny, his story completed, slapped Bartholomew on the back.

'I heard you have secreted a woman in the College . . .'

Abigny's voice was loud, and several students looked at him speculatively. Brother Michael's eyebrows shot up, his baggy green eyes glittering with amusement. The Franciscans paused in their debate and looked at Bartholomew disapprovingly.

'Hush!' Bartholomew chided Abigny. 'She is in the care of Agatha, and not secreted anywhere.'

Abigny laughed, and draped his arm round Bartholomew's shoulders. Bartholomew pulled away as wine fumes wafted into his face. 'I wish I were a physician and not a philosopher. What better excuse to be in a woman's boudoir than to be leeching her blood.'

'I do not leech the blood of my patients,' said Bartholomew irritably. They had been down this path before. Abigny loved to tease Bartholomew about his unorthodox methods. Bartholomew had learned medicine at the University in Paris from an Arab teacher who had taught him that bleeding was for charlatans too lazy to discover a cure.

Abigny laughed again, his cheeks flushed pink with wine, but then leaned closer to Bartholomew. 'But you and I may not be long for our free and easy lives if our new Master has anything to say. He will have us taking major orders as he and his two sycophants over there plan to do.'

'Have a care, Giles,' said Bartholomew nervously. He was acutely aware that the students' conversation at the nearest table had stopped, and Bartholomew knew that some of the scholars were not above telling tales to senior College members in return for a lenient disputation, or spoken exam.

'What will it be for you, Matt?' Abigny continued, ignoring his friend's appeal for discretion. 'Will you become an Austin Canon and go to work in St John's Hospital? Or would you rather become a rich, fat Benedictine, like Brother Michael here?'

Michael pursed his lips, but humour showed in his eyes. Like Bartholomew, being the butt of Abigny's jokes was nothing new to him.

Abigny blundered on. 'But, my dear friend, I would not want you to take orders with the Carmelites, like good Master Wilson. I would kill you before I would let that happen. I . . .'

'Enough, Giles!' Bartholomew said sharply. 'If you cannot keep your council, you should not drink so much. Pull yourself together.'

Abigny laughed at his friend's admonition, took a deep draught from his goblet, but said no more. Bartholomew sometimes wondered about the philosopher's behaviour. He was fair and fresh-faced, like a young country bumpkin. But his boyish looks belied a razor-like mind, and Bartholomew had no doubt that if he dedicated himself to learning he could become one of the foremost scholars in the University. But Abigny was too lazy and too fond of the pleasures of life.

Bartholomew thought about Abigny's claim. Most Cambridge masters, including Bartholomew, had taken minor holy orders so that they were ruled by church law rather than secular law. Some, like Brother Michael and the Franciscans, were monks or friars and had taken major orders. This meant that they could not marry or have relations with women, although not all monks and friars in the University kept these vows as assiduously as they might.

As a boy, Bartholomew had been educated at the great Benedictine Abbey at Peterborough, and, as one of their brightest students, had been expected to take his vows and become a monk. His sister and brother-in-law, acting *in loco parentis*, had other ideas, and a marriage was planned that would have benefited their cloth trade. Bartholomew, however, had defied them both, and had run away to Oxford and then Paris to study medicine. Since leaving Peterborough, Bartholomew had not given a monastic vocation another thought, other than taking the minor orders that would protect him from the rigours of secular law. Perhaps, a few months ago, the prospect of never having a relationship with a woman would not have mattered, but Bartholomew had met Philippa Abigny – Giles's sister – and was not at all sure that a vow of chastity was what he wanted.

The evening dragged on, speeches were made, and the candles gradually dipped lower in their silver holders. The guests began to leave. First the Bishop made his exit, sweeping out of the hall in his fine robes, followed as ever by his discreet chain of silent, black-robed clerics. The Chancellor and the Sheriff left together, and Bartholomew wondered what they had been plotting all evening. Edith, Bartholomew's sister, earned a nasty look from Wilson when she kissed her brother on the cheek and whispered an invitation to dine with her and Sir Oswald the following day.

The noise level in the hall rose as more wine was consumed, especially by the students and the commoners. Bartholomew began to grow drowsy, and wished Wilson would leave the feast so he could go to bed. It would be considered bad manners for a Fellow to leave the high table before the Master, and so Bartholomew waited, struggling to keep his eyes open and not to go face down in his food like Francis Eltham.

He watched expectantly as Alexander, the College Butler, made his way to Wilson, hoping that some urgent College business might draw him from the hall, so that the Fellows might leave. Wilson spun round in his chair to gaze at Alexander in shock. He then looked at Bartholomew, and whispered in the Butler's ear. Alexander nodded, and moved towards the physician.

'Begging your pardon, sir,' he began softly, 'but it is Master Augustus. I think he is dead.'

11

BARTHOLOMEW STARED UP AT ALEXANDER IN disbelief. He half suspected a practical joke by Abigny, but realised that even Abigny's sometimes outrageous sense of humour would not allow him to stoop to such a prank.

'What happened?' he asked hoarsely.

Alexander shrugged, his face pale. 'I went to take him and Brother Paul some wine, since Master Wilson thought they were too ill to attend the feast.' Bartholomew grimaced. Wilson did not want Augustus at the feast because he was afraid the old man's ramblings might embarrass him. 'I went to Brother Paul first, but he was already asleep. Then I went in to Augustus. He was lying on his bed, and I think he is dead.'

Bartholomew rose, motioning for Brother Michael to go with him. If Augustus were dead, then Michael would anoint the body and say prayers for his soul, as he had for the two men outside the College gates. Although Michael was a monk and not a friar – and would therefore not usually have been authorised to perform priestly duties – he had been granted special dispensation by the Bishop of Ely to give last rites and hear confessions. This was because, unlike the Franciscan and Dominican friars, Benedictine monks were scarce in Cambridge, and the Bishop did not want his few monks confessing their sins to rival Orders.

'What is going on?' panted Michael, as he hurried to keep up with Bartholomew. Michael was a man who loved his food, and, despite Bartholomew's advice to moderate himself for the sake of his health, he was grossly overweight. A sheen of sweat glistened on his face and soaked into his lank brown hair just from the exertion of leaving the hall so quickly.

'Alexander says Augustus is dead,' Bartholomew replied tersely.

Michael stopped abruptly, and gripped Bartholomew's arm. 'But he cannot be!'

Bartholomew peered at Michael in the darkness of the courtyard. His face was so deathly white that it was almost luminous, and his eyes were round with horror.

'I went to see him after I had finished with those town lads,' Michael went on. 'He was rambling like he does, and I told him I would save him some wine from the feast.'

Bartholomew steered Michael towards Augustus's room. 'I saw him after you, on my way to the hall. He was sound asleep.'

Together they climbed the narrow wooden stairs to Augustus's tiny chamber. Alexander was waiting outside the door holding a lamp that he passed to Bartholomew. Michael followed the physician over to the bed where Augustus lay, the lamp and the flames from the small fire in the hearth casting strange shadows on the walls. Bartholomew had expected Augustus to have slipped away in his sleep, and was shocked to see the old man's eyes open and his lips drawn back over long yellow teeth in a grimace that bespoke of abject terror. Death had not crept up and claimed Augustus unnoticed. Bartholomew heard Michael take a sharp breath and his robes rustled as he crossed himself quickly.

Bartholomew put the lamp on the window-sill and sat on the edge of the bed, putting his cheek to Augustus's mouth to see if he still breathed – although he knew that he would not. He gently touched one of the staring eyes with his forefinger to test for a reaction. There was none. Brother Michael was kneeling behind him intoning the prayers for the dead in his precise Latin, his eyes closed so he would not have to look at Augustus's face. Alexander had been sent to fetch oil with which to anoint the dead man.

To Bartholomew it seemed as if Augustus had had some kind of seizure; perhaps he had frightened himself with some nightmare, or with some of his wild imaginings – as when he had tried to jump out of the window two nights before. Bartholomew felt sad that Augustus had died afraid: three generations of students had benefited from his patient teaching, and he had been kind to Bartholomew, too, when the younger man had first been appointed at Michaelhouse. When Sir John had arranged Bartholomew's fellowship, not all members of the College had been supportive. Yet Augustus, like Sir John, had seen in Bartholomew an opportunity to improve the strained relationship between the College and the town; Bartholomew had been given Sir John's blessing to work among the poor and not merely to pander to the minor complaints of the wealthy.

The gravelly sound of Michael clearing his throat jerked Bartholomew back to the present. Sir John was dead, and so, now, was Augustus. Michael had finished his prayers, and was stepping forward to anoint Augustus's eyes, mouth and hands with a small bottle of chrism that Alexander had fetched. He did so quickly, concentrating on his words so that he would not have to see Augustus's expression of horror. Bartholomew had seen many such expressions before: his Arab master had once taken him to the scene of a battle in France, where they had scoured the field looking for the wounded among the dead and dying, and so Augustus's face did not hold the same horror for him as it did for Michael.

While waiting for Michael, Bartholomew looked around the room. Since the commotion two nights before, Wilson had decreed that Augustus should not be allowed the fire he usually had during the night. Wilson said, with good reason, that it was not safe, and that he could not risk the lives of others by allowing a madman to be left alone with naked flames.

Bartholomew suspected that Wilson was also considering the cost, because he had questioned Sir John on several occasions about the necessity of the commoners having a fire in July and August. Michaelhouse was built of stone, and Bartholomew knew that Augustus was not the only old man to complain of being cold, even in the height of summer. That a small fire burned merrily in the hearth suggested that one kind-hearted servant had chosen to ignore Wilson's orders and let Augustus have his comfort.

'Matt, come away. We have done all we can here.'

Bartholomew glanced up at Michael. His face was shiny with sweat, and had an almost greenish hue. The chrism in the small bottle he held shook as his hands trembled, and he was looking everywhere except at Bartholomew and Augustus.

'What is the matter with you?' asked Bartholomew,

perplexed. Michael had often accompanied Bartholomew to pray for patients beyond his medicine
and had seen death many times. He had not been
especially close to Augustus, and so his behaviour could
not be explained by grief.

Michael took a handful of Bartholomew's gown
and pulled hard. 'Just come away. Leave him be, and
come with me back to the hall.' Bartholomew resisted
the tug, and the small bottle fell from Michael's hand
and bounced onto the floor.

'Pull yourself together, man,' Bartholomew said,
exasperated, and leaned down to retrieve the bottle,
which had rolled under the bed. He picked it up to
hand back to Michael, and was startled to see the hem
of the monk's robes disappearing through the door.
Michael had, quite literally, fled.

Bartholomew looked to Alexander, who appeared
as bewildered as Bartholomew felt. 'Go back to the feast,'
he said, seeing the steward's unease. 'You will be needed
there. I will see to Augustus.'

Alexander left, shutting the door behind him, and
Bartholomew heard his feet clattering down the stairs
and the outside door slam shut. He chewed on his lower
lip, bemused. What had been the matter with Michael?
They had known each other since Bartholomew had
been made a Fellow, and Bartholomew had never seen
him in such a state before. Usually the obese monk was
well in control of his emotions, and he rarely allowed
himself to be so discomfited that he was unable to come
up with a sardonic remark or cutting response.

As Bartholomew put the bottle of chrism down on
the window-sill, he noticed that the lid had come off and
that his hand was greasy with the highly scented oil. He

wiped it on a napkin that lay on a desk under the window, and dropped to his hands and knees with the lamp to look for the bottle-top. It had rolled to the far side of the bed, and Bartholomew had to lie flat to reach it. As he stood up, he noticed that his clothes were covered with small flecks of black. Puzzled, he peered closely at some of the bits that clung to his sleeve. They looked like flakes of burned parchment. He brushed them off; they must have come from the fire in the hearth. He was about to leave when the edge of the bedclothes caught his eye. On the light green blanket was a pale scorch mark about the size of his hand. Curious, he inspected the rest of the covering, and found a similar spot at the corner.

Augustus's screams of two nights before came tearing into his mind. Augustus had claimed that devils had come to burn him alive! Bartholomew shook his head. He was being ridiculous. Agatha had probably burned the blanket while it was being laundered, although he would not wish to be the one to ask her. Nevertheless, he took the lamp, and, lying flat on his back, he inspected the wooden slats underneath the bed. He swallowed hard. The boards were singed, and one was even charred. Augustus had not been imagining things. There *had* been a fire under his bed.

Still lying on his back, he thought about the events of two days before. It had been deep in the night, perhaps one or two o' clock, when Augustus had started to yell. Bartholomew had thrown on his gown and run to the commoners' dormitory, which was diagonally opposite his own room across the courtyard. By the time he had arrived, Alcote, Alexander, and Father William were already there with Wilson's book-bearer, Gilbert, and the commoners from the next room. Alcote and William said that they had been working together in William's rooms on material for a public debate they were to hold the next day, and since William's room was directly below that of Augustus, had been the first to arrive. Gilbert, always ferreting information and gossip for Wilson, had materialised from nowhere, and Alexander never seemed to sleep.

Bartholomew screwed up his eyes. But one other person had also arrived before him. Brother Michael had been there. He had been dishevelled, as was Bartholomew, having been woken from his sleep, but Michael's room was above Bartholomew's, so he must have moved with uncharacteristic haste to have arrived first. Unless he had been there already. The thought came unbidden into Bartholomew's mind. Michael was dishevelled. Had he been involved in a tussle with Augustus and set a fire under the bed? Was Brother Michael the devil of Augustus's mind? But Augustus's door had been locked from the inside, and Michael had helped Bartholomew to break it down.

It made no sense. Why would Michael wish Augustus harm? Michael was a monk: a rarity in the University, where friars and priests abounded, but Benedictine monks were uncommon. Bartholomew reached for the damaged wood and scratched it with his fingernail. It was quite deeply burnt, not merely singed, so whoever had started the fire had meant business. Bartholomew thought again. The room had been horribly smoky, enough to make his eyes smart, but the windows were open, and the draught was sucking the smoke back down the chimney where it was billowing into the room. He remembered asking Alexander to douse the fire to allow some fresh air to circulate. Any evidence of smoke from under the bed would have been masked by the fire in the hearth.

He felt angry at himself. He had not believed for an instant that there could have been any degree of truth in Augustus's story. But what if his other ramblings held grains of truth? What of his statements today? What had he said? Something to the effect that evil was afoot and would corrupt them all, especially those who were unaware, and that Sir John had begun to guess and look what had happened to him.

Bartholomew felt his blood run cold. Sir John's sudden demise had taken everyone by surprise; he had certainly not seemed suicidal the night of his death as Bartholomew could attest. What if he had not committed suicide? What if there was truth in senile Augustus's mumblings, and Sir John had begun to guess something? But what? Michaelhouse had its petty rivalries and bids for power, as, no doubt, every other College and hostel in the University did. But Bartholomew found it hard to imagine that there could be anything so important as to warrant the taking of lives. And anyway, Michael and Bartholomew had seen Augustus alive before the feast, and none of the Fellows, commoners, or students had left the hall before Bartholomew had been summoned by Alexander.

He slid out from under the bed for a second time and dusted himself off. He looked down at Augustus's sprawled corpse, at the horrified look on the face. Sitting on the bed, he began a rigorous inspection of the body. He sniffed at the mouth to check for any signs of poison; he ran his fingers through Augustus's wispy hair to see if he had been struck on the head; he lifted the bed-gown to look for any small puncture marks or bruises; and, finally, he examined the hands. There was nothing, not even a fibre trapped under the fingernails. There was not a mark on the body, and not the merest hint of blood. Aware that the chrism may have masked the smell of poison, Bartholomew prised the dead man's mouth open again, and, holding the lamp close, looked carefully for any redness or swelling on the tongue or gums. Nothing.

He began to feel foolish. It had been a long day, and he was tired. Henry Oliver's attempt to leave him to the mercies of the town mob must have upset him more than he had thought, and it had not been pleasant to see the loathsome Wilson sit so smugly in Sir John's chair. I am as bad as old Augustus with his imaginings, Bartholomew thought irritably. The old commoner had most likely set the bed alight himself, not realising what he had done.

Bartholomew straightened Augustus's limbs, pulled the bed-gown down over the ancient knees, and covered him decently with the blanket. He kicked and poked at the fire until he was sure it was out, fastened the window-shutters, and, taking the lamp, left the room. He would ask Father Aelfrith to keep vigil over the body. It was getting late, and the feast should almost have run its course by now.

As he made his way down the stairs, he thought he saw a shadow flit across the doorway, and his heart almost missed a beat. But when he reached the courtyard, there was nothing to be seen.

The feast seemed to have degenerated somewhat since he had left, and the floor and tables were strewn with thrown food and spilt wine. Abigny was standing on one of the students' tables reciting ribald poetry to a chorus of catcalls and cheers, while the two Franciscans looked on disapprovingly. Brother Michael had returned to his place, and gave Bartholomew a wan smile. Alcote and Swynford were deep in their cups, and Wilson, too, was flushed, although with wine or the heat of the room Bartholomew could not tell.

'You have been a damned long time!' Wilson snapped at Bartholomew as he approached. 'What of old Augustus? How is he?'

'Dead,' Bartholomew said bluntly, watching for any reaction on the smug face. There was nothing, not even a flicker of emotion.

'Well, it is for the best. The man had lived his threescore years and ten. What kept you?'

Bartholomew suddenly found himself being examined closely by Wilson's heavily-lidded eyes. He stared back, hoping that the dislike he felt for the man did not show in his face. 'I had to make my examinations,' he responded.

The lazy hooded eyes were deceptive, and Wilson pounced like a cat. 'What examinations?' he said sharply. 'What are you saying? Michael returned ages ago. What were you doing?'

'Nothing that need concern you, Master Wilson,' replied Bartholomew coldly. He resented being questioned so. For all Wilson knew, he might have been visiting a patient, and that was none of his business.

'Everything in the College concerns me, Doctor Bartholomew. You may have had a loose rein under Babington, but you are under my authority now. I ask again: what examinations?'

Bartholomew felt like emptying a nearby pitcher of

wine over Wilson's head and walking out, but he had no wish to lose his fellowship over the likes of Wilson. He swallowed down several retorts of which the facetious Brother Michael would have been proud, and answered calmly, 'Augustus had not died in his sleep as I thought he might. His eyes were open and he looked terrified. It is my duty to make sure that the causes of death were natural.'

'"Causes of death were natural",' Wilson mimicked with a sneer. 'And? What did you find?'

'Nothing.'

'Of course you found nothing,' spat Wilson. 'Augustus probably frightened himself to death with one of his flights of imagination. What did you expect?' He turned to Swynford and gave one of his superior smiles, as if mocking the skills of medicine over his own common sense.

'There could be all manner of causes, Master Wilson,' said Bartholomew, masking his anger with cold politeness. 'What if he had died of the plague that is said to be sweeping towards us from the west? I am sure you would want to be the first to know such things.'

Bartholomew had the satisfaction of seeing Wilson blanch when he mentioned the plague. Good, he thought, with uncharacteristic malice, now I know how to get under the skin of this arrogant man.

Wilson recovered his composure quickly. 'I hope you are not so poor a doctor as to confuse plague with old age,' he said, putting his elbows on the table and placing together flabby hands shiny with grease from his dinner.

Bartholomew smiled. 'Let us hope not, for all our sakes,' he replied. 'And now, sirs, I bid you good-night,' and with a small bow took his leave of the new Master. If Wilson really did doubt his skills, Bartholomew hoped he would spend some restless nights wondering whether he was as safe as he might be from the plague that was rumoured to be devastating the West Country.

He paused to ask Aelfrith if he would keep vigil over Augustus. The friar looked straight ahead of him while Bartholomew imparted his news, and then rose and left the hall without a word.

Bartholomew walked back past Brother Michael and heard the monk follow him out into the cool night air.

'Are you well, Brother?' Bartholomew asked, trying to sound casual.

'Now, yes. I do not know what happened to me in there. Something about the old man's face. I am sorry I left in a rush, but I thought I was going to be sick.'

Michael had looked sick in the room. Perhaps he had over-eaten at the feast. It would not be the first time the monk had made himself ill with his greed for food and wine. 'I think some of the students will be sick in the morning, by the look of them now,' said Bartholomew, with a smile. 'I am willing to wager that none of them attend your lecture at six tomorrow morning.'

'And neither will I,' replied Michael. 'Our fine new Master has given all Michaelhouse scholars and masters tomorrow off. Is this the way he intends to continue the academic tradition of Michaelhouse?'

'Michael!' laughed Bartholomew. 'You are too incautious by far. Watch what you say, for shadows may have sharp hearing.'

Brother Michael's fat face suddenly became serious. 'More than we think, Matt. Heed your own words!' With that, he hurried over to the stairs that led up to his room, leaving Bartholomew standing in the courtyard alone.

Bartholomew rose with the first grey light of dawn the next morning to find that a small core of students were still enjoying Wilson's wine; he could hear them singing in the hall. Many had not been in their beds for more than two or three hours, Abigny among them. The philosopher lay sprawled on his back snoring loudly as Bartholomew went to find some breakfast.

As he walked across the courtyard, Bartholomew breathed in deeply. The air was cold and fresh, quite different from how it would be later when the hot sun would make the flies swarm over the putrid ditches that criss-crossed Cambridge.

He walked slowly along the cobbled footpath that ran around the courtyard, savouring the early morning, and admiring, as he often did, the fine building that was the centre of Michaelhouse. The north wing, in which Bartholomew lived, was the newest part, and was two storeys of dark yellow stone with slender arched windows. Regularly spaced along the front were three doorways leading to barrel-vaulted porches. Each porch contained doors leading to the two rooms on the lower floor, and a wooden staircase leading to two more rooms on the upper floor. The rooms were small, cramped, and in short supply, and Bartholomew felt himself fortunate that he shared his room with Abigny, and not three students, as did Father William.

The oldest part of Michaelhouse was the south wing, where the commoners, William, Swynford, and Aelfrith lived, and was, Bartholomew thought, the finest building.

It was also built around three staircases and contained twelve rooms of different sizes on two floors, but the original simple arched windows had been recently replaced by larger, wider ones that filled the scholars' rooms with light. Delicate traceries in stone had been carved at each window apex, each bearing the initials 'HS' in honour of Michaelhouse's founder, Hervey de Stanton, Edward II's Chancellor of the Exchequer. Unlike the north wing, the staircases in the south wing were built of stone, with brightly painted vaulted ceilings.

Joining the two wings was what had once been the house of a wealthy merchant, who had bequeathed it to the newly founded College. It was dominated by its handsome entrance, with the arms of Hervey de Stanton picked out in blue and gold above. The lower floor comprised a handsome reception room with a large spiral staircase leading to the hall on the upper storey, and the service rooms and kitchens, shielded from guests by a carved oak screen. The upper floor displayed a long line of arched windows that allowed light into the hall, and the little conclave, or combination room, at the far end. The hall was built of a pale, honey-coloured stone that changed with the light; at sunset it glowed a deep rose pink, while at noon it often appeared almost white.

Out of the corner of his eye, Bartholomew caught a flicker of light through the closed shutters on the upper floor of the south wing, and remembered Aelfrith and his vigil. He retraced his steps, thinking he would offer to relieve the friar for a while. He opened the door at the base of the stairs quietly, for he did not wish to awaken anyone who might have only recently retired to bed. Because the stairs were stone, Bartholomew found it easy to walk soundlessly. The stairway was dark and he kept one hand on the wall to feel his way upwards. Reaching Augustus's little chamber, he opened the door, and stopped dead.

Aelfrith, his back to Bartholomew, was squatting in the middle of the floor, vigorously scratching at the floorboards by the light of a single candle. Augustus's body lay next to him in a tangle of bedclothes and strewn pieces of parchment. In the dim light, Bartholomew could see that, here and there, parts of the plaster covering the walls had been chipped away.

Bartholomew took a step backwards, but shock made his movements clumsy, and he bumped into the door. Aelfrith jumped to his feet, spinning round to face him. Bartholomew was only aware of his dark robes, and the light was too weak to allow him to make out any expression on the face, enveloped as it was in a deep hood.

'Aelfrith!' Bartholomew exclaimed in a horrified whisper. 'What are you doing?'

Aelfrith turned to point at something, and then, before Bartholomew had time to react, dived forward, slamming him backwards into the door. Bartholomew felt all the breath rush out of him, and scrabbled at the billowing robes ineffectually as Aelfrith grabbed a handful of his hair. Bartholomew, numb with disbelief, saw the silhouette of something sharp in Aelfrith's free hand. The sight of it jolted him out of his shock, and he twisted out of Aelfrith's grip so that the knife screeched harmlessly against the wall.

Bartholomew grasped the hand holding the knife, and, for a few seconds, the struggle was at a stalemate. Then Aelfrith, perhaps made strong by panic, gave an almighty heave that sent Bartholomew sprawling backwards down the stairs. For a few moments, Bartholomew's world spun in all directions, until a sharp ache from a knee twisted in the fall brought everything back into focus. He was dimly aware of footsteps, although he had no idea from where they came. He picked himself up slowly, wincing at the pain in his leg. His fall had wedged him against the door, and so Aelfrith could not have left the building.

Cautiously, he hobbled up the stairs with as much silence as he could manage. The door to Augustus's room was still open, and the body still lay on the floor entangled in the blankets. Beyond, the door to the commoners' room was also ajar. Bartholomew swallowed, and began to inch forward. Aelfrith had to be in the commoners' room: there was no way out of this part of the building other than the door against which Bartholomew had fallen. He pushed the commoners' door so that it lay flat against the wall, and edged his way along it.

The commoners' room was lighter than Augustus's, because all the shutters had been thrown open to keep the room cool through the summer night. The commoners slept on pallets, simple mattresses of straw, that could be piled up on top of each other during the day to make more room. Bartholomew could see that all the commoners were there, and all asleep. He could see enough of their faces or bodies to know that none of them was Aelfrith, and there were no alcoves or garderobes in which to hide. Aelfrith was not there.

He backed out, and went to Augustus's room. He was totally mystified. There was nowhere for Aelfrith to hide, and he could not have left the building without passing Bartholomew on the stairs. Bartholomew leaned against the wall. Now that the first danger appeared to be over, he was beginning to shake with the shock, and his knee ached viciously. Legs trembling, he sank down onto the bed.

His heart leapt into his mouth as Augustus gave a long, low groan. Bartholomew stared at the body in horror. With a shaking hand, he reached out slowly, and grasped the bedcovers that had wrapped themselves around the corpse, easing them off the face.

He recoiled in confusion as the unmistakable bristly tonsure of Aelfrith emerged from under the tangle of blankets. For a few seconds, Bartholomew sat stupefied, just staring at the inert form on the floor. If this was Aelfrith, who was the man who had attacked him? And more to the point, where was Augustus? He crouched down beside the man on the floor. Gently, he eased him onto his side, noting the deep gash on the side of his head. Aelfrith's eyes fluttered open, and Bartholomew helped him to a sitting position. For a few minutes, all Aelfrith did was to hold his head in his hands and moan. Bartholomew limped to the table, and soaked a napkin in water from the nightstand to press against the swelling. Eventually, Aelfrith squinted up at him.

'What happened?' he croaked.

Bartholomew stared at him, trying to make sense out of the happenings of the last few minutes. 'You tell me,' he said finally, easing himself back down onto the bed. 'Where is Augustus?'

Aelfrith turned his head sharply to look at the bed, wincing at the quickness of the movement. He gazed at the empty bed, and then peered underneath it. He looked back at Bartholomew, his eyes wide with shock. 'Where is Augustus?' he repeated.

Bartholomew watched as Aelfrith hauled himself to

his feet and threw open the shutters. Both men looked around the small room in the better light. It was a mess. Augustus's few possessions had been scattered, his spare clothes pulled from the shelf and hurled to the ground, and a small box on the table ransacked so that odd bits of parchment lay everywhere. Bartholomew recalled that his attacker had been doing something in the middle of the floor, and leaned forward to see that the floorboards had been prised up in places. The sharp knife that had almost been the end of Bartholomew had evidently been used to scratch loose plaster from the walls, for small piles of dust and rubble lay all around the room.

'Tell me what happened,' said Bartholomew.

Aelfrith shook his head, and sank down onto the bed next to him. 'I do not know. I was kneeling, facing the crucifix next to the window, when I heard a sound. I thought it might be Brother Paul; he has taken a turn for the worse recently, so I went to make sure he was sleeping. He was curled up under his blanket fast asleep, so I came back here. I knelt down again, and that is all I can remember. The next thing I knew was that you were helping me up from the floor, and that Augustus was gone.' He turned suddenly, and gripped Bartholomew's arm. 'Matthew, are you sure that Augustus was . . .' he faltered.

Bartholomew nodded, remembering the extensive examination he had made. Not only was Augustus dead, but rigor mortis had begun to set in, and no drugs or poisons, however sophisticated, could mimic that.

'But who would do this?' Aelfrith blurted out. 'What could anyone want to gain from poor old Augustus? And where is the man who attacked me?'

Bartholomew leaned back against the wall and

closed his eyes. He thought about Augustus's previous claims and the burnt bed; about the unexpected death of Sir John; about Brother Michael's strange behaviour; and about the other Fellows' reactions – Wilson's lack of emotion when told that Augustus was dead, Swynford's dismissal of Augustus as a senile old man, and even Aelfrith's expressionless acceptance.

He began to feel sick in the pit of his stomach. All his suspicions of the night before came clamouring back to him. There were too many questions, and too many unexplained details. Suddenly, he had no doubts about the validity of Augustus's statements, and that, because of them, someone had wanted him out of the way. But who? And why? And even more urgent, where was Augustus's body? Why would anyone want to remove the body of an old man?

'Matthew?' Bartholomew opened his eyes. Father Aelfrith's austere face was regarding him sombrely, his normally neat grey hair sticking up in all directions around his tonsure. 'Look in the commoners' room to see if Augustus was moved there, then look down the stairs . . .'

Bartholomew sighed. 'Whoever attacked you also attacked me. I was knocked down the stairs, and I know Augustus is not there. I looked in the commoners' room and know that he is not there either. We will check again together, but whoever attacked us also seems to have taken Augustus.'

'That does not necessarily follow, my son,' said Aelfrith. 'You have no proof for such a statement.'

Bartholomew pulled a face. Aelfrith, one of the University's foremost teachers of logic, was right, but both attacks and the removal of Augustus had occurred in or near Augustus's room, and if the same person was not responsible, then at least both events must have been connected to the same cause.

'We should fetch Master Wilson,' he said. 'He should come to decide what should be done.'

'Yes. We will,' said Aelfrith. 'But first I want to find Augustus. He cannot be far. We will look together, and undoubtedly find that he has been moved for some perfectly logical reason.'

Aelfrith rose, looking under the bed a second time as he did so. In the interests of being thorough, Bartholomew also glanced under the bed, but there was nothing there, not even the black fragments of wood he had examined the night before. He looked closer. The dust that had collected under the bed had gone. It looked as though someone had carefully swept underneath it. He looked at the floor under the small table, and found that that too had been swept.

'You will not find him under there, Matthew,' said Aelfrith, a trifle testily, and began to walk to the commoners' room. Bartholomew followed, looking at the gouge in the wall where he had deflected the knife blade away from himself.

Both men stood in the doorway looking at the nine sleeping commoners. All along the far side of the long room were tiny carrels, or small workspaces, positioned to make use of the light from the windows. The carrels had high wooden sides so that, when seated, a scholar would not be able to see his neighbour; for most scholars in medieval Cambridge, privacy for studying was regarded as a far more valuable thing than privacy to sleep. All the carrels were empty, some with papers lying in them, one or two with a precious book from Michaelhouse's small library.

Bartholomew walked slowly round the room, checking each of the commoners. Five of them, including Paul, were old men, living out their lives on College hospitality as a reward for a lifetime of service. The man who had attacked Bartholomew had been strong, and of a height similar to his own. Bartholomew was above average height, and sturdily built. He was also fitter and stronger than the average scholar since a good part of his day involved walking to see patients, and he enjoyed taking exercise. The attacker could not have been any of the old men, which left four.

Of these, Roger Alyngton was Bartholomew's size, but had one arm that was withered and useless, and Bartholomew's attacker had two strong arms. So the number was down to three. Father Jerome was taller than Bartholomew by three inches or more, but was painfully thin and was constantly racked by a dry rattling cough. Bartholomew suspected a wasting disease, although Jerome refused all medicines, and would be far too weak to take on someone of Bartholomew's size. That left two. These were the Frenchman, Henri d'Evéne and the brusque Yorkshireman, Jocelyn of Ripon. D'Evéne was slight, and, although it was conceivable that he could have attacked Bartholomew, it was doubtful that he would have the strength to overcome him. Jocelyn was a recent visitor to Michaelhouse, and had come at the invitation of Swynford. He was a large man with a ruddy face and a shiny bald head. Bartholomew had not seen him sober since he had arrived, and he had been admonished several times by Sir John for his belligerent attitude when College members gathered in the conclave for company in the evenings. He certainly would have the strength to overpower Bartholomew.

Bartholomew stood looking down at him. Even in sleep, Jocelyn scowled. Could he be the assailant? Bartholomew bent close to him and caught the fumes of the previous evening's wine. His attacker had not had alcoholic fumes on his breath. Of course, this could be a ruse, and he could easily have downed a glass of wine as a cover for his actions. D'Evéne lay on the pallet next to him curled up like a child.

Bartholomew straightened, and tiptoed out of the dormitory, wincing at his sore knee. He joined Aelfrith who was still standing in the doorway, looking grey-faced and prodding cautiously at the gash on his head.

'How long was it before you were attacked?' Bartholomew asked of the friar.

Aelfrith thought carefully. 'I am not sure. The feast became very noisy after I left. I expect the other Fellows left shortly after us for it would not be seemly to continue to carouse when one of our number lay dead. The students, though, would have enjoyed their freedom and the wine. None of the commoners had returned, however,' he said suddenly. 'It is not every day that the commoners are treated to such food and wine, and, like the students, they intended to wring every drop of enjoyment out of it that they could.'

'So you, Paul, and Augustus were the only ones in this part of the building?' asked Bartholomew. 'And all the others were in the hall?'

'I do not know that they were in the hall,' replied the logician, 'but they were not here. The feast became noisy, as I said, and I found that it was distracting me from my prayers. I rose, perhaps shortly after midnight, to close the door to the room, and continued with my prayers. I may have nodded off for a while,' he admitted, 'but I would have woken if the commoners had returned.'

'Did you hear any sounds, other than the noise from the hall?'

'None,' said Aelfrith firmly. 'And what about you? How did you come to be in the commoners' room so early?'

'I rose at my usual time,' replied Bartholomew, 'and I saw a flicker of light coming from Augustus's room. I came because I thought you might like to be relieved for a while.'

Aelfrith acknowledged this with a bow of his head. 'Pray continue,' he said.

'I came as quietly as I could so as not to wake anyone, opened the door, and saw what I assumed to be you kneeling on the floor prising up the floorboards. What I thought was Augustus lay on the floor. As I entered, whoever it was that I thought was you leapt to his feet and came at me before I had the chance to react. He had a knife, and we grappled together. Then he pushed me down the stairs, and I heard footsteps. He did not come down the stairs because I fell against the door and he could not have opened it without moving me. I went back up the stairs, but could find no trace of him, either in Augustus's room or the dormitory. Then you came round and I realised that Augustus was missing.'

Aelfrith frowned. 'These commoners sleep very soundly,' he said. 'I am knocked on the head, and probably fell with quite a clatter. You have a fight on the landing virtually outside their room, and none of them wake. Now, we stand here speaking to each other, and not a soul stirs. Curious, would you not say?'

He strode into the centre of the commoners' dormitory, and clapped his hands loudly. Jocelyn's snores stopped for a second, but then resumed. Aelfrith picked up a pewter plate from a table, tipping off some wizened apples, and banged it as hard as he could against the wall, making an unholy row. Jocelyn groaned, and turned onto his side. D'Evéne and Jerome began to stir, but did not wake.

The cold feeling of unease that had earlier been in Bartholomew's stomach returned. He knelt down by Alyngton and felt his neck. His life beat was rapid and erratic. He pulled back his eyelids, noting how the pupils responded slowly to the light. He moved to one of the old men, and went through the same process.

He looked up at Aelfrith. 'They have been drugged,' he said. 'Of course! How else could an intruder hope to ransack a room and steal a body?'

Aelfrith stared back. 'My God, man,' he whispered. 'What evil is afoot in this College? What is going on to warrant such violence?'

Augustus's words of the previous day came back to Bartholomew: '"Evil is afoot, and will corrupt us all, especially those who are unaware."'

'What?' asked Aelfrith, and Bartholomew realised he had spoken aloud. He was about to explain, when something stopped him. He was confused. The events of the past few hours seemed totally inexplicable to him, and the brightness of the day seemed suddenly dulled, as suspicion and distrust settled upon his thoughts.

'Just quoting,' he mumbled dismissively, rising to check on the others.

'Here!' exclaimed Aelfrith. Bartholomew spun round. 'This must be it!' He held a large pewter jug in his hands, similar to the ones used to serve the wine at meals in the hall. Bartholomew took it gingerly. At the bottom were the dregs of the wine, and a few cloves. Evidently, Master Wilson's good wine had been replaced with inferior stuff that needed spicing when the feast had reached a certain point. But there was something else too. Swirling in the dregs and drying on the side of the jug were traces of a grey-white powder. Bartholomew smelled it carefully and detected a strong hint of laudanum. The commoners must have been drunk indeed not to have noticed it, and, at this strength, mixed with the effects of a night's drinking, would ensure that the commoners slept at least until midday.

He handed the jug back to Aelfrith. 'A sleeping draught,' he said, 'and a strong one too. I only hope it was not too strong for the old folks.' He continued his rounds, lying the torpid commoners on their sides so they would not choke, and testing for the strength of their pulses. He was concerned for one, a tiny man with a curved spine who was known simply as 'Montfitchet' after the castle in which he had been born. Montfitchet's pulse was far too rapid, and he felt clammy to the touch.

'I wonder whether it was consumed here, or in the hall,' said Aelfrith thoughtfully. 'We will find out when they awake. When will that be, do you think?'

'You can try to wake Jocelyn now,' said Bartholomew. 'I suspect he may be more resistant to strong drink than the others, and he almost woke when you banged the plate.'

Bartholomew reached Brother Paul. Paul had not attended the feast, and if he too had been drugged, the chances were that the wine had been sent to the commoners' dormitory to be consumed by them there. Bartholomew felt Paul's neck for a life beat, his mind on the mysteries that were unravelling all around him. He snapped into alertness, quickly dragged the thick covering from the pallet, and stared in horror. Aelfrith came to peer over his shoulder.

'Oh, sweet Jesus,' he breathed. He crossed himself and took a step backwards. 'My God, Matthew, what is happening here? The Devil walked in Michaelhouse last night!'

Bartholomew stared down at the blood-soaked sheet on which Paul lay. The knife that had caused his death still protruded from his stomach, and one of his hands was clasped loosely round the hilt. Bartholomew pulled at it, a long, wicked Welsh dagger similar to those that he had seen carried by Cynric and the soldiers at the Castle.

'Another suicide?' whispered Aelfrith, seeing Paul's hand on the hilt.

'I do not think so, Father. The knife was stabbed into Paul with such force that I think it is embedded in his spine. I cannot pull it out. Paul would never have had the strength for such a blow. And I do not think his death was instant. I think he died several minutes after the wound. Look, both hands are bloodstained, and blood is smeared over the sheet. I think he was trying to pull the knife out, and I think the murderer waited for him to die before arranging the bedclothes in such a way that no one would notice he was dead until the morning. And by then,' he said, turning to face Aelfrith, 'whatever business was going on last night would be completed.'

'Or would have been,' said Aelfrith, 'had you not

been an early riser and an abstemious drinker!' He shuddered, looking down at the pathetic body of Brother Paul. 'Poor man! I will say a mass for him and for Augustus this morning. But now, we must inform the Master. You stay here while I fetch him.'

While Aelfrith was gone, Bartholomew inspected Paul. He was cold, and the blood had congealed. Aelfrith had said that he had heard a sound and had gone to check Paul. Had he already been dead then? Was it the murderer Aelfrith had heard? Bartholomew had heard Paul cough when he had looked in on Augustus before he went to the feast, so he must have died later than that. Had Paul seen something and called out? Or had he just been dispatched as a caution to ensure the strange events of the previous evening were kept secret?

Bartholomew put his head in his hands. Two murders in his College. And what of Sir John? Bartholomew was beginning to have serious doubts that Sir John had committed suicide, and was inclined to believe that he had been murdered for something he knew or was about to find out. It seemed that Augustus was killed because he also knew, or someone thought he knew, something. And poor, gentle Brother Paul was murdered because he was too ill to attend Wilson's wretched feast! Bartholomew went to check on Montfitchet. Perhaps it would be four murders before the day was out, for the tiny man showed no signs of improving, and was beginning to turn blue around the mouth.

III

BARTHOLOMEW HEARD WILSON'S VOICE CARRYING across the courtyard. Wilson was due to move into Sir John's spacious room that day, and the College servants had been working furiously to prepare it to his fussy requirements. So the previous night, he had been in his old room, which he shared with Roger Alcote. Bartholomew looked out of the window and saw that Alcote was hurrying over the courtyard behind Wilson, and that Aelfrith had awakened Father William, too. Michael, a light sleeper, was peering out of his window to see what was going on, and Gilbert had evidently been dispatched to fetch Robert Swynford and Giles Abigny.

Wilson swept importantly past Bartholomew, paused briefly to look into Augustus's ransacked room and stopped as he saw Brother Paul's body. Bartholomew had left him as he had been found, the knife protruding from his stomach, and Wilson paled at the sight.

'Cover him up, damn you,' he snarled at Bartholomew. 'Leave the poor soul with some dignity!'

Bartholomew drew the bedcover over Paul's body, while Wilson looked around at the commoners in disdain.

'They are all drunk!' he proclaimed. 'We will not have such debauchery while I am Master!'

Bartholomew barely restrained himself from telling Wilson that if they were drunk, it was due to the copious amounts of wine he himself had supplied the night before, and that such 'debauchery' would most certainly not have been tolerated under Sir John's Mastership.

'Now,' Wilson said, sweeping some discarded clothes from a bench and sitting down, 'tell me what happened.'

Bartholomew looked at Aelfrith. As Senior Fellow, it was his prerogative to speak first. Aelfrith shook his head sorrowfully. 'I cannot begin to say what evil has walked in these rooms,' he began. Alcote and Swynford, in anticipation of a lengthy explanation, followed Wilson's lead and sat on the bench. Father William stood next to Aelfrith, silently offering his support, while Brother Michael, his black robes askew, leaned against the door. Abigny, less the worse for wear than Bartholomew would have expected, slipped into the dormitory noiselessly and stood next to him. All the Fellows were present.

Wilson folded his arms over his ample paunch and waited imperiously. 'Well?' he demanded.

'It is complex,' Aelfrith began. Bartholomew edged his way nearer to Montfitchet, partly so he could keep an eye on the old man, and partly so he would be able to see all the faces of the gathered Fellows. It was possible that one or more of them had committed some terrible acts, and he wanted to watch them all closely. He felt rather ashamed: these were his colleagues, and some of them, like Michael and Abigny, his friends whom he had known for years. None of them had any history of violence that he knew. He thought of Sir John, and his mangled body, and he looked across at the covered body of Paul, and steeled himself. They would be no friends of his if they had killed Sir John and Brother Paul!

'This is what I perceive to have happened,' Aelfrith continued. He looked over at Bartholomew. 'You must interrupt if you think I have left something out. Augustus died during the feast, and Matthew came to check the body at Master Wilson's request. He declared Augustus dead, and Brother Michael came to pray for his soul. Michael returned to the hall first, and Matthew came later.'

Wilson snorted, his eyes boring into Bartholomew. The physician had not realised that the Fellows had been so intrigued as to why he had taken so much longer than Michael. Well, he was certainly not going to reveal that he suspected Augustus had been murdered. Aelfrith continued.

'He made his report to the Master, and asked if I would keep vigil for Augustus. I went to Augustus's room, and kept vigil there until I was attacked from behind and knocked senseless. I have the wound to prove it. When I came round, Matthew was helping me to rise. Augustus's body was gone, and his room had been ransacked. I have no idea as to the reasons for either. Matthew and I made a quick search of this part of the building for Augustus and for the attacker. It was then that Matthew discovered that the commoners, who had been remarkably oblivious to all these goings-on, had been drugged. While examining them, he found that Brother Paul, God rest his soul, had been murdered. And that is all I know.' His story completed, he stood with head bowed and hands folded in front of him.

There was a silence among the Fellows, and then a

clamour of questions. Wilson tried to restore order, first by waving a pudgy hand in the air, and next by shouting. Bartholomew saw one or two of the drugged commoners stir, and bent down to examine Montfitchet.

'Well, Doctor Bartholomew,' said Wilson unpleasantly, 'what have you to say for yourself? You spend a considerable amount of time alone with Augustus before returning to the hall; you are standing over Father Aelfrith when he regains his senses after being knocked on the head by an unseen assailant; you discover the commoners have been drugged; and you uncover poor Brother Paul's body. What have you to say?'

Bartholomew looked at him in disbelief. The Master clearly thought that he had something to do with the sinister events of the night, an accusation not lost on the other Fellows who looked uneasy.

He took a deep breath, and recounted his story as he had done to Aelfrith, omitting nothing but his suspicions and speculations. When he mentioned his struggle at the top of the stairs, Alcote went to check the knife mark in the plaster.

Wilson watched Bartholomew closely as he gave his account of events. His unblinking eyes made Bartholomew uncomfortable, and he wondered whether this was a tactic employed by lawyers on their victims in court. The others listened with a mixture of horror and fascination, but Bartholomew could gauge nothing from their expressions other than shock.

When he had finished, Wilson stared at him for several long moments. 'Have you told us everything?' he asked. 'Is there anything you are keeping back?'

Bartholomew hoped his discomfiture did not show. 'I have told you everything I know. And everything I have told you is the truth,' he said. Bartholomew considered himself an appalling liar, but his statements to Wilson had been meticulously truthful. He had told the new Master only what he knew to have happened, and had omitted merely to speak of his growing suspicions. And how could he do otherwise? He had no real evidence, only a collection of strange coincidences and suppositions. But, he promised himself, he would have something more than unfounded suspicions soon.

'This is ludicrous!' exclaimed Abigny. 'Disappearing corpses, ransacked rooms of madmen, fights in the darkness! For heaven's sake, this is a College, not the London stews! Bodies do not just disappear. There must be some purely rational explanation.'

'Such as?' asked William.

'Such as,' said Abigny, exasperated, 'a secret exit! Some door unknown to us that allowed the murderer to escape, or to hide.' He began to look around him as though such a door would suddenly become apparent.

'Do not be ridiculous!' said Wilson aggressively. 'A secret door! Where? This is not a castle. The walls are less than a foot thick. Where could there possibly be such a door?'

'I do not know!' Abigny snapped back, his voice beginning to rise. 'It was only a suggestion. Maybe Augustus is not dead and is off wandering somewhere. Maybe some burglar came into the College, attacked Matt and Father Aelfrith and escaped out of a window.'

'You try jumping out of any of the windows here,' said Michael. 'You would need to be very agile, and,' he said looking ruefully down at his rotund form, 'very slender.

All the windows have stone mullions which would make them very difficult to squeeze through, and the drop is enough to break a leg. Perhaps Augustus or a burglar might have wriggled his way out, but he would not have landed undamaged.'

Wilson seized on Abigny's statement like a drowning man on a rope. 'Of course! Augustus was not dead and it was he who attacked Father Aelfrith and Doctor Bartholomew in the dark. That would explain everything.' He looked around triumphantly, considering the mystery to be solved. With an air of finality, he rose to leave.

'Augustus was dead!' said Bartholomew firmly. 'And he most certainly would not have had the strength to push me down the stairs. The man I fought with was a man of my size. And it also does not explain Paul's murder and the drugging of the commoners.'

'Yes, it does,' Wilson said. 'Augustus was mad, we all know that. He feigned his death to you, and then hit Father Aelfrith on the head when he came to keep vigil. He then, in his madness, went into the commoners' room and killed Paul – let us remember that he *was* insane,' he continued, looking around at each Fellow in turn. 'Perhaps he left the drugged wine for the others to drink when they returned, perhaps they are not drugged at all, but insensible after a night of debauchery.' At this he cast a scathing glance around at the comatose figures of the commoners still motionless on their pallets. 'But regardless, he returned to his room and began his foolish searching for the Lord knows what. When the Doctor surprised him, he attacked, made strong by insanity. Then, knowing his game was up, he jumped out of the window and escaped.'

'Escaped where?' asked Bartholomew. 'The gates are still locked.'

'Then he is hiding in the College,' said Wilson. 'I will order a thorough search to be made.' He looked behind him to where he knew Gilbert would be hovering, and raised his eyebrows. Gilbert disappeared immediately, and the Fellows could hear him summoning the College servants from their other duties. 'Do not worry,' he said to the Fellows, 'Augustus will be found and brought to justice. Paul's death will not go unavenged!' He turned to Bartholomew. 'I suppose *he* is dead, Physician?' he added with a sneer.

Bartholomew shrugged. 'Check for yourself,' he invited. 'And then check poor Montfitchet too.'

'What?' Wilson was momentarily thrown from his pomposity. The Fellows clustered around Montfitchet's pallet. His face had a bluish tinge to it and a small trickle of blood came from the corner of his mouth. Bartholomew gently closed the half-open eyes. Wilson elbowed him roughly out of the way to look for himself.

'Dead!' he proclaimed. 'Augustus has two murders to pay for!'

Outside, Bartholomew heard the servants clattering up the stairs and banging doors as they made their search of the College.

'Now,' began Wilson, taking matters in hand, 'Father Aelfrith, have your wound attended to – by our esteemed Master of Medicine if you trust him not to pronounce you dead. Of course, I will understand perfectly should you wish to consult another physician.'

Bartholomew raised his eyes heavenward. Now Wilson had his theory, he would hang onto it like a dog with a bone, and would take every opportunity to undermine Bartholomew's skills as a physician to give it more credence.

'Doctor Bartholomew will attend to me,' said Aelfrith quietly. 'I see no need to call upon the services of another physician.'

'That is your own choice, Father,' responded Wilson disparagingly, his tone making it clear that he would have no hesitation in taking his patronage elsewhere. Bartholomew studiously avoided Wilson's gaze, not trusting himself to speak civilly. He saw clearly that many of the objections that Wilson had raised to his appointment four years before would now be voiced; indeed, would be used against him at every opportunity, and perhaps Wilson would succeed in bringing about his dismissal from the College. Wilson gazed at Bartholomew in a hostile manner for several moments before continuing.

'Father William, would you arrange to have the bodies moved to the church? Then you and Brother Michael must do what is necessary for their souls. Master Alcote, I would like you to take the news to the Bishop, for we will need his services when our murderer is caught.' Since, like most scholars at the University, Augustus had taken minor orders, any crimes of which he might be accused would be dealt with by Church, rather than secular, law. 'Master Swynford, Master Abigny, perhaps you would oversee the search. Make sure that every nook and cranny is investigated. Augustus must be found!'

The Fellows scurried off to do his bidding. Bartholomew and Aelfrith made their way down the stairs together, heading for Bartholomew's room. As they reached the courtyard, Bartholomew went to look at the ground under Augustus's window. If anyone had managed to squeeze out of the first-floor window and jump, there would be some evidence, but there was nothing to be seen. There were a few tendrils of bindweed creeping up the wall: had someone leaped from the window, the plants would have been damaged or displaced. Bartholomew saw nothing that indicated anyone had made an escape from Augustus's window.

He stood up slowly, wincing at his stiffening knee. Wilson gave him a cold glance as he left, guessing what he was doing and disapproving of it. Bartholomew knew that Wilson would regard his action as a direct challenge to his authority, but was disturbed by Wilson's eagerness to accept the first excuse that came along and to dismiss any facts that confounded it.

Aelfrith waited, his hands folded in the voluminous sleeves of his monastic robes. 'Our new Master seems to dislike you, my son,' he said.

Bartholomew shrugged, and began to limp towards his room. Aelfrith caught up with him, and offered his arm for support. The tall friar was surprisingly strong, and Bartholomew was grateful for his help.

They arrived at the tiny chamber Bartholomew used to store his medicines. It had been used originally to store wood, but Sir John had ordered it cleaned for Bartholomew's use because he thought it was not healthy for him to sleep with the smell of his medicines.

The blacksmith still slept on the pallet bed, snoring noisily. Bartholomew had forgotten about him. He would have to send Cynric to ask his family to come to collect him. Aelfrith wrinkled his nose in disgust at the smell of stale wine fumes, and went to Bartholomew's own room next door. Abigny had thrown the shutters open before he had left, and the room was bright and sunny. Neither Bartholomew nor Abigny had many possessions – a few clothes, some writing equipment, and Bartholomew had a book he had been given by his Arab master when he had completed his training; all were stored out of sight in the large chest that stood at one end of the room.

Aelfrith looked around approvingly. The room was clean, with fresh rushes and herbs scattered on the floor, and a servant had already put the bedding out of the window to air. Bartholomew had been taught that dirt and disease went hand in hand – his insistence on cleanliness was another reason he was regarded as an oddity.

He sank down onto a stool. He had not realised what a wrench he had given his knee, and he knew it would slow him down for a few days. He made to stand again, remembering that he should be tending Aelfrith's head. Aelfrith pushed him back down firmly.

'Tell me what you need, Matthew, and I will get it. I am sure you can doctor me as well sitting as standing.'

As Aelfrith fetched water, linen, and some salves, Bartholomew thought about Augustus, Paul, and Montfitchet. He had been fond of Paul, and only now did the shock of his cruel death register. He took a shuddering breath, and blinked away tears.

Aelfrith drew a stool up next to him, and laid a hand on his shoulder comfortingly. Bartholomew smiled weakly, and began to tend to the wound in the friar's scalp. It was a nasty gash, and Bartholomew was not surprised that Aelfrith had been rendered unconscious. He could easily have been insensible for several hours. Aelfrith, like Bartholomew, was showing signs of delayed shock, with shaking hands and sudden tiredness.

Bartholomew inspected the ragged edges of the wound, and prodded gently to ensure no splinters were left that might fester. Satisfied that it was clean, he bathed it carefully, and tied a neat bandage around the tonsured head. Aelfrith rose to leave. He leaned out of the window, looked both ways, and closed the shutters and the door.

'I am too befuddled to think now,' he said in a low voice, 'but I am appalled at the wickedness that has been perpetrated in this house of learning. Our Master is mistaken in his explanation, and I, like you, know that Augustus was dead last night. I believe there is sinister work afoot, and I suspect that you think the same. Now, I will say no more, but you and I will meet later today to talk when we are both more ourselves. Trust no one, Matthew. Keep your counsel to yourself.'

His calm grey eyes looked steadily at Bartholomew. Bartholomew's blood ran cold and he suddenly felt inutterably tired. He was a physician, dedicated to healing, and here he was being sucked into some vile intrigue where the taking of life appeared to be of little consequence. Aelfrith seemed to detect Bartholomew's feelings, for he gave one of his rare smiles, his eyes kindly.

'Rest now, Matthew. We will deal with this together, you and I.'

He was gone before Bartholomew could respond. Bartholomew put cold wraps around his knee and hobbled over to his bed to lie down. It was gloomy in the room with the shutters closed, but he could not be bothered to get up to open them again. He thought of the drugged commoners. He should really go to see to them. And he should check the blacksmith's leg. And Agatha would be wondering what to do with the woman he left with her last night. And he had promised his sister he would visit today. With his thoughts tumbling around inside his head, Bartholomew fell into a restless doze.

Bartholomew awoke, the sun full on his face, to the sound of the bell ringing to announce that the meal was about to be served in the hall. Like most of the Colleges and hostels, the main meal at Michaelhouse was between ten and eleven o'clock in the morning, with a second, smaller meal around four, and bread and ale for those that wanted it later in the evening.

He was disoriented for a moment, since he seldom slept during the day. Then the events of the morning came flooding back to him, and some of the brightness went out of the sunshine. Abigny had returned and opened the shutters, and was sitting at the table writing. He turned when he heard Bartholomew moving, his face lined with concern.

'At last!' he said, 'I have never known you to sleep a day away before. Are you ill?'

Bartholomew shook his head. His knee felt better already from the rest. He sat quietly for a moment, listening to the scratching of Abigny's quill as he finished what he was writing, and Brother Michael's footsteps as he moved about in the room above. Brother Michael shared a room with Michaelhouse's two Benedictine students, but Michael's footsteps were distinct from the others' because of his weight. After a few moments, he came thundering down the stairs, bent on being the first to the meal. Bartholomew heard him puffing as he hurried across the courtyard.

Upstairs, the other brothers moved about much more quietly, their sandalled feet making little sound. Suddenly, something clicked in Bartholomew's memory.

As he had lain at the bottom of the stairs after being pushed, he had heard footsteps, presumably those of his attacker. He could not tell where they came from, but they had been very distinct. The south wing, where the commoners roomed, was better built than the north wing where Bartholomew lived – he had climbed the stairs that morning without making a sound, which was why he had taken his attacker by surprise. While Bartholomew could usually hear sounds from the upstairs rooms in the north wing, he had noticed that the south wing was very much quieter, and the ground-floor residents were seldom disturbed by the people above them.

So how was it that he had heard footsteps? Had he imagined it? Bartholomew had the feeling that if he could work out why hearing the footsteps bothered him, he would be much nearer to solving the mystery. For now, the answer eluded him, and he told himself that mysterious footsteps in the night were the least of his concerns compared to the murders of his colleagues.

He hauled himself up, splashed some water on his face, tried to restore some order to his unruly black hair, and made his way out. Abigny watched him.

'Well, you are in a mess,' he observed. 'No gallivanting off today, Physician. And I was going to ask you to come to St Radegund's with me to see my sister!'

Bartholomew glowered at him. Abigny's sister had been committed to the care of the nuns at St Radegund's following the death of her father a year before. It had not taken Abigny long to observe that his pretty, fair-haired sister and his scholarly chamber-mate seemed to find a lot to talk about. Philippa would give her brother no peace when he visited without Bartholomew in tow, though, for the life of him, Abigny could not imagine what his sister, who had spent the greater part of her life in convents, could ever have in common with the world-wise Bartholomew.

'Well, perhaps I should invite her to Michaelhouse,' he said playfully. 'You brought a woman here yesterday. I must tell Philippa about that; I am sure she would find it most amusing.'

Bartholomew shot him another withering glance.

'I am going,' Abigny said cheerfully, and waved a folded piece of parchment at Bartholomew. 'One advantage that a philosopher has over a physician is that he can write decent love poetry. So first, I am away to deliver this little work of genius to the woman of my dreams!'

'On which poor soul do you intend to prey this time?' asked Bartholomew drily. Abigny's innocent, boyish looks had cost many a girl her reputation, and Abigny seemed to move from relationship to relationship with staggering ease. He was playing with fire, for if Wilson had any inkling of what Abigny was doing, the philosopher would be forced to resign his fellowship and would have grave problems finding a teaching position elsewhere.

'That lovely creature from the Laughing Pig over in Trumpington,' replied Abigny, tapping Bartholomew on the shoulder gleefully. 'Now, do not look like that! I met her at the house of your very own sister, so she must be a woman of stainless reputation.'

'At Edith's?' queried Bartholomew. Edith's large household in the village of Trumpington, two miles away, was run with the style and elegance that befitted her husband's wealth and status. Bartholomew could not imagine how Abigny had met a tavern-maid there.

'Three weeks ago, at the farewell meal she had for young Richard going to Oxford,' said Abigny, seeing Bartholomew's confusion. 'I met her in the kitchens where she was delivering eggs. She has invited me to sample the fine ale that she has been brewing.'

'Giles, have a care! If you are caught frequenting drinking houses, Wilson will drop on you like a stone. He wishes himself rid of you only slightly less than he wishes himself rid of me.'

'Oh, come, Master Physician,' laughed Abigny, 'not so gloomy on such a wonderful day. The sun is shining, the birds are singing, and I am in love!'

Bartholomew looked dubiously at Abigny's piece of parchment. 'Can this barmaid read?' he asked.

Abigny laughed again. 'Of course not! So she will never know that the words here are actually a list of books I made for my students last term, now embellished with a few decorated capitals for appearance's sake. Parchment is expensive!'

Bartholomew noted that Abigny was wearing his best robe and hose, implying that his intentions towards the barmaid were serious, if not honourable. Abigny set off, jauntily waving his hat in the air before disappearing through the door. He put his head back a moment later. 'By the way,' he said, 'your smelly patient has gone. I sent Cynric to tell his family to come and remove him. I could not bear to have him lying about here all day! He said to tell you he would keep his side of the bargain whatever that might mean.'

He had disappeared a second time before Bartholomew had a chance to reply. Bartholomew saw that Alcote had emerged from his room on the next staircase, and, since his window shutters were open, had probably heard their entire conversation. Of all the Fellows, Alcote was the one who most strongly disapproved of women having anything to do with the College. Bartholomew wondered if he had once been married and the experience had driven him to extremes. Alcote was a small, fussy man who reminded him of a hen. He was impatient with his less-able scholars, and most of his students lived in fear of his scathing criticisms.

Bartholomew made his way slowly round the court-yard, Alcote walking silently next to him.

'Has Augustus's body been found?' Bartholomew asked.

Alcote looked sharply at him. 'Augustus has not been found yet,' he said. 'We are still searching and will bring him to justice, never fear. He could not possibly have left the College grounds, because the porters at the main gates were awake all night owing to the racket the students were making in the hall, and they are positive no one went past them. And your woman kept Mistress Agatha awake all night weeping, and she says no one went out of the back gate.'

'How are the commoners?'

Alcote smiled gloatingly. 'Waking with dreadful heads and sick stomachs, and it serves them right,' he said. 'Next time they will beware of the sin of gluttony.'

Bartholomew stopped and grasped Alcote's wrist. 'Are they really sick? Why did no one wake me? I may be able to give them something to relieve the symptoms.'

Alcote freed his wrist. 'There is nothing you can do. They will live.'

Aelfrith joined them. 'How is your head?' Bartholomew asked.

'My years of learning must have given me a tough skull,' said Aelfrith with a smile, 'for I feel no ill effects at all.'

They reached the main building and climbed the wide spiral stairs to the hall. The borrowed tapestries that had adorned the walls the night before had been removed, but evidence of the festivities was still apparent in the scraps of food that littered the rushes on the floor, and in the smell of spilled wine.

'Master Abigny?' asked Wilson, his voice loud in the otherwise silent hall.

'Visiting his sister,' replied Brother Michael. It had become a standard excuse. Sir John had not been too particular about whether his Fellows chose to eat in College or not, but, judging from the way Wilson's mouth set in a firm line of displeasure, from now on Fellows would be required to attend meals in hall.

Alcote whispered something to Wilson that made the master's eyes glitter with anger. Bartholomew had no doubt that Alcote was telling him about what he had overheard. Spiteful little man, he thought, and turned to see Michael raising his eyes heavenwards, much to the amusement of the students at the end of the table.

'Silence!' Wilson banged a pewter goblet on the table, making everyone jump, and the giggles of the students stopped instantly. Wilson glared around. 'Two of our members lie foully murdered,' he said. 'It is not a time for frivolous laughter.' Some of the students hung their heads. Gentle Paul would be missed. Throughout the summer he had sat in the sun in the courtyard and had been only too happy to while away the hours by debating with the students to help them develop their skills in disputation, and by patiently explaining points of grammar, rhetoric, and logic to those who had stayed on to try to catch up.

Wilson intoned the long Latin grace, and then nodded to the Bible scholar to begin the recital that would last throughout the meal. Sir John had encouraged academic debate, and had chaired some very lively discussions, all aimed to hone and refine the College's reputation of academic excellence. Wilson was more traditional in approach, and considered it fitting for scholars to listen to tracts from the Bible while they ate, so that they could improve their spiritual standing.

Bartholomew studied his colleagues. Brother Michael, on his right, hunched over his trencher, greedily cramming pieces of meat into his mouth. Bartholomew offered him the dish of vegetables seeped in butter, and received, as always, a look of disbelief. Michael firmly believed that vegetables would damage his digestion and lived almost entirely on large quantities of meat, fish, and bread. Bartholomew thought back to Michael's odd behaviour of the night before. Was it illness as he had claimed, or did he know something about Augustus's death? Bartholomew had never seen the fat monk in such a state, but whatever had upset him was obviously not affecting his appetite now.

Aelfrith sat between Bartholomew and Father William. When speaking was permitted at meals, the Franciscans would usually discuss theology in Latin. Bartholomew compared the two men. Aelfrith was tall and thin, with a sallow face and grey eyes that were often distant. Bartholomew did not find him a warm man, but he was compassionate, discreetly generous to many of Bartholomew's poorer patients, and devoted to his teaching. Father William was of a similar height, but much heavier. Like Aelfrith, he was in his late forties, but his hair was thick and brown. His eyes often burned with the passion of the fanatic, and Bartholomew could believe the rumours that he had been appointed to search out heresy by his Order, and had been sent to Cambridge because he was over-zealous.

Wilson was the oldest Fellow, probably just past fifty, and was a singularly unattractive individual. His dry brown hair released a constant dusting of dandruff that adorned all his gowns, and his complexion was florid with a smattering of spots that reached right down to his array of chins. Swynford leaned towards him and whispered. Swynford was distantly related to the powerful Dukes of Norfolk, and held considerable sway in University circles. In a place where a College depended on the seniority and authority of its Fellows and Master, Michaelhouse owed much of its influence to Swynford. Wilson would need to keep him happy. Swynford was a handsome man around the same age as the Franciscans, but his bearing was more military than monastic, his manner confident and assured. His hair was grey, thick, and neat, and his beard always well groomed. He was the only Fellow, other than the Master, to have the luxury of a room and a servant of his own, and he paid the College handsomely for the privilege. Beside his impressive figure, Alcote looked like a small bird.

Bartholomew speared a slice of turnip on his knife and chewed it thoughtfully. Alcote had said that the porters and Agatha were prepared to swear that no one had left the College, other than the guests, once the gates had been locked after the Oliver brothers had attempted to provoke the riot. This meant that, unless someone had entered the College early and stayed until after the gates were unlocked the following morning, the murderer was a College member. There were few places to hide in Michaelhouse: all the rooms were occupied by students, Fellows, commoners, or servants, and all, except Swynford, shared a room with at least one other person. It would be difficult to hide in a small room where two or more people slept. There had been students in the hall and the conclave all night, which meant that no one could have hidden there, and the servants would have noticed anything untoward in the kitchens and other service rooms.

The more Bartholomew thought about it, the more his instincts told him that the murderer was a College man, who knew the habits and routines of its members. Bartholomew glanced along the table at his colleagues. Which one, if any, had murdered Paul, Augustus and possibly Sir John, and attacked him and Aelfrith? From size alone it could not have been Alcote or Abigny – they were too small. Brother Michael was fat, and since he deplored exercise of any kind, Bartholomew thought it unlikely that Michael could best him in a tussle, although it was possible. That left William, Wilson, and Swynford, all of whom were tall and probably strong enough. Then there were the commoners, Henri d'Evéne and Jocelyn of Ripon.

The only way he could reduce the list would be by establishing who was where, when, and with whom. Michael and Bartholomew had seen Augustus alive before the beginning of the feast, which meant that he had died at some point between the time when Bartholomew left him and Alexander had found him. All the Fellows and commoners had been at the feast the entire time that Bartholomew had been there. There were privies between the hall and the conclave, so no one had needed to leave the hall for that reason.

Bartholomew rubbed his eyes. Had Augustus been murdered? He had spent a long time looking for evidence that he had been, and had found nothing. But it was all too coincidental – Augustus dying the night Paul was stabbed and the commoners drugged. And for what had Bartholomew's attacker been searching?

And what of Paul? When had he died? Assuming that Aelfrith was telling the truth, Paul had probably been killed about the same time that the Franciscan had been knocked on the head. Bartholomew remembered that Paul's blood had congealed slightly, and the body was cold and beginning to grow stiff. If all the Fellows had retired to their beds around the same time as had Bartholomew, any of them could have slipped over to the south wing, murdered Paul, and drugged the commoners' wine.

But why? What could be so important as to warrant murder? Why was Augustus's room ransacked? And where was his body? Why would anyone want to take it? And how did all this tie in with Sir John's death? The more Bartholomew thought about it, the more confused and inexplicable the possibilities became.

The meal took longer than usual because some of the servants were still employed in searching for Augustus. The Bible scholar droned on and Bartholomew grew restless. He should question the commoners about the drugged wine, and visit Agatha and Mistress Atkin. He had badgered a fellow physician, Gregory Colet, to lend him a scroll containing some of the writings of the great physician Dioscorides, and Bartholomew was anxious to begin reading it. Despite being a centre for learning, copies of books and scholarly writings were scarce in Cambridge, and each was jealously guarded. Colet would not wait too long before he wanted his scroll back. If the students were to pass their disputations, they had to know Dioscorides's lists of healing plants. But for Bartholomew merely knowing was not enough: he wanted his students to understand the properties of the potions they used, the harmful and beneficial effects these might have, and how they might affect the patient when they were taken over a long period of time. Before he began teaching them this, he wanted to refresh his memory.

At last the meal was over and the scholars rose for the final grace. Then the Fellows clustered around Wilson, who had just been listening to Gilbert.

'Still nothing,' he informed his colleagues. 'But I have alerted the porters to watch both gates for Augustus, and we will continue our search for the rest of the day if necessary. The man must be found. The Bishop will be here this evening, and I will turn this miserable business over to him, as is my duty. Doubtless he will want to see us all when he arrives.'

Bartholomew was glad to leave the hall and go out into the fresh air. It was not yet noon, but the sun was already scorching. He leaned against the wall for a minute, enjoying the warmth on his face, with his eyes closed. The air in the courtyard felt still and humid, and Bartholomew was acutely aware of the stench from the ditches west of the College. He thought of one of his patients, Tom Pike, who lived down by the wharves on the river and had a lung disease. This weather would make life unbearable for him. The smells and the insects were always worse by the river and the King's Ditch than elsewhere in the town. He wondered if bad smells and foul air were responsible for the spread of the plague that was ravaging Europe.

He saw the commoners, Jocelyn of Ripon and d'Evéne the Frenchman, coming out of the hall together and hailed them over.

'Are you better now?' he asked, looking closely at the rings under their eyes and the way they winced at the brightness of the sun.

'My head aches something rotten,' grumbled Jocelyn. 'Master Swynford told me the wine may have been tampered with, and I can tell you, Doctor Bartholomew, that it would come as no surprise to me if it were. I have not had a hangover like this since I was ten years old!'

Bartholomew could well believe it of this rough man who drank so much. D'Evéne coughed cautiously. 'That is the last time I drink French wine,' he said, a weak attempt at a joke.

'Do you recall which jug of wine it was that contained the drug?' asked Bartholomew.

Jocelyn looked at him in disbelief. 'Of course I do not!' he said. 'Do you think I would have drunk it if I thought it had been poisoned?'

Bartholomew smiled, acknowledging the absurdity of his question. D'Evéne interrupted. 'I remember,' he said. 'I have a natural aversion to wine – it brings on blinding headaches – so I avoid it whenever possible, and drink ale instead. Last night, a good while after you Fellows left, the commoners were all together enjoying the atmosphere, the food, the drink, when poor Montfitchet started to complain about feeling ill. We ignored him until he really was sick, which made us all begin to question the states of our own stomachs. We decided to leave, and went across to our room together. When we were there, before going to sleep, someone said it would be right and proper to toast Master Wilson and his new role with his best wine. Montfitchet and I declined the wine, but everyone else said we were being churlish, and that we should drink Master Wilson's health with his fine red wine. I had consumed a good deal of ale by then, and so I allowed myself to accept when I should have declined. So did Montfitchet. I have no idea how the wine came from the hall to our dormitory, but it was there.'

Jocelyn looked at him. 'Yes, by God!' he said. 'The wine in the jug. I poured it out. It was my idea to drink the Master's health. I do not recall how it arrived in our room. It was just there, and I saw it was fairly distributed among the lot of us.'

'When did you start to feel the effects?'

'It is difficult to say,' d'Evéne replied, with a shrug. 'Perhaps half an hour? The older folks had already dropped off to sleep, but Jerome, Roger Alyngton, Jocelyn and I were still chatting. We were already merry, and I do not think any of us felt that the sudden soporific feeling was anything more than too much strong drink. Although perhaps poor Montfitchet felt different.'

Bartholomew spoke to Alyngton, Father Jerome, and two of the old men. None of them could add to d'Evéne's story, although all claimed to have gone back to the dormitory together.

Bartholomew sat again, resting his back against the pale apricot stone, his head tipped back and his eyes closed against the brightness of the sun. A shadow fell across him, and he squinted up.

'We must talk, Matthew, but not here. Meet me

shortly, in the orchard.' Aelfrith, after a furtive glance round, glided off towards his room.

'Give me a hand up, Brother,' Bartholomew said to Michael, emerging last from the hall, his jaws still working on a scrap of food. Michael extended a hand and pulled. Bartholomew was momentarily taken aback by the strength of Michael's arm. He had always imagined the large monk to be flabby and weak, but Bartholomew was hauled to his feet with effortless ease.

'I am away to Barnwell Priory this afternoon,' Michael said, wiping his mouth on his sleeve. 'Want to come? We could stop off at St Radegund's on the way.' He gave a most unmonklike leer. Had Abigny told everyone of Bartholomew's interest in his sister?

'I cannot, Brother. I am going to talk to Aelfrith.' Michael gave him an odd glance. 'What about?'

'This business about Augustus, I suppose,' said Bartholomew. 'Do you believe me, Michael? Do you think Augustus was dead last night?'

'Oh, yes,' said Michael fervently, 'Augustus was dead. I saw you do your usual checks, and I saw him myself. Look, Matt,' he said suddenly, seizing Bartholomew's wrist with a clammy hand, 'you must be cautious.' He glanced about him, as furtive as Aelfrith had been. 'I do not understand what is going on, but I am afraid. Afraid for me and afraid for you.'

'Afraid of what?' asked Bartholomew in a hushed voice.

'I do not know,' said Michael, exasperated, tightening his grip on Bartholomew's arm. 'Perhaps it is the work of the Devil. Augustus thought so, and now his body has disappeared.'

'Come now, Brother,' said Bartholomew reasonably.

'You cannot believe that. You have always told me that the only Devil is man himself. And what do you mean about Augustus and the Devil?'

Michael shook his head. 'I do not know. He spoke of it just before he died.'

'When exactly?'

Michael shook his head again and released Bartholomew's arm. 'I do not remember. But you must be cautious. Go to meet Aelfrith, but remember what I say.'

He scurried off and disappeared into the dark doorway of his staircase. Bartholomew watched him thoughtfully. What was bothering Michael? What was going on in the College?

IV

HEN BARTHOLOMEW RETURNED TO HIS ROOM, there was a message from one of the wealthy cloth merchants in Milne Street asking him to visit. Bartholomew glanced up at the sun, trying to estimate whether he had sufficient time before he was due to meet Aelfrith. He hesitated for a moment, but then set off, swinging his heavy bag of potions and instruments over his shoulder, aware that he should walk slowly to avoid straining his knee. Since the merchant had never asked for him before, Bartholomew imagined that his brother-in-law must have recommended him.

He found the house, a rambling building gleaming under fresh whitewash, and knocked at the door. A servant directed him up the stairs and into a sumptuous room hung with cloth of blue and gold. There was even glass in the windows, and the sun filtered through it to make patterns on the wooden floor. Bartholomew introduced himself, and sat on the bed to listen to his new patient's problem. It did not take him long to discover that if Nathaniel the Fleming had been more abstemious with Master Wilson's wine at the Michaelhouse feast the night before, he would not have been lying in his bed complaining of pains in his head and stomach cramps. Bartholomew listened gravely to Nathaniel's list of ailments, and prescribed large quantities of watered ale and a cold compress for his head. Nathaniel looked aghast.

'But you have not consulted my stars. And should you not leech me?'

Bartholomew shook his head. 'There is no need for leeches, and I do not need to read your stars to understand the nature of your . . . affliction.' He rose to take his leave.

'Wait!' Nathaniel, with a burst of energy that made him wince, grabbed Bartholomew's arm. 'Oswald Stanmore told me you were the best physician in Cambridge. Is watered ale and wet cloths all that you prescribe? How do you know about the state of my humours?'

Bartholomew felt a flash of impatience. 'Of course, I could spend the afternoon consulting charts and learning of your humours. But at the end of the day, my advice to you would be the same: drink lots and apply a cool cloth to soothe your head. Time will heal the rest.'

Nathaniel half rose from his bed. 'But that is not enough! What kind of physician are you that you choose not to use the tools of your trade?'

'An honest one, Master Nathaniel,' retorted Bartholomew. 'I do not seek to charge you for services you do not need.'

'But how do you know?' argued Nathaniel. 'And I feel the need for leeches.'

'Then I cannot help you,' said Bartholomew, turning to leave.

'Then I will send for Master Colet,' said Nathaniel. 'He knows his leeches. You need not tend to me again.'

Bartholomew left, biting his tongue to prevent himself from telling Nathaniel he was a fool. As he clattered down Nathaniel's fine staircase, he heard the merchant ordering a servant to fetch Colet. Clenching his fists in frustration, he wondered whether he should have complied with Nathaniel's request – applied leeches to his arm to remove the excess of humours, and read his stars to see what other treatment they might suggest. But the man only had a hangover! Why should Bartholomew waste his time applying treatments that were unnecessary? And why should Nathaniel pay for them? As he walked home, his frustration and anger subsided. Once again, he had lost the chance of a wealthy patient because he tried to give him what he knew was best, rather than what the patient expected. Sir John had been wise when he encouraged Bartholomew to work among the poor – they seldom questioned his skills, even if they did not always follow his advice.

Bartholomew stopped at the kitchen for something to drink, and by the time he had limped to the orchard, Aelfrith was already waiting. It was pleasant in the shade of the trees, with the rich scent of ripe apples. Bartholomew made his way to the ancient tree-trunk that lay against the wall, and had been used by countless students to study in solitude or to enjoy a nap in the sun.

'I have made sure that we are the only ones here,' Aelfrith said. 'I want no one to overhear us.'

Bartholomew watched him warily, Michael's warnings ringing in his ears. Aelfrith took a deep breath. 'There is an evil loose in the College,' he said, 'and we must try to stamp it out.'

'What is the evil, and how do we stamp it out?' Bartholomew asked. 'And why all the secrecy?'

Aelfrith looked hard into Bartholomew's eyes, as if searching for something. 'I do not want to tell you what I am about to,' he said. 'Until last night I would have said you were better not knowing. But now things have changed, and I have been instructed to tell you for your own good.'

He paused and squinted up into the leafy branches of the apple trees, as if his mind was wrestling with itself. 'There is an evil afoot that threatens not only the College, but the whole University, and perhaps even all England,' he blurted out. Bartholomew studied him. He was deeply agitated about something, and perspiration beaded on his face. 'Satan is trying to destroy us.'

'Oh come, Father,' said Bartholomew, his patience beginning to wane. 'Surely you did not bring me here to tell me that. You sound just like Augustus!'

Aelfrith's head whipped round to look at him. 'Exactly,' he whispered. 'Augustus saw, but his wits were gone, and he was unable to keep his secret. Look what happened to him!'

'What happened to him, Father?' asked Bartholomew. He had spoken to no one about his suspicions that Augustus had been murdered. Perhaps now he would hear them confirmed.

'Augustus was taken by the Devil,' Aelfrith said in a whisper. Bartholomew tried not to show his irritation. He personally concurred with Michael that the only devils to exist were those within man himself, and he had considered Aelfrith beyond common superstitions about devils and demons.

'Is that all?' asked Bartholomew, beginning to rise. Aelfrith tugged him back down. 'No, that is not all,' he said coldly. 'You must be patient. This is most difficult for me.' He clasped his hands together, and muttered some prayer, trying hard to compose himself. Bartholomew picked up a fallen apple from the ground and began to eat it. It was sharp, and not quite ripe.

'It is a complex story, so you must be patient. You must remember that I am telling you this because it may be necessary for your own safety, and not because I wish to entertain you.'

Bartholomew nodded, intrigued, despite himself.

'A little more than a year ago, the master of King's Hall died. You probably remember. He is said to have hanged himself, although the official story is that he fell down the stairs and broke his neck.'

Bartholomew remembered the incident well, and had heard the rumours that his death had been suicide. Had that been true, then the Master of King's Hall would not have been buried in consecrated ground, as with Sir John. But he had died in the privacy of his own College, and his scholars had been able to hide the manner of his death from outside eyes. So he had been laid to rest in a fine alabaster tomb in All Saints' Church. Sir John had chosen a public place for his suicide, and, however much the Fellows wished the details of his death silenced, it had become public knowledge within a few hours.

'Within a few weeks, two more Fellows of King's Hall died, of summer ague. These three deaths disturbed the scholars of King's Hall, but a new Master was elected, and life returned to normal. About the same time, one of the Deans at Peterhouse was found dead in the fish-ponds. He was thought to have fallen in and drowned while in his cups.'

Bartholomew wondered where all this was leading.

Aelfrith continued, 'The Dean was a close friend, a Franciscan like myself. He did not like alcoholic beverages; he said they clouded his thoughts. I do not believe that he would have ever allowed himself to become drunk enough to drown in a fish-pond! A few days after the Dean, two Fellows at Clare lay dead from eating bad food.'

Bartholomew recalled the two deaths at Clare. He had been called to help by Gregory Colet, the teacher of medicine at Rudde's Hostel, who had been a guest of the Master of Clare that night. He and Colet had been mystified by the case. The two Fellows had eaten some oysters sent by the grateful parent of a successful student. Others, including Colet, had eaten the oysters, too, and although some complained of sickness, only the two young men had died. Colet and Bartholomew had stood by helplessly, and had watched them die.

'For several months there were no further deaths, but then, a few weeks ago, the Hall of Valence Marie, founded this most recent year, lost two Fellows to summer ague. Now, I know as well as you do that deaths from accidents and agues are not infrequent in Cambridge. But add these deaths to our four at Michaelhouse, and we have an unnaturally high figure: twelve in the Colleges in the last year.'

'So what exactly are you telling me?' Bartholomew asked, the unease that he had experienced in Augustus's room the previous night returning.

'That not all these deaths were natural, and that some of them are connected.'

The feeling of unease intensified. 'But why?'

'Not everyone wants the University to flourish,' Aelfrith said. 'There are those who wish to control it, or to stamp it out altogether. You know what happened to the University at Stamford in 1334. It was becoming a rival to Oxford and Cambridge, and the King suppressed it. He closed down all the hostels and forbade the masters to teach there. Many tried to go back to Oxford or Cambridge, but found that they were not granted licences to teach. If you remember your history, you will know that Henry III did the same to the University of Northampton in 1265. The University of Oxford is larger, older, and more powerful than Cambridge, but Cambridge is growing and is increasing its influence . . .'

'Are you saying that the University at Oxford is murdering our Fellows?' Bartholomew said incredulously. 'That is the most ridiculous thing I have ever heard! I am sorry, Father, but what kind of nonsense have you been listening to . . .?'

'It is not nonsense, and we have proof!' Aelfrith snapped back. 'Just listen to me! Every single Fellow who died had been an Oxford student before he came to Cambridge.'

'That is not proof, Father, that is coincidence. I went to Oxford first, and so did you!'

'Which is why I am telling you this,' replied Aelfrith, regaining his calm with difficulty. 'About thirty years ago, King Edward II founded King's Hall. He gave it money, buildings, and sent to it scholars and boys destined to be some of the most powerful men in England. Many scholars at Oxford considered this a great insult to them – the King should have endowed this great foundation in Oxford, not Cambridge. But the City of Oxford had refused to help Edward's – well, let us say "friend" – Piers Gaveston when he was imprisoned, and the man was later killed. Edward had no cause to love Oxford. The present

King has continued to give money and influence to King's Hall, and with its growing prestige and power, so grows the University of Cambridge. King's Hall is the largest and most influential of all the Colleges and hostels in Cambridge.

'There are many who believe that there is a secret group of Oxford men who have come to Cambridge to try to bring about the downfall of the Colleges, and when the Colleges fall, the University will crumble with them.'

'Come now, Father!' said Bartholomew, disbelievingly. 'The University would not crumble without the Colleges! Without the hostels, maybe, since there are more of them, and they house the majority of the masters and scholars.'

'Think, man!' said Aelfrith, his agitation rising again. 'The loudest and most frequently heard voices in the University are not from the hostels, they are from the Fellows of the five Colleges. The Colleges own their own buildings, their own land, and the hostels do not. The hostels rely on the good graces of the town – a landlord only need say he wants to reclaim the hostel because he wishes to live in it, then the hostel is finished, its scholars and masters no more than homeless vagrants. It is rumoured that Edmund Gonville will found another College soon, and so might the Bishop of Norwich. The Colleges are becoming powerful in the University – they are its future – and as the Colleges increase in power, so does the University.'

'But there are scholars enough for both Oxford and Cambridge, and we take them from different parts of the country anyway,' protested Bartholomew.

Aelfrith shook his head impatiently, and continued his narrative. 'You know the stories that a terrible pestilence is coming. For seven years it has been coming, from the lands in the Far East and across Europe. Many said it would not come across the waters that separate us from France, but it is already in the West Country. It is said that whole villages will be wiped out, and that it is a sign of God's wrath for the sin of man. It is said that God is especially angry with his priests and monks, and that many of us will perish for our sins.'

'With good reason,' muttered Bartholomew, thinking of the wealthy monasteries and the heavy Church taxes on the poor.

'You are failing to see the point!' said Aelfrith, exasperated. 'If there is a huge reduction in the clergy, then the two Universities *will* be competing for scholars. And who will teach them if we are to lose most of our masters? There are many, both in Oxford and Cambridge, who believe that the Universities will be fighting for their very existences before the year is out. Cambridge, being the smaller, is the more vulnerable. The weaker Cambridge is, the greater chance for survival Oxford will have. Ergo, some Oxford scholars are waging a secret war against us in anticipation of the events to come.'

'You really believe this, don't you?' said Bartholomew, incredulously.

'Yes, I do. And so should you. I spoke of evidence. We are not without our own spies, and we have documents from Oxford scholars stating their intentions very clearly.'

'You say "we",' said Bartholomew. 'Who else knows of this?'

'I cannot say,' said Aelfrith, 'because we do not know who is truthfully for Cambridge, and who may have been sent by Oxford. I can only tell you that seven of the Fellows whose deaths I mentioned earlier were of the same mind as me, including Sir John and the two young lads you tried to treat for food poisoning. This network of spies is nothing recent – there is nothing inherently wrong in watching the moves of the opposition, and we have had people who have traded information for as long as University records exist. But there has never been any violence, especially murder. Poor Augustus knew of the threat and he must have been killed because it was thought he might know something – someone believed he should not have done.'

'By whom? By Oxford people to strike at the Colleges, or by Cambridge people to keep him from spilling their secrets?'

'That is my problem, Matthew. I do not know.'

Bartholomew looked at him through narrowed eyes. 'Good company you keep, Priest, if you think them capable of murder.'

Aelfrith rose restlessly, and began to pace back and forth. Bartholomew caught a sparkle of tears in his eyes as he walked, and was sorry for his comment. Aelfrith was a virtuous man, and Bartholomew was sure that he had allowed himself to become embroiled in the murky world of University politics for the purest of reasons, and probably for what he considered to be the good of the College.

'You saw Augustus's room,' the friar said, after a moment. 'Someone was looking for something. Whoever attacked us had chipped loose plaster from the walls and had tried to prise up the floorboards. I have an idea of what the person may have been looking for.'

'What could possibly be worth the killing of two old men?'

Aelfrith smiled. 'You are a good man, Matthew, but you have been out into the world and you should know better than to ask a question like that. The lives of two old men are worth nothing to those that we are dealing with – on either side.' He stopped pacing and came to sit next to Bartholomew again. 'The spy system uses coded messages. We are dealing with some of the best minds in England here, so the codes have become very intricate and complex. All coded messages are affixed with a specific mark, or seal, so that their authenticity can be assured. Each time a message is sent, the seal is attached.

'You probably did not know that Sir John acted as an agent for the King for many years. Essentially, his task was to act as a link, passing information up and down the chain of communication. Each contact had a different sign that only he and Sir John knew, to ensure that only authentic information would be passed on. About a year ago – the same time as the first deaths in King's Hall – one of Sir John's contacts started to send messages about a group of scholars at the University of Oxford who are dedicated to bringing about the downfall of the University here.

'The sign Sir John used with this contact was an elaborate knot design carved into a gold signet ring – they had one each, exact duplicates in every detail. When a message came, Sir John only needed to match his seal with the one on the message to know that it was authentic. The design of the seals was very complex, and Sir John would have known if a message was marked with an imitation. Sir John carried this seal with him always, on a thick cord around his neck. After Sir John died, the seal he used to send his messages disappeared.'

Bartholomew nodded, a little impatient at the lengthy explanation. He had seen the ring Aelfrith was talking about. It always hung on a robust length of leather around Sir John's neck. Bartholomew had asked him about it once, and Sir John had given him the impression that it was a trinket of no inherent value, but of great personal significance. Bartholomew supposed, in the light of what Aelfrith had just told him, that Sir John had spoken the truth.

'On the night of his death Sir John visited Augustus, and may have hidden the seal in his room. I am sure Sir John was killed because someone wanted to steal the seal, but I am also confident that he was not wearing it when he died.'

'How can you be sure of that?'

'The manner of his death. He is said to have thrown himself into the mill race so that he would be either crushed or drowned by the water-wheel.'

Bartholomew swallowed hard and looked away. Aelfrith continued.

'There were two odd things about Sir John's death. The first is that when you, Swynford, and I dined with him on the night of his death, he did not seem like a man about to take his own life. Would you agree?'

Bartholomew assented. It was a fact that had played on his mind, increasing his sense of helplessness about Sir John's death. Had the Master seemed ill or depressed, Bartholomew could have offered his support and friendship.

'The second odd thing was the clothes he was wearing. Now,' Aelfrith held up his hand as Bartholomew began to protest, 'I am not going to say anything that will harm Sir John's reputation further. He was wearing the habit of a Benedictine nun. Correct?'

Bartholomew refused to look at Aelfrith. It had been the most disturbing aspect of Sir John's death. It was bad enough to imagine him being in a state of mind where he could hurl himself under the water-wheel. But that his own clothes were nowhere to be found, and that he was clad in the gown of a nun, drew much speculation on Sir John's sanity and personal life.

'I do not think Sir John was in disguise as has been suggested,' said Aelfrith. 'I believe his clothes were stolen so that they could be thoroughly searched for the seal. I think he was killed – perhaps by a knock on the head – and his clothes taken after he had died. The nun's habit was specifically chosen to bring Michaelhouse into disrepute. Its Master wearing nun's clothes to commit suicide at the mill! The plan succeeded: the town people still nudge each other and grin when Michaelhouse is mentioned, and scholars in Oxford claim that there, the masters are men in men's clothing.'

Bartholomew winced, but said nothing. Aelfrith saw his discomfiture, and hurriedly changed the subject.

'But whoever killed Sir John did not find the seal, and came to look for it in Augustus's room, assuming that Sir John had hidden it there because it was the only place he had been between dining with us and leaving the College. I was knocked on the head, Paul stabbed, and the commoners drugged to allow time to make a thorough search. You interrupted that search, and were attacked.'

Bartholomew was about to dismiss Aelfrith's explanation as inadequate, when he recalled Augustus's words on the afternoon of Wilson's installation. He had spoken of an evil in the College that would corrupt all, but there was something else, too. 'Just remember John Babington, hide it well.' Bartholomew's thoughts raced forward. Perhaps Aelfrith was right, and Sir John had hidden the seal with Augustus, and Augustus had watched him. So, did that mean that Augustus had been killed so that the discovery of the seal would remain a secret? Was he killed because he had refused to reveal where it was hidden? But Bartholomew had seen no marks on Augustus's body to support the possibility that he was forced to do anything.

'But this does not explain what happened to Augustus's body,' he said. He began to have hopes that the bizarre manner of Sir John's death might be explained, and his good reputation restored.

Aelfrith sighed. 'I know. But one of the last messages Sir John received from Oxford said that our protagonists are in league with witches and warlocks,' he said. 'I do not think we will see our Brother Augustus again.'

Bartholomew disagreed. 'Bodies do not just disappear, Father,' he said. 'His will be found, especially if it is hidden away in this heat!'

Aelfrith pursed his lips in disgust. 'This is the part that disturbs me most of all,' he said. 'I believe the disappearance of Augustus's body was the work of the Devil, and that the Devil has a servant in this College!'

Bartholomew was surprised that Aelfrith would so readily accept witchcraft as an answer. He had also been surprised with Brother Michael for the same reason. It was too convenient an answer.

'So who do you think attacked us and killed Paul and Montfitchet?' he asked, to move the discussion on. Bartholomew could believe that the Devil had a servant in the College easily enough – someone who was committing murder and stealing bodies – but the idea that the Devil was responsible he found too hard to accept. He sensed he would not agree with Aelfrith on this point, and that if he questioned it further they might end up in the orchard for hours discussing it as a point of theology.

'The Devil's servant,' replied Aelfrith in response to Bartholomew's questions. He turned to Bartholomew. 'I have told you all this because I wish you to be on your guard – for your own life and for the security of your University.'

'Do the other fellows know all this?' asked Bartholomew.

'Master Wilson does. He thinks you are a spy because you have a degree from Oxford, because your practice takes you out of College a lot, and because he was suspicious of your relationship with Sir John. He warned Sir John about you many times. He does not like you, and now he is Master, he will undoubtedly try to see that your days as a Fellow here are numbered.'

That Wilson thought the worst of him, and might attempt to rid Michaelhouse of him, did not come as any great shock to Bartholomew. 'Who else knows?' he asked.

'Michael seems to know some of it, although he did not learn it from me. William and Alcote know. It was William who told me to warn you. Alcote is in Wilson's pocket, and believes you are a spy. They both think you were looking for the seal when you took so long with Augustus.'

'And what do you think, Father?'

'That you are innocent in all this, and that you should

remain so. I also reason that you grieve too deeply for Sir John to have been involved in any way with his death, and that you have continued to be a good friend after most others have abandoned him.'

Bartholomew squinted up into the apple trees. He wished Sir John were with him now, to help him reason out all this subterfuge and plotting. 'What of the others? Swynford and Giles Abigny?'

'Swynford is aware of the Oxford plot, but declines to become involved. His family have lands near Oxford, and he says it is in his interests to remain neutral. Sir John's contact has already reported that Swynford declined Oxford when they tried to recruit him. Abigny would not find the time between his love affairs for matters of such seriousness, and in any case, I could not trust his judgement nor his discretion. He has no connections with Oxford anyway, and would make them a poor spy. He does not move in the right circles to be of interest to them, unless they are concerned with tavern gossip.'

Bartholomew smiled. The flighty Abigny was from a different world than the austere Franciscan friars, and they would never see eye to eye. But Aelfrith was right. Abigny was appallingly indiscreet, and would never manage to remain sober long enough to do spying of any value. Aelfrith stood to leave.

'If you think of anything, however small, that might throw light onto this wretched affair, will you let me know?'

Bartholomew nodded. 'I will, but I have thought it over many times, and have not deduced the tiniest shred of evidence that could be of value. I think I would be as much a loss as a spy as would Giles!'

Aelfrith reached out to touch Bartholomew on the

shoulder, a rare gesture of affection for the sombre friar, and walked out of the orchard.

Bartholomew sat for a while, pondering what Aelfrith had told him. He still found it difficult to believe that Oxford and Cambridge scholars would play such dangerous games, and he would not accept that Augustus's body had been stolen by the Devil. The sun was hot, and he thought back to what he had said to Aelfrith. Bodies did not just disappear, so Augustus's corpse must have been either hidden or buried. If it were hidden, the heat would soon give it away; if it were buried, perhaps it would never be found.

The bell began to ring for the afternoon service at St Michael's, and Bartholomew decided to go to pray for the souls of his dead friends.

Bartholomew made his way slowly back from the church down St Michael's Lane. A barge from the Low Countries had arrived at the wharf earlier that day, and all the small lanes and alleys leading from the river to the merchants' houses on Milne Street were full of activity.

At the river the bustle was even more frenzied. A Flemish captain stood on the bank roaring instructions in dreadful French to his motley collection of sailors who yelled back in a variety of languages. At least two were from the Mediterranean, judging from their black curly hair and beringed ears, and another wore an exotic turban swathed around his head. Further up-stream, fishermen were noisily unloading baskets of eels and the slow-moving water was littered with tails and heads that had been discarded. Overhead, the gulls swooped and screeched and fought, adding to the general racket.

Behind the wharves were the rivermen's houses, a dishevelled row of rickety wooden shacks that leaked when it rained, and often collapsed when it was windy. Bartholomew saw an enormous rat slink out of one house and disappear into the weeds at the edge of the river where some small children were splashing about.

'Matt!' Bartholomew turned with a smile at the sound of his brother-in-law's voice. Sir Oswald Stanmore strode up to him. 'We were worried about you. What has been happening at Michaelhouse?'

Bartholomew raised his hands in a shrug. 'I do not know. The clerics are mumbling about evil walking the College, but Wilson thinks it was only Augustus.'

Stanmore rolled his eyes. 'Wilson is a fool. You should have heard him pontificating to us last night, telling us everything we would ever need to know about the wool trade, and about French cloth. The man would not know French cloth from homespun. But we have heard terrible rumours about Michaelhouse! How much did you all drink last night?'

Ever practical, Stanmore had put everything down to drunkenness, not such an unreasonable assumption considering the amount of wine that had flowed.

'Nathaniel the Fleming seems to have had his share too,' said Bartholomew, turning as one of the swimming children emitted an especially piercing shriek.

Stanmore laughed. 'I told him last night he would need your services this morning. Did he call you?'

Bartholomew nodded, and told him what had happened. Stanmore threw up his hands in despair.

'Lord save us, Matt! I provide you with one of the wealthiest men in the town as a patient, and you cannot even subdue your unorthodox thoughts long enough to treat him. I know,' he said quickly, putting up a hand to quell the coming objection, 'what you believe, and I understand, even applaud, your motives. But for the love of God, could you not even try to placate Nathaniel? You need to be far more careful now Wilson is Master, Matt. Even a child can see that he loathes you. You no longer have the favoured protection of Sir John, and securing a patient such as Nathaniel might have served to keep his dislike at bay for a while.'

Bartholomew knew Stanmore was right. He gave a rueful smile.

'Edith told me to call on you today to make certain you were well,' Stanmore continued. 'What have you done to your leg? What debauchery did your feast degenerate into once the sobering effects of your town guests had gone?' He was smiling, but his eyes were serious.

'Tell Edith I am fine. But I do not understand what is happening at Michaelhouse. The Bishop is due to arrive today and will take matters in hand.'

Stanmore chewed his lower lip. 'I do not like it, Matt, and neither will Edith. Come to stay with us for a few days until all this dies down. Edith is missing Richard; if you came, it would take her mind off him for a while.'

Richard, their only son, had left a few days before to study at Oxford, and the house would be strangely empty without him. Bartholomew was fond of his sister and her husband, and it would be pleasant to spend a few days away from the tensions of the College. But he had work to do: there were students who had returned before the Michaelmas term so that they could be given extra tuition, and he had his patients to see. And anyway, if he left now, Wilson would probably see it as fleeing the scene of the crime, and accuse him of the murders. Regretfully he shook his head.

'I would love to, I really would. But I cannot. I should stay.' He grabbed Stanmore's arm. 'Please do not tell Edith all you hear. She will only worry.'

Stanmore smiled understandingly. 'Come to see us as soon as you can, and talk to her yourself.' He looked round as loud shouts came from a group of apprentices, followed by a splash as someone fell in the river. 'I must go before they start fighting again. Take care, Matt. I will tell Edith you will visit soon.'

As Bartholomew made his way back up the lane, he saw a small cavalcade of horses trot into Michaelhouse's yard, and knew that the Bishop had arrived. Servants hurried to stable the horses, while others brought chilled ale and offered to shake dust out of riding cloaks. Wilson hurried from his new room to meet the Bishop, soberly dressed in a simple, but expensive, black gown.

The two men stood talking for a while, while students, commoners, and Fellows watched out of the unglazed windows. Eventually, Wilson led the way into the main building, through the hall and into the smaller, more private conclave beyond. Alexander was sent to fetch wine and pastries, and the College waited.

First, the servants were sent for. Then it was the turn of the students, and then the commoners. It was nearing the time for the evening meal when the Fellows were summoned. The Bishop sat in the Master's chair, which had been brought from the hall, while his clerks and assistants were ranged along the benches on either side of him. Wilson sat directly opposite, and, judging from his pallor and sweaty jowls, had not had an easy time of it.

The Bishop stood as the Fellows entered and beckoned them forward to sit on the bench with Wilson. Bartholomew had met the Bishop before, a man who enjoyed his physical comforts, but who was able to combine a deep sense of justice with his equally deep sense of compassion. He was known to be impatient with fools, severe with those who told him lies, and had no time at all for those unwilling to help themselves. Although Bartholomew thought he probably would not enjoy an evening in the Bishop's company, he respected his judgement and integrity.

The Fellows sat on either side of Wilson, Bartholomew at the end so he could stretch his stiff knee. He felt as if he were on trial. The Bishop started to speak.

'Master Wilson and Fellows of Michaelhouse,' he began formally. 'It is my right, as Bishop of this parish, to investigate the strange happenings of last night. I must tell you now that I am far from satisfied with the explanation I have been given.' He paused, and studied the large ring on his finger that contained his official seal. 'These are difficult times for the Church and for the University. There is news that a terrible pestilence is sweeping the land, and may be here before Christmas, and relations between the Church and the people are far from ideal. Neither the University nor the College can afford to have scandals. Much damage was done to both following the unfortunate death of Master Babington. You cannot allow another unsavoury incident to occur if you wish your College to survive.

'Now, two College members have been murdered,

perhaps by another, although I do not care to guess who the perpetrator of the crime might be. The College has been searched, and has revealed nothing. All the commoners, students, and servants have alibis – assuming that Brother Paul was slain during or after the feast. The commoners were all together, and each can vouch for every one of the others. Since the regular term's lectures have not yet begun, there are only fifteen students in residence, and all, like the commoners, can give alibis for each other. The servants had a hard night of work, and one missing pair of hands would have been immediately noticed. After the feast, they all retired exhausted to bed, and the good Mistress Agatha, who was kept awake by a grieving woman, swears that none left the servants' quarters until woken by the Steward this morning.

'That leaves the Fellows. Please understand that I am accusing no one, but you will each tell me where you were last night, and with whom. Master Wilson, perhaps you would set the example and begin.'

'Me?' said Wilson, taken aback. 'But I am the Master, I . . .'

'Your movements, please, Master Wilson,' said the Bishop coldly.

Wilson blustered for a few moments, while the Bishop waited like a coiled snake for him to begin. 'After Doctor Bartholomew told us that Augustus was dead, I felt it inappropriate to continue at the feast. Father William, Master Alcote, and Master Swynford left with me. Bartholomew and Brother Michael had already retired, and Master Abigny stayed, although I did not condone this.' A glint of pleasure crossed his features at having expressed his disapproval of Abigny to the Bishop.

SUSANNA GREGORY

'On the contrary, Master Wilson,' the Bishop intervened smoothly, 'I hope you did condone it. After all, you
were going to leave students in your hall with seemingly
unlimited quantities of wine, and a riot narrowly averted
earlier in the day. I would consider it an act of prudence
to leave a Fellow to oversee affairs. Why did you not end
the feast?'

Bartholomew hid a smile. He knew that many
students disliked Wilson and he had been trying to
win them round with his generosity with the wine. He
would not have wished to negate any positive points he
might have gained by ending the feast when the students
were still enjoying themselves.

Wilson opened and shut his mouth a few times,
before Swynford intervened. 'We discussed that, my
Lord Bishop. We felt that Augustus would not wish such
a joyous occasion to be brought to an early conclusion
on his account.'

The Bishop looked at Swynford narrowly before
returning his attention to Wilson. 'And what did you do
after you left the hall, Master Wilson?' he continued.

'I walked with Master Alcote to our room. I only
moved into the Master's room today; last night I was
in my old room. We talked for a while about Augustus,
and then we went to sleep.'

'Does this tally with your memory?' the Bishop asked
Alcote.

The nervous little man nodded, looking even more
like a hen than usual. 'Yes, we talked until the candle
expired, and then went to sleep. Neither of us went out,
or knew any more, until the next morning.'

'Father Aelfrith?'

'I left the hall and went straight to Augustus's room,

where I stayed all night. At some point, I heard a noise and went to check Brother Paul, who had been ill. He was asleep, and none of the other commoners had yet returned. I went back to my prayers, and was hit on the head from behind. I heard nothing and saw nothing. The next thing I recall was being helped up by Doctor Bartholomew.'

'Master Swynford?'

'I left the hall with Father William, and Masters Alcote and Wilson. I saw Brother Michael and Doctor Bartholomew walking together across the courtyard to their staircase. I went straight to my room and went to sleep. I am afraid that because I room alone, I have no alibi,' he said with an apologetic smile.

'Who else lives on your staircase?' the Bishop enquired.

'Father William lives downstairs from me.'

'Father, what were your movements?'

'I left the hall and went directly to my room. I saw Master Swynford go past moments later and disappear up the stairs. I share a room with three others of my Order, students, who left the feast when I did. All four of us prayed throughout the night for Augustus's soul, as did Father Aelfrith.'

'If Master Swynford had left his room during the night, would you have heard him?'

'I believe so, my Lord Bishop,' said William, after a moment's consideration. 'The night was humid. We did not want our voices to disturb others who were sleeping, and so the window shutters were closed, but the door was open to allow us some air. I am certain we would have heard if Master Swynford came down the stairs.'

'There is your alibi, Master Swynford,' said the Bishop. 'Doctor Bartholomew, where were you?'

'I went back to my room, checked on the blacksmith – he had had his leg broken in the skirmish outside the gates,' he added hastily, seeing the Bishop raise his eyebrows. 'I was tired and went to sleep straight away. I do not know when Giles returned. I rose while it was still quite dark, and, seeing the candle in Augustus's room, went to offer to relieve Father Aelfrith. I fought with someone and was pushed down the stairs. I could find no trace of him when I went to look, and then discovered that what I had assumed to be Augustus's body lying on the floor was actually Father Aelfrith, and Augustus had gone.'

'So you have no one who can confirm where you were all night?' asked the Bishop.

Bartholomew shook his head and saw Wilson exchange smug glances with Alcote.

'Brother Michael?' said the Bishop.

Michael shrugged. 'Like our physician, I have no alibi. We walked to our staircase together. I saw him check the disgusting man with the broken leg, and go into his own room. I went upstairs. My room-mates were enjoying Master Wilson's good wine in the hall, and were still enjoying it when dawn broke this morning. I was alone all night.'

'And finally you, Master Abigny. What have you to say?'

'I was in the company of Michael's two room-mates and the other students until I was too drunk to stay awake any longer,' Abigny announced cheerfully, ignoring Wilson's look of anger. 'The same two Benedictines took time from their roistering to help me to my room, where I remember nothing until woken by Alexander with stories of missing bodies and murder.' He sat back indolently, and Bartholomew knew that his entire demeanour was carefully calculated to annoy Wilson as much as possible.

'Let us summarise,' said the Bishop, ignoring Abigny's display. 'Everyone's movements can be vouched for except Bartholomew, Aelfrith, and Michael. Aelfrith could not have hit himself on the head from behind, and Bartholomew saw him lying on the floor before he engaged in his struggle.

'So, what we have left is a mystery. There is no doubt that evil deeds were committed, and that two men died. I find it difficult to believe that Doctor Bartholomew would mistake a living man for a corpse, but these things happen, especially after copious amounts of Master Wilson's good wine.' He raised his hand to stall the objection that Bartholomew was about to voice. He had had very little to drink the night before, chiefly because he did not feel Wilson's succession of Sir John good cause for celebration.

'Augustus, whether dead or alive, has gone. We may never know whether he was innocent or guilty of murder. It is imperative that this business is done with as quickly as possible. Neither your College nor the University can afford to have gossip about missing corpses and murders. You know what would happen – wealthy families would decline to send their sons here, and the University would eventually cease to exist altogether.'

Bartholomew shot a quick look at Aelfrith sitting next to him, echoes of their conversation coming back to him. Perhaps Aelfrith was right, and the whole affair was a plot by rivals to strike at the very foundations of the University.

The Bishop looked at each of the Fellows in turn before continuing. 'Neither you nor I has a choice in this matter. I have already spoken with the Chancellor and he agrees with me as to the course of action that must be taken. I repeat that you have no choice in this matter. There will be a funeral service for Augustus the day after tomorrow. It will be said that his body was discovered in the orchard, where he had been hiding. The excitement of the installation was too much for him, and had addled his wits. There are, I believe, medical conditions that make a living man appear as a corpse. Augustus was afflicted by this and was pronounced dead by the College physician. He later awoke from this trance, and struck Aelfrith from behind while he was praying. He ran down the stairs and slipped through the College buildings to the orchard, where he later died. Brother Paul, who had become depressed with his illness, took his own life. The other commoner . . .' The Bishop waved his hand impatiently.

'Montfitchet,' offered Wilson in a small voice, the enormity of what was being asked shaking him out of his usual smugness.

'Montfitchet, yes. Montfitchet died of his own excesses. The commoners have already attested to that. The man made a pig of himself all night, despite complaining of stomach pains caused by his gluttony. And that, Fellows of Michaelhouse, is what the world will be told happened here. There will be no rumours of evil in the College,' he said, looking hard at the Franciscans, 'and no tales of dead bodies walking in the night to murder their colleagues.'

He sat back to indicate that he had finished speaking. The conclave was totally silent, as the Fellows let his words sink in. The clerks, usually furiously scribbling when the Bishop spoke, sat ominously still. No record was being made of this meeting.

Bartholomew looked at the Bishop aghast. So, the Church and the University were prepared to cover the whole thing up, to smother the truth in a thick blanket of lies.

'No!' he cried, leaping to his feet, wincing as his injured knee took his weight. 'It would be wrong! Brother Paul was a good man, and you cannot condemn him to a grave in unconsecrated soil and allow his and Montfitchet's murderer to walk free!'

The Bishop rose, his eyes hard with anger, although his face remained calm. 'Brother Paul will be buried in the churchyard, Doctor,' he said. 'I will grant him a special dispensation in view of his age and state of mind.'

'But what of his murderer?' Bartholomew persisted, unappeased.

'There was no murderer,' said the Bishop softly. 'You heard what I said. One suicide, and two deaths by misadventure.'

'The servants already know Paul was murdered! They saw his body! And there are already rumours around the town.'

'Then you must make certain that no such rumours are given credence. You must prey on people's sympathies – a poor old man, lying alone listening to the celebrations in the hall. He decides to release his soul to the Lord so that he will no longer be an encumbrance to his College. Master Wilson tells me that there was a note saying as much found in Paul's hand.'

Bartholomew stared at Wilson in shock. The plan was becoming more and more elaborate with each passing moment. Wilson refused to meet Bartholomew's eyes and busied himself twisting the rings on his fat fingers.

'I agree with Bartholomew.' Swynford was also on his feet. 'This plan is not only foolhardy, but dangerous. If ever the truth were to be found out, we would all hang!'

'You will hang for treason if you do not comply,' said the Bishop casually, sitting down again. 'I have already informed you that the University cannot afford a scandal. There are many at King's Hall who enjoy the King's protection, who will consider any dissent in this matter to be a deliberate act of defiance towards the Crown.'

Swynford sat down hastily. He was well-enough connected with the University's power-brokers to know that this was not an idle threat. Bartholomew thought back to Aelfrith's words. The King, and his father before him, had invested money and power in King's Hall; any weakening of the University would injure their institution too, and no King liked to discover that he had made a poor choice in where he invested his authority.

'But what if Augustus's body is discovered after we "bury" it?' Bartholomew asked anxiously, his mind running through a wealth of possibilities in which the Michaelhouse Fellows would be discovered and exposed.

'Augustus will not be recovered, Doctor Bartholomew,' said the Bishop smoothly. 'I am sure I can rely on you all to see to that.'

Bartholomew swallowed. 'But this is against the laws of the Church and the State, and I will not do it,' he said quietly.

'Against the laws of the Church and the State?' said

the Bishop musingly. 'And who do you think makes these laws?' His voice became hard. 'The King makes the laws of the State, and the Bishops make the laws of the Church. You have no choice.'

'I will resign my fellowship,' persisted Bartholomew, 'rather than be a part of this.'

'There will be no resignations,' said the Bishop. 'We can afford no scandal. Now, we must come to some arrangement. Master Wilson informs me that you wish for a larger room for your medical consultations and an increase in your stipend . . .'

'And I will not be bribed!' retorted Bartholomew angrily.

The Bishop's face turned white with anger and Bartholomew knew that his protestations had touched a raw nerve. He stood again and advanced on Bartholomew.

'I see you have a bad leg, Doctor. Perhaps you would like to return with me to Ely so that my barber-surgeon can treat it? Perhaps there we can persuade you of your wisest course of action.' He gave Bartholomew one of the coldest smiles the physician had ever seen, and pushed him back down onto the bench.

William grabbed Bartholomew's arm as the Bishop walked back to his chair. 'For God's sake, man!' he hissed. 'The Bishop is being more than patient! He could hang you for treason right now, and if you force him to take you with him to Ely, you can be sure that you will not return the same man!'

Aelfrith nodded vigorously. 'Remember what I said to you,' he whispered. 'There are forces at work here of which you have no idea. Your life will not be worth a fig if you do not comply.'

'Now,' the Bishop began again, having controlled himself somewhat, 'I will require all here to take an oath that you will act as I have suggested. Master Wilson.'

The Bishop extended his hand, and Wilson stood slowly and knelt in front of the Bishop. He took the proffered hand.

'I swear, by all that I hold holy, that I will do everything in my power to save the College, the University, and the King's name from disrepute. I will tell no one of the events of last night other than as you suggest.' He kissed the seal on the Bishop's ring, bowed, and left the hall without looking back. For the first time since he had known him, Bartholomew felt sorry for Wilson. As Master, he had obviously been held responsible for the events of the night, and would have a formidable task in ensuring the Bishop's fabric of lies was accepted outside the College.

The Bishop eyed Swynford, who rose and swore the same oath. Bartholomew's thoughts were in turmoil. How could he make such a promise? It would be a betrayal of Sir John, Augustus, Paul, and Montfitchet. He would be saying that he, one of the most highly qualified physicians in the country, was unable to tell the difference between a living man and a dead one! He watched as Alcote scurried forward when Swynford left. What could he do? Perhaps he had already signed his death warrant with the Bishop, or with some of the forces about which Aelfrith had warned him.

Alcote left, and William stepped forward. Aelfrith seized his arm. 'You must take the oath! You will not live another day if you do not! Do it for the College, for Sir John.' He broke off as the Bishop gestured for him to approach. Michael slid along the bench towards Bartholomew, his eyes frightened in his flabby face.

'For God's sake, Matt! None of us like this, but you are putting us all in danger. Do you want to be hanged, drawn, and quartered at Smithfield? Just swear this wretched oath! You do not need to do anything else. You can always go away until all this dies down.'

Abigny stepped forward. Michael's grip became painful. 'Not to take the Bishop's oath will be treason, Matt. I understand the position you are taking, but it will cost you your life if you persist!' He stood as the Bishop gestured for him to advance, swore his promise, and left. Bartholomew reflected that his colleagues seemed very keen that he should take the Bishop's oath. Was this out of concern for him, or did they have other, more sinister reasons for wanting his silence concerning the deaths at Michaelhouse? The conclave was silent. The Bishop and Bartholomew regarded each other.

The Bishop suddenly snapped his fingers, and, in an instant, parchment was cleared away, inkhorns sealed, and pens packed. The clerks filed out in silence, leaving the Bishop alone with Bartholomew.

Bartholomew waited, and was surprised when the Bishop sat heavily at one of the tables and put his head in his hands. After a few moments, the Bishop looked up, his face lined and grey with worry, and gestured for Bartholomew to sit next to him.

'I have become so involved in the interests of the Church, and of upholding the law, that I have failed to see some things,' he said. 'I know what I am asking you to do is wrong on one level, and yet, on another it is absolutely right. This pestilence is at the centre of it. Have you heard the news? In Avignon, our Pope has had to consecrate the River Rhône because there were too many bodies for the graveyards. In Paris, the dead lie stinking in their houses and the streets because there are none left to bury them. All over Europe, villages lie silent. Many great abbeys and monasteries have lost more than half their brethren.

'Some say it is a visitation from God, and they may be right. The people will need their faith to deal with this terrible plague, and they will need their priests, friars, and monks to help them. If the same happens in England as has already happened in France, there will be a desperate shortage of clergy, and we will need every religious house and the universities to train more.

'Do you not see, Matthew? We must prepare ourselves, and gather our forces. We cannot allow the University to flounder now, just before the people will need it more than ever before. You may have been told that some scholars at Oxford would like very much to see Cambridge fall so that they will have a monopoly over students and masters. This may well be true, but I cannot allow that to happen. We must offer as many places of training as possible, so that we can produce learned clergy to serve the people.

'You made me angry earlier, and I am sorry. I had to threaten you because I could not allow your stand to cause the others to waver. I will not force you to take the oath, because you, of all the Fellows, would not want the people to suffer from a lack of spiritual comfort during this terrible plague and the years to follow. I have heard that you choose to work with the poor, when you could easily become rich by healing the wealthy. I know that you understand why I was forced to ask the others to protect the University.'

The Bishop was no longer the splendid figure in purple who had ridden in at the gates, but a man struggling to reconcile his actions with his conscience. Bartholomew's anger was still very much at the surface, and he had had too many dealings with crafty patients not to be aware that some people possessed powerful skills at lying.

'So where does this leave us?' he said suspiciously.

'It leaves us in your hands, Matthew,' said the Bishop. 'If you will not give outsiders the explanation I have offered, then say nothing. In a few weeks it may not matter anyway, and you and I could be dead.'

He sighed and stood up to leave. 'Go in peace, Matthew,' he said, sketching a benediction in the air above Bartholomew's head. 'You continue God's work in your way, and I will continue in mine, and may we both learn from each other.'

The Bishop walked out of the room, and by the time Bartholomew had limped over to the window to watch him leave Michaelhouse, he had regained his regal bearing. He sat upright in his saddle, and clattered out of the yard with his clerks and monks trailing behind him.

The door of the conclave burst open and Brother Michael shot in, his chest heaving with exertion. 'Oh, thank God!' he said, fervently crossing himself. 'I expected to find you here with a knife in your ribs!' His words brought back a memory of Brother Paul, and he visibly paled. 'Oh lord,' he groaned, flopping into Wilson's chair, 'we really are going to have to be careful!'

V

December 1348

ROTHER PAUL, AUGUSTUS, AND MONTFITCHET
were laid to rest in the little cemetery behind
St Michael's Church two days after the Bishop's
visit. The official explanations for their deaths were
given to any who asked, and, although speculation was
rife for several weeks, the Fellows' consistent rendering
of the same story began to pay off. Bartholomew, when
asked specific questions, replied that he did not know
the answer, although whenever possible he avoided the
subject. Eventually, the excitement died down and the
incident seemed to be forgotten. Term started at
the beginning of October, and, although student numbers were low because of the fear of the impending
plague, the Michaelhouse Fellows found themselves as
busy as ever with lectures, disputations, and readings.

Bartholomew tried to forget about the events of
August; even if he had discovered anything, what could he
have done about it? He considered confiding his thoughts
to his brother-in-law, but was afraid that if he involved
Stanmore, he might endanger him somehow. For the same
reason, he did not wish to involve any of his friends.

Rachel Atkin had regained her wits after the death of her son. As well as his manor in Trumpington, Sir Oswald Stanmore owned a large house at his business premises in Milne Street in which his brother Stephen lived with his family. Bartholomew persuaded Stephen to take Rachel as a laundress, and she seemed to settle well enough into his household.

The Oliver brothers remained a problem. They seldom attended lectures, and Wilson would have sent them down had not the College's acquisition of the property on Foul Lane depended on their academic success. Bartholomew occasionally saw Henry glowering at him, but it became so commonplace that eventually he came not to notice it.

Bartholomew spent many of the final days before term in the company of Philippa Abigny. They rode through the rich meadows to Grantchester, and watched the archery competitions in Barton, sometimes alone, but often in the company of her brother and one of his latest loves. Brother Michael or Gregory Colet occasionally acted as chaperons, prudently disappearing on business of their own once outside the sight of the nunnery, leaving Bartholomew and Philippa alone together. Edith also acted as chaperon, and was only too pleased to encourage her younger brother in his courting. She had been nagging him for years to find a wife and settle down. Bartholomew and Philippa often strolled together in the pleasant grounds of St Radegund's Priory, careful not to touch each other, for they knew that behind the delicate arches of the nunnery windows the Abbess watched with hawklike eyes.

On several days they attended the great Stourbridge Fair, which ran for most of September and drew huge crowds of people from the countryside for miles around. They saw fire-eaters from Spain, jugglers from the Low Countries, and jongleurs from France, who sang of deeds of daring. Men and women hawked pies, pastries, drinks of fermented apple, crudely made wooden flutes, and cloths and ribbons of all colours. The smell from roasting meat mingled with that of damp straw and horse manure. Animals bleated and squealed, children screamed in delight, jousting knights clashed their weapons, and here and there a lone voice shouted warnings of the terrible pestilence that swept over Europe and would soon claim all whom God deemed unholy.

The threat of the coming plague cast a grim shadow over their lives. Stories came to Cambridge of settlements like Tilgarsley in Oxfordshire where every inhabitant had died, leaving behind a ghost village. A third of the population of the city of Bristol was said to have perished, and in October the first cases began to appear in London. Bartholomew spent long hours consulting his fellow physicians and surgeons about how to deal with the pestilence when it came, although the truth of the matter was that they really did not know. The town officials tried to impose some sort of control on who was allowed into the town in an attempt to prevent the disease from spreading, but it was impossible to enforce, and those barred from entering merely crossed the ditches, swam the river, or hired a boat.

The first snows fell early, powdering the ground with white before the end of November, and Bartholomew saw an increasing number of elderly patients with chest troubles brought on by the cold. Then, just before term ended, he saw his first case of the plague.

*　　　*　　　*

It was a cold morning, with a raw wind howling from the fens, with the promise of more of the persistent drizzling rain that had been dogging Cambridge for the past three days. Bartholomew had risen at five, while it was still dark, and attended Father William's high-speed mass. Lectures started at six, and his students, perhaps sensing the role they might soon have to play, bombarded him with questions. Even Francis Eltham, whom Bartholomew doubted would ever make a physician, had joined in the lively discussion.

Lectures finished around nine, and the main meal of the day was at half-past ten. It was a Friday, and so the meal was fish, freshly baked bread, and vegetables. Bartholomew tuned out the reading of the Bible scholar and thought about the debate on contagion in which he had just led his students. He wondered how he could convince them that there was a pattern to whom infectious diseases affected, and they were not merely visitations from God. He had risked the wrath of the clerics by refusing to allow the students to consider 'struck down by God' as a determinant for contagious disease. They had to think for themselves. 'Struck down by God' was a convenient excuse for not working out the real causes.

After the meal, all members of College were obliged to attend the midday service in St Michael's Church. Bartholomew walked back to the College with Michael, who was grumbling about the cold.

'Right! I am away,' said Abigny, coming up behind them and slapping them both on the shoulders. 'It is too damned cold at that College. I am going over to St Radegund's, where they have warm fires to toast pretty little feet.' He raised an eyebrow at Bartholomew. 'Coming? Philippa specifically told me to ask you.'

Bartholomew smiled. 'Tell her I will come later. I have two patients to see first.'

Abigny tutted. 'But will she wait until later, Physician? I, for one, would not wish to embrace you after you had been in those shabby hovels you like to frequent.'

'Then it is just as well you will not get the chance, Philosopher,' retorted Bartholomew.

Michael nudged him. 'Just go, man. Your patients will wait; your love might not.'

Bartholomew ignored them and went to collect his leather sack of medicines and instruments. He was in good spirits as he set off towards the Trumpington Gate, despite the bitter wind and the promise of rain. His first call was to the family of tinkers that lived near the river; the other call was on Bridge Street, near the church of the Holy Trinity, to one of Agatha's numerous relatives. Afterwards, he could go straight to the Priory and visit Philippa while Abigny was still there, since the nuns would not allow Bartholomew to see Philippa unless she was chaperoned.

The first drops of rain were beginning to fall when he reached the tinker's house. A group of children waited for him, standing barefoot in the mud. He followed them to the ramshackle pile of wood and earthen bricks that was their home. It was cold inside, despite the fire that billowed smoke so that Bartholomew could barely see. He knelt down on the beaten earth floor next to a child who lay in a tangle of dirty blankets, and began his examination. The child was obviously frightened, and Bartholomew found himself chattering about all manner of inane subjects to distract her. The other children clustered round, giggling at his banter.

The child was about six years old, and, as

Bartholomew had thought, was suffering from dehydration resulting from severe diarrhoea. He showed the mother how to feed her with a mixture of boiled water and milk and gave her specific instructions about the amounts she should be given. He discovered that the child had fallen into the river two days earlier, and suspected that she had swallowed bad water.

The rain was falling persistently as he walked back along the High Street towards Shoemaker Row, and he was drenched by the time he reached Holy Trinity Church. It was the third time he had been soaked in a week, and he was running out of dry clothes. The only fires Wilson allowed in the College were in the kitchens and, on very cold days, in the conclave, and there was not enough room for all the scholars to dry their clothes. Bartholomew began to invent a plan to warm stones on the hearths so that they might be wrapped round wet clothes.

The house of Agatha's cousin, a Mistress Bowman, was a small half-timbered building, with whitewashed walls and clean rushes on the floors. Mistress Bowman ushered him in fearfully.

'It is my son, Doctor. I do not know what is wrong with him, but he is so feverish! He seems not to know me!' She bit back a sob.

'How long has he been ill?' asked Bartholomew, allowing her to take his wet cloak.

'Since yesterday. It came on so fast. He has been down in London, you know,' she said, a hint of pride in her voice. 'He is a fine arrow-maker, and he has been making arrows for the King's armies in France.'

'I see,' said Bartholomew, looking at her closely, 'and when did he return from London?'

'Two days ago,' said Mistress Bowman.

Bartholomew took a deep breath and climbed up the steep wooden stairs to the room above. He could hear the laboured breathing of the man before he was half-way up. Mistress Bowman followed him, bringing a candle because, there being no glass in the windows, the shutters were closed against the cold and it was dark. Bartholomew took the candle and bent down towards the man on the bed. At first, he thought his dreadful suspicions were unfounded, and that the man had a simple fever. Then he felt under the man's arms and detected the swollen lumps there like hard unripe apples.

He gazed down at the man in horror. So this was the plague! He swallowed hard. Did the fact that he had touched the man mean that he would now succumb to the disease himself? He fought down the almost overwhelming urge to move away and abandon him, to flee the house and return to Michaelhouse. But he had discussed this many times with his fellow physician, Gregory Colet, and both had come to the conclusion – based on what little fact they could distil from exaggeration or rumour – that their chances of contracting the plague were high regardless of whether they frequented the homes of the victims. Bartholomew understood that some people seemed to have a natural resistance to it – and those that did not would catch it whether they had the slightest contact with a victim, or whether they exposed themselves to it totally.

Would Bartholomew die now – merely from touching the man who writhed and groaned in his delirious fever? If so, the matter was out of his hands, and he could not, in all conscience, abandon the victims of the foul disease to their suffering. He and Colet had agreed. While, all over the land, physicians were fleeing towns and villages for secluded houses in the country, Bartholomew and Colet had decided to stand firm. Bartholomew had nowhere to flee in any case – and all his family and friends were in Cambridge.

Bartholomew braced himself and completed his examination. Besides the swellings in the arms, there were similar lumps, the size of small eggs, in the man's groin and smaller swellings on his neck. He was also burning with fever, and screamed and writhed when Bartholomew gently felt the buboes.

Bartholomew sat back on his heels. Behind him, Mistress Bowman hovered worriedly. 'What is it, Doctor?' she whispered. Bartholomew did not know how to tell her.

'Did he travel alone?' he asked.

'Oh, no! There were three of them. They all came back together.'

Bartholomew's heart sank. 'Where do the others live?' he asked.

Mistress Bowman stared at him. 'It is the pestilence,' she whispered, looking down at her son with a mixture of horror and pity. 'My son has brought the pestilence.'

Bartholomew had to be sure before an official pronouncement was made, and before people started to panic. He stood. 'I do not know, Mistress,' he said softly. 'I have never seen a case of the pestilence before, and we should check the other lads before we jump to conclusions.'

Mistress Bowman grabbed his sleeve. 'Will he die?' she cried, her voice rising. 'Will my boy die?'

Bartholomew disentangled his arm and took both her hands in his firmly. He stood that way until her shuddering panic had subsided. 'I do not know, Mistress. But you will do him no good by losing control of yourself. Now, you must fetch clean water and some linen, and sponge his face to bring his fever down.'

The woman nodded fearfully, and went off to do his bidding. Bartholomew examined the young man again. He seemed to be getting worse by the minute, and Bartholomew knew that he would soon see scores of cases of such suffering – perhaps even among those he loved – and be unable to do anything about it.

Mistress Bowman returned with her water and Bartholomew made her repeat his instructions. 'I do not wish to frighten you,' he said, 'but we must be careful. Do not allow anyone in the house, and do not go out until I return.' She had gathered her courage while she had been busy, and nodded firmly, reminding him suddenly of Agatha.

He left the house and went to Holy Trinity Church. He asked the priest if he could borrow a pen and a scrap of parchment, and hurriedly scribbled a note to Gregory Colet at Rudde's Hostel, telling him of his suspicions and asking him to meet him at the Round Church in an hour. Outside, he threw a street urchin a penny and told him to deliver the note to Colet, who would give him another penny when he received it. The lad sped off while Bartholomew trudged to the house of one of the other men who had travelled from London.

As he arrived, he knew that any attempt he might make to contain the disease would be futile. Wails and howls came from within and the house was thronged with people. He elbowed his way through them until he reached the man lying on the bed. A glance told Bartholomew that he was near his end. He could scarcely draw breath and his arms were stuck out because of the huge swellings in his armpits. One had burst, and emitted a smell so foul that some people in the room covered their mouths and noses with scraps of cloth.

'How long has he been ill?' he asked an old woman, who sat weeping in a corner. She refused to look at him, and went on with her wailing, rocking back and forth.

'God's anger is visited upon us!' she cried. 'It will take all those with black, sinful hearts!'

And a good many others besides, thought Bartholomew. He and Colet had listened carefully to all the stories about the plague that flooded into Cambridge in the hope of learning more. For months, people had spoken of little else. First, it was thought that the infection would never reach England. After all, how could the foul winds that carried the disease cross the waters of the Channel? But cross they did, and in August, a sailor died of the plague in the Dorset port of Melcombe, and within days, hundreds were dead.

When the disease reached Bristol, officials tried to cut the port off from the surrounding areas to prevent the disease from spreading. But the wave of death was relentless. It was soon in Oxford, and then in London. Bartholomew and his colleagues discussed it deep into the night. Was it carried by the wind? Was it true that a great earthquake had opened up graves and the pestilence came from the uncovered corpses? Was it a visitation from God? What were they to do if it came to Cambridge? Colet argued that people who had been in contact with plague victims should stay away from those who had not, but even as Colet's words of warning rang in his ears, Bartholomew saw that such a restriction was wholly impractical. Among the crowd was one of

Michaelhouse's servants – even if Bartholomew avoided contact with the scholars, the servant would be among them. And what of those who had already fled?

Thomas Exton, the town's leading physician, declared that none would die if everyone stayed in the churches and prayed. Colet had suggested that applying leeches to the black swellings that were purported to grow under the arms and in the groin might draw off the poisons within. He said he meant to use leeches until his fellow physicians discovered another treatment. Bartholomew argued that the leeches themselves might spread the infection, but agreed to try them if Colet could prove they worked.

Bartholomew pulled himself out of his thoughts and slammed the door, silencing wailing and whispering alike.

'How long has this man been ill?' he repeated.

There was a gabble of voices answering him, and Bartholomew bent towards a woman dressed in grey.

'He was ill when they came home the night before last,' she said. 'He had been drinking in the King's Head tavern on the High Street, and his friends brought him back when he began to shake with this fever.'

Bartholomew closed his eyes in despair. The King's Head was one of the busiest taverns in the town, and, if the rumours were true and infection spread on the wind, then those who had been in contact with the three young men were already in danger. A hammering on the door stilled the buzz of conversation, and a thickset man in a greasy apron forced his way in.

'Will and his mother are sick,' he yelled. 'And one of Mistress Barnet's babies has turned black!'

There was an immediate panic. People crossed

themselves, the window shutters were thrown open, and some began to climb out screaming that the plague was there. Rapidly, only the sick man, Bartholomew, and the woman in grey were left in the house. Bartholomew looked at her closely, noting a sheen of sweat on her face. He pulled her into the light and felt under her jaw. Sure enough, there were the beginnings of swellings in her neck; she was already infected.

He helped her up the stairs to a large bed, and covered her with blankets, leaving a pitcher of water near her, for she was complaining of a fierce thirst. He went to look at the young man downstairs on his way out, and saw that he was already dead, his face a dark purple and his eyes starting from his face. The white shirt under his arms was stained with blood and with black and yellow pus. The stench was terrible.

Bartholomew let himself out of the house. The street was unusually silent as he made his way to the Round Church of the Holy Sepulchre, where Gregory Colet was waiting anxiously.

'Matt?' he said, stepping towards him, his eyes fearful.

Bartholomew held up his hand, warning him to come no closer. 'It has come, Gregory,' he said softly. 'The plague has come to Cambridge.'

The next few weeks passed in a whirlwind for Bartholomew. At first, there were only a few cases, and one of them even recovered. After five days, Bartholomew began to hope that the pestilence had passed them by, and that the people of Cambridge might have escaped the worst of the fever, or that it had burned itself out. Then, without warning, four people became infected one day, seven the next day, and thirteen the day after that. People began to die and Bartholomew found himself with more requests for help than he could possibly answer.

Colet called an urgent meeting of the physicians and surgeons, and Bartholomew described the symptoms he had seen first-hand while he stood in the gallery of St Mary's Church, as far away from the others as possible. There was much to be done. Gravediggers needed to be found, and collectors of the dead. There were few who wanted such tasks, and there was an argument between the medics on the one hand and the Sheriff on the other about who should pay the high wages to entice people to do it.

The number of cases of the plague continued to rise dramatically. Some people died within a few hours of becoming ill, while others lasted for several days. Others still seemed to recover, but died as their relatives began to celebrate their deliverance. Bartholomew could see no pattern as to who lived and who died, and he began to doubt his fundamental belief that diseases had physical causes that could be identified and removed. He and Colet argued about it, Colet claiming that he had more success with his leeches than Bartholomew had with his insistence on clean water and bedding, and use of various herbs. To a certain extent that was true, but Colet's patients were wealthier than Bartholomew's, and suffered and died in warm rooms where lack of food was not a problem. Bartholomew did not consider the comparison a fair one. He discovered that in some cases he could ease the discomfort from the buboes by incising them to let the putrescence out, and that probably one in four of his patients might survive.

Term at the University was immediately suspended, and scholars who would usually have stayed in Cambridge for the Christmas break thronged the roads leading north, some taking the plague with them. Bartholomew was horrified that many physicians went too, leaving dozens of sick people to the care of a handful of doctors.

Colet told Bartholomew that the royal physician, Master Gaddesden, had also fled London, going with the King's family to Eltham Castle. The plague was not a disease that would profit the medical profession, for there seemed to be no cure and much risk. In Cambridge, three physicians had already perished, including the master of medicine from Peterhouse and Thomas Exton, who had proclaimed that praying in the churches would deliver people.

The plague seemed to bring with it unending rain. Bartholomew trudged through the muddy streets constantly wet and in a daze of exhaustion, going from house to house to watch people die. He sent a note to Philippa urging her to stay in St Radegund's, and it was advice that all the nuns seemed to take, for none were seen ministering to the sick. The monks and friars at Barnwell and St Edmund's did their duty by administering last rites, and they too began to fall ill.

College life changed dramatically. The remaining students and teachers gathered together in the church to attend masses for the dead and to pray for deliverance, but there were looks of suspicion everywhere. Who had been in contact with the sick? Who might be the next to be struck down? The regular assembling for meals began to break down, and food was left in the hall for scholars to take back to their rooms to eat alone.

Bartholomew wondered whether unchanged rushes on the floors and discarded scraps of food in the scholars' rooms might be responsible for the sudden increase in the number of rats he saw around the College. Master Wilson withdrew completely, and remained in his room, occasionally leaning out of his window to shout orders.

Swynford left to stay with a relative in the country, and Alcote followed Wilson's lead, although Bartholomew occasionally saw him scuttling about in the dead of night, when everyone else was asleep. The three clerics did not shirk from their religious duties, and were tireless in burying the dead and giving last rites.

Abigny made Bartholomew move out of their room and sleep on the pallet bed in his storeroom.

'Nothing personal, Matt,' he said, his face covered with the hem of his gown as he spoke, 'but you are a dangerous man to know since you frequent the homes of the sick. And anyway, you would not wish me to visit Philippa if I had been near the Death.'

Bartholomew was too tired to argue. Master Wilson had tried to isolate the College so that no one could enter. There were plenty of supplies in the storeroom, he had called to the assembled College members from his window, and clean water in the well. They would be safe.

As if to belie his words, one of the students suddenly pitched to the ground. Bartholomew ran over, and noted the symptoms with despair. Wilson's shutters slammed abruptly, and the plan was not mentioned again.

College members began to die. Oddly, the old commoners who Bartholomew thought would be the first to succumb, because they were the weakest, were the last to become infected. The Frenchman Henri d'Evéne died on the eve of his planned departure for France. He had been careful to touch nothing that might have been infected by plague bearers; he had drawn his own water from the well, and ate little from the kitchens. He bribed Alexander to let him use Swynford's room while he was gone, because the room faced north, and it was said that north-facing rooms were safe from the plague.

But, as the bell was ringing for Compline, Bartholomew heard a dreadful scream from d'Evéne's quarters. He ran up the stairs and hammered on the door.

D'Evéne opened it, his face white with terror. He was shirtless, and Bartholomew saw the swellings under his armpits, already turning black with the poisons within. He caught the young man as he swooned in his arms and laid him on the bed. D'Evéne tossed and turned with a terrible fever for two days, Bartholomew tending him as much as he could, and died as dawn broke, writhing in agony.

Bartholomew had noticed that the swellings took two forms. If they were hard and dry, and emitted little putrescence when lanced, the patient might survive if he could withstand the fever and the pain. If they were soft, and contained a lot of fluid, the patient would invariably die, regardless of whether the swelling was lanced or not.

Bartholomew and Colet not only had to tend the sick, they had to oversee the removal of bodies from houses and streets. Both knew that if these were not removed as quickly as possible, the streets would become so unhealthy that people would die from other diseases. The first few men who took on the unwholesome, but handsomely paid, task of removing the dead, quickly caught the plague and died, and it bccame more and more difficult to find people willing to take the risk. Bartholomew, walking along the wharves one night after tending people in the rivermen's homes, heard shuffling and muttering at one of the small piers. Going to investigate, he found two dead-collectors dumping their load into the river so that they would not have to go to the cemetery in the dark.

Bartholomew watched the pathetic corpses bob off downstream as they were caught in the current.

'You have committed them to an unhallowed grave,' he whispered. The dead-collectors shuffled uneasily. 'And now their bodies might carry the Death to villages down the river.'

'It is already there,' said one of the men defensively. 'It is at Ely already. At least fifteen monks have died so far.'

When they had gone he walked to the churchyard and peered into the pit. It would soon be full. He and Colet had asked that a larger pit be dug, just outside the Trumpington Gate, because the cemeteries of the parish churches were too small to cope with the dead, and there was not enough available labour to dig individual graves. Since no one knew how the plague spread, Bartholomew did not want bad humours seeping from the bodies into the river from where some people, despite his warnings, drew their drinking water. There were fields outside the Gate that were well away from the river and its ditches, and away from homes.

As he reached the gates at Michaelhouse, the porter greeted Bartholomew cautiously, a huge pomander stuffed with herbs over his mouth.

'Brother Michael asks if you will go to his room,' he said, backing away as far as possible.

Bartholomew nodded. He did not blame the man. Perhaps Bartholomew was doing more harm than good by visiting the sick in their homes. Perhaps he was aiding the spread of the Death by carrying it in his clothes or in the air around him.

Slowly he climbed the stairs to Michael's room and pushed open the door. Brother Michael knelt next to his bed giving last rites to Father Aelfrith.

'Oh, no!' Bartholomew sank down onto a stool and waited for Michael to finish. 'When?'

'He was well enough this morning, but collapsed in the yard just as I came home,' said Michael, his voice muffled.

Bartholomew went over to the bed, and rested his hand on Aelfrith's brow. He was barely breathing, but seemed to have been spared the terrible agony that some victims went through. It was a risk, visiting the sick and giving last rites, and physicians and clerics had all known that they too might be stricken. Seeing Aelfrith so near the end reminded Bartholomew, yet again, of his own mortality. His thoughts went to Philippa, hopefully secure in the convent, and of their brief spell of happiness at the end of summer.

'I will go again to see if I can find William,' said Michael, furtively rubbing a sleeve over his eyes.

Bartholomew tried to make Aelfrith more comfortable. He had found that stretching the arms out helped relieve pressure on the swellings, and so caused the patient less pain. He was surprised to find that Aelfrith had no swellings. He looked again more carefully, inspecting his neck and his groin. There was no trace of swelling anywhere, and none of the black spots that afflicted some victims, although there was evidence that he had been violently sick. Bartholomew hoped this was not some new variation of the plague.

Aelfrith's eyes fluttered open. He saw Bartholomew and tried to speak. Bartholomew bent closer to hear him, straining to hear the voice that was no more than a rustle of breath.

'Not plague,' he whispered. 'Poison. Wilson.'

He closed his eyes, exhausted. Bartholomew wondered whether the fever had made him delirious. Aelfrith waved his hand weakly in the air. Bartholomew took it and held it. It was cold and dry. Aelfrith's eyes pleaded with Bartholomew, who bent again to listen.

'Wilson,' he whispered again.

Bartholomew, his mind dull from tiredness and grief, was slow in understanding. 'Are you saying that Wilson poisoned you?' he asked.

Aelfrith's lips drew back from his teeth in an awful parody of a smile. And then he died. Bartholomew leaned close and smelled Aelfrith's mouth. He moved back sharply. There was an acrid odour of something vile, and he noticed that Aelfrith's tongue was blistered and swollen. He *had* been poisoned! By Wilson? Bartholomew could not see how, because the lawyer had not left his room for days. Bartholomew sometimes saw him watching the comings and goings in the courtyard through his window, although he would slam the shutter if Bartholomew or any of the clerics so much as glanced up at him.

Bartholomew felt all the energy drain out of him as the significance of Aelfrith's death dawned on him. Another murder! And now of all times! He thought that the plague would have superseded all the dangerous political games that had been played in the summer.

And what was Aelfrith doing in Michael's room anyway? Had Michael poisoned him? He began to look around for cups of wine or food that Michael may have enticed Aelfrith to take, but there was nothing.

He almost jumped out of his skin as the door flew open and Michael came back with Father William in tow.

'Sweet Jesus, we are too late,' groaned Michael, visibly sagging.

'Too late for what?' asked Bartholomew, his tone sharp from the fright he had just had.

'For Father William to give him the Host,' said Michael.

'I thought you had already done that,' said Bartholomew. Surely Michael would not have poisoned the Host? He would surely be damned if he had chosen that mode of execution for one of God's priests.

'I am a Benedictine, Matt,' said Michael patiently. 'He wanted to have the last rites from one of his own Order. I looked for William, but could not find him. I gave Aelfrith last rites because he was failing fast and I thought he might die before William was back.'

Bartholomew turned his attention back to Aelfrith. Was he being unfair to Michael? He thought back to Michael's reaction at the death of Augustus. Was Michael one of those scholars so dedicated to the future success of Cambridge that he would kill for it? Or was he one of those who wanted to see Cambridge fail and Oxford become the foremost place of learning in the land? Or had Wilson slipped out of his room in the dark and left poison for Aelfrith? Was Aelfrith telling him he should go and tell Wilson that he had been poisoned?

Bartholomew was just too tired to think properly.

Should he go to Wilson? Or would the wretched man think Bartholomew was trying to give him the plague? Bartholomew could not blame people like Wilson, Swynford, and Alcote who hid away to save themselves. Had he not been a physician, he might well have done the same thing. The College had divided down the middle, four Fellows going among the plague victims to do what they could, and four remaining isolated. In the other colleges, the division was much the same.

He felt his mind rambling. What should he do? Should he tell Michael and William that Father Aelfrith had been poisoned, and had not died of the plague at all? And then what? The Bishop had his hands too full with his dying monks to be able to investigate another murder. And he probably would not want to investigate it. He would order it covered up, like the others. Well, let us save the Bishop a journey, then, thought Bartholomew wearily. He would say nothing. He would try to see Wilson later, and he would try to question Michael. He wondered why someone had gone to the trouble of committing murder now of all times, when they could all be dead anyway by the following day.

Michael and William had wrapped Aelfrith in a sheet while Bartholomew had been thinking, and together they carried him down the stairs. Bartholomew followed them. What should he do about Aelfrith's burial? He had not died of the plague and so there was no reason why he should be put in the plague pit. He decided to ask Cynric to help him dig a grave in St Michael's churchyard.

The stable was being used as a temporary mortuary in which dead College members awaited collection by the plague carts. Bartholomew saw that there were already two others there, and closed his eyes in despair.

'Richard of Norwich and Francis Eltham,' said Michael in explanation.

'Not Francis!' exclaimed Bartholomew. 'He was so careful!' Eltham had been like Wilson and had shut himself in his room. His room-mates had left Cambridge, so he had been alone.

'Not careful enough,' Michael said. 'This Death has no rhyme nor reason to it.'

Father William sighed. 'I must go to Shoemaker Row. The sickness is in the home of Alexander's sister and they are waiting for me.'

He disappeared into the night, leaving Michael and Bartholomew alone. Bartholomew was too drained to be anxious about Michael's possible murderous inclinations, and too tired to talk to the fat monk about Aelfrith's dying words. Bartholomew wished he had spoken again to Aelfrith about his suspicions, but Aelfrith had taken his oath to the Bishop seriously and had never again mentioned the business to Bartholomew.

Next to him, Michael sniffed loudly, his face turned away from Bartholomew. They stood silently for a while, each wrapped in his own thoughts, until Michael gave a huge sigh.

'I have not eaten all day, Matt. Did you ever think I would allow that to happen?' he said in a frail attempt at humour. He took Bartholomew's arm, and guided him towards the kitchen. Michael lit a candle and they looked around. The big room was deserted, the great fireplace cold. Many of the staff had left the College to be with their families, or had run away northwards in an attempt to escape the relentless advance of the plague. Pots had been left unwashed and scraps of old food littered the stone-flagged floor. Bartholomew wrinkled his nose in disgust as a large rat wandered boldly into the middle of the floor.

As Michael and Bartholomew watched, it started to twitch and shudder. It emitted a few high-pitched squeals before collapsing in a welter of black blood that flowed from between its clenched teeth.

'Now even the rats have the plague,' said Michael, his enthusiasm for foraging for food in the kitchen wavering.

'Now why would God send a visitation down upon rats?' said Bartholomew mockingly. 'Why not eels or pigs or birds?'

Michael gave him a shove. 'Perhaps he has, Physician. When did you last have the time to watch birds and fish?'

Bartholomew gave him a weak smile, and sat at the large table while Michael rummaged in the storerooms. After a few minutes, he emerged with a bottle of wine, some apples, and some salted beef.

'This will do,' he said, settling himself next to Bartholomew. 'This is a bottle of Master Wilson's best claret. It is the first time I have been able to get near it without Gilbert peering over my shoulder.'

Bartholomew looked askance. 'Stealing the Master's wine? Whatever next, Brother!'

'Not stealing,' said Michael, uncorking the bottle and taking a hearty swig. 'Testing it for him. After all, how do we know that the plague is not spread by claret?'

And how do we know that it was not claret that poisoned Aelfrith? thought Bartholomew. He put his head in his hands. He liked Michael, and hoped he was not one of the fanatics of whom Aelfrith had warned him. He suddenly felt very lonely. He would have given anything for a few moments alone with Philippa.

'You must eat,' said Michael gently, 'or you will be no good to yourself or to your patients. Drink some wine, and then try some of this beef. I swear to you, Matt, it is no older than eight months, and only a little rancid.'

Bartholomew smiled. Michael was trying to cheer him up. He took the proffered piece of meat and choked some of it down. He rifled through the apples, looking for one that was not home to families of maggots. Finding one, he presented it solemnly to Michael, who took it with equal gravity and cut it in half.

'Never let it be said that Michaelhouse scholars do not share their good fortunes,' he said, presenting a piece to Bartholomew. 'When do you think this will be over?' he asked suddenly.

'The plague or the murders?' said Bartholomew. The strong wine on his empty stomach had made him answer without thinking.

Michael stared at him. 'Murders?' he asked, nonplussed. Understanding suddenly showed in his eyes. 'Oh no, Matt! Do not start on that! We swore an oath!'

Bartholomew nodded. He had told no one, not even his sister or Philippa, about the conversation he had had with the Bishop, despite probing of varying degrees of subtlety by Wilson, Alcote, and Michael.

'But we know the truth,' he said quietly.

Michael was horrified. 'No! No, we do not,' he insisted. 'We never will. We should not be talking of this!' He looked over his shoulder as if he expected the Bishop to be there.

Bartholomew stood up and walked over to the

window, where he stood staring out into the darkness of the yard.

'But murder is murder, Brother,' he said softly. He turned to look at Michael, whose fat face still wore an expression of disbelief.

'Perhaps so,' Michael said, nervously, 'but it is over and done.'

Bartholomew raised his eyebrows. 'Is it?' he asked gently, watching Michael for any slight reaction that might betray guilt.

'Of course!' Michael snapped. 'Over and done!'

Bartholomew turned back to the window. Michael had always loved the intricate affairs of the College, and took a strange delight in the petty plays for power. On occasions, Bartholomew and Abigny had found his persistent speculations tiresome, and had actively avoided his company. Bartholomew wondered whether his refusal to discuss them now meant that he took the Bishop's oath very seriously and really believed that the murders were over, or whether he had other reasons for maintaining his silence. Did he know that Aelfrith had been murdered? Bartholomew decided he would gain nothing by questioning Michael further, except perhaps to arouse his suspicions. If Michael did know more than he was telling, then Bartholomew would be foolish indeed to allow his suspicions to show.

Michael went to sit next to the fire in the large chair from which Agatha usually ran her domain. He shifted his bulk around until he was comfortable, stretching his feet out as if the fire were blazing. Bartholomew went back to the bench and lay flat, folding his hands over his stomach, looking up at the cobwebs on the ceiling. He would rest just a little while before going to his bed.

'Not only have I missed a good many meals,' said Michael, 'but I have been too busy to complain about my perpetually cold feet!'

'Missed meals will do you no harm, my fat monk,' said Bartholomew drowsily. It was freezing in the kitchen, and they were both wet from being out in the rain all day. They should not lie around in the cold, but should go back to their respective beds and sleep in the warm.

'When will it end?' asked Michael again, his voice distant, as if his thoughts were elsewhere.

Did he mean the plague or the murders in the College? wondered Bartholomew a second time, his thoughts beginning to tumble through his tired brain again. He asked himself why he was lying in a cold kitchen alone with someone whom he thought might know more than was safe about at least one murder.

'Why was Aelfrith in your room?' Bartholomew asked sleepily. Gradually, he was relaxing for the first time in days; it was a pleasant feeling, and he felt himself beginning to fall asleep.

'Mmm?' said Michael. 'Oh, I took him there. He collapsed in the yard. His room was locked, so I took him to mine.'

'Locked?' asked Bartholomew, now struggling to stay awake.

'Yes,' came Michael's voice from a long way off. 'I thought it was odd, too. But locked it was, and I could not get in. Perhaps one of his students saw him collapse and did not want him brought to their room.'

Bartholomew thought about that. It was possible, and he knew that Aelfrith's three Franciscan novices had been concerned that the work he was doing among the plague victims might bring the disease to them.

'When do you think this plague will end?' he asked in response, wriggling slightly to ease the ache in his back.

'When the Lord thinks we have learned,' said Michael.

'Learned what, for God's sake?' asked Bartholomew, settling down again. 'If this continues, perhaps there will be no one left to learn anything.'

'Perhaps not,' said Michael. 'But if He wanted us all to die, He would not have bothered to send the signs.'

'What signs?' Bartholomew felt his eyes begin to close, no matter how hard he struggled to keep them open. He tried to remember when he had last slept; a couple of hours two nights before?

'When the plague first started in the Far East, there were three signs,' began Michael. Bartholomew gave up on keeping his eyes open, and just listened.

'On the first day, it rained frogs and serpents. On the second day, there was thunder so loud that people hearing it were sent mad, and lightning that came as sheets of fire. On the third day a great pall of black smoke issued from the earth, blotting out the sun and all the light. On the fourth day, the plague came.

'There have been other signs too,' Michael continued after a moment. 'In France, a great pillar of fire was seen over the Palace of the Popes in Avignon. A ball of fire hung over Paris. In Italy, when the plague arrived, it came with a terrible earthquake that sent noxious fumes all over the surrounding country and killed all the crops. Many died from famine as well as the plague.'

'There have been no such signs here, Brother,' said Bartholomew, almost asleep. 'Perhaps we are not so evil as the French or the Italians.'

'Perhaps not,' said Michael. 'Or perhaps God does not want to waste His signs on the irredeemable.'

Bartholomew woke with a start. He was cold and very stiff, and still lying on the bench. Wincing, he eased himself up, wondering why he had not gone to bed to wake warm and rested. Daylight was flooding in through the window, and there was a crackle of burning wood. He looked behind him.

'Oh, you are awake, lazy-bones,' grunted Agatha. 'Sleeping in the kitchen indeed! Master Wilson will not be impressed.'

The kitchen had been cleaned since the previous night: the food swept away and the dead rat removed. One of the fireplaces had been cleared out and a warm blaze replaced the cold ashes. Stiffly, Bartholomew went to sit beside it on a stool, smelling the fresh oatcakes cooking on the circular oven next to the fire. Brother Michael still slept in Agatha's chair, black circles under his eyes and his mouth dangling open. Bartholomew's suspicions of the night before seemed unreasonable. Even if Michael had been connected with the death of Aelfrith in some way, he obviously meant Bartholomew no harm, when he could easily have dispatched him as he lay sleeping on the bench.

Bartholomew stretched himself and filched an oatcake when he thought Agatha was not looking. The sudden movement woke Michael, who sat looking around stupidly. 'What time is it?' he asked, blinking the sleep from his eyes and rubbing his cold hands together.

'A little before eight, I would say,' said Agatha. 'Now you sit down,' she continued, pushing Michael back in his chair. 'I have made you some oatcakes – if this greedy physician has not eaten them all.'

'But I have missed Prime,' said Michael, horrified. 'And I did not say Matins and Lauds last night.'

'Your stomach must still be asleep,' said Bartholomew, 'if you are considering prayers before breakfast.'

'I always say prayers before breakfast,' snapped Michael, and then relented. 'I am sorry, Matt. I cannot stick knives in boils and try to relieve fevers like you do. My way of fighting this monstrous pestilence is to keep my offices, no matter what happens. I hope it may make a difference.' He gave a rueful look. 'This will be the first time I have failed since this business began.'

'I was thinking yesterday that the clerics were doing more good than the physicians ever could,' said Bartholomew, startled by Michael's confession. 'Do not be too hard on yourself, Brother. Or, as you said to me last night, you will be no good to yourself or your patients,' he said in a very plausible imitation of Michael's pompous voice that made Agatha screech with laughter.

Michael laughed too, more at Agatha's reaction than at Bartholomew's feeble attempt at humour. 'Oh lord, Matthew,' he said. 'I never thought we would laugh again. Give me the oatcakes, Mistress Agatha. I had nothing but maggoty apples last night.'

Agatha pulled the oatcakes out of the oven and plumped herself down on a stool next to Bartholomew. 'I am gone for three days to tend to my relatives, and the College falls apart,' she said. 'Filth in the kitchens, rats in the rooms, and the food all gone.'

Michael coughed, his mouth overfull of fresh warm

oatcake. 'The servants have mostly left,' he said. 'That great lump of lard in the Master's room will not stir himself to take charge as he should, and the College is ruled by chaos.'

'Not any more,' said Agatha grandly, 'for I am back. And make no mistake, young sirs, no pestilence is going to get me! I have been three days going from house to house, seeing my relatives die, and I am still free from the pestilence. Some of us will not be taken!'

Bartholomew and Michael stared at her in astonishment. 'You may be right,' said Bartholomew. 'Gregory Colet and I wondered whether some people may have a natural resistance to the plague.'

'Not resistance, Master Bartholomew,' said Agatha proudly, 'I am one of God's chosen.' She shifted her ample skirts importantly. 'He strikes down those that anger him, and spares those he loves.'

'That cannot be, Mistress,' said Bartholomew. 'Why would God strike down children? And what of the monks and friars who risk themselves to give comfort to the people?'

'Monks and friars!' spat Agatha. 'I have seen the lives they lead: wealth, rich foods, women, and fine clothes! God will direct them to hell first!'

'Thank you for your kind words, Mistress,' said Michael, eyeing her dolefully. 'And how long would you say I have before God banishes me to hell?'

Agatha grinned sheepishly. 'I did not say he would take you all. But what other reason can there be that some die and some live? The physicians do not know. Gregory Colet told me I may be right, and the priests believe some are chosen to live and others to die.'

'Perhaps some people have a balance of humours

in their bodies that gives them a resistance to the plague,' mused Bartholomew, taking another oatcake.

'And have you compared the humours of those that live with those that die?' asked Michael.

Bartholomew nodded, frustrated. 'But I can see no pattern in it as yet.'

Michael patted his shoulder. 'Well, perhaps the balance is too fine to be easily seen,' he said. 'But if your theory is true, I do not want to know, for it would mean that I am doomed – to live or die – as my body directs, and that nothing I do – no matter how I pray or try to live a godly life, will make a difference. And then I would be without hope and without God.'

Bartholomew raised his hands. 'It would be no kind of answer anyway,' he said. 'I want to know how to cure this foul disease, not forecast for people whether they will live or die.'

Michael stood up, stuffing the rest of the oatcakes in his scrip for later. 'As much as I like your company, sitting here discussing the causes of the Death with two people who have no more idea why it has come than I have will benefit no one. I must say my prayers and visit the people.'

He marched out of the kitchen, and Bartholomew heard his strong baritone singing a psalm as he went to the porter's lodge. He also glimpsed Wilson's white face at his window, surveying the domain he dared not rule.

'You can stay a while, if you do not mind me clattering,' said Agatha. Bartholomew recognised this as a rare compliment, for Agatha did not approve of idle hands in the kitchen. She was already beginning to reimpose her order on the chaos, for the boys who worked in the scullery had been set to work washing floors, and Cynric and Alexander were collecting the bedclothes of those who had died to be taken to the laundry.

'Thank you, Mistress, but I must meet with Gregory Colet to see that the new pit is dug.'

He left Agatha to her work, and went to draw some water from the well. Back in the room where he stored his medicines, he washed quickly in the freezing water and changed his clothes. His clean ones were not quite dry, but it was going to rain again anyway, he thought. As he emerged from the storeroom, he saw Father William and hailed him over. He looked tired, and his eyes were red-rimmed.

'Nathaniel the Fleming has the plague,' he said. 'I have been called to give him last rites.'

'Not leeches?' asked Bartholomew, his own weariness making him obtuse.

William looked askance at him. 'Doctor Colet has already leeched him, but the poisons were too deep in his body to draw out.' He reached a meaty hand towards Bartholomew. 'What of Aelfrith? Will you see him taken to the plague pit?'

Bartholomew looked up at the pale blue sky. Did William know? Should he tell him? What if William and Wilson were in league, and had poisoned Aelfrith together? Bartholomew looked at the friar's face, grey with fatigue, and recalled also that Aelfrith and William had been close friends. 'Shall I bury him in the churchyard instead?' he asked, to buy himself more time to think.

William looked startled. 'Can we? Is it not safer for the living to bury him in lime in the plague pits?'

'I do not see why,' Bartholomew said, watching

William closely. 'Others were buried in the churchyard before the plague came in earnest.'

William pursed his lips. 'I have been thinking about that. Perhaps it is their corrupted flesh lying in hallowed ground that is causing the contagion to spread. Perhaps the way to stop the Death is to exhume them all and rebury them in the plague pits.'

Now it was Bartholomew's turn to be startled. Here was a theory he had not encountered before. He mulled it over in his mind briefly, reluctant to dismiss any chance of defeating the plague without due thought, no matter how unlikely a solution it might seem. But he shook his head. 'I suspect that would only serve to put those that perform the exhumation at risk, if not from the plague, then from other diseases. And I cannot see that they are a danger to the living.'

William looked at him dubiously. 'Will you bury Aelfrith, then? In the churchyard?'

Bartholomew nodded, and then hesitated. If William were involved in Aelfrith's murder, incautious questioning would only serve to endanger his own life, and if he were not, it would be yet another burden for the exhausted friar. 'Were you . . . surprised that he was taken?' Bartholomew asked, before realising how clumsy the question was.

William looked taken aback. 'He was fit enough at the midday meal,' he replied. 'Just tired like us all, and saddened because he had heard the deathbed confession of the Principal of All Saints' Hostel. Now you mention it, poor Aelfrith was taken very quickly. It was fortunate that Brother Michael was near, or he might have died unshriven.'

He began to walk away, leaving Bartholomew less

certain than ever as to whether he was involved. Were his reactions, his words, those of a killer? And what of Wilson? What was his role in Aelfrith's death?

Before leaving, he decided to see Abigny briefly. He pushed the door open slowly, and a boot flew across the room and landed at his feet. Bartholomew pushed the door all the way open and peered in.

'Oh. It is you, Matt. I thought it was that damned rat again. Did you see it? It is as big as a dog!' Abigny untangled himself from his bed. 'What a time I had last night, Physician. What delights I sampled! None of the young ladies want to meet their maker without first knowing of love, and I have been only too happy to oblige. You should try it.'

'Giles, if you are sampling the delights of as many poor ladies as you say, I hope you do not plan to visit Philippa,' said Bartholomew anxiously. 'Please do not visit her if you are seeing people who may be infected.'

'Poppycock! She will die if it is her time,' said Abigny, pulling on some of his brightest clothes. Bartholomew knew only too well that this meant he was planning on impressing some female friends.

'And you will die before it is yours if you take the pestilence to her!' he said with quiet menace. He had always found Abigny rather shallow and selfish, although he could be an entertaining companion, but he had always believed the philosopher to be genuinely fond of his sister. Through the past few black weeks, it had been the thought of Philippa's face that had allowed Bartholomew to continue his bleak work. He could not bear to think of her falling prey to the filthy disease.

Abigny stopped dressing and looked at Bartholomew. 'Matthew, I am sorry,' he said with sincerity. 'You should know better than to think I would harm Philippa. No, I do not have the plague . . .' He raised his hand to stop Bartholomew from coming further into the room. 'Hugh Stapleton died last night.'

Bartholomew leaned against the door. Stapleton had run Bene't Hostel, and had been a close friend of Abigny's. Abigny spent more time at the Hostel than he did at Michaelhouse, and regularly took his meals there.

'I am sorry, Giles,' he said. He had seen so many die over the last several days, including Aelfrith, that it was difficult to sound convincing. He wondered whether he would be bereft of all compassion by the time the plague had run its course.

Abigny nodded. 'I am away to enjoy the pleasures of life, and I will not see Philippa,' he said. 'I was with Hugh when he died, and he told me to enjoy life while I had it. That is exactly what I am going to do.'

He flung his best red cloak over his shoulders and walked jauntily out of the yard. Bartholomew followed him as far as the stable where Father Aelfrith's body lay. While Abigny enjoyed life, Bartholomew had a colleague to bury. He glanced up and saw Wilson lingering at the window. Had he killed Aelfrith?

'Father Aelfrith is dead,' Bartholomew yelled up at him, drawing the attention of several students who were walking around the yard to the hall. 'Will you come to see him buried, Master Wilson?'

The shadowy shape disappeared. Bartholomew took a spade from the stable and walked to St Michael's churchyard.

VI

CHRISTMAS AT CAMBRIDGE WAS USUALLY A TIME for celebration and for a relaxing of the rules that governed scholars' lives. Fires would be lit in the conclave, and students and Fellows could gather round and tell each other stories, or even play cards. Since it was dark by four o'clock in the evening, a night by the fire in a candle-lit conclave was a pleasant change from the usual practice of retiring to dark, unheated rooms.

But the plague was still raging in Cambridge at Christmas, and few felt like celebrating. Bedraggled groups of children stood in the snow singing carols for pennies. Food was scarce because many of the farmers who grew the winter vegetables or tended the livestock were struck with the plague. Many who were fit did not wish to risk a journey into the town, where they might come into contact with infected people.

The cart patrolling the streets collecting the dead became a common sight. Old women who had lost entire families followed it around, offering prayers for the dead in return for money or food. Houses stood empty, and at night, after the curfew bell had rung and the depleted and exhausted patrols of University beadles and Sheriff's men slept, small bands of vagrants and thieves would loot

159

the homes of the dead and the sick. The thieves soon became bolder, coming in from surrounding villages and even attacking during the daylight hours.

To make matters worse, it was a cold winter, with gales howling across the flat land, bringing with them driving snow. On clear days and nights, the temperature dropped so low that sick people had to go out foraging for sticks to build fires to melt ice for water to drink.

The monks at Barnwell Priory lost a third of their number, although St Radegund's fared better and only three nuns became ill. More than half of the monks at the great monasteries at Ely and Norwich perished, and Bartholomew began to appreciate the Bishop's point as he saw more and more people die without being given last rites. Some did not care, but only wished to end their agony; others died in terror of going straight to hell as a punishment for various petty sins. The church walls were full of paintings of the damned being devoured by demons in hell, so Bartholomew did not wonder that people were afraid.

It was impossible to tell how many members the University lost. At the first sign of the plague, some left the town and did not return. As the numbers of deaths rose, harried clerks began to lose count, and many people ended up in the plague pits without any record being made. By January, King's Hall lost ten of its scholars, and Michaelhouse lost eleven. Bartholomew had thought that perhaps the scholars might fare better than the townspeople because they were younger, fitter, and usually better fed. But the plague struck indiscriminately, and by Christmas the old commoners were still alive and well, but several healthy young students were dead.

However much Bartholomew thought and studied and worked, he could not understand why some people died and others recovered, or why, in the same household, some people caught the disease while others remained healthy, even after being in contact with the sick. He and Colet compared experiences regularly, and argued endlessly and without conclusion. Colet had given up leeching buboes, and incised them where he could, like Bartholomew. But he still believed that leeching after the incisions caused the recovery of his patients. Bartholomew believed the keys were rest, a warm bed, and clean water. Since neither had a better record of success than the other, each refused to adopt the other's methods. But Colet's patients were generally wealthy, with warm homes and clean bedding. Bartholomew's patients were poor, and warmth and cleanliness were not always easy to attain.

Bartholomew continued on his rounds, lancing the black swellings whenever he thought it might ease a patient's pain. Two more physicians died, and another two fled, so that only Bartholomew, Colet, and Simon Roper from Bene't Hostel were left. They found they could not trust the town officials to carry out their recommendations and had to supervise virtually everything, from the digging of the pits and the proper use of lime, to the cleaning of the streets of the dead rats and refuse that built up.

Bartholomew, arriving home at dawn after staying with a family that had five of seven children dying, was awoken within minutes by hammering on the door. Wearily, he struggled out of bed to answer it. A young man stood there, his long, unruly hair at odds with his neat scholar's tabard.

'I thought you would have been up by now,' said the man cheekily.

'What do you want?' Bartholomew asked thickly, so tired he could barely speak.

'I have been sent to fetch you to St Radegund's.'

Bartholomew's blood ran cold, and he was instantly awake. 'Why, what has happened?' he asked in a whisper, almost afraid to ask. 'Is it Philippa Abigny?'

'Oh, no,' said the student. 'A man wants you. But you had better hurry up or he said you will be too late.'

Bartholomew hastened back inside to dress. When he emerged, the tousle-haired man was leaning against the wall chatting to the porter. Bartholomew ignored him and made his way up St Michael's Lane at a steady trot. He heard footsteps behind him, and the young man caught him and tried to match his pace.

'If you want to travel quickly, why do you not take a horse?' he asked between gasps.

'I do not have a horse,' answered Bartholomew. 'Who has asked for me? Is it Giles Abigny?' The fear he felt earlier returned. He hoped Abigny had not become ill and gone to the convent for help. St Radegund's had escaped lightly until now, perhaps because the Prioress had determined on a policy of isolation, and no one was allowed in; money in a pot of vinegar was left outside the gates for all food that was delivered. Bartholomew hoped the Prioress had managed to continue so, not only because Philippa was inside, but also because he wanted to know if the plague could be averted in this way.

'You do not have a horse?' queried the student, losing his stride. 'A physician?'

'Who asked for me?' Bartholomew asked again. He was beginning to be annoyed.

'I do not know, just some man. I am only the messenger.'

Bartholomew increased his speed, and quickly left the student puffing and wheezing behind him. It was only a matter of moments before the walls of St Radegund's loomed up out of the early morning mist. He pounded on the door, leaning against the wall to get his breath, his legs unsteady from a brisk run on an empty stomach and anticipation of what was to come.

A small grille in the door snapped open. 'What do you want?' came a sharp voice.

'It is Matthew Bartholomew. I was sent for,' he gasped.

'Not by us,' and the grille slammed shut.

Bartholomew groaned and banged on the door again. There was no reply.

'You are unlikely to get an answer now.'

Bartholomew spun round, and the student found himself pinned against the wall by the throat. 'Hey! I am only the messenger!' he croaked, eyes wide in his face.

Bartholomew relented and loosened his grip, although not by much.

'Who sent for me?' he asked again, his voice dangerously quiet.

'I do not know his name. I will have to show you,' the student said, trying to prise Bartholomew's hands from his throat, some of his former cockiness gone.

He led the way around the walls towards the convent gardens. 'My name is Samuel Gray,' he said. Bartholomew ignored him. 'I am a medical student at Bene't Hostel.'

Bartholomew saw they were heading for a small shack where garden tools were kept. He and Philippa had sheltered there from a summer thunderstorm once as they had walked together among the fruit bushes. That had been only a few short months before, but to Bartholomew it seemed in another lifetime. Gray reached the hut first, and pushed open the door. Bartholomew took a step inside and peered into the gloom, trying to see what was inside.

'Philippa!' She was kneeling in a corner next to a figure lying on the floor.

'Matt!' She leapt to her feet, and before Bartholomew could prevent her, she had thrown herself into his arms. His first instinct was to force her away, lest he carried the contagion with him somehow in his clothes, but the shack was already rank with the smell of the plague, so there was little point. He allowed all else to be driven from his mind as he enjoyed the first contact he had had with Philippa since the plague began.

Suddenly she pushed him away. 'What are you doing here?' she said. 'Who asked you to come?'

Bartholomew gazed at her in confusion. He looked around at Gray, who stood at the door looking as surprised as Bartholomew.

'I do not know,' Gray said. 'It was a man. He told me to bring you here, and that he would be waiting to meet you.'

Bartholomew looked back at Philippa. 'I do not know of any man,' she said. 'I have been here since dawn. I had a message to come, and I found Sister Clement here. She has the plague.'

'But who told you to come? And how did you get out? I thought the convent was sealed.'

'I do not know, to answer your first question. A message came written on a scrap of parchment pushed under the door. I came here immediately. In answer to your other question, there is a small gate near the kitchens that is always open, although few know of it. Sister Clement has been using it regularly to slip out and go among the poor.' Her voice caught, and Bartholomew put his arms round her again.

He said nothing while she sobbed quietly, and Gray shuffled his feet in the doorway. On the floor, Sister Clement was near the end, her laboured breathing almost inaudible. Philippa looked at her, and raised her eyes pleadingly to Bartholomew. 'Can you help her?'

Bartholomew shook his head. He had seen so many similar cases during the last few weeks that he did not even need to examine her to know that there was nothing he could do. Even lancing the swellings at this point would do no more than cause unnecessary suffering.

'But you are a physician! You must be able to do something!'

Bartholomew flinched. These were words he heard every day, but they hurt nevertheless. He went over to look at the old lady, and arranged her arms so that the pressure on the swellings under them would be reduced. The buboes in her groin had burst, emitting the smell which Bartholomew had come to know well, but that still filled him with disgust. He sent Gray to find a priest to give her last rites, and sat back helplessly. Behind him, Philippa cried softly. He took her hand and led her outside into the clean morning air.

'Why did you come, Matt?' asked Philippa.

'That student came and said I was needed at St Radegund's. He does not seem to know by whom.'

'I receive a message to come here, sent by an unknown person, then you do. What is going on? Who wants us here together?' Philippa looked around her as if expecting the unknown person to emerge from the bushes.

'Friend or foe?' asked Bartholomew absently. He was horribly afraid that it was the latter, someone who wanted Philippa to come into contact with a plague victim, and Bartholomew to know it. He felt a sudden anger. Who would want to do such a thing? What had either of them done to harm anyone else?

'Now I am out of that horrid place, I will not go back,' said Philippa with a sudden fierce determination. 'I refuse. I can stay with you and Giles. I can sleep in your medicine room.'

'There is plague at the College, Philippa,' said Bartholomew. 'You would not be safe.'

'There is plague here!' said Philippa vehemently, gesturing to the shack behind them. 'And anyway,' she continued, 'I do not approve of the way the nuns skulk behind the convent walls. Sister Clement was the only one with any decency.'

'Do you want to die like that?' asked Bartholomew, gesturing back at the old lady.

'Do you?' countered Philippa. 'You see plague victims every day, and you are well. So is Gregory Colet. Not everyone who touches someone with the Death catches it.'

Bartholomew wondered what to do. It was out of the question to take Philippa to Michaelhouse. Even though Master Wilson was not in a position to do anything about it, the clerics would object. And she could not possibly sleep in the medicines room. The shutters did not close properly, and there were no separate privies that she would be able to use. He would have to take her to

Edith's house. Edith had not heeded his advice and locked herself away, and Stanmore was still trying to conduct his trade. Philippa would not be as protected there from the plague as she had been in the convent, but it was the best he could do.

Gray came back over the fields bringing with him an Austin Canon from Barnwell whom he had waylaid. They listened to his murmurings as he administered last rites to the old nun. After a few minutes he came out, told them that Sister Clement was dead, and went on his way. For him, it would be the first in a long day of such prayers, and who knew whether he would live to see another such day tomorrow?

Bartholomew took Philippa's hand, and together they began to make their way back to Barnwell Causeway. Gray tagged along behind.

Bartholomew decided to go to Edith's house in Trumpington immediately. They would have to walk because he knew of nowhere where he would be able to hire horses. All the usual places had been struck by the plague, and the horses turned to graze unattended in the fields. Bartholomew turned to Gray.

'Can you tell me anything else about this man who gave you the message? What did he look like?'

Gray shrugged. 'He was wearing a Dominican habit, and his cowl was over his face. He had ink on his fingers, though, and he tripped on the hem of his gown as he left.'

Ink on his fingers. He could be a clerk or a student, unfamiliar enough in the friar's long habit to fall over it when he walked. Were the fanatical scholars after him now? Was this a warning to him that he was vulnerable through Philippa, even though he had thought her safely tucked away in her convent? He wondered why on earth they were bothering. No one who watched the sun rise these days could be certain of seeing it set in the evening. All they had to do was wait. Why had they taken the trouble to poison Aelfrith? As Bartholomew's thoughts of murder came tumbling back, he clutched Philippa's hand tighter, glad to feel something warm and reassuring. She smiled at him, and they began to walk towards Trumpington.

Edith was delighted to see Bartholomew and surprised to see Philippa. She fussed over them both, and found Philippa a small room in the garret where she could have some privacy. Oswald Stanmore was just finishing a late breakfast in the parlour, and chatted to Bartholomew while Edith whisked Philippa away.

'She will be glad of some company,' he said, jerking his thumb towards the stairway where Edith had gone. 'She frets over Richard. We have had no word since the plague came. I keep telling her that she should look on this as a positive sign and that definite news might mean he has been buried.'

Bartholomew said nothing. He did not want to remind Stanmore of the dozens of unnamed bodies he saw tipped into the pits. People often died in the streets, were collected by the carts and their names were never discovered. He was sure that Stanmore must have seen this as he did his business around the town. He tried not to think about it; Bartholomew did not want to imagine Richard tipped into some pit in Oxford, never to be traced by his family.

'How are the figures?' asked Stanmore.

'Another fifteen died yesterday, including eight

children,' said Bartholomew. 'I have lost count of the total number, and the clerk who is supposed to note numbers of bodies going into the pits is drunk half the time. We will probably never know how many have died in Cambridge.'

'You look exhausted, Matt. Stay here for a few days and rest. You cannot keep going at this pace.'

'The plague will not last forever,' said Bartholomew. 'And how can I leave Colet and Roper to do everything?'

'Simon Roper died this morning,' said Stanmore. He noticed Bartholomew's shock. 'I am sorry, lad. I thought you would have known.'

Now Bartholomew and Colet were the only ones left, with Robin of Grantchester, the town surgeon, whose methods and hygiene Bartholomew did not trust. How would they manage? Because there had been cases where Bartholomew had lanced the black swellings and the patient had lived, he wanted to make sure that as many people as possible were given this tiny chance for life. If there were fewer physicians and surgeons, fewer people would be treated, and the plague would take those who might have been able to survive.

'Stay here with Philippa,' said Stanmore persuasively. 'She needs you, too.'

Bartholomew felt himself wavering. It would be wonderful to spend a few hours with Philippa and to forget all the foulness of the past weeks. But he knew that there were people who needed him, perhaps his friends, and he would not forgive himself if one of them died when he might have been able to help. He shook his head.

'I must go back to the College. Alexander was

unwell last night. I should check on him, and I must make sure that the pits are being properly limed, or we may never escape from this vile disease.' He stood up and stretched.

'Ride with me then,' said Stanmore, gathering scrolls of neat figures from the table and stuffing them in his bag. 'One of the apprentices can bring the horse back again tonight.'

Edith came in and told them that Philippa was resting. Apparently the death of the old nun had upset her more than Bartholomew had thought. He had become so inured to death that he had made the assumption that others had too, and had not considered that Philippa would be so grieved.

Edith gave Bartholomew a hug. 'Take care,' she whispered. 'Do not take too many chances. I could not bear to lose you.'

She turned away so that he would not see the tears in her eyes, and bustled around the fireplace. Bartholomew reached over and touched her lightly on the shoulder before following her husband into the yard. It was beginning to snow again, and the wind was bitterly cold. The muddy ruts in the track back to Cambridge had frozen, and the covering of snow made the travelling treacherous. Both horses stumbled several times, and the snow swirled about them so that they could barely see the way.

After a few minutes, Stanmore reined in. 'This is insane, Matt. We must go back. We can try again later.'

'You return. I have to go on,' said Bartholomew.

'Be sensible! We can barely see where we are going. Come home with me.'

'But I am worried about Alexander. And I promised the miller I would look in on his boy.'

'Go if you must, but I think you are mad. Take the horse. Please do not stable the poor beast at Michaelhouse, but take it to Stephen. He knows how to care for horses, unlike your dreadful porter.'

Bartholomew nodded and with a wave of his hand urged the horse on down the track, while Stanmore retraced his steps. The snow seemed to be coming horizontally, and Bartholomew was quickly enveloped in a soundless world of swirling white. Even the horse's hooves barely made a sound. Despite being cold and tired, he admired the beauty and tranquility of the countryside. The soft sheets of brilliant white stretching in all directions seemed a long way from the putrid black buboes and blood-laden vomit of the plague victims. He stopped the horse, so that he could appreciate the silence and peace.

He was startled to hear a twig snapping behind him. He twisted round in the saddle and saw a shadow flit between the trees. He hoped it was not robbers; he had no wish to be attacked for the few pennies in his pocket. He jabbed his heels into the horse's side to urge it forward, and it broke into a brisk trot. Glancing behind himself frequently, Bartholomew saw nothing but snow-laden trees and the hoof marks of his horse on the path.

He reached the Priory of St Edmund's, its buildings almost invisible in the swirling snow, and continued to Small Bridges Street. The miller was waiting for him, peering anxiously through the snow. As Bartholomew dismounted, he raced to meet him.

'He is well, Doctor, he lives! You saved him! You

said he had a chance, and you were right. He is awake now, asking for water.'

Bartholomew gave a brief smile and went to see his small patient. His mother had died of the plague three days before, followed by one of his sisters. The boy looked as though he would recover now, and the rest of the family seemed healthy enough. Leaving them with stern warnings not to drink the river water just because the well was frozen, he mounted and rode back to Michaelhouse, his spirits a little higher. As he turned to wave to the miller, he thought he saw a shadow dart into the long grass by the side of the stream, but it was no more than the merest flash of movement, and however hard he looked, he could see nothing else.

Bartholomew took the horse to Stephen Stanmore's house on Milne Street and stayed for a cup of mulled wine. Stephen looked tired and strained and told him that three of the apprentices had died. Rachel Atkin, whom Bartholomew had persuaded him to take, was proving invaluable in helping to nurse others with the sickness.

When Bartholomew returned to College, Alexander had already died, and Brother Michael was helping Agatha to sew him into a blanket. Cynric was also ill, shivering with fever, and muttering in Welsh. Bartholomew sat with him until the light began to fade, and went out to check on the plague pits.

Cynric was more friend than servant. They had first met in Oxford when they had been on opposing sides in one of the many town-and-gown brawls. Each had bloodied the other, but rather than continue, Bartholomew, who had had enough of his foray into such senseless behaviour, offered to buy the short Welshman some ale. Cynric had narrowed his eyes suspiciously, but had gone with Bartholomew, and the two had spent the rest of the day talking and watching their fellow brawlers being arrested. Bartholomew had arranged for the itinerant Cynric to work in the hostel where he studied, and, later, had invited him to Cambridge. Officially, Cynric was Bartholomew's book-bearer, although he did other tasks around the College and had a considerable degree of freedom.

Bartholomew walked back down the High Street to the scrap of land that had been hastily consecrated so that plague victims could be buried. He peered into the pit in the growing gloom, and ordered that the dead-collectors be told to use more lime.

It was still snowing heavily as he walked back to College. The snow was almost knee-deep in places, and walking was hard work. Bartholomew began to feel hot, and paused to wipe the sweat from his face. He also felt dizzy. Probably just tiredness, he thought impatiently, and he tried to hurry through the snow to return to Cynric. Walking became harder and harder, and Bartholomew was finding it difficult to catch his breath. He was relieved when he finally reached Michaelhouse, and staggered through the gates. He decided that he needed to lie down for a few moments before sitting with Cynric again.

He made his way over to his room, and pushed open the door. He stopped dead in his tracks as Samuel Gray rose languidly from his bed, where, judging from his half-closed eyes and rumpled hair, he had been sleeping.

Bartholomew desperately wanted to rest, and his

body felt stiff and sore. It must have been the unaccustomed riding. He took a step forwards, and Gray moved cautiously backwards.

'I have been waiting for you,' said Gray.

Bartholomew swallowed. His throat felt dry and sore. 'What for? Not more messages?'

'No, no, nothing like that,' said Gray.

Bartholomew felt his knees begin to give way. As he pitched forward into the surprised student's arms, he knew he had become a victim of the plague.

Epiphany came and went. Brother Michael, Father William, and a mere handful of students celebrated mass. Alcote slipped into the back of the church, and skittered nervously from pillar to pillar as a few parishioners straggled in. When one of them began to cough, he left and scuttled back to the safety of his room. Of Wilson, there was no sign.

Cynric had a burning fever for two days, and then woke on the third morning claiming he was well. Agatha, who had been nursing him, heaved a sigh of relief and went about her other duties, secure in her belief that she was immune. When a peddler came to the College selling crudely carved wooden lions covered in gold paint that he assured her would protect her from the plague, she sent him away with some ripe curses ringing in his ears.

The dead-collectors failed to come for Alexander, and so Agatha loaded him onto the College cart with the reluctant help of Gilbert, and took him to the plague pit herself. Agatha had heard that Gregory Colet, devastated by the death of Simon Roper and Bartholomew's sickness, had given up visiting new plague victims and no longer supervised the liming of the plague pits or the cleaning of the streets.

More of the dead-collectors died, and it became almost impossible to persuade people to take their places. Several friars and Canons from the Hospital offered their services, but these were not enough, and soon bodies lay for two or three days on the streets or in houses before they were taken away.

Many people believed that the end of the world was near, and that the plague was a punishment for human sin. It was said that entire villages were wiped out, and that in the cities, at least half the population had perished. Trade was virtually at a standstill, and civil disorder was rife in the cities and towns.

Bartholomew knew little about the days he was ill. Occasionally he was conscious enough to hear low voices, and he heard the College bell ringing for meals and for church services. The swellings on his neck, groin, and under his arms gave him intense pain, and he was usually aware of little else.

After five days, he saw a candle flickering on the shelf under the window. He watched it for a while, wondering why the shutters were closed and a candle burning when he could see daylight seeping under the door. As he tried to turn his head, a searing pain in his neck brought everything back to him. He remembered walking back from the plague pit and finding the obnoxious student sleeping on his bed, and recalled meeting Philippa in the shack in the convent grounds.

'Philippa!' he said, his voice no more than a whisper.

'She is well, but worried about you, as is your sister.' The student had appeared, and was leaning over him, dark rings under his eyes, and his hair even more rumpled than Bartholomew remembered.

'What are you doing here?' Bartholomew croaked.

'Tsk, man! The lad has been looking after you day and night! Show a little gratitude.'

Bartholomew gave a weak grin. 'Cynric! Thank God! I thought you might be gone.' He reached for Cynric's hand to assure himself his imagination was not playing tricks.

Cynric, touched, became brusque. 'Lie still, or those incisions will start bleeding again.'

'What incisions? Did Gregory Colet come?'

'Master Colet has given up on the world, and spends his days on his knees with the monks. It is young Samuel who has been looking after you.'

Bartholomew looked appalled, and winced as he tried to move his arms to check where the swellings on his neck would have been. 'I feel as though I have been savaged by a dog,' he groaned. 'What has he done to me?'

'He cut the swellings open to drain them. Just as you have been doing to others, Master Physician. Now you know how it feels,' said Cynric, ruefully rubbing his own lacerated neck.

Bartholomew looked at the student. 'Who are you?' he asked, wondering why a fit and healthy young man would opt to care for a plague victim he did not know.

'Samuel Gray,' said the student, promptly.

'Yes, from Bene't Hostel. But that is not what I meant. What do you want from me?'

Gray looked at the floor. 'I followed you to Trumpington, and then back in the snow. When you returned from seeing the miller's boy, I came here while you went off to see to Cynric. I was waiting for you, but you were such a long time, I fell asleep.' He looked up and met Bartholomew's eyes. 'I was Master Roper's student, and he is dead, so I would like to study under you.'

His speech over, he tried to look nonchalant, as if Bartholomew's response was not that important to him anyway, but in the silence that followed, his face grew anxious and he watched Bartholomew intently.

'I see.' Bartholomew was suddenly very tired, and could not stop his eyes from closing. Then he was shaken awake again. 'Will you have me?' the student asked insistently.

Bartholomew struggled to free himself from Gray's grip, but was as weak as a kitten. 'Why me? What have I done to deserve this?' he said, his voice heavy with sleepiness.

Gray looked at him narrowly, trying to assess whether there was a hidden insult in the question. 'There are not many of you left,' he said rudely.

Bartholomew heard Cynric laughing. He could feel himself drifting into a deep and restful slumber. Gray's voice brought him awake again.

'Will you have me? I have a good degree, you can ask Hugh Stapleton. Oh . . .' his voice trailed off. Stapleton was dead. 'Master Abigny!' he exclaimed jubilantly. 'You can ask him, he knows me!' He gave Bartholomew another gentle shake.

Bartholomew reached up and grabbed a handful of Gray's tunic, pulling him down towards the bed. 'You will never be a good physician unless you can learn when to let your patients rest,' he whispered, 'and you will never be a good student unless you learn not to manhandle your master.'

177

Releasing Gray's clothing, he closed his eyes and was instantly asleep. Gray looked at Cynric. 'Was that a yes or a no?' he asked.

Cynric, still smiling, shrugged and left the room, closing the door softly behind him. Gray stood looking down at Bartholomew for several minutes before tidying the bedclothes and blowing out the candle. He lay down on the pallet bed Cynric had given him and stared into the darkness. He knew that Bartholomew would live now, so long as he rested and regained his strength.

Bartholomew coughed in his sleep, and Gray raised himself on one elbow to peer over at him. He believed he had taken no risk in tending Bartholomew, for he was one of the plague's first victims in Cambridge and had survived. He did not think he would catch the disease a second time, and had been making a good deal of money by offering to tend plague victims in the houses of rich merchants. But that was nothing compared to what he may have earned by nursing Bartholomew. He had heard about Bartholomew's methods and ideas, and had longed to study with him when he was an undergraduate, but the physician already had as many students as he could manage.

Gray knew exactly what he wanted from life. He intended to become an excellent physician and have a large number of very wealthy patients. Perhaps he might even become the private physician of some nobleman. Regardless, he intended to find himself a position that would bring him wealth and enough free time to be able to enjoy it. He knew Bartholomew worked among the poor, but to Gray that meant he would gain far more experience of diseases than from a physician who tended the rich. He would be happy to work among the poor during his medical training, but then he would be off to make his fortune in York or Bristol, or perhaps even London.

Gray smiled to himself and lay back down, his arms behind his head. He and Cynric had been caring for Bartholomew continuously for five days and nights, and several times had thought their labours were in vain. Brother Michael had actually given Bartholomew last rites before the fever suddenly broke.

Once Bartholomew had slept almost twenty-four hours without waking, his recovery was rapid. He was out of his bed and taking his first unsteady steps around the College yard within a day, and felt ready to begin his work again within three days. Michael, Cynric, and Gray urged him to rest more, but Bartholomew insisted that tossing restlessly on his bed was more tiring than working. Bartholomew decided that all plague victims in the College should be in one room so that they could have constant attention. He set about converting the commoners' dormitory into a hospital ward, relocating the few surviving commoners elsewhere. Brother Michael's Benedictine room-mates willingly offered their services, and Bartholomew hoped that this arrangement might reduce the risks to others.

As soon as he could, Bartholomew went to see Gregory Colet. As he walked through the wet streets to Rudde's Hostel, he was shocked at the piles of rubbish and dead animals that littered them. There were three bodies, crudely wrapped in filthy rags, at the doors of St Michael's Church that Bartholomew judged to have been there for several days. Around them, several rats lay dead and dying, some half-buried in mud and refuse.

Brother Michael walked beside him, his cowl

pulled over his head in an attempt to mask the stench.

'What has happened here, Michael?' said Bartholomew in disbelief. He watched a ragged band of children playing on a huge pile of kitchen waste outside Garret Hostel, occasionally stopping to eat some morsel that they considered edible. On the opposite side of the street, two large pigs rooted happily among a similar pile of rubbish. He shook his head in despair at the filth and disorder.

Michael shrugged. 'There is no one left to do anything. Now that Colet has given up, you and Robin of Grantchester are the only medics here. All the others are dead or gone.'

'What about the priests? Can they not see that the streets need to be cleared and the bodies removed?'

Michael laughed without humour. 'We are in the business of saving souls,' he said, 'not bodies. And anyway, so many clerics have died that there are barely enough to give last rites. Did you know that there are only three Dominicans left here?'

Bartholomew gazed at him in shock. The large community of Dominicans had continued to work among the poor after the outbreak of the plague, and it seemed that their adherence to their way of life may have brought about their virtual demise.

Gregory Colet was not in his room at Rudde's, and the porter told them that he would be in one of the churches, usually St Botolph's. Bartholomew had always admired St Botolph's, with its slate-grey stone and windows faced with cream ashlar, but as Michael pushed open the great oak door and led the way inside it felt damp and cold. The stained glass that he had coveted for St Michael's Church no longer seemed to imbue it with soft colour, but served to make it dismal. The feeling of gloom was further enhanced by the sound of muted chanting. Candles were lit in the sanctuary and half a dozen monks and friars from various Orders knelt in a row at the altar. Colet sat to one side, his back against a pillar and his eyes fixed on the twinkling candles. One of the monks saw Bartholomew and Michael and came down the aisle to meet them.

Michael introduced him to Bartholomew as Brother Dunstan of Ely. Dunstan expressed pleasure to see Bartholomew well again.

'God knows we need you now,' he said, his eyes straying to Colet.

'What is wrong with him?' Bartholomew asked.

Dunstan tapped his temple. 'His mind has gone. He heard that Roper had died and that you had the sickness, and he gave up. He sits here, or in one of the other churches, all day and only goes home to sleep. I think he may be willing himself to die.'

Michael crossed himself quickly while Bartholomew looked at Dunstan in horror.

'No! Not when there are so many others that are being taken who want to live!'

Dunstan sighed. 'It is only what I think. Now I must go. We have so many masses to say for the dead, so much to do . . .'

Michael followed Dunstan to the altar rail, leaving Bartholomew looking at Colet, still gazing at the candles with vacant eyes. Bartholomew knelt down and touched Colet on the shoulder. Reluctantly Colet tore his eyes from the candles to his friend. He gave the faintest glimmer of a smile.

'Matt! You have escaped the Death!'

He began to look back towards the candles again, and Bartholomew gripped his shoulder.

'What is wrong, Gregory? I need your help.'

Colet shook his head. 'It is too late. You and I can do no more.' He became agitated. 'Give it up, Matthew, and go to the country. Cambridge will be a dead town soon.'

'No!' said Bartholomew vehemently. 'It is far from over. People have recovered and others have escaped infection. You cannot give up on them. They need you and so do I!'

Colet shook Bartholomew's hand away, his agitation quickly disappearing into a lethargic gloom. 'I can do no more,' he said, his voice barely audible.

'You must!' pleaded Bartholomew. 'The streets are filthy, and the bodies of the dead have not been collected in days. I cannot do it all alone, Gregory. Please!'

Colet's dull eyes looked blankly at Bartholomew before he turned away to look at the candles. 'Give it up,' he whispered. 'It is over.'

Bartholomew sat for a moment, overwhelmed by the task he now faced alone. Robin of Grantchester might help, but he would do nothing without being paid and Bartholomew had very little money to give him. He glanced up and saw Michael and Dunstan watching him.

'You can do nothing here,' said Dunstan softly, looking at Colet with pity. 'It is best you leave him be.'

Depressed at Colet's state of mind, Bartholomew ate a dreary meal in Michaelhouse's chilly hall, and then went to visit the building where Stanmore had his business.

Stephen greeted Bartholomew warmly, looking so like his older brother that Bartholomew almost mistook him. Bartholomew was urged inside and made to sit near a roaring fire while Stephen's wife prepared some spiced wine. Stephen reassured him that everyone was well at Trumpington, but there was a reservation in his voice that made Bartholomew uneasy.

'Are you sure everyone is well?' he persisted.

'Yes, yes, Matthew. Do not worry,' he said, swirling the wine in his cup, and assiduously refusing to look Bartholomew in the eye.

Bartholomew leaned over and gripped his wrist. 'Has anyone there had the plague? Did it come with Philippa?'

Stephen sighed. 'They told me not to tell you, because they did not want you to go rushing over there before you were well enough. Yes. The plague struck after you brought Philippa. She became ill before you were scarcely gone from the house. Then Edith was stricken, and three of the servants. The servants died, but Philippa and Edith recovered,' he said quickly as Bartholomew leapt to his feet. 'Sit down again and listen. They were not ill as long as you. They got those revolting swellings like everyone else, but they also got black spots over their bodies.'

He paused, and Bartholomew felt his heart sink. 'They are well now,' Stephen said again, 'but . . .' His voice trailed off.

'But what?' said Bartholomew. His voice was calm and steady, but he had to push his hands into the folds of his robe so that Stephen would not see them shaking.

'The spots on Edith healed well enough, but Mistress Philippa has scars.'

Bartholomew leaned back in his chair. Was that it? He looked perplexed, and Stephen tried to explain.

'There are scars on her face. She will not let anyone see them, and she refuses to speak to anyone. She wears a veil all the time, and they have to leave her food outside the door . . . where are you going?'

Bartholomew was already at the door, drawing his hood over his head. 'Can I borrow a horse?' he said.

Stephen grabbed his arm. 'This is difficult for me to say, Matt, but she specifically asked that you not be allowed to see her. She does not want to see anyone.'

Bartholomew shook him off. 'I am a physician. There may be something I can do.'

Stephen grabbed him again. 'She does not want you to go, Matt. She left a note saying that you were not to come. No one has seen her for the past week. Leave her. In time she will come round.'

'Can I borrow a horse?' Bartholomew asked again.

'No,' said Stephen, maintaining his grip.

'Then I will walk,' said Bartholomew, pushing him away and striding out into the yard. Stephen sighed, and shouted for an apprentice to saddle up his mare. Bartholomew waited in silence, while Stephen chattered nervously. 'Richard is back,' he said. Bartholomew relented a little, and smiled at Stephen.

'Thank God,' he said softly. 'Edith must be so happy.'

'As a monk in a brothel!' said Stephen grinning. The apprentice walked the horse over and Bartholomew swung himself up into the saddle. Stephen darted into his house and returned with a long blue cloak. 'Wear this, or you will freeze.'

Bartholomew accepted it gratefully. He leaned down

to touch Stephen lightly on the shoulder, and was gone, kicking the horse into a canter that was far from safe on the narrow streets.

Once out of the town, he had to slow down out of consideration for Stephen's horse. The road to Trumpington had been well travelled, and the snow had been churned into a deep slush. The weather was warmer than it had been before Christmas, and the frozen mud had thawed into a mass of cold, oozing sludge. The horse slipped and skidded, and had to be urged forward constantly. Bartholomew was beginning to think he would have to lead it, when the path became wider, and he was able to pick his way around the larger morasses.

He tried not to think about what he might encounter when he reached Edith's house. He thought, instead, of Gray's amazement when he discovered that Bartholomew did not own a horse. He wondered, not for the first time since his recovery, whether Gray was the kind of person he wanted to teach.

Bartholomew knew that he owed Gray his life. It was doubtful whether Bartholomew would have recovered without Gray's clumsy surgery and constant care. The student had taken quite a risk in lancing the swellings himself; he had not done it before, and had only seen Master Roper do it once. Bartholomew would bear the scars of Gray's inexperience for the rest of his life.

But Bartholomew remained unsure of Gray. He did not like the fact that it had been Gray who had been sent to bring him to meet Philippa, and did not like the feeling of being in debt to the flippant young man. In fact, he did not like Gray. He was confident to the point of arrogance, and was perpetually estimating how much each patient should pay as opposed to how much Bartholomew charged. Bartholomew's charges usually fell short of the cost of the medicines, and he was constantly aware of Gray's disapproving presence in the background. It was like having Wilson with him.

At last he reached the village and Edith's house. Richard came racing out to meet him, and Bartholomew was almost knocked off his feet with the force of the embrace. Richard was only seventeen, but was already almost as tall as Bartholomew. Richard chattered on in his excitement, forgetting the dignity, as befitting an under-graduate at Oxford, that he had been trying to cultivate. Bartholomew listened, Richard's descriptions bringing back vivid memories of his own time in Oxford.

Edith hurried out from the kitchen, wiping her hands on her apron before giving him a hug, and Stanmore came to slap him on the shoulders.

'Matt, you look thin and pale,' Edith said, holding him at arm's length. She hugged him again. 'It was horrible,' she whispered, so that only he could hear. 'We heard you were ill, and there was nothing we could do. I was so afraid for you.'

'Well, I am fine now. But you have been ill, too?'

Edith waved a hand dismissively. 'A couple of days in bed, that is all. But you should not have come.' Her face grew fearful, and she clung onto his arm. 'We told Stephen not to tell you,' she said.

'My lord, Matt! What on earth have you been doing with Stephen's horse?' Stanmore, for whom horses were a passion, was looking in horror at the bedraggled, mud-spattered mare.

Bartholomew groaned. He had not realised what a

state the horse was in. 'Stephen will have my hide. Can you clean it up?'

Richard went off with the stable boy to supervise, and Bartholomew followed his sister and her husband into the house. Once away from Richard, all three grew serious. Edith explained how she had gone to check on Philippa immediately after Bartholomew had left, and had found her feverish. Edith had become ill the same night, and the three servants by the following day. The fever had not seemed as intense as that of some of the plague victims, but had included a rash of black spots. Edith showed Bartholomew some faint pink marks on her arm.

Philippa's spots had been mainly on her face. She had asked Edith for a veil, and since then had locked herself in her room. That had been seven days before. Edith had spent many hours trying to get her to unlock the door, but she had eventually refused even to speak.

Bartholomew stood. 'She will not see you, Matt,' said Edith. 'She left a note that you specifically should not come to see her. Poor girl. I cannot imagine that she can be so badly scarred.'

Neither could Bartholomew. At least, not so badly scarred that he would not still want her. He thought of Colet. What terrible things this pestilence was doing to people's minds. He gave his sister the faintest of smiles before making his way up the stairs to Philippa's room. Edith did not try to stop him; she knew him too well. At the back of her mind lingered the hope that the sound of his voice might serve to pull Philippa out of her depression.

He stood outside the door for a few moments before

knocking. There was a rustle from inside the room, and then silence.

'Philippa?' he called softly. 'It is Matthew. Please open the door. There is no cause to be afraid.'

There was silence. He knocked again.

'Philippa. If you open the door and talk to me, I promise I will not try to touch you or look at you,' he called. 'Just give me a few moments with you.'

There was nothing. Bartholomew sat on the chest that was in the hallway and reflected. He would not have normally considered invading someone's privacy, but he wondered whether Philippa's mind, somehow affected by her illness, might mean that she was unable to look after herself properly. If this were the case, then she needed help, even though she might not know it herself.

Edith had married Stanmore when she was eighteen, and had come to live in Trumpington. Bartholomew had been eight, and whenever he had been permitted out of the abbey school in Peterborough, he had come to stay in Edith's rambling house. He knew every nook and cranny, and also knew that the lock on the door, behind which Philippa hid, was faulty. He knew that a sharp stick in the right place would open the door in an instant because he had played with the lock on many a wet afternoon as a boy.

He decided to try once more. 'Philippa. Why will you not answer me? Just let me talk to you for a few moments, and I promise to leave when you ask.'

There was no sound at all, not even a rustle. Bartholomew was worried, and was sure that there must be more wrong with her than a few scars. He took a sharpened piece of metal that was part of his medical equipment, and pushed it into the lock the way he had done so many years before with a stick. He had not lost his touch, and the door sprung open with ease.

Philippa jumped violently as he took a step towards her, and Bartholomew stopped. She huddled on the bed, swathed in the cloak he had given her when they had walked from the convent to Trumpington. It was still spotted with mud. Her face was turned towards him, but was covered by a long piece of gauze so that he could not make out any features. She was crouched over like an old hag, a piece of embroidery on her lap.

Bartholomew felt his breath catch as he looked at the embroidery. Philippa hated sewing and would do almost anything to avoid it. She most certainly would not be doing it voluntarily. He looked at her more closely. Her posture was wrong: something in the way she held herself was not right, and her feet were bigger than Bartholomew remembered.

'I asked you not to come.' The voice was the merest whisper, intended to deceive.

'Who are you? Where is Philippa?' Bartholomew demanded. Her head came up with a jerk when she realised she was found out, and Bartholomew caught the glint of eyes under the thick veil. He stepped forward to pull the veil off, but stopped short as she threw the embroidery from her lap and pointed a crossbow at his chest. Bartholomew took a step back. How ironic, he thought, to escape the plague and to die from a crossbow bolt.

The figure beckoned Bartholomew forward, waving the crossbow in a menacing gesture when he did not move.

'Who are you?' Bartholomew asked again. He wondered whether he would die before he found out, and whether the woman would have the courage to shoot him as he stood there.

'No questions, and turn around slowly,' she said in her dreadful whisper.

'Where is Philippa?' Bartholomew demanded, his concern making him desperate.

'One more question, and I will shoot you. Turn round.'

The whisper held a menace that was chilling, and Bartholomew had no doubt that this was not an idle threat. He turned round slowly, knowing what was coming next, and bracing himself for it.

He was not wrong. There was a sudden rustle of clothes and the crossbow came crashing down, aimed at his head. He half turned and was able to escape the full force of the blow, although it stunned him for vital seconds. The woman shot out of the door and tore down the stairs. Bartholomew staggered to his feet and lurched after her. She tore across the courtyard to where Richard was talking to the stable-boy, with Stephen's horse now clean and still saddled. Bartholomew could see what was going to happen.

'Stop her!' he yelled. He was too far behind to catch her, and ran instead towards the great oak gate, intending to close it so that she would not be able to escape.

Richard and the stable-boy gaped at the spectacle of Philippa racing across the yard clutching a crossbow, and Richard only pulled himself together at the last minute. He lunged at the would-be rider.

Meanwhile, Bartholomew was hauling at the gate with all his might. Stanmore seldom closed his gate by the look of the weeds that climbed about it, and it was stuck fast. He saw Richard hurled to the ground as the woman reached the horse. She was mounted in an instant, and wrenched the reins away from the stable-boy in a great heave that all but pulled the lad's arms out of their sockets. Bartholomew felt the gate budge, and heaved at it with every ounce of his strength. The woman wheeled the horse around, trying to control its frenzied rearing and aim it for the closing gate.

Bartholomew felt the gate move again, and was aware of blood pounding in his temples. The woman brought the horse under control, and began to urge it towards the gate. Bartholomew felt the gate shift another inch, but then he knew it would not be enough. The horse's iron-shod hooves clattered on the cobbled yard as it headed towards the gate.

Bartholomew suspended his efforts as the horse came thundering down on him. He made a futile attempt to grab at the rider, but was knocked from his feet into a pile of wet straw. The rider swayed slightly, and, as she glanced back, the wind lifted the veil, giving Bartholomew a clear view of her face. Richard shot through the gate after her, and raced down the track before realising a chase was hopeless. The rider turned the corner and was gone from sight.

'After her!' Stanmore cried, and his yard became a hive of activity as horses were saddled and reliable men hastily picked for pursuit. Bartholomew knew that by the time Stanmore was ready, their quarry would be long gone. Still, it was always possible that the horse might stumble and throw its rider, especially that miserable horse, he thought. Edith hurried up to him as he picked himself up.

'What happened? What did you say to her?' she cried.

'Are you all right, Uncle Matt? I am sorry. He was just too strong for me.' Richard looked forlorn at having failed. Bartholomew put a hand on his shoulder.

'For me too,' he said with a resigned smile.

Edith looked from one to the other. 'What are you saying?' she said. '*He?*'

Bartholomew looked at Richard. 'Did you see his face?' he asked.

Richard nodded. 'Yes, but why was he here? Where is Philippa?'

'Who was it, if not Philippa?' asked Edith, perplexed.

'Giles Abigny,' said Bartholomew and Richard together.

VII

BARTHOLOMEW LOOKED OUT OF THE WINDOW FOR at least the tenth time since Stanmore and his men had set off in pursuit of Abigny.

'Perhaps it was Giles all along, and you just thought it was Philippa you met outside the convent,' Richard said to him.

'I kissed her,' said Bartholomew. Seeing his nephew's eyebrows shoot up, he quickly added, 'And it *was* Philippa, believe me.'

Richard persisted in his theory. 'But you could have been mistaken, if you were tired, and . . .'

'Giles has a beard,' said Bartholomew, more patiently than he felt. 'Believe me, Richard, I would have noticed the difference.'

'Well, what do *you* think is going on?' demanded Richard. 'I have been sitting here racking my brain for answers, and all you have done is tell me they are wrong.'

'I do not know,' said Bartholomew, turning to stare into the fire. He saw Richard watching him and tried to pull himself together. He asked his nephew to tell him everything that had happened since he had left Philippa with the Stanmores ten days ago, partly to try to involve

Richard and partly to make sure that the sequence of events was clear in his own mind.

Philippa had become ill almost as soon as he had left, and either Edith or one of the servants had been with her through the two nights of her fever. On the morning of the third day, she seemed to have recovered, although she was, of course, exhausted. In the evening, she had asked for a veil and had closed her door to visitors, communicating by notes the day after that. Edith had not kept any of them, and so Bartholomew was unable to see whether the writing had been Philippa's or her brother's. No one could prove whether it had been Philippa or Giles who had been living in Edith's house for at least the last seven days.

Richard, with an adolescent's unabashed curiosity, had crouched behind the chest in the hallway to glimpse her as she emerged to collect the trays of food that had been left. Even with hindsight, he was unable to say whether the person who came from the room, heavily swathed in cloak and veil, was man or woman.

Bartholomew considered Richard's recital of events. What could be happening? Giles had behaved oddly ever since the death of Hugh Stapleton. Had he completely lost his mind and embarked on some fiendish plot to deprive Philippa of potential happiness because he had lost his? Had he secreted her away somewhere, either because he thought she would be safer with him, or because he meant her harm?

Richard and Bartholomew made a careful search of the garret room, but found nothing to provide them with clues to solve the mystery. There were some articles of clothing that Edith had lent her, and the embroidery, but virtually nothing else. The room had its own privy that emptied directly into the moat, but there was nothing to indicate how long Giles had been pretending to be Philippa.

Bartholomew thought carefully. There was not the slightest chance that Abigny would return to College if he thought Bartholomew might be there. He would hide elsewhere, so Bartholomew would need to visit all Abigny's old haunts – a daunting task given his dissolute lifestyle. Abigny had a good many friends and acquaintances, and was known in virtually every tavern in Cambridge, despite the fact that scholars were not permitted to frequent such places. Bartholomew grimaced. The company Abigny kept was not the kind he relished himself – whores and the rowdier elements of the town. Gray would probably know most of these places, Bartholomew thought uncharitably; after all, he had mentioned he knew Abigny.

A clatter in the yard brought Bartholomew to his feet again. Richard darted out of the door to meet his father, with Bartholomew and Edith close on his heels.

'Got clean away,' said Stanmore in disgust. 'We met a pardoner who had been on the road from Great Chesterford. He said he saw a grey mare and rider going like the Devil down towards the London road. We followed for several miles, but he will be well away by now. Even if the horse goes lame or tires, he will be able to hire another on the road. Sorry, Matt. He has gone.'

Bartholomew had expected as much, but was disappointed nevertheless. He clapped Stanmore on the shoulder. 'Thank you for trying anyway,' he said.

'Poor Stephen,' said Stanmore, handing his horse over to the stable-boy. 'He was attached to that mare.

And his best cloak gone with it! I suppose I must lend him one of mine until he can have another made.'

Bartholomew walked slowly back into the house. Stanmore was right. Given such a good start, Abigny was safely away. If he hired a fresh horse, reverted to another disguise, and joined a group of travellers as was the custom, it would be unlikely that Bartholomew would ever trace him. London was a huge sprawl of buildings and people, and it would be like looking for a needle in a haystack.

Edith put her hand on his arm. 'There is nothing you can do now,' she said. 'Stay here tonight, and Oswald will ride into town with you tomorrow.'

Bartholomew shook his head, trying not to compare Edith's warm and comfortable house with his chilly room at Michaelhouse. 'I must get back tonight. Colet has lost his mind, and there is much still to be done.'

'Then at least drink some warmed wine before you go,' said Stanmore. Before Bartholomew could object, Stanmore had taken his arm and was leading him up the flagged stairs to the solar. Richard followed. A fire burned steadily in the hearth, and the woollen rugs scattered on the floor muffled their footsteps. A sudden gust of wind rattled the shutters, and Bartholomew shivered.

'You will need help with the town,' said Stanmore. 'Stay here tonight and we will discuss what must be done.'

Bartholomew smiled at his brother-in-law's guile. They all knew he had overstretched himself on his first real day out. He would have been most disapproving had a patient done the same thing, and Edith was correct in that there was nothing he could do to help Philippa that night. He sat on a stool near the fire and picked up a stick to poke at the flames. Richard drew up a stool next to him, and Stanmore settled himself in a large oak chair covered in cushions and furs. For a while, no one spoke.

'How has Trumpington fared with the plague?' asked Bartholomew eventually, stretching outspread hands towards the fire.

'Twenty-three dead,' replied Stanmore, 'and another two likely to follow. Our priest died on Sunday, and one of the Gilbertine Canons is staying here until a replacement can be found.' He shook his head wearily. 'What is happening, Matt? The priests say this is a visitation from God, but they are dying just like those they accuse of sinning. The physicians can do nothing. I sent for Gregory Colet when Edith and Philippa became ill, since you, too, were stricken. He told me to put hot tongs in their mouths to draw the demons out. When I asked him to do it, because I was so concerned for Edith I would have tried anything, he refused because he said he was afraid the demon would enter him. What kind of medicine is that?'

Bartholomew stared into the fire. 'Colet has lost his mind. I suppose seeing so many die must have been too much for him to bear.'

'Colet?' exclaimed Richard in disbelief. 'Surely not! He always seemed so . . . cynical.'

'Perhaps that is why he has become so afflicted,' said Bartholomew glumly. 'I cannot understand it. And I do not understand the plague. Agatha walks among the victims daily and is fit and well; Francis Eltham and Henri d'Evéne hid themselves away and were taken. The old and sick cling to life, while the young and healthy die within hours. Some recover, some do not.'

'Then perhaps the priests are right,' said Stanmore. 'But why do they die too? Take Aelfrith. I heard he is dead, and he was as saintly a man as you could hope to meet.'

'The plague did not take him,' said Bartholomew, and then could have kicked himself for his thoughtless indiscretion. He drew breath to make amends, but it was too late.

'What do you mean?' asked Stanmore. 'Michael said the Death took him.'

Bartholomew hesitated. It would be a relief to tell Stanmore all he knew – about Sir John, Aelfrith, Augustus, Paul, and Montfitchet, and about the plot to suppress Cambridge University. But men had been killed, and it was likely that others would follow: the plague had not prevented Aelfrith from being murdered. Bartholomew could not risk Stanmore's safety merely to satisfy his own longing for someone with whom to share his thoughts. Edith entered the solar with a servant who carried a jug of steaming wine. She stood next to her husband, and Bartholomew's resolve strengthened. He had no right to put Stanmore's life or Edith's happiness at stake. After all, he had already lost five friends and colleagues to murder, many more to the plague, Colet to madness, and Giles and possibly Philippa to something he did not yet understand. There was only his family left. He changed the subject, asking Stanmore about his ideas for dealing with the plague in the town.

By the time Stanmore had finished outlining his plans for clearing the town of the plague dead, the day was too far advanced for Bartholomew to think of returning to Michaelhouse – as Stanmore had known it would be. Bartholomew spent the night in the solar, wrapped in thick, warm blankets, enjoying the rare luxury of the fire.

Bartholomew rose early the next day feeling much stronger. He rode into Cambridge with Stanmore, who offered to break the news of the stolen horse to Stephen. Bartholomew dismounted at St Botolph's and went to see Colet. He had to step over two bodies that had been dumped next to the door to await collection by the plague-cart. He buried his nose and mouth in his cloak against the smell and slipped into the dim church.

The monks were still there, different ones than last time, praying in a continuous vigil for deliverance from the plague and saying masses for the dead. Colet was there too. He sat on a bench wrapped in a blanket to protect himself from the damp chill of the church and playing idly with a carved golden lion that he wore on a long chain around his neck.

'Look at this, Matt,' he said, turning his face with its vacant grin to Bartholomew. 'Is it not pretty? It will protect me from the plague.'

Bartholomew sat beside him, and looked at the carving. He had seen others wearing similar icons, and had heard from Agatha that some rogue had been selling them in the town, claiming that anyone who wore one would be protected from the pestilence.

'It will not work, Gregory,' he said. 'We need to clean up the streets and bury the dead more quickly.'

Colet stared at him, and a thin drool of saliva slipped from his mouth onto the blanket. 'We should not do that. It is God's pestilence, and we should not try to fight His will by trying to reduce its effects.'

Bartholomew looked at him, aghast. 'Where on earth did you conceive that notion? You cannot believe that any more than I do.'

'But it is true, it is true,' Colet sang to himself, rocking back and forth.

'In that case,' Bartholomew said sharply, 'why are you hanging on to that ridiculous lion?'

He immediately regretted his words. Colet stopped rocking and began to cry. Bartholomew grabbed him firmly by the shoulders. 'Help me! I cannot do it all alone. Have you seen the streets? There are piles of rubbish everywhere, and the dead have not been collected in days.'

Colet snuffled into his blanket. 'If you stay with me, I will lend you my lion.'

Bartholomew closed his eyes and leaned back against the wall. Poor Colet. He had been one of the best physicians in Cambridge, and was now reduced to little more than a drooling idiot. He had acquired a large practice of rich patients, including some of the most influential men in the town, as well as teaching at Rudde's Hostel. Because of this, he was wealthy and had the ears of many powerful men. In short, he was at the beginning of what would have been a brilliant career.

Bartholomew made one last try. 'Come with me today. Help me with the sick.'

Colet shrank backwards against the pillar, fear stark on his face. 'No, Master Roper, I cannot go out there with you. I have heard there are people with the plague!' He began to twist the lion through his fingers again, staring unseeingly at the row of kneeling monks. He seemed to have forgotten Bartholomew was there at all.

* * *

Bartholomew went back to Michaelhouse. After a moment's hesitation, he opened the chest where Abigny kept his belongings and rummaged around. Nothing appeared to have gone: Abigny, it seemed, had not intended to flee Michaelhouse. Bartholomew stood for a moment looking out over the yard as he thought about what he should do first. His instinct told him to drop everything and go to the taverns and hostels in search of news of Abigny. Reluctantly, he put that aside; his first duty was to organise collection of the bodies and cleaning of the streets.

Stanmore had said already that he would put out a general message that good wages would be paid to anyone willing to rid the streets of rubbish. Since there were a number of people without employment because their masters had died, he anticipated that there would not be too much of a problem in attracting applicants. Even if it did not prevent the spread of the plague, it would reduce the spread of other, equally fatal, diseases.

Bartholomew's task was to arrange a better system of collecting the dead. Since he had been ill, the number of deaths seemed to have levelled off somewhat, although this did not mean that the plague had lessened its grip on the town. He walked to the Castle to see the Sheriff, who, pale-faced and grieving for his wife, was pliable to Bartholomew's demands. Bartholomew wondered if his mind had gone the same way as Colet's. He left the Sheriff morosely polishing his helmet and repeated his instructions to an able-looking sergeant-at-arms. The sergeant gave a hearty sigh.

'We cannot collect the dead,' he said. 'We have lost a third of the men already, and we do not have enough to patrol the town for these bloody robbers, let alone for collecting bodies. We cannot help you. Did you know that everyone in the little settlement near All Saints-next-the-Castle is dead? Not a soul has survived. The men are terrified of the place and believe that it is full of ghosts. Even if I did have the men to help, they would probably rather hang than collect the dead.'

Bartholomew left feeling depressed. He went to the settlement the sergeant had told him about and wandered through the pathetic little shacks that had been people's homes. The sergeant was right: there was not a living soul in the community. He left quickly, gagging on the smell of putrefaction.

There were more bodies in Bridge Street, although the area around St John's Hospital was relatively clean thanks to the Austin Canons. Bartholomew talked to the Canons and they agreed, albeit reluctantly, to pick up bodies they saw on the way to the plague pits when they took their own dead there. He walked on to St Edmund's Priory and obtained a similar agreement there, along with the promise of a lay-brother to supervise the filling of the plague pits.

Bartholomew's plans to keep the town free from plague-ridden bodies were beginning to come together. He still needed volunteers to drive the carts each day and collect up the piles of dead. He knew the risk of infection was great, but it was a job that had to be done.

He stood looking at the plague pit that he and Colet had organised almost two weeks before. It was so full that there was scarcely room to add the quicklime over the last layer of corpses, let alone cover it with earth afterwards. He shivered. It was a desolate spot, even though it lay only a short distance from the town gates. The wind seemed colder near the pit, and whistled softly through the scrubby trees and bushes that partially shielded it from the road. He went to a nearby tavern and offered to buy ale for any who would help him dig a new pit. At first, there was no response. Then a man stood, and said he would buy ale for any who could dig faster or deeper than he could. This met with catcalls and hoots, but the man strode out of the tavern rolling up his sleeves, and others followed.

In a short time, a new pit was dug, larger than the previous one and about twice as deep. Men competed with each other to show off their strength while, more sedately, women and even small children helped, ferrying stones from the pit to the ever-growing pile of earth to one side. Bartholomew took his turn in digging and heaving great stones out of the way. During a brief respite, Bartholomew went to speak to the man who had instigated the competitive spirit.

'Thank you, Master Blacksmith,' he said. 'I thought I might have to dig it alone.'

The blacksmith grinned, revealing the yellow-black teeth that Bartholomew remembered from the night of the riot. 'It will cost you in ale,' he said.

When the new pit had been dug, Bartholomew's helpers began to drift away. He handed over all the money he had to buy the promised ale and was pleasantly surprised to receive half of it back again with mutters that it was too much. He shovelled lime into the pit, and watched as it bubbled and seethed in the water at the bottom. The blacksmith helped him bury the first bodies, a pathetic line of ten crudely-wrapped shapes. Bartholomew covered them with more lime, and leaned on the spade wiping the sweat from his eyes.

The blacksmith came to stand beside him. 'I am

sorry,' he said, and pushed something into Bartholomew's hand. Bartholomew, bewildered, looked at the greasy black purse in his hand, and then back at the blacksmith. Abruptly the blacksmith turned away and began to walk back to the tavern. Bartholomew caught up with him, and swung him round.

'What is this?'

The blacksmith refused to meet Bartholomew's eyes. 'I did not want to do it. I told them it was wrong,' he mumbled, trying to head for the tavern. Bartholomew held him fast.

'What was wrong? What are you talking about? I do not want your money.'

The blacksmith looked up at the low clouds scudding overhead in the growing dusk. 'It is the money I got for the riot,' he said. 'I kept it all this time. I only spent enough to get some of my lads drunk enough to be brave on the night, and some to bury Mistress Atkin's son. It is Judas money and I do not want it.'

Bartholomew shook his head in bewilderment. 'What are you talking about?' he said. 'Did someone pay you to start the riot?'

The blacksmith looked Bartholomew full in the face, his eyes round. 'Yes, they paid me to get some of the lads excited. You know how it was that day – that pompous bastard throwing his wealth around while us poor folk stood and watched and waited for scraps like dogs.' He spat on the ground. 'They seemed to know how it would be, and they paid me to make sure there was a fight. Once the fight was started, I was to find you and warn you off.'

He paused, and searched Bartholomew's face, earnestly looking for some reaction to his confession.

Bartholomew thought back to the riot, of his last-minute dash into the College with the enraged mob behind him, and of Abigny telling him that Henry Oliver had ordered Francis Eltham to lock him out. Surely the whole thing had not been staged to get at him? Bartholomew shook his head in disbelief. What could he have done that people wanted him dead? He racked his brain for patients who might have died in his care, wondering whether his unorthodox treatment might have seemed to have killed when leeches might have saved, but he could think of none. Unbidden, Sir John's benign face came into his mind. But what had Sir John done, or Augustus and Aelfrith, to warrant their murders? He recalled Henry Oliver's looks of hatred at him since the riot every time they inadvertently met.

The blacksmith, watching Bartholomew's brows drawn down in thought, continued. 'It seemed like an easy way to earn some decent money at first, and trade had been poor, with the threat of the Death coming. I did a good job, getting people roused up against Michaelhouse. But it went wrong. It all got out of control before I could do anything, and the two lads died. Then you helped Rachel Atkin, and you set my leg. I have felt wrong ever since, which is why I have not spent the money. My broken leg was God's judgement on me for my actions. The men who gave me the money came to see me while my leg was mending, and I told them that I had warned you as they asked, just to get them out of my house.'

'Get who out?' asked Bartholomew, the whole mess slowly revolving in his mind, a confused jumble.

The blacksmith shook his head. 'I wish I knew, because I would tell you. These are evil men, and

I would wish you to be on your guard against them.'

'Where did they approach you?'

The blacksmith nodded over to the tavern. 'In there. I was having a quiet drink, and I got a message telling me that if I went outside, I could be a rich man. I went, and there were two men. They told me to cause a bit of a fight on the day of old fatso's ceremony, and to get you alone and warn you off.'

'What exactly did they say?'

The blacksmith closed his eyes and screwed up his face as he sought to recall the exact words. 'They said that I should just say to you "stay away". Those were their very words!' he said triumphantly, pleased at his feat of memory.

'What were these people like?'

'I could not say. Only one spoke, but I do not recall his voice. He was quite big, about your size, I would say. The other was smaller, but both of them wore thick cloaks with hoods, and I could not see their faces.'

Bartholomew and the blacksmith stood side by side in the darkness for several moments before the blacksmith spoke again. 'If I knew who they were, I would tell you. The only thing I can think of, and it is not much, is that the purse they gave me is nice. See?'

Bartholomew took a few steps to where he could see the purse in the faint light from the tavern windows. The purse had been fine in its time, but weeks in the blacksmith's grubby hands had begrimed its soft leather and all but worn away the insignia sewn in gold on the side. Bartholomew examined it more closely, turning it this way and that to try to make the gold thread catch the light. As he did so, the insignia suddenly stood out clearly. 'BH' – the initials of Bene't Hostel! He had seen Hugh Stapleton with a purse almost identical when he had been out with Abigny once.

He tipped the money out of the purse into his hand. About five marks, an enormous sum of money for a blacksmith. He turned round again. 'You keep this,' he said, pushing the money towards the blacksmith and slipping the empty purse into his belt. 'What is done is done. Thank you for telling me all this. I had no idea that I had such powerful enemies.'

The blacksmith gave a short laugh devoid of humour. 'Oh, they are powerful right enough. I could tell that just by the way they spoke to me. They are people used to ordering others about.' He put a mud-stained hand on Bartholomew's shoulder. 'I wish I had told you this before, but you seemed to be doing well enough. I do not want the money, though. I might go to hell if I take it knowing what it was for – and these days, a man cannot be sure of getting the chance to confess before he is taken.' He looked in distaste at the silver coins in his rough hand.

Before Bartholomew could stop him, he flung them all in the direction of the pit. Bartholomew saw some of them glitter as they plunged into its steaming depths. The blacksmith smiled. 'It is all right now,' he said quietly. 'The blood money is where it belongs.'

Bartholomew offered his thanks again, and made for home. He hoped that all the coins had disappeared into the quicklime. He did not want to think of people climbing into the pit to fetch them out.

He walked slowly, breathing in the cold night air in an attempt to clear his reeling mind. He was wholly confused. Someone had tried to warn him to stay away the same night that Augustus, Paul, and Montfitchet were murdered. But stay away from what? Had it been Hugh Stapleton who had issued the warning? Were there others with Bene't Hostel purses? Was it Abigny who had hired the blacksmith, since he was so often at Bene't Hostel and was apparently involved in something that had led him to pretend to be Philippa? But Michael had witnessed that it had been Abigny who had kept Francis Eltham from closing the gates until Bartholomew was safely inside. Gray had been at Bene't's too. Was he involved? It did not make sense. He wished Sir John or Aelfrith were alive so that he could tell them the whole insane muddle and they could help him to sort it out. He had already decided not to confide in his family, but who else could he trust? Michael? Bartholomew did not understand the monk's role in the death of Augustus, nor his position in the wretched Oxford plot. Abigny was clearly involved and, anyway, he had fled. The loathing he felt for Wilson was mutual, and how could he trust a man who skulked in his room and left the College to its own devices when it needed a strong Master? He considered the Chancellor and the Bishop, but what did he have to tell them? There was only his word that Aelfrith had been poisoned, and that Augustus had been dead when he disappeared. And the Chancellor and Bishop were unlikely to be impressed with him for producing the blacksmith as a witness, a self-confessed rabble-rouser and a man notorious for his drunkenness. With a heavy sigh, Bartholomew arrived at the same conclusion he had reached at Stanmore's house: that there was no one with whom he could speak, and he would have to reason through the muddle of facts alone.

Having reached St Michael's Church, he walked

across the churchyard and stood looking down at the pile of earth that marked Aelfrith's grave.

'Why?' he whispered into the night. 'I do not understand.'

He rethought the blacksmith's words as he crouched down in the long grass that grew over Aelfrith's mound. He had no reason to believe the man was lying. Were the mysterious men at the tavern ordering Bartholomew to stay away from Augustus? The blacksmith suggested that one of the men was educated and used to giving orders. Could it have been Wilson, suspecting that something might happen to Augustus and wishing to conceal the entire matter before it had occurred? He had certainly tried to hide the truth later.

Bartholomew stood, and stretched his aching limbs. It had been a long day, and the more he thought about it, the more loose ends there were and the murkier the matter became. He was tired and wanted to concentrate on finding Philippa. She might be in danger, and his feeble attempts at trying to unravel University business would not help her. Wearily he walked down the lane to Michaelhouse, intending to ask Gray to help him search the taverns for news of Abigny.

When he reached his room, there was no sign of Gray, and Bartholomew was uncertain how to begin questioning people in taverns. He knew that the wrong questions would not bring him the information he needed, and might even be dangerous. He heard a creak of floorboards in the room above, and an idea began forming in his mind. Philippa's disappearance was no secret, and it was only natural that he would want to find her. Why should he not enlist Michael's help for that? He would not need to reveal that he knew anything of the alleged Oxford plot, only that he wished to find Philippa.

Grateful that he had something positive to do, he slipped out of his room and up the stairs to Michael's chamber. He pushed open the door and saw that Michael's bed was empty. The two Benedictines who shared his room were sleeping, one of them twitching as if disturbed by some nightmare. Disappointed, he turned to leave.

As he closed the door, a scrap of parchment fluttered to the floor from one of the high shelves, caught by a sudden draught from the door downstairs. Bartholomew picked it up, and strained to read the words in the darkness. They were in Michael's bold, round hand, the letters ill-formed and clumsy with haste. 'Seal must still be in College. Will look with Wilson.'

Bartholomew stared at it. Michael had obviously written this message and been unable to deliver it, or had been disturbed while he was writing. Whatever the reason, it proved beyond a shadow of a doubt that Michael was embroiled in all this intrigue. Bartholomew felt his hands shaking. Michael may have been the very one who had paid the blacksmith to warn him away.

He gasped in shock as the note was snatched from his hand. He had been so engrossed in his thoughts that he had not heard Michael coming from the room opposite. He saw the monk's face in the gloom of the hallway. It was contorted with rage, and he was controlling himself with difficulty. Bartholomew could think of nothing to say. He had not been prying in Michael's room, and had not searched for the scrap of parchment, but there was no reason for Michael to believe that.

Words would be meaningless now: what could be

said? Bartholomew pushed his way past Michael into the hallway. In the room opposite, he could hear the muffled voices of the three students that lived there. One of them must have become ill and called for help. Bartholomew poked his head round the door and saw the student writhing on his pallet bed, his room-mates staring at him fearfully in the light of a flickering tallow candle. Bartholomew felt the sick boy's head, and told the others to carry him to the commoners' dormitory.

He went back down the stairs to his own room and closed the door. His hands still shook from the fright he had had when Michael had snatched the note away. He should not be surprised by what he had learned, bearing in mind Michael's very old behaviour on the night of Augustus's death. At the unpleasant interview with the Bishop, Michael had had no alibi for the night of the murders. Perhaps it was he who had struck down poor Paul and drugged the commoners after all.

So what should he do now? Should he tell Wilson? Or the Chancellor? But what could he tell them? He had not a single solid scrap of evidence to lay against Michael except the note, and that was doubtless a pile of ashes by now.

He froze as the door of his room swung slowly open and Brother Michael stood there holding a fluttering candle. The light threw strange shapes on the walls and made Michael look even larger than he was, as his voluminous robes swung about him. He stood in the doorway without saying a word for several moments. Bartholomew began to feel the first tendrils of fear uncoiling in his stomach.

Wordlessly, Michael closed the door, and advanced on Bartholomew, who stood, fists clenched, prepared for an attack. Michael gave an odd smile, and touched one of Bartholomew's hands with a soft, clammy finger. Bartholomew flinched and felt as though Michael must be able to hear his heart pounding in the silence of the room.

'I warned you to beware, Matthew,' he said in a low whisper that Bartholomew found unnerving.

Bartholomew swallowed. Was Michael's warning the one the blacksmith had been paid to give? Or was Michael merely referring to his words outside their staircase the night of Augustus's murder, and in the courtyard the following day?

'By prying you have put yourself in danger,' Michael continued in the same chilling tone.

'So what are you going to do?' Bartholomew was surprised at how calm his own voice sounded.

'What do you expect me to do?'

Bartholomew did not know how to answer this. He tried to get a grip on his fear. It was only Michael! The fat monk may have been bulkier and stronger, but Bartholomew was quicker and fitter, and since neither of them had a weapon, Bartholomew was sure he would be able to jump out the window before Michael could catch him. He decided an offensive stance might serve him to better advantage.

'What have you been meddling in?' he demanded. 'What have you done with Philippa?'

'Philippa?' Michael's sardonic face showed genuine astonishment. He regained his composure quickly. 'Now there, my friend, I have sinned only in my mind. The question is, what have *you* been meddling in?'

They stood facing each other, Bartholomew tensed

and ready to react should Michael make the slightest antagonistic move.

Suddenly the door flew open and Gray burst in, his face bright with excitement in the candlelight.

'Doctor Bartholomew! Thank God you are here! Brother Michael, too. You must come quickly. Something is going on in Master Wilson's room.'

He darted across the room, and grabbed Bartholomew by his sleeve to pull him out the door. Bartholomew and Michael had time to exchange glances, in which each reflected the other's confusion. They quickly followed Gray across the courtyard, and Brother Michael began to pant with the exertion.

'We will say no more of this,' he said in an undertone to Bartholomew. 'You will tell no one of what you read on the note, and I will tell no one that you read it.' He stopped and clutched Bartholomew's shirt. 'Do you agree, on your honour?'

Bartholomew felt as though his brain was going to explode, so fast were the questions pouring through it. 'Do you know anything about Philippa?' he asked. He watched Michael's flabby face wrinkle with annoyance at what he obviously perceived as an irrelevancy.

'I know nothing of her, nor of her wastrel brother,' he said. 'Do you swear?'

'I will swear, if you promise to me you know nothing of Philippa's disappearance, and if you hear anything, no matter how trivial it might seem, you will tell me.'

Gray bounded back to them. 'Come on! Hurry!' he cried.

'Oh, all right, I promise,' Michael said irritably. Bartholomew turned to go, but Michael held him fast. 'We are friends,' he said, 'and I have tried to keep you out of all this. You must forget what you saw, or your life and mine will be worth nothing.'

Bartholomew pushed the monk's sweaty hand away from his shirt. 'What dangerous games are you playing, Michael? If you live in such fear, why are you involved?'

'That is none of your business,' he hissed. 'Now swear!'

Bartholomew raised his hand in a mocking salute. 'I swear, o meddling monk,' he said sarcastically. Michael looked angry.

'You see? You think this is trivial! Well, you will learn all too soon what you are dealing with if you do not take care. Like the others!'

He turned and hurried to where Gray was fretting at the foot of Wilson's staircase, leaving Bartholomew wondering what the obese monk was involved in to have him scared almost out of his wits.

'Come on, come *on*!' called Gray, almost hopping from foot to foot in his impatience.

Bartholomew followed Michael and Gray up the stairs, and the three of them stood in the little hallway outside Wilson's room. Bartholomew moved away from Michael, not totally convinced that this was not some plot cooked up by Michael and Gray to harm him.

'What is it?' whispered Michael.

Gray motioned for him to be quiet. Bartholomew had not been up this staircase since Sir John had died, and he felt odd standing there like a thief in the dark. Gray put his ear to the door and indicated that the others should do likewise. At first, Bartholomew could hear nothing, and then he could make out low moaning noises, like those of an animal in pain. Then he heard some muttering, and the sound of something tearing. He moved away so that Michael could hear, almost ready to walk away and leave them there. He did not feel comfortable listening at the Master's door like this; what Wilson got up to in his own room, however nasty, was his own business, and Bartholomew wanted none of it.

All three leapt into the air as a tremendous crash came from inside the room. Michael leaned against the wall, his hand on his chest, gasping for breath. Gray stared at the door with wide eyes. Suddenly, Bartholomew became aware of something else. He crouched down near the bottom of the door and inspected it carefully. There was no mistake. Something was on fire in Wilson's room!

Yelling to the others, he pounded on the door, just as terrified screams started to come from within. Brother Michael shoved his bulk against the door, and the leather hinges gave with a great groan. It swung inwards, and Bartholomew rushed inside. He seized a pitcher of water from atop a chest, and dashed it over the figure writhing on the floor. He was aware of Michael and Gray tearing the coverings from the walls to beat out the flames that licked across the floor. Bartholomew used a rich woollen rug to smother the flames that continued to dance over Wilson.

It was all over in a few seconds. The fire, it seemed, had only just started and so had not gained a firm hold. Gray went round carefully pouring Wilson's stockpile of wine and ale over the parts that still smouldered. They had averted what could have been a terrible disaster.

Bartholomew carefully unrolled Wilson from the rug. One or two tendrils of smoke rose from his clothes, but the fire was out. Michael helped Bartholomew lift their Master onto the bed, where Bartholomew began to examine him. Michael wandered around the room picking up pieces of charred paper, watching them crumble in his hands, and muttering something about the College accounts.

The commotion had brought others running to see what had happened. Alcote was first; Jocelyn of Ripon, Father Jerome, Roger Alyngton, and the surviving commoners, were close on his heels. They stopped dead when they saw the Master lying on the bed in his burned gown and Bartholomew kneeling next to him.

'What have you done?' Alcote demanded.

Gray intervened, and Bartholomew admired his poise and confidence. 'I was just returning from Bene't's, and I saw flickering coming from the Master's room. I was worried there was a fire, so I went up the stairs and listened outside the door. I could not smell any smoke, but I could hear someone crying. He was crying with so much pain that it almost hurt to hear. I went to fetch Doctor Bartholomew, because I thought maybe the Master had lost his mind like poor Gregory Colet, and the Doctor might be able to help. Brother Michael was with him, so he came too.'

Michael took over. 'I heard no crying,' he said, 'but moaning. Then there was a crash, which must have been the Master knocking that table over, and the table had the lamp on it. We were just in time to put out the flames. It seems the Master was busy burning documents.' He held up a handful of charred remains for Alcote to see.

Alcote stepped dubiously inside the room. The floor was awash with spilled ale and wine, and cinders of Wilson's parchments lay everywhere. 'Why was he burning his documents?' he demanded. 'Why did he knock the table over? It is heavy. He could not knock it over with ease.'

'He probably fell against it,' said Bartholomew, looking up from his patient. 'He has the plague.'

Alcote gasped and shot back outside the room, fumbling for a piece of his robe with which to cover his mouth and nose. 'The plague? But that is not possible! He has been in his room since it started and no one has touched him!'

Bartholomew shrugged. 'He has it nevertheless. Come and look.'

Alcote shrank back further still, and disappeared into the group of students that had assembled outside. Bartholomew rose from Wilson's bed.

'It is all over,' he said to the onlookers. 'There was a fire, but it is out now. Go back to your beds.' He nodded to Gray, indicating that he should disperse them. Alyngton and Jerome stared in horror at one of Wilson's burned feet that stuck out of the end of the bed. Jocelyn bent down to pick up one of the pieces of burned paper.

'I have heard the plague turns people's minds. Poor man. He has burned the College accounts!' He took the arms of his fellow commoners, and led them away gently. Bartholomew wondered if Jocelyn had been a soldier, for he was remarkably unmoved by the ghoulish foot that poked out, red and blistered.

Michael closed the door and came to peer over Bartholomew's shoulder. 'How is he?' he asked.

Bartholomew bent to listen to Wilson's heart again. It still beat strongly, but his injuries were terrible. The fire had caught the edge of his gown, and had spread quickly up to his waist before Bartholomew had been able to put out the flames. Wilson's legs were a mass of blackened flesh and bleeding blisters, and even now his toes felt hot to Bartholomew's hand. As if that were not enough, Wilson had great festering buboes under his arms, on his neck, and in his groin. One had burst, and a trickle of pus and blood dripped onto his burned legs.

'Will he live?' asked Michael, deliberately not looking at Wilson's legs.

Bartholomew moved away, so that if some part of Wilson's brain were conscious, he would not be able to hear. 'No,' he said. 'He will die before the night is over.'

Michael looked over at Wilson's still figure. 'Why did he burn the College accounts?' he asked.

'Evidence of payments to people he wished kept secret?' mused Bartholomew, without really considering the implications.

'Such payments would not be written down,' Michael said scathingly. 'They would come out of a separate account, the records of which any sensible master would keep only in his head. These accounts,' he continued, waving a fistful of charred parchment in the air, scattering tiny cinders, 'are nothing. They are only records of the College's finances. There is nothing here to warrant burning!'

Bartholomew shrugged, and turned his attention to his patient. He guessed Michael had expected to find some documents relating to this miserable University business. Wilson lay quietly, and Bartholomew moistened his lips with the few drops of water remaining at the bottom of the pitcher. He placed a clean piece of linen over Wilson's burned legs, but saw no point in putting him through painful treatment when he was going to die in a few hours. If he regained consciousness,

Bartholomew could give him medicine that would dull his senses.

Since Gray was still busy dispersing the curious scholars, Bartholomew went to his storeroom to fetch the medicine himself. Recently, he had rarely needed to use such powerful potions – he did not use it for victims of the plague because it tended to make them vomit. He kept all such medicines in a small, locked chest at the back of the room and usually carried the key on his belt. He took it now, and leaned down impatiently when it would not fit. He turned the small chest to the light and looked in horror.

The lock on the chest was broken. Someone had prised it off completely. With a feeling of sick dread, Bartholomew opened the box and looked inside. He kept a very careful written record of these medicines, with dates, times, and amounts used. Most of the potions were still there, with one glaring exception. Bartholomew looked in shock at the near-empty bottle where the concentrated opiate had been. Was this what had been used to kill Aelfrith? There was certainly enough missing to kill.

Bartholomew leaned over the chest, feeling sick. Was all this never going to end? Had Wilson sneaked down to Bartholomew's room in the depths of some night to steal poison with which to kill Aelfrith? If Wilson were the murderer, he did not have long to wait before he was judged for it. Feeling appalled at the pointlessness of it all, he put a few grains of the remaining white powder in a spare bottle, marked it down in his record book, and returned to Wilson.

He told Gray to find another chest in which to lock the poisons and sat next to Wilson. Michael went to fetch the accoutrements he needed to give Wilson last rites.

Bartholomew dipped a corner of a cloth into some water, and wiped Wilson's face with it. He noted that even on his deathbed, Wilson still managed to look pompous. Bartholomew tried to stop himself thinking such uncharitable thoughts, and wiped Wilson's face again; to his shock, Wilson opened his eyes.

'Rest now, Master Wilson,' he said, trying not to think about whether the man had murdered Aelfrith. 'Try to sleep.'

'Soon, I will sleep all too much,' came the whispered reply. 'Do not try to fool me, Physician. I know I have only a short while left.'

Bartholomew did not argue. He rubbed the soaking end of the cloth over Wilson's parched lips, and reached for the medicine that might give him some relief. Wilson's white hand flapped about pathetically.

'No! I want none of your medicines!' he grated. 'I have things I must say.'

'Brother Michael will be here soon,' Bartholomew said, putting the stopper back on the bottle. 'You can make your confession to him.'

'I do not want to talk to him,' said Wilson, his voice growing stronger as he spoke. 'I have things I want to say to you alone.'

Bartholomew felt the hair on the back of his neck rise, and he wondered whether Wilson was about to confess to murder. Wilson's hand flapped again, and enveloped one of Bartholomew's. The Physician felt revulsion, but did not pull his hand away.

'It was me,' said Wilson. 'I fought with you in the

dark on the night of Augustus's death. It was me who pushed you down the stairs.'

Bartholomew snatched his hand back. 'Then it was also you who murdered Brother Paul!' he said. 'Poor Brother Paul! Murdered while he lay defenceless on his pallet bed!'

Wilson gave an awful grimace that Bartholomew took to be a smile. 'No! You have that wrong, Physician. You always were poor at logic. Listen to me and learn.'

Bartholomew gritted his teeth so that he would not allow his distaste for the lawyer to show.

Wilson continued wheezily. 'After I left the feast, I went back to the room I shared with Alcote. We talked for a while, and he went to sleep, as we told the Bishop the next day. But I did not sleep. Alcote was almost senseless with the amount of wine he had drunk. It was a simple thing to slip out of the room once it began to ring with his drunken snores. He woke only when Alexander came to fetch us when you had raised the alarm, and by then I was back in my bed. There was my alibi!'

He stopped speaking, and lay with his eyes closed, breathing heavily. After a few moments, Wilson opened his eyes again, and fixed Bartholomew with an unpleasant stare.

'I allowed quite some time to pass before I went to Augustus's room that night,' he continued, his voice weaker than before. 'I was going to send Aelfrith away and offer to pray for Augustus until dawn. I went up the stairs, but saw that Augustus's room had been ransacked, and that he was gone. Aelfrith was unconscious on the floor. The shutters were open, and in the light from outside, I could see that there was an irregularity in the wooden floor. It is doubtful I ever would have noticed it in ordinary light. I closed the shutters and had just prised up the board, when you came. We fought, and you lost.'

He paused, coughing weakly. Bartholomew wiped away a thin trail of blood that dribbled from his mouth and thought back to that struggle. Wilson, like Michael, was flabby, and was well-endowed with chins, but that did not mean to say he was also weak. If Wilson had been desperate and panic-stricken, Bartholomew believed he could have been overpowered by him.

'I assume your intention in going to Augustus's room was not to pray?' asked Bartholomew.

Wilson sneered. 'Damn right it was not to pray! I wanted to find the seal. I am certain that whoever murdered Sir John did not get it from his body.'

Bartholomew caught his breath. 'You say Sir John was murdered?'

Wilson sneered again. 'Of course he was! He was killed for the seal he always carried, and without which no further messages would come from his contact in Oxford. It was imperative I found that seal. I saw it round his neck as he went for dinner the night of his death. The way in which his body was dressed indicated that it had not been round his neck when he died, or his murderers would not have bothered taking his clothes – they would merely have thrown his body into the mill stream. No murderer stays too long at the site of his crime,' he said with a superior smile.

'The only place Sir John went between dinner and when he left College for the last time was to see Augustus,' Wilson continued. 'So, the seal had to be in Augustus's room. When you told me he had died, I decided to look for the seal before someone else did.'

'But you did not find it,' said Bartholomew. He thought of Augustus's senile ramblings the afternoon before the feast, exhorting John Babington to 'hide it well'. If Sir John had not hidden the wretched seal as well as he apparently had, Augustus, Paul, and Montfitchet might still be alive.

'I did not,' said Wilson. 'I had just felt about in the small hole in the floorboards when you came blundering in. But,' he continued, fastening a cold, but sweaty, hand round Bartholomew's wrist, 'I did not hit Aelfrith, I did not drug the wine, and I did not kill Paul.' He looked at Bartholomew. 'I also do not know what happened to Augustus, although I do not believe he was responsible for the happenings that night. The poor old fool was far too senile to have effected such a well-considered plan.'

'Well-considered?' said Bartholomew in disgust. 'You call the murder of Paul and Montfitchet well-considered?'

Wilson ignored him and lay silent for a while.

'So how did you escape?' asked Bartholomew after a while. 'You did not pass me on the stairs.'

'You are observant, Master Physician,' said Wilson facetiously. 'Had you looked up instead of down, you may have noticed where I was, although I doubt it, for it is very cunningly concealed. The south wing of Michaelhouse was designed with two trap-doors in the ceilings of the upper floor. It is a secret passed on from Master to Master should the need ever arise for him to listen to the plottings of his fellows.'

'Sir John died before you became Master. How did you find out about this?'

'The day the Chancellor told me I was to be Master, he gave me various documents locked in a small chest.

I had to return the box to him immediately after I had read the documents, lest I die without passing certain information to my successor. Reference to these secret doors was included with a stricture that only Masters should be informed of their presence. I immediately went to Augustus's room to look for one of them. He watched me, but did not understand what I was doing.'

'Who else knows about these trap-doors?'

'When you know that, you will know the murderer.'

Bartholomew's mind began to mull through this information. Wilson's callous dismissal of Augustus had probably brought about his death. Augustus had very possibly babbled to someone else, in one of his senile ramblings, about the trap-door he had watched Wilson uncover, and had thus endangered himself. So, who might he have told? Evidently not Aelfrith or he would have guessed where his attacker might have hidden himself, and would not have searched with Bartholomew. Was it Michael? Or another Fellow?

Wilson watched him trying to reason the muddle out, his expression smug, as if Bartholomew were one of his students trying to resolve some legal point for which there was no solution. He continued. 'All I had to do once I had pushed you down the stairs was to stand on the window-sill, and pull myself through the opening. I could hear you looking for me and knew you would never be able to spot the trap-door, especially in the poor light. Whoever killed Paul and took Augustus evidently also knew about the trap-doors.'

Bartholomew sat back and thought. It made sense. As Aelfrith had prayed over Augustus, the murderer had slipped through the trap-door – or perhaps even dropped something on the friar – and knocked him senseless. The wine was drugged, and Paul murdered so that the commoners would know nothing about what was going on. A search of the room was made, but, not finding the seal, and perhaps hearing Wilson coming, the murderer took Augustus's body through the trap-door to hide it.

'But why steal a body?' asked Bartholomew, still thwarted in his attempt to make sense of the new information.

Wilson sighed. 'You are intractable, Physician. It would not take long to search a corpse, and so the answer is obvious. Augustus was alive, and was taken so that he would reveal where the seal was hidden to the murderer!'

Bartholomew shook his head. 'Augustus was dead, Master Wilson. He was probably murdered too.'

'Rubbish,' said Wilson dismissively. 'He was alive. Why would anyone wish to steal a corpse? Think, man! Your supposition that Augustus was dead is not a reasonable one.'

He lay back on his pillow, his face red with effort. Bartholomew sponged it again while he let all Wilson's claims sink in. Wilson was right. It would make sense for the murderer to take a living person with him to be questioned later, but not a dead one. But Bartholomew knew Augustus had been dead! He had touched his eyes, and made a careful examination of the body. Nevertheless, apart from that, Wilson's story made matters a little clearer, and also explained why the Master had been prepared to put about the Bishop's lies. The Bishop had probably known exactly what Wilson had been doing in Augustus's room, and approved of it.

The door swung open on its broken hinges, and Michael entered, bringing the things he would need to give Wilson last rites and to hear his confession.

'Get out!' hissed Wilson, lifting his head from the pillow. 'Get out until I am ready!'

Michael looked annoyed, but left the room without arguing. Wilson waited until he heard his footsteps going down the wooden stairs.

'Why did you want this seal?' Bartholomew asked.

Wilson's eyes remained closed. The effort of sending Michael away had exhausted him. His voice was little more than a whisper when he finally spoke. 'Because the University is under threat from scholars at Oxford,' he said. 'Babington's seal would have enabled us to continue to receive reports on their activities from his contact there. Since the seal has gone missing, we have heard nothing, and we are missing out on vital information. I had to find it and could let nothing stop me!'

'Even murder?' asked Bartholomew softly.

'I assure you I did not murder anyone,' said Wilson tiredly. 'Although I did try to kill you when you found me in Augustus's room. I do not like you, Master Physician. I do not like the way you mix learning and dealing with those filthy thieves in the town you call your patients. I do not like the way your life and loyalties are divided between the College and the town. And I did not like the way Babington encouraged you to have it so.'

Bartholomew felt like telling Wilson that he did not like him either, but there was nothing to be gained from such comments at this point.

'Do you know anything about Aelfrith's death?' he asked instead. Wilson was fading fast, and he had many questions he wanted answered.

'No, why should I? The foolish man went out among plague victims. What did he expect?'

'He was murdered too. He was killed with medicines from my poisons chest. His last words were "poison" and "Wilson". What do you make of that?'

Wilson fixed bloodshot eyes on Bartholomew. 'Nonsense,' he said after a moment. 'You misheard him. Aelfrith was told about the seal, but he was an innocent, who should never have been allowed to know the secret. He was too . . . willing to believe good of people. Do not make up mysteries, Bartholomew. You have enough to do with those that already exist.'

'What were you doing when you set yourself alight?' asked Bartholomew. He remained uncertain whether Wilson really knew nothing of Aelfrith's murder and so was dismissing it out of hand, or whether he knew far too much but was refusing to say so. Bartholomew had to lean close to Wilson to hear his words, trying not to show repugnance at his fetid breath.

'I was burning the College records,' he said. 'My successor will probably be Swynford, and I will not make things easy for the likes of him by leaving nicely laid-out ledgers and figures. Oh, no! He can work it all out for himself! I was going to burn all the records, then send for you, but I was overcome with dizziness, and must have knocked the table over with the lamp on it.'

So, Wilson's motive for burning the ledgers had been spite, and Michael was wrong in assuming that it was anything more sinister or meaningful. Bartholomew looked down at Wilson with pity. How could a man, knowing he was going to die, perform such petty acts of meanness with his last strength? He thought of others he had seen die during the last weeks, and how many had died begging him to take care of a relative, or asking him to pass some little trinket to a friend who had not had the chance to say goodbye. Bartholomew felt sick of the University and its politics, and particularly sick of Wilson and his pathetic vengeance.

He moved away. He had one more question to ask, one that meant more to him than the others. He had to put it casually, because he sensed if Wilson knew it was important to him, he might not answer.

'Does any of this have anything to do with Giles or Philippa Abigny?' he asked, looking at where the door hung at an odd angle on its damaged hinges.

Wilson gave a nasty wheezing chuckle. 'Your lady love? It is possible. I have been thinking for some time now that Abigny might be one of the Oxford spies. He spends too much time away from the College, and I never know where he is. Perhaps it was he who found the seal. I heard that your lady has gone. She should have stayed in her convent. Probably ran off with some man who will make her richer and happier than you, Physician.'

Bartholomew fought down the urge to wrap his hands round the man's neck and squeeze as hard as he could. So, Abigny could be one of Oxford's spies. Was that why he had been hiding in disguise at Edith's house? But that did not explain where Philippa was. Bartholomew could see no option other than to become embroiled in this seething pit of intrigue and spies in order to find out about Abigny's possible role.

'Do you know for certain that Philippa ran away with a man?' asked Bartholomew as calmly as he could.

Wilson gave another breathy cackle. 'I am almost tempted to say yes because I would like to see the expression on your face,' he said. 'But the answer is no. I have no idea where your woman is, and I have no information whatsoever about her disappearance. I wish I had, because I want you to do two things for me, and I would like to make you feel obliged to do them by giving you information in return.'

Bartholomew grimaced. He wondered why Wilson had chosen him to do his bidding. 'What are they?'

Wilson's lips parted in his ghastly grin. 'First, I want you to find the seal.'

Bartholomew spread his hands helplessly. 'But how can I find it if you could not? And why me and not one of the others?'

'Swynford is gone, and I would not trust him anyway. Aelfrith is dead. Father William is too indiscreet, and would go about his task with so much fervour that he would surely fail. Brother Michael knows more than he is telling me, and I do not trust that he is on the right side. The same goes for Abigny, who has fled the nest anyway. Alcote is too stupid. That leaves only you, my clever Physician! You have the intelligence to solve the riddle, and Aelfrith assured me that you were uninvolved with all this before he died.'

Wilson lifted his head from the pillow and reached for Bartholomew's arm. 'You must find it, and pass it to the Chancellor. He will see you amply rewarded.' He released Bartholomew's arm, and sank back.

So Wilson thought that any of the surviving Fellows might be involved, although he thought it less likely of William or Alcote. Abigny and Michael were plainly embroiled. But the entire Oxford business seemed so far-fetched, especially now when towns and villages were being decimated with the plague. Why would Oxford scholars bother to waste their time and energy on subterfuge and plotting when they all might be dead in a matter of weeks anyway?

'It seems so futile,' he blurted out. 'Now of all times there are issues far more important to which scholars should devote their attention.'

Wilson sneered again. 'What is more important than the survival of the College and University? Even you must see that is paramount! You must have some love of learning, or you would not be here, exchanging comfort and wealth for the cramped, rigid life of a scholar. Your arrogance has not allowed you to see that there are others who love learning, and would do anything to see it protected. I sacrificed a glowing future as a cloth merchant to become a scholar, because I believe the University has a vital role to play in the future of our country. You are not the only one to sacrifice yourself for a love of knowledge and learning.'

Bartholomew watched the guttering candle. 'But the University at Oxford is stronger, bigger, and older than Cambridge. Why should they bother?'

Wilson made an impatient sound, and slowly shook his head. 'You will not be convinced, I see. Aelfrith said as much. But you will see in the end. Anyway, it matters not why you choose to seek the seal, only that you do so. Believe it will lead you to your woman if you wish. Believe it will avenge Babington's death. But find it.'

He closed his eyes, his face an ashen-grey.

'And the second thing?' Bartholomew asked. 'You said there were two things you wanted done.'

'I want you to see that I am not thrown into one of your filthy plague pits. I want to be buried in the church near the high altar, and I want an effigy carved in black marble. I am choosing you to do this because I know you are dealing with burials these days, and because you have already had the plague and might now survive the longest. Any of the others might catch it, and I cannot rely on them to carry out my wishes. You will find money for the tomb in my purse in the College chest.'

Bartholomew stared at him in disbelief, and almost laughed. Wilson was incorrigible! Even with so little time left, his mind was on pomp and ceremony. Bartholomew wanted to tell him that it would give him great pleasure to see his fat corpse dumped into the plague pit, but he was not Wilson, and so he merely said he would do what he could.

Wilson seemed to be fading fast, now he had completed his business. Sweat coursed down his face and over his jowls, and Bartholomew noticed that one of the swellings on his neck must have burst when he was moving his head. Thankfully, he did not seem to be in any pain. Perhaps the shock of the burns had taken the feeling from his body, or perhaps Wilson was able to put it to the back of his mind while he tied up the loose ends in his life.

'Tell Michael to come,' he whispered. 'I have done with you now.'

Bartholomew was peremptorily dismissed with the characteristic flap of the flabby hand that had been the cause of so much resentment among the College servants. He went to the door and called for Michael. Michael huffed up the stairs and spread out his accoutrements, obviously still indignant about his dismissal from the room earlier.

Bartholomew left so that Wilson could make his

confession in private, and went to examine the other plague cases in the commoners' room. He was summoned back by Michael after only a few minutes.

'The Master had little to confess,' said Michael in amused disbelief. 'He says he has lived a godly life, and has done no harm to anyone who did not deserve it. God's teeth, Matt.' Michael shook his head in wonder. 'It is as well he has asked you not to put him in the plague pit. In a tomb of his own, the Devil will be able to come to claim him that much quicker!'

VIII

WILSON DIED SHORTLY AFTER HE WAS ABSOLVED of his sins. Bartholomew helped Cynric stitch the body into one of the singed wall-hangings that Michael and Gray had used to put out the flames. Bartholomew did not want the body to stay in the College, nor did he want it lying in the church where it might infect others. The only solution was to dig a temporary grave so that it could be retrieved when the tomb was ready.

Gray went to purchase a coffin at an extortionate price – they had become a rare commodity – and at dawn that day, Cynric and Gray dug a deep grave at the back of the church. Agatha, Cynric and Gray watched from a distance as Bartholomew and Michael lowered the coffin, while William muttered a requiem mass at top speed.

When it was over, they went into the church for the morning service and then back to College for breakfast. The hall was cold and gloomy, and Bartholomew suggested that they all eat in the kitchen, where it was warm and Cynric would not have so far to carry the food. The other scholars had tended to prepare their own breakfasts in their rooms since the onset of the plague, to avoid unnecessary contact.

William gulped down some bread and watered wine, and went to take the news of Wilson's death to the Chancellor. Agatha watched him go.

'Would it be an unchristian thing to be thankful that that pompous old windbag was dead?' she asked Michael.

'Yes,' replied Michael, his hands full of chicken and his face covered in grease.

'Well, then,' she said, 'you have advance warning of what I will say in my confession. The College will be better without him. What will happen now?'

Michael swallowed a huge mouthful of food, and almost choked. Bartholomew pounded him on the back. 'The Fellows choose two names from their number, and the Chancellor picks one of them,' Michael said between coughs. As soon as he stopped coughing, he crammed as much food into his mouth as would fit, and went through the same process again.

'So, which two Fellows will you choose?' asked Agatha, beginning to clear away the table.

Michael swallowed hard, tears coursing down his cheeks. 'Dry, this chicken,' he remarked, making Bartholomew laugh. 'One nomination will have to be Swynford, I suppose. I would like you to be the other, Matt.'

'I am not doing it,' Bartholomew gasped in amazement. 'I do not have time.'

'Well, who else then?' asked Michael.

'You, Swynford, William, Alcote. Any of you would do well.' Bartholomew wondered which of them would promote the cause of the University, and which might be Oxford's spies. He rose and washed his hands in a bowl of water near the fire. Behind him, he could hear the cracking of bones as Michael savaged the remains of his chicken. Gray dabbled his hands quickly in the cold water, and wiped them on his robe. He did not see why Bartholomew was always washing his hands; they only became dirty again, especially in the shabby hovels that Bartholomew frequented.

Bartholomew's first duty of the day was to examine Alyngton and five students in the commoners' room. He lanced the swellings that looked as though they would drain, and left Michael's Benedictine room-mates with instructions on how to keep the sick scholars comfortable. That done, he visited three patients in the rivermen's houses down by the wharf.

Gray followed him from house to house carrying the heavy bag that contained Bartholomew's instruments and medicines. Bartholomew could feel the student's disapproval as he entered the single-roomed shacks that were home to families of a dozen. The only patient of which Gray did not disapprove was the wife of a merchant. She was one of the few cases with which Bartholomew had had success, and was lying in a bed draped with costly cloths, tired, but still living. The grateful merchant pressed some gold coins into Bartholomew's hand. Bartholomew wondered whether they would be sufficient to bribe people to drive the carts that collected the dead.

Once the urgent calls were over, Bartholomew turned to Gray.

'I need to discover what happened to Philippa,' he said. 'I am going to try to see if anyone knows Giles Abigny's whereabouts.'

Gray's face broke into a smile. 'You mean you plan to visit a few of his favourite spots?' he asked cheerfully.

'Oh, good. Beats traipsing around those dismal hovels. Where shall we begin?'

Bartholomew was thankful that Gray had so readily agreed to help. 'The King's Head,' he said, saying the first place that came into his head.

Gray frowned. 'Not a good place to start,' he said. 'We would be better going there later when it is busier. We should visit Bene't's first – that is where he spent most of his time outside Michaelhouse. Hugh Stapleton's brother, Cedric, is ill and now Master Roper is dead, they have no physician. We could see him first and then wheedle an invitation to eat there.'

Bartholomew saw he had a lot to learn in the sleazy ways of detection. He walked with Gray up the High Street to Bene't Street. Gray strolled nonchalantly into Bene't Hostel and a notion went through Bartholomew's mind that the scholars there might consider him to have poached Gray from them. The student had attached himself to Bartholomew with gay abandon, and Bartholomew had not asked whether he had sought permission from the Principal – whoever that was now that Hugh Stapleton had died.

The hostel was little more than a large house, with one room enlarged to make a hall. Bartholomew assumed that the hall would be used for communal meals as well as teaching. The hostel was far warmer than the chilly stone rooms of Michaelhouse, and the smell of boiled cabbage pervaded the whole house. Drying clothes hung everywhere, and the entire place had an aura of controlled, but friendly, chaos. No wonder Abigny had felt more at home here than in the strict orderliness of Michaelhouse.

Gray made for the small hall on the first floor of the

building. He stopped to speak to a small, silver-haired man, and then turned to Bartholomew. 'This is Master Burwell, the Sub-Principal,' he said. 'He is very grateful for your offer to attend Cedric Stapleton.'

Bartholomew followed Burwell up some narrow wooden steps into the eaves of the house. 'How long has Master Stapleton been ill?' he asked.

'Since yesterday morning. I am sure there is little you can do, Doctor, but we appreciate you offering to help.' Burwell glanced round to smile at Bartholomew, and opened the door into a pleasant, slant-sided room with two dormer windows. The windows were glazed, and a fire was lit, so the room was remarkably warm. Bartholomew stepped in and went to the man who lay on the bed. A Dominican lay-brother was kneeling by him, alternating muttered prayers with wiping his patient's face with a napkin. Bartholomew knelt next to him to peer at the all-too-familiar symptoms.

He took a knife and quickly made criss-cross incisions on the buboes in Stapleton's armpits and groin. Immediately, a foul smell filled the room, and the lay-brother jerked backwards with a cry of disgust. Bartholomew asked for hot water, and set about cleaning the swellings. It seemed that Bartholomew's simple operation had afforded Stapleton some relief, for his breathing became easier and his arms and legs relaxed into a more normal position.

Bartholomew sat for a while with Stapleton, then went in search of Gray. He found him holding court in the small hall, in the middle of some tale about how he had sold a pardoner some coloured water to cure him of his stomach gripes, and how the pardoner had returned a week later to tell him that the wonderful medicine had worked.

Bartholomew sat on the end of a bench next to Burwell. Burwell raised his eyebrows questioningly.

'It is too soon to tell,' Bartholomew said in response. 'You will know where you stand with Master Stapleton by nightfall.'

Burwell looked away. 'We have lost five masters and twelve students,' he said. 'How has Michaelhouse fared?'

'Sixteen students, three commoners, and two Fellows. The Master died last night.'

'Wilson?' asked Burwell incredulously. 'I thought he was keeping to his room so he would not be infected.'

'So he did,' said Bartholomew. 'But the pestilence claimed him all the same.' He was wondering how to breach the subject of Abigny without sounding too obvious, when Burwell did it for him.

'We heard about Giles Abigny,' he said. 'We heard from Stephen Stanmore that he had been hiding in your sister's attic, and then ran off with Stanmore's horse.'

'Do you have any ideas where Giles might be?' Bartholomew asked.

Burwell shook his head. 'I never understood what was going on in Giles's head. A strange combination of incredible shallowness mixed with a remarkable depth of learning. I do not know where he might be.'

'When was the last time you saw him?' asked Bartholomew.

Burwell thought carefully. 'He was very shocked at Hugh's death. After that he went wild, trying to squeeze every ounce of pleasure from what he thought might be a short life. He continued in that vein for perhaps a week. Then he seemed to quieten down, and we saw less of him. Then, about two weeks ago, after going to the King's Head, he regaled us with a dreadful tale about cheating at dice and stealing the wages of half the Castle garrison. He had an enormous purseful of money, so perhaps there was some truth in it. He went off quite late, and I have not seen him since.'

Bartholomew tried to hide his disappointment. A sighting two weeks ago did not really help. He stood to leave, and beckoned to Gray.

'Please send someone for me at Michaelhouse if I can be of any more help to Cedric,' he said to Burwell. 'And thank you for your assistance with Giles.'

Burwell smiled again, and escorted them to the door. He watched as they made their way down Bene't Street and the smile faded from his face. He beckoned to a student, and whispered in his ear. Within a few moments, the student was scurrying out of the hostel towards Milne Street, his cloak held tightly against the chill of the winter afternoon.

Bartholomew and Gray spent two fruitless hours enquiring after Abigny in the town's taverns. They came up with nothing more than Burwell had told them, except that Abigny's idiosyncrasies seemed to be notorious among the townspeople.

Bartholomew was ready to give up, and retire to bed, when Gray, with a display of energy that made Bartholomew wonder whether he had been at the medicine store, suggested they walk to Trumpington to visit the Laughing Pig.

'It is best we visit at night,' he said. 'More people

will be there, and they will have had longer for the ale to loosen their tongues.'

So the two set off for Trumpington. Although it was only two miles, Bartholomew felt he was walking to the ends of the Earth. A bitter wind blew directly into their faces and cut through their clothes. It was a clear night, and they could hear the crack and splinter of the water freezing in the ruts and puddles on the track as the temperature dropped.

Bartholomew breathed a sigh of relief when the Laughing Pig came into sight. Within a few minutes they were seated in the tavern's large whitewashed room with frothing tankards of ale in front of them. The tavern was busy, and a fire crackled in a hearth in the middle of the room, filling it with pungent smoke as well as warmth. The floor was simple beaten earth, which was easier to keep clean than rushes.

Bartholomew was well known in Trumpington, and several people nodded at him in a friendly fashion. He struck up a conversation with a large, florid-faced man who fished for eels in the spring and minded Stanmore's cows for the rest of the year. The man immediately began to gossip about the disappearance of Philippa. Bartholomew was dismayed, but not surprised, that her flight had become the subject of village chatter – doubtless by way of Stanmore's party of horsemen who had tried to catch up with the fleeing Abigny.

Overhearing the discussion, several others joined in, including the tavern maid with whom Abigny had claimed he was in love back in the summer. She perched on the edge of the table, casting nervous glances backwards to make sure the landlord did not catch her skiving.

'How long do you think Giles Abigny was pretending

to be his sister?' Bartholomew asked casually, in a rare moment of silence.

There was a hubbub of conflicting answers. Everyone, it seemed, had ideas and theories. But listening to them, Bartholomew knew that was all they were. He stopped paying attention and sipped at the sour ale.

'Giles was odd a long time before he did this,' whispered the tavern maid, who, as Abigny had said, was indeed pretty. She glanced towards the next table where the landlord was serving and pretended to clean up near Bartholomew. 'The last time I saw him was at the church two Fridays ago. He was hiding behind one of the pillars. I thought he was playing around, but when I grabbed him from behind, he was terrified! He ran out, and I have not seen him since.'

Two Fridays before. That was three days after Philippa had become ill. So Abigny had not been impersonating her at least until then.

'Do you know where he went?' Bartholomew asked.

The tavern maid shook her head. 'I ran after him, but he had gone.'

The landlord shouted for her to serve other customers, and she left. Bartholomew thought about what she had told him: Abigny had been in the church at Trumpington terrified of something.

He tried to bring the general conversation round to what Abigny's reasons could be, but the suggestions were so outrageous that he knew no one had any solid facts to add. Bartholomew and Gray talked with the locals for a while longer, and decided to stay with Edith for the night. Perhaps he would have more luck with his search tomorrow.

*   *   *

Gray was already up and admiring the horses in Stanmore's stable by the time Bartholomew awoke. He threw open the window-shutters and looked out over the neat vegetable patches to the village church. He could see the Gilbertine Canon, standing outside the porch talking to the early risers who had been to his morning mass. The weak winter sun was shining, glittering on the frost that lay over everything like a white sheet of gauze. Bartholomew took a deep breath, and the air was clean and fresh. He understood why Stanmore preferred not to live at the house in Milne Street so near the stinking ditches and waterways of Cambridge.

He went to the garderobes and broke the ice on a bowl of water. Shivering and swearing under his breath, he washed and shaved as fast as he could, and borrowed one of Stanmore's fresh shirts from the pile on the shelf in the corner. He went down to the kitchens, where a large fire blazed, and he and Edith sat on stools and discussed Philippa's disappearance. It seemed he could have saved himself a walk, because she had been busy on his behalf, collecting scraps of information from the Trumpington folk.

She, too, had spoken to the tavern girl, and had also questioned the Canon. He had told her that Abigny had frequented the church a great deal following Philippa's arrival. Abigny had seemed restless and agitated, and once the Canon had alarmed him by standing up suddenly from next to the altar where he had been meditating. Abigny had turned so white that the Canon had been genuinely concerned for his health. The day after, he had disappeared. The Canon had assumed that Abigny had been waiting while Philippa was ill, and as soon as she was well again, he had returned to Michaelhouse.

'So,' said Edith, 'Giles may have been in the house pretending to be Philippa as early as the day her fever broke, since that was when either of them was last seen. I do not understand why he did not just come here. He has stayed with us before.'

Bartholomew nodded in agreement.

'Of course,' she continued, 'since none of us actually saw Philippa once her fever had gone, there is no reason to assume that she was alone in the room.'

Bartholomew stared at her. 'What do you mean?' he asked.

'Perhaps as soon as Philippa was out of danger from the plague, he climbed up to her window to be with her. Perhaps there were two people in the room for some of the time, not just one. I thought she had rather a voracious appetite; she always ate everything we left on the trays outside the door, and we began leaving her larger and larger amounts. I thought it was just a reaction to the fever, or even boredom, making her eat so much.'

'And you know what that means?' Edith continued, after a pause. 'It means that he probably nursed her himself for a time, before she left and he took her place. It means that she was not spirited away while she was still weak, but when she was stronger. So she probably went voluntarily.'

Bartholomew was not sure whether this was good or bad. 'But why was she spirited anywhere? Why did she not stay here? Why did Abigny feel obliged to keep up such a pretence? And why did Philippa and Giles not feel that they could trust us enough to tell us what was going on?'

Edith patted his hand. 'These are strange times, Matt,' she said. 'Oswald told me that one of his apprentices hanged himself two days ago, because he had accidentally touched a plague victim. He was so afraid he might catch it, he decided he would rather die by his own hand. Do not question too much. I am sure you will find Philippa eventually. And Giles.'

But even if he did, Bartholomew thought, things would never be the same. If Edith was right, and Philippa had gone from the house willingly, it meant that she had not trusted him enough to tell him her motives. The same was true of Giles.

Edith stood up. 'I must do some work,' she said. 'Did you know that we have the children from the village who have been orphaned in our stable loft? It is warm and dry there, and we can make sure they are fed properly. The bigger ones are helping to tend the vegetable plots, and I take care of the little ones here. Labour is becoming scarce, Matt. We will all starve if we do not continue to look after the fields.'

Bartholomew was not surprised at his sister's practicalities, nor of her carefully concealed charity. She would not offend the children's dignity by giving them meals and a place to stay for nothing, but provided them with small duties that would make them feel they were earning their keep.

Stanmore took a small cart into Cambridge so that Bartholomew and Gray would not have to walk. Richard went too, sitting in the back interrogating Gray about life as a student in Cambridge, and making comparisons with his own experiences in Oxford.

Bartholomew alighted at St Botolph's Church to see Colet, while the others went on to Milne Street.

The monks knelt in a line before the altar, although Bartholomew noted that there were fewer than there had been previously. Colet, however, was not there. Bartholomew went to Rudde's Hostel in search of him, but was told by the porter that he had gone out early that morning, and had not been seen since. Bartholomew's spirits rose a little. Did this mean that Colet had recovered and was visiting patients again?

The porter, seeing the hopeful look on Bartholomew's face, shook his head.

'No, he is as addled as ever. He had his hood pulled right over his face, and said he was going out to pick blackberries. At this time of year! He has been saying that every day recently. He will be back later to sit and dribble in the church.'

Bartholomew thanked him, and walked back to Michaelhouse. On the way, he met Master Burwell who asked if there was any news of Abigny. Bartholomew shook his head, and asked whether Giles had seemed afraid of anything on the last few occasions that Burwell had seen him. Burwell scratched his head.

'Yes. Now that you mention it. The hostel is a noisy place, and he was constantly jumping and looking round. I just assumed it was fear of the plague. Several of the students are in a similar state, and I have heard Master Colet is far from well in his mind.'

'Was there anything specific?'

Burwell thought again. 'Not that I can put a finger on. He was simply nervous.'

After Bartholomew had enquired after Cedric Stapleton, they parted, and Bartholomew returned to his room. He looked around carefully to see if Abigny had been there, but the minute fragments of rushes that he had secretly placed on Abigny's belongings were still in place. Gray burst in, full of enthusiasm, but he was less so when Bartholomew dispatched him to buy various herbs and potions from the town herb-seller, known locally as 'Jonas the Poisoner' following an incident involving several poorly-labelled bottles some years before.

Bartholomew went to examine his patients in the commoners' dormitory, to find that three students had died in the night. Roger Alyngton was no better, but no worse. That morning, the frail Father Jerome had complained of a fever, and was lying restlessly next to him. Bartholomew wondered whether Jerome would have the strength or the will to fight the sickness.

When the patients were all resting, Bartholomew slipped out and went into the room that had been Augustus's and that was now used to store clean blankets and linen. He carefully closed the door. The shutters were already fastened, but the wood had swollen and warped over many years, and were ill-fitting enough to allow sufficient light for Bartholomew to see what he was doing.

He crouched on the window-sill and peered up at the ceiling. He had never really noticed the ceilings in the south wing before. They were really quite beautiful, with elaborate designs carved into the fine dark oak. Looking carefully, Bartholomew could see no evidence whatsoever of a trap-door. He wondered if Wilson had been lying to him. He jumped down and lit one of the supply of candles he had appropriated from the hall for use in the sickroom. Climbing back onto the window-sill, he held the candle up and looked again. He could still see nothing.

He put the palm of his hand against the ceiling and

pushed gently, and he was startled to feel it move. He pushed again, and an entire section of the ceiling came loose. He had to drop the candle to catch the heavy wood and prevent it from crashing down onto his head. Carefully, he lowered the loose panel onto the floor, relit his candle, and cautiously poked his head into the space beyond.

At first he could make nothing out, but then gradually he saw that the trap-door, as Wilson had called it, did little more than conceal a way into the attic. He did not know what he had expected – a cramped secret passage, perhaps, with dusty doorways leading away from it. Still holding the candle he hauled himself up, bemused to think that Wilson had been fit enough to do the same.

There was not sufficient room for him to stand upright, so he walked hunched over. The candle was not bright enough to illuminate the whole of the attic, and it faded into deep shadows at the edges. There was an unpleasant smell too, as if generations of small animals had found their way in, but had become trapped and died. Bartholomew shook himself. He was being fanciful. The attic was basically bare, the wooden floor covered in thick dust, scuffed here and there by some recent disturbances. He walked carefully along the length of the south wing, his way lit by small holes in the floor, although whether these were for providing light or for spying on the people in the rooms below, he could not say. Over the commoners' room, he could clearly hear the Benedictine whispering comforting words to Alyngton, while over what had been Swynford's room – where d'Evéne had died – he could even read the words on a book that lay open on the table. At the very end of the attic, he found the second trap-door. It was marked by a large metal ring, and when Bartholomew pulled it up, he saw that it gave access to the last staircase. Wilson could easily have climbed into the attic, walked along to the second door, and slipped away down the stairs and back to his own room. So could the murderer of Paul, Montfitchet, and Augustus.

He lowered the door and retraced his steps, carefully examining the floor for any more entrances and exits. He found none, but at the far end, where the south wing abutted onto the hall, he found a tiny doorway. He squeezed through it, and down a cramped passageway that was so full of dust and still air that Bartholomew began to feel as though he could not breathe. The passageway turned a corner, and Bartholomew faced a blank wall. He scratched at the stones and mortar with his fingernail. It was old, and had evidently been sealed up many years before. He stooped to look for any signs that it had been tampered with in recent days, but there was nothing. The passageway must have run in the thickness of the west wall of the hall, and perhaps emerged in the gallery at the back. He vaguely recalled Sir John complaining that an old door had been made into the ugly window that was there now, so perhaps the secret passageway had been blocked up then. Regardless, it seemed that the sturdy wall blocking the passage was ancient, and would have no bearing on the current mysteries.

He turned round, and began to squeeze his way down the narrow passage again. As he reached the point where the passage turned the corner, he saw that one of the stones had been prised loose about the level of his knees, and that something had been stuffed into the space. Gingerly, he bent towards it, and eased it out. It was a very dirty green blanket that smelled so rank that Bartholomew obeyed his instinct, and hurled it away from him. As it lay on the floor, something caught his eye. It was a singe mark, about the size of his hand.

Heart thumping, he picked it up by the hem, and took it back into the attic where he spread it out on the floor. It was the blanket that Bartholomew had inspected on the night of Augustus's death. There were the singe marks that had made Bartholomew think that Augustus had not been imagining things when he had claimed someone had tried to burn him in his bed. And there were other marks too – thick, black, encrusted stains ran in a broad band from one end of the blanket to the middle. Bartholomew knew old blood-stains when he saw them, and their implication made him feel sick.

Augustus must have been taken from his room and hidden up in the attic before Wilson conducted his clandestine search below. Perhaps the murderer had watched Wilson through the spy-holes, or perhaps he had hidden Augustus's body in the small passageway, so that Wilson would not have seen it when he effected his own escape. If Wilson had already explored the attic as he claimed, he would have known the little passage was blocked, and would not have tried to use it to get away.

And then what? When Wilson had gone? Augustus had been dead, and no counter-claims from anyone would make Bartholomew disbelieve what he knew. Had the murderer believed Augustus was still alive, and battered him when he lay wrapped in the blanket? Had Wilson been lying, and it was he who had returned later and battered the poor body? And regardless of which solution was the right one, where was Augustus now?

Bartholomew retraced his steps, carefully exploring every last nook and cranny of the attic, half hoping and half afraid that he would find Augustus. There was nothing: Augustus was not there. Bartholomew went back to the passage. The dust had been disturbed, and not just by his own recent steps. It was highly likely that Augustus had been hidden here until the hue and cry of his death and disappearance had died down.

The candle was beginning to burn low, and Bartholomew felt as though he had gained as much information from the attic as he was going to. At the last minute, he stuffed the blanket back into the hole in the wall again, as he had found it. He did not want the murderer, were he to return, to know about the clues he had uncovered.

He lowered himself through the trap-door back into Augustus's room and replaced the wooden panel. As it slid into place, Bartholomew again admired the workmanship that had produced a secret opening that was basically invisible, even when he knew where to look. He brushed himself off carefully and even picked up the lumps of dust that dropped from his clothes. He did not want anyone to guess what he had been doing. He put his ear to the door, and then let himself out silently.

He glanced in at his patients, and went down the stairs. The sky had clouded over since the morning, and it was beginning to rain. Bartholomew stood in the porch for a moment, looking across the courtyard. It was here he had fallen when Wilson had pushed him down the stairs. He closed his eyes, and remembered the footsteps he had heard as he lay there. That must have been Wilson effecting his escape across the attic floor. In his haste to get away, he had obviously forgotten to move with stealth, and Bartholomew had been able to hear him running.

Bartholomew thought about the night that Augustus had claimed there were devils in his room wanting to burn him alive. It was clear now: someone had climbed through the trap-door into Augustus's room, locked the door, and tried to set the bed alight. Whoever it was had escaped the same way when Bartholomew and Michael had broken the door down. But that still did not mean that Michael was innocent. He could easily have let himself out of the attic through the other trap-door and run round to Augustus's staircase to be in time to help Bartholomew batter the door. It would even explain why Michael had been virtually fully dressed in the middle of the night.

Cynric was taking food from the kitchen to the hall for the main meal of the day. Bartholomew walked briskly across the yard, and went up the stairs to the hall. It was cold and gloomy. Cynric had lit some candles, but they only served to make the room seem colder and darker as they flickered and fluttered in the draughts from the windows.

Bartholomew took some leek soup from a cauldron and sat next to Jocelyn of Ripon, more for company than from any feeling of friendship. Jocelyn made room for him and began telling him how the landowners were having to pay high wages to labourers to make them work on the farms. Because so many labourers had died from the plague, those left were in great demand and were able to negotiate large payments.

Jocelyn rubbed his hands gleefully as he described the plight of the rich landowners. He then outlined his plans for gathering groups of people together and selling their labour *en masse*. This would mean that the labourers would have a good deal of sway over the landowners and could obtain better pay and working conditions. If one landowner treated them unfairly, they would go to another who would be willing to make them a better offer. Jocelyn saw himself in the position of negotiator for these groups of people. Bartholomew, uncharitably, wondered what percentage of the profits the avaricious Jocelyn would take for his efforts. He tried to change the subject.

'Do you have plans to travel back to Ripon?'

'Not while there is money to be made here,' Jocelyn said.

Bartholomew tried again. 'What made you come to Cambridge last year?' he asked, taking a piece of salted beef that had less of a green sheen to it than the others.

Jocelyn looked irritated at being sidetracked, and poured himself another generous cup of College wine. 'I contacted Master Swynford. We are distantly related by marriage, and I came here because I plan to start a grammar school in Ripon, and I wanted to learn how it might best be done. I have a house that I can use, and because it will be the only grammar school for miles around, I know it will be successful.'

Bartholomew nodded. He knew all this, because Swynford had talked about it when he had asked the other Fellows whether his relative could come to stay in Michaelhouse in return for teaching grammar. Jocelyn's plan had sounded noble, but, having met him, Bartholomew was convinced that the school would be founded strictly as an economic venture and would have little to do with promoting the ideals of education.

As the most senior member present, it was

Bartholomew's responsibility to say the Latin grace that ended all meals in College. This done, he escaped to his room.

Gray had not been able to buy all the medicines that Bartholomew needed, and there was no choice but to walk to Barnwell Priory to see what he could borrow from their infirmarian. Bartholomew waited for Gray to eat, and then set off for the Priory in the rain.

'You need not come,' said Bartholomew, when Gray started grumbling. 'You can stay in College and help in the sick-room.'

'I do not mind going to the Priory, and I want to learn about the medicines. I just do not like all this walking. Miles last night, and miles today. Why do you not get a horse?'

Bartholomew sighed. 'Not again, Samuel! I do not have a horse because I do not need one. By the time the thing was saddled and ready to go, I could have walked where I was going.'

'Well, what about when you go to Trumpington?' Gray demanded petulantly.

Bartholomew felt his exasperation turning to irritation. 'I usually borrow or hire one.'

'But you cannot hire them now, not with all the stable-men dead of the plague. And Stephen Stanmore will never lend you another after what happened to the last one.'

Bartholomew whipped round and grabbed Gray by the front of his gown. 'Look! You do not like walking. You do not like my patients. You do not approve of what I charge them. Perhaps you should find yourself another master under which to study if you find my affairs so disagreeable!'

He released the student, and walked on. After a few paces, he heard Gray following him again. He glanced round, and Gray looked back at him sullenly, like a spoilt child. Gray sulked all the way to the Priory, until listening to Bartholomew and the infirmarian discussing the plague took his mind away from his moodiness. Bartholomew regretted his outburst; the lad had saved his life after all. He made an effort to include Gray in the discussion, and tried to ensure that Gray understood which medicines he was taking from the infirmarian and what they were for.

Bartholomew and the infirmarian left Gray packing the herbs and potions into a bag, and walked out into the drizzle.

'How many monks have you lost?' asked Bartholomew.

The infirmarian bowed his head. 'More than half, and Father Prior died yesterday. Perhaps our communal way of life promotes the sickness in some way. You have heard that all the Dominicans are dead? But what else should we do? Forsake our Rule and live in isolation like hermits?'

There was no answer to his question.

When Gray was ready, they took their leave of the infirmarian, and walked back along the causeway to the town. Gray had recovered completely from his attack of the sulks, and chattered on about what he planned to do once he had completed his training. Bartholomew grew dispirited listening to him. Did people think of nothing other than making money?

Gray tugged at his cloak suddenly. 'We should go to St Radegund's!' he said.

'Whatever for? They will refuse us entry.'

'Maybe Philippa went back there after she left your sister's house.'

Bartholomew stared at him. Gray was right! Why had he not considered it earlier? Gray had already set off down the causeway, and was hammering at the convent door by the time Bartholomew caught up with him. While they waited for the door to be answered, Bartholomew fretted, wiping the rain from his face impatiently. Gray hopped from foot to foot in an attempt to keep warm. Bartholomew looked at the door, and, despite his preoccupation, saw that several tendrils of weed had begun to grow across it. The nuns were taking their isolation seriously.

The small grille in the door was snapped open. 'What?' came a sharp voice.

'I want to speak with the Abbess,' said Bartholomew. His voice sounded calm, but his thoughts were in turmoil. Perhaps he would find Philippa safe and sound back in the convent, and all his worrying would be over.

'Who are you?' snapped the voice again.

'Matthew Bartholomew from Michaelhouse.'

The air rang with the retort of the grille being slammed shut vigorously. They waited a few moments, but nothing happened.

Gray looked almost as disappointed as Bartholomew felt. 'Oh, well. That is that,' he said.

Abruptly, the grille shot open again, and Bartholomew could see that this time there were two people on the other side.

'Well?' came the first voice, impatient and aggressive.

Bartholomew was so surprised that the Abbess had

come to the door, that he was momentarily stuck for words.

'Is it Henry?' the Abbess's voice was deep for a woman, and she was tall enough that she had to bend her head slightly to look through the grille. Her reasons for coming to answer the door were suddenly clear to Bartholomew. She thought he was coming to bring her news of her nephews, the Oliver brothers.

'Henry is well, Mother,' Bartholomew replied. He moved nearer to the door so that he could see her more clearly.

'Come no closer!' she said, her voice hard and distant. 'I hear that you walk freely among the contagion. I do not want you to bring it here. What do you want of me?'

Bartholomew was taken aback by her hostility, but it was not the first time he had been repulsed because of his contact with plague victims, and doubtless it would not be the last.

'I came to ask whether you had news of Philippa Abigny,' he said, watching the beautiful, but cold, face of the Abbess carefully.

Bartholomew saw a flash of anger in the ice-blue eyes. 'How dare you come here to ask that when you stole her away from us! You have fouled her reputation by your actions.'

He had expected such a response, although he had not imagined it would be given with such venom. But he did not wish to get into an argument with the Abbess about whether he had sullied Philippa's reputation, and so he tried to remain courteous.

'I am sorry if you think that,' he said, 'but you have not answered my question.'

'Do you think I am so stupid as to answer?' The Abbess virtually spat the words out. 'You stole her away once. If I told you she was here, you would try to do the same again.'

Bartholomew shook his head. 'You misunderstand my intentions. She came with me of her own free will, although I wished her to go back to where she would be protected from the plague. I only want to know that she is safe.'

'Then you can continue in your agony of doubt,' said the Abbess. 'For I will not tell you of the news I have, nor of her whereabouts.'

'Then do you know where she is?' Bartholomew cried.

The Abbess stepped back from the grille and smiled at him with such coldness that Bartholomew felt himself shudder. He was suddenly reminded of the looks of hatred Henry used to throw at him. What a family, all consumed with hate and loathing! He saw a large shadow fall over the Abbess, and watched her turn towards it, the coldness evaporating from her smile in an instant. Bartholomew glimpsed the hem of a highly decorated black cloak, and knew that Elias Oliver was there.

'Where is she?' Bartholomew shouted. The Abbess began to walk away, tall and regal, smiling at the tall figure beside her and ignoring Bartholomew. Bartholomew rattled the door in frustration, but the grille was slammed shut, and no amount of shouting and battering would induce the nuns to open it again.

Bartholomew slumped against the wall in defeat. Gray sat down beside him.

'Do not fret so,' he said. 'I have an idea.'

Bartholomew fought to regain control of his temper.

Did the wretched woman know where Philippa was, or was she merely pretending in order to have revenge for his 'stealing' her? He had had very little to do with the nuns of St Radegund's. They lived secluded in their cloisters, and even when he had visited Philippa, he had seen little of the Priory or its inmates.

Gray stood up and set off round the Priory walls. Bartholomew followed, sharply reminded of what had happened when he had last followed Gray around the walls of the convent. Gray slipped in and out of trees until he reached a point where the walls were totally obscured by thick undergrowth. Without hesitating, he led the way down a tiny path until he reached a door in the wall. He knocked twice, softly.

Bartholomew watched in amazement as the door opened and a young woman in a nun's habit peeped out. Seeing Gray, she checked no one was looking, and stepped out, closing the door carefully behind her.

'This is my cousin, Sister Emelda,' said Gray, turning to Bartholomew.

The young woman smiled shyly at Bartholomew, and then looked at Gray. 'I knew you would come! I cannot stay long, though, or I will be missed.' She glanced around her, as if expecting the spectre of the Abbess to appear through the trees. Gray nodded, and passed her something wrapped in a cloth. Emelda took it quickly, and secreted it in her robes. She reached up and kissed him quickly on the cheek. 'Thank you,' she whispered.

Gray flushed. 'The doctor has something to ask you,' he said, to cover his embarrassment.

Emelda smiled at Bartholomew again. 'I know you from when you used to come to court Philippa. Poor

Philippa! She hated it here, especially in the winter months, and even more when you stopped coming.'

'Is she here now?' he asked.

Emelda quickly shook her head. 'No. She has not been seen since you took her away. If she were here, I would know, because I do the cooking, and food is very carefully rationed. I would know if there were another person hidden away.'

'Have you heard anything from her?'

Again, a shake of the head.

'Do you know if the Abbess has heard of her whereabouts?'

'She has not! And she is very angry about it.' Emelda giggled. 'It is hard to keep secrets in a small community like this, and I know that she has those beastly nephews of hers trying to find out where Philippa is. I hope you find her before they do.'

Inside the convent, a bell began to ring. 'Terce,' said Emelda. 'I must go.' She smiled at the two men and slipped quickly through the door again.

Gray led the way through the undergrowth and back to the road. Bartholomew was full of questions. 'That was the door Philippa spoke about, the door that Sister Clement used when she went out to work among the sick. How did you know about it?' he demanded. 'And you did not tell me you had a cousin in the convent! What was it you handed to her in that package?'

Gray raised his hand to slow the stream of questions, reminding Bartholomew unpleasantly of Wilson. 'Emelda has been at St Radegund's since we were children, and she told me about the gate. I never told you about her because you have never asked about my family. And what I gave her was my business.'

Gray knew he had overstepped his bounds before Bartholomew said a word. 'Sorry, sorry,' he muttered. 'I will tell you, but you have to promise not to fly into a temper.'

'I will promise no such thing,' said Bartholomew coldly.

Gray sighed. 'All right,' he said. 'It is medicine for my mother. She is in there too. She took orders when I was old enough to look after myself, but now she has a wasting sickness and every week I take her medicine to relieve her pain.'

He looked defiantly at Bartholomew before continuing. 'That was one of the reasons why I had to become apprenticed to you. I was making a lot of money nursing rich plague victims, but Jonas refused to sell me the medicine. I stole it from Roper when I was with him, and now I steal it from you.'

He stopped walking, and looked at Bartholomew belligerently, waiting. Bartholomew stopped too, and studied this strange young man. 'Why did you not just ask me?' he said gently.

'Because you are always too busy, and because my mother comes from a rich priory and I thought you might rather give the medicine to the poor.'

Bartholomew was shocked. Did he really appear so insensitive to Gray? 'I have never refused medicine to anyone, rich or poor,' he said.

Gray suddenly lost his belligerence, and looked at the ground. 'I know. I am sorry,' he said in a quavering voice. 'It just seemed easier to steal the medicine than to ask for it.'

Bartholomew realised that this was why Gray had persuaded him to go to St Radegund's – not to ask about Philippa, but to deliver medicine for his mother. Perhaps the strain of his mother's illness accounted for his dreadful behaviour earlier that day. 'Perhaps I could examine her . . .?' he suggested.

Gray grimaced. 'I wish you could, but that old bitch, the Abbess, will not let anyone in or out, and my mother is too ill to be moved now. The medicine is the only thing that helps.'

'Which medicine is it?' asked Bartholomew.

Gray told him. 'My God, man!' Bartholomew exploded. 'Concentrated opiates can be a powerful poison! No wonder Jonas refused to sell it to you! It does have pain-relieving powers, but if someone gives her too much, she could die!'

Gray winced and took a step back. 'I know,' he said defensively, 'but I know how much she can have. I watched Roper giving it out to one of his sons when he had a similar wasting disease. I measure it out and put it in little packets for Emelda to give her.'

'Oh, lord!' groaned Bartholomew. 'What have I done to deserve a student like this?' He looked at Gray. 'I suppose you knew my supply was running low, and that I have been wondering where it had gone, and that is why you have chosen now to tell me?'

The answer was in the way Gray hung his head and refused to meet his eyes.

Bartholomew began walking again. Gray followed. On the one hand Bartholomew was relieved that his medicines had not been the cause of Aelfrith's death; on the other hand, he was disturbed that Gray had stolen such a powerful drug from him and prescribed it to someone.

'You are a disreputable rascal, Gray. You lie and

steal, and I cannot trust you. We will go to Jonas now, together, and replenish my stocks of this wretched stuff. Then *I* will measure it out for your mother, and we will go together and discuss with Emelda what else we can do to make your mother's life more bearable. Medicine is not just giving out potions, you know. There are many other things that can be done to effect a cure or to relieve symptoms.'

Detecting that a lecture was about to begin, Gray skipped a little to catch up to him to listen properly. He would need to work hard to gain the trust of his teacher, but at least he knew Bartholomew was prepared to allow him to try.

Bartholomew, meanwhile, glanced at Gray walking beside him – a liar and a thief. He could not possibly confide in the student, and, excluding his family, there was not a single person left in the world whom he could trust.

It was dusk by the time Bartholomew and Gray arrived back at Michaelhouse. The rain had turned the beaten earth of the yard into a quagmire, and the honey-coloured stones of the buildings looked dismal and dirty in the fading light. Like a skull, Bartholomew thought suddenly, and the windows and doors were like eyeless sockets and broken teeth. He pinched himself hard, surprised at his morbid thoughts; he was becoming preoccupied with death.

As if to reinforce his thoughts, Father William emerged from the staircase leading to the plague room. He was dragging something behind him, a long shape sewn into a blanket. Bartholomew went to help.

'Who is it?' he asked, taking a corner of the

blanket and helping William to haul it through the mud. He wondered what he would have thought of this manhandling of the body of a colleague before the plague had struck and inured him to such things.

'Gilbert,' said William shortly, oblivious to the muddy puddles through which he dragged the body. 'Like his master, isolation did not keep him from the Death.'

The stables, used as a mortuary for College plague victims, smelled so strongly of death and corruption that William backed out so fast he fell. Bartholomew went to help him up.

'Holy Mother!' the friar exclaimed, clambering to his feet with his wide sleeve firmly pressed to his nose. 'Thank the Lord we have no horses! They would have died breathing that stench!' He walked away as quickly as he could, turning to shout at Bartholomew, 'Get rid of the corpses, Doctor. Do your job!'

Bartholomew went back into the stables, covering his nose and mouth with his cloak. William was right: the odour was terrible. The porter, hearing William's shouting, came over to say that the carts had not been for the bodies for several days, and so it was not surprising that they were beginning to smell. Bartholomew tipped rushes from a hand-cart so he could begin to load the bodies onto it. The scholars would have to take their colleagues to the plague pit themselves if the official carts did not come.

Gray came to help, but gagged and complained so much that Bartholomew told him to wait outside. Bartholomew hated what he was doing. These ungainly lumps sewn tightly into rough College blankets had been people he had known. There were five College students, two of the commoners, and now Gilbert. Eight College members who had been his friends and colleagues. But there were nine shrouded bodies. He frowned and counted again, running through the names of the dead scholars one by one. He must have forgotten someone.

He took a body by the feet, and began to drag it to where Gray waited outside by the empty cart.

'Who has died since we buried Wilson?' Bartholomew asked.

Gray looked taken aback. 'I thought you kept a note of all these things,' he said. Seeing a flash of annoyance pass across Bartholomew's face, he recited the names.

'Eight,' said Bartholomew. 'Who died just before Wilson?'

Gray named the others, nineteen in all. He thought he saw which way the conversation was leading, assumed he was being criticised, and began to object. 'You told me to take them to the plague pit, and I did. Ask Cynric. He helped. We took all of them!'

Bartholomew held up his hand to quell Gray's indignant objections. 'I believe you,' he said. 'But we seem to have an extra body here now.'

Gray looked at the one Bartholomew still held by the feet. 'One of the townspeople probably slipped it in here so that we would take it to the pits with the others,' he suggested.

'Unlikely,' said Bartholomew, 'unless they stole one of our blankets as well.'

Gray and Bartholomew looked at each other for a moment, and then back to the stables. Bartholomew began to drag the body back inside again.

'This had best be done out of sight,' he said over

his shoulder to Gray. 'I do not want anyone to see what I am going to do. Will you bring a lamp?'

Gray was gone only briefly, returning with a lamp and a needle and thread. He lit the lamp and closed the door against prying eyes. 'You cut the shrouds open, and I will sew them up,' he said, swallowing hard as he steeled himself for the grisly task.

Bartholomew clapped him on the shoulder, and made a small cut along the seam of the first body. It was Gilbert. He sat for a moment, looking at his face, more peaceful than most of his patients, but blackened with the plague nevertheless. Gray, kneeling next to him, nudged him with his elbow.

'Hurry up,' he urged, 'or someone will come and ask what we are doing.'

He began stitching the blanket back together while Bartholomew moved to the next one. It was one of the law students who had been studying under Wilson. He resisted the urge to think about the scholars as their faces appeared under the coarse blanket-shrouds, and tried to concentrate on the task in hand. The third was another student, and the fourth one of the old commoners. As he came to the fifth, he paused. The blanket was exactly the same as the others, but there was an odd quality about the body inside that he could not define. Instinctively, he knew it was the one that did not belong to Michaelhouse.

Carefully he slit the stitches down one side of the blanket, noting that they were less neat than the others he had cut. He peeled it back and cried out in horror, leaping backwards and almost knocking the lamp over.

'What? What is it?' Gray gasped, unnerved by Bartholomew's white face. He went to look at the body, but Bartholomew pulled him back so he should not see.

They went to the door for some fresh air, away from the stench of the bodies. After a few moments, Bartholomew began to lose the unreal feeling he had had when he looked into the decomposed face of Augustus, and rubbed his hands on his robe to get rid of their clamminess. Gray waited anxiously.

Taking a last deep breath of clean air, Bartholomew turned to Gray. 'It is Augustus,' he said. Gray looked puzzled for a moment, and then his face cleared.

'Ah! The commoner who disappeared after you had declared him dead!' He looked at the stables. 'He is dead now, is he?'

'He was dead then,' snapped Bartholomew, trying to control the shaking of his hands. 'And he is very dead now.'

Bartholomew led Gray back inside the stables again, noticing how the student's eyes kept edging fearfully over to the bundle that was Augustus. 'You must not tell anyone of this,' Bartholomew said. 'I do not understand what is happening, why his body has been put here now after all this time. But I think he was murdered, and his murderer must still be alive or Augustus's body would still be hidden. We must be very careful.'

Gray nodded, his usually cheerful face sombre. 'Just sew him back up again, and let us pretend to anyone who is watching that we have not noticed the extra one,' he said, going to the door and trying to peer out through the gaps in the wood.

It was possibly already too late for that, Bartholomew thought, if the murderer had seen them take Gilbert's body back inside again once they had realised that something was amiss. He collected his thoughts. Bartholomew could see why Augustus's body had reappeared. It had been no secret that Wilson had spent some time talking alone to Bartholomew before he died. The murderer had assumed, correctly, that Wilson would tell him about the trap-door to the attic – where Augustus had probably lain since his body had been taken. That would explain the unpleasant smell that Bartholomew had noticed there. If, as Bartholomew supposed, the body had been hidden in the passageway, Wilson would have been unlikely to have found it because he would have no reason to search a passageway he knew was blocked off. Unless, he thought, Wilson had known, and had deliberately told Bartholomew about the trap-door, knowing that he would find Augustus. What had Wilson said? Discover who in the College knew about the trap-door and he would find the murderer?

Bartholomew rubbed a hand over his face. He realised that once the murderer became aware that Bartholomew knew of the trap-door and would be likely to search the attic, he would have to dispose of the corpse that had lain there for several months. In many ways, it was an ideal time. When better to dispose of a body than when there were bodies of so many others to be taken away? Had William not complained, then Bartholomew might well have left the bodies to be collected by the dead-cart the following day, and no one would have known that one of them had not died of the plague at all.

So the person who had brought Augustus's body to the stables must also have been the person who had killed him. It could not have been Aelfrith, since he was long dead. It could not have been Wilson, because

Augustus's body had been placed in the stable after he had died – and Bartholomew was certain Gray was not lying to him about removing the previous corpses. Was it Abigny? Had he come back from wherever he was hiding when he had heard that Bartholomew knew about the trap-door? Could it have been Swynford, back from his plague-free haven? Was it Michael, who had reacted so oddly at Augustus's death? Was it William, who had prompted him to look at the bodies in the first place, or Alcote, skulking in his room?

Gray was handing him the needle and thread so he could sew up Augustus's shroud again. But Bartholomew had one more task he needed to do.

'Start taking the others out to the cart,' he said. 'I need to take a closer look.'

Gray's eyes widened in horror, but he began to drag the bodies outside to the cart as Bartholomew had instructed. Bartholomew knelt down by Augustus, and slit the shroud down the side, pulling it back to reveal the grey, desiccated body. Augustus was still dressed in the nightshirt he had been wearing when Bartholomew had last seen his body, but it was torn down the middle to reveal the terrible mutilations underneath. Bartholomew felt anger boil inside him. Whoever had taken the body had slashed it open, pulling out entrails, and slicing deeply into the neck and throat.

All Bartholomew could assume was that Augustus had led the murderer to believe he had swallowed that wretched ring of Sir John's, and the murderer had desecrated his body to find it. Bartholomew was beginning to feel sick. Augustus's blackened and dried entrails had been stuffed crudely back into his body with a total disregard for his dignity. The horrific mess made

Bartholomew wonder whether the murderer would ever have found the ring anyway.

He had seen enough. Hastily, he began to resew the bundle, hiding the terribly mangled body from his sight – and from Gray, who was becoming bolder and inching forward. Bartholomew looked at Augustus's face. The warmth of the attic in the top of the house in late summer must have sucked the moisture from the body, for the face was dry and wizened rather than rotten. The skin had peeled back from the lips, leaving the teeth exposed, and the eyes were sunken, but it was unmistakably Augustus.

As Bartholomew covered up the face, he whispered a farewell. His mind flashed back to Augustus's funeral back in September, when a coffin filled with bags of earth had been reverently laid to rest in the churchyard. He sat back on his heels, staring down at the shapeless bundle in front of him, and wondered if the requiem mass said for him by Aelfrith had truly laid his soul to rest. Bartholomew had often looked at the simple wooden cross in the churchyard, and wondered about the body that should have lain beneath it. At least in the plague pit the old man would rest in hallowed ground and no one would come again to desecrate his body.

IX

February 1349

JANUARY ENDED IN A SUCCESSION OF BLIZZARDS THAT coated everything in white. With February came wetter, warmer weather that turned the snow into icy brown muck that seeped into shoes and chilled the feet. Bartholomew still trudged around the houses of plague victims, incising buboes where he could, but mostly doing little more than watching people die. He and Gray had visited the last of Abigny's known haunts, and then revisited his favourite ones, but had learned nothing. Philippa and Abigny seemed to have vanished into thin air.

Bartholomew heard that Stanmore's older sister, her husband, and all seven of their children were dead, while at Michaelhouse he buried Roger Alyngton, two more students, and four of the servants. Colet still sat in St Botolph's Church and drooled his days away. Bartholomew had lain in wait for him one day, and dragged him along when he went to visit his patients – hoping to shock him back to rationality – but his patients had been disconcerted, and Colet had become so distressed that Bartholomew was forced to take him home.

It was mid-afternoon, but already growing dark because of the overcast skies, when Bartholomew and Gray were met on the way home by Master Burwell, who asked them to attend a student who was dying. Bartholomew did all he could, but the student died without regaining consciousness. Three other Bene't Hostel students were ill, and Bartholomew helped Burwell set up a separate room in which they could be cared for. It was a large room compared to the others, and Jacob Yaxley, Master of Law, who had had it to himself since the death of his room-mates, clearly resented being moved. He muttered and grumbled as his students helped him carry his books and papers to another chamber.

As they walked back to the College, Bartholomew thought he saw one body, all wrapped in its shroud, move, and went to investigate. He took his knife and slit open the crude sheet. The woman inside was still alive, although barely. Her neighbour shouted that the woman had sewn herself into the winding sheet when she knew she had the plague, because there was no one left to do it for her.

'What about you?' Bartholomew shouted.

The neighbour crossed himself quickly, and slammed the window shut. The woman muttered incoherently as Bartholomew carried her back inside. He had heard from Michael that some people, the last surviving members of their families, were preparing themselves for burial with their dying strength but he had dismissed it as yet another plague story intended to horrify. He sat back on his heels, patting the woman's hand abstractedly, unable to stop his mind running through the dreadful outcomes of such actions:

supposing the cart had come while she was still alive, and she had been smothered in earth or burned by the quicklime? He wondered if others had not already suffered that fate. The woman slipped away quietly while he was thinking, and he and Gray resewed the shroud and left her on her doorstep again.

It was dark by the time they arrived back at Michaelhouse. Bartholomew went to see his patients in the commoners' room. Jerome had recovered from the plague, but it had weakened him, and he was dying slowly from the wasting disease in his chest. As Bartholomew entered the room, he saw Father William was helping one of the Benedictine novices to sew someone into a blanket. A quick glance around the room told him it was Nicholas, at fifteen Michaelhouse's youngest student, who looked that morning as if he might recover. Bartholomew sat heavily on a stool.

'His end was so quick that there was no time to call you,' William said. The fanatical gleam that was usually in his eyes had dulled, and he looked exhausted. 'I have listened to so many dreadful confessions that hell will soon be running out of space.'

Bartholomew wondered if the Franciscan were making a joke, but there was no humour in his face. 'Then perhaps there will be an overspill into heaven,' he replied, standing up.

William grabbed at his sleeve and pulled him down again, whispering angrily in his ear. 'That is heresy, Doctor, and I advise you against such fanciful remarks!'

'So is your belief that hell has limited space,' Bartholomew retorted. He remembered the rumours when William had first arrived at Michaelhouse that he had been an inquisitor for the Church.

William let go of Bartholomew's sleeve. 'Do not worry,' he said, and Bartholomew saw the gleam come back into his eye as his mind ran over the implications of Bartholomew's reply. 'I will not entrap you in a theological debate. But I miss the company of Aelfrith. There was a man with a lively mind!'

Bartholomew agreed, and wished Aelfrith were alive, so that he could confide his thoughts and feelings to him at that moment. He could have trusted Aelfrith – unlike William or Alcote or Michael – with his concerns about the plague and the College. And thinking of Michael, Bartholomew had not seen him since the previous day. He asked if William had.

A curious expression passed over William's face. 'No,' he said. 'He has gone somewhere. He has left me with quite a burden, you know.'

Bartholomew thought it curious that Michael had told no one where he was going, but let it pass. He stood up from his stool, stretched his aching limbs, and helped William to carry Nicholas downstairs and across the courtyard to the stables. They placed the body near the door and left as quickly as possible. Bartholomew knew he would never enter the stables again without thinking about Augustus.

The following day, as he walked back along the High Street with Gray, Bartholomew felt the first huge drops of rain from a storm that had been threatening all morning. Gray hailed a student he knew, who invited them into Mary's Hostel to shelter from the worst of the rain. Like Bene't Hostel, Mary's was warm, steamy, and smelled of boiled vegetables. The student brought them spiced wine, and Bartholomew began to relax from the warmth of the fire and the effects of the wine.

He was virtually asleep when he became aware that Gary was introducing him to someone. Embarrassed, he jumped to his feet, and bowed to the scholar who was being presented to him. From Gray's words, he found it was the new Principal of Mary's, Neville Stayne. Bartholomew had known the previous Principal quite well, but he had died of the plague before Christmas. His successor was a man in his forties with a shock of oddly wiry black hair that seemed to want to be as far away from his scalp as possible.

Stayne gestured for him to sit again, and perched on a stool next to him, asking him about the progress of the plague in the town. After a while, Stayne brought the subject round to Giles Abigny, who, it seemed, had also spent a good deal of time at Mary's. The members of the hostel were anxious for his safety.

'Have you any idea where he might be?' asked Bartholomew, expecting the same range of speculation and unfounded rumour he had been given everywhere else.

The fire popped and crackled, and Stayne watched it for a moment before answering. 'I do not know where he is now, but I believe I saw him two nights ago in Cambridge.'

Bartholomew's stomach lurched. 'Where? What happened?'

'Well, I think I saw him coming out of the alehouse near the Dominican Friary the night before last. I had heard about him taking his sister off somewhere, and so seeing him stuck in my mind.' The Principal leaned back and closed his eyes as he tried to recall what he had seen. 'He was wearing a heavy cloak, and he turned when I called his name. Then he began to walk away from me quickly. He turned a corner, and I ran after him, but when I got there, the street was empty.' He shrugged. 'That is all, I am afraid. If asked to swear in a court of law, I would not be able to say it was definitely Giles. But it certainly looked like him, and he did turn and then run away when I called his name. Draw your own conclusions.'

Bartholomew and Gray took their leave as soon as the rain had eased. Stayne closed the door behind them and waited. From the small chamber to one side of the hallway, Burwell emerged. The two men spoke together in low tones for a short time, and then Burwell left, his face grim.

There were two alehouses near the Dominican Friary, but no one in either could remember Giles Abigny. When Bartholomew began to describe him, the fat landlord shook his head.

'We are on a main road, and our trade is excellent, even with this pestilence. I cannot remember everyone who buys ale from me. He may have been here, but I cannot be certain.'

The landlord at the other alehouse knew Abigny and was more helpful, but said Abigny had most definitely not been there two nights before. He smiled ruefully, and said that Abigny had once been caught cheating at a game of dice with two of the locals, and had not dared to show his face again for fear of what might happen to him.

They walked back to Michaelhouse, and, after a silent meal, Bartholomew went to the sick-room. The dim light of the grey winter afternoon made it feel gloomy, and Bartholomew stoked up the fire. He was sure that Wilson would have been appalled at the waste of fuel on dying men. He smiled to himself as a picture of Wilson in hell, telling the Devil not to waste wood on his fires, sprang into his mind. He felt someone touch him on the shoulder, and looked up to see William bending over him. He felt slightly uncomfortable. Was the ex-inquisitor reading his mind and seeing heretical thoughts within?

William beckoned him outside, and stood waiting in the chilly hallway outside Augustus's room.

'We have been sent a message from the Chancellor at last,' he said. 'He has chosen Robert Swynford to be our next Master.'

'No great surprise, and he will make a good Master,' Bartholomew said. 'Will he come back from the country?'

William shook his head. 'Robert also sent a message saying that there has been plague in the house of his relatives and most of the menfolk have died. He asks our indulgence that we allow him to remain away for a few weeks until he is sure the women will be properly cared for. He has asked Alcote to act as his deputy until then.'

Bartholomew wondered if leaving the College in the care of a man who had just been deprived of the position might not be a risky move. Then he thought of Robert Swynford's easy grace and confidence, and knew that he would have no problem whatsoever in wresting delegated power back from Alcote.

'But Alcote is hiding in his room like Wilson was,' said Bartholomew. 'How can he run the College?'

'I assume Swynford has not been told that,' said William. 'Alcote has asked for various documents to be sent to him, so it seems he will at least see to the administration.'

Bartholomew went outside for some air and to stretch limbs cramped from bending over his patients all afternoon. The rain had stopped, and the clouds were beginning to clear. The porter saw him and scuttled over, stopping a good ten feet from Bartholomew, a large pomander filled with powerful herbs pressed to his face. Bartholomew realised that he had not seen the porter's face since the day he had returned from the house of Agatha's cousin and announced to Michaelhouse that the plague had come. The man held a note that he placed on the ground so he would not have to go nearer to Bartholomew than necessary. When he saw Bartholomew pick it up, he scurried back into the safety of his lodge. Bartholomew watched as he slammed the door. Perhaps the porter was right, and Bartholomew did carry a dangerous miasma around with him. He felt well enough, but how did he know he did not carry the contagion with him, in his breath, his clothes? He sighed heavily and turned his attention to the scrap of parchment in his hand which, in almost illegible writing, said that he was needed at the tinker's house near the river.

Bartholomew collected his cloak and bag of medicines, and set off. A wind was getting up, and it seemed to be growing colder by the moment. Bartholomew wondered whether the river would freeze over, as it had done the year before. As first, he had welcomed this, because it had cut down the smell. But then people just threw rubbish onto the ice rather than into the water, and it was not long before the smell was worse than it had been when the river was running.

He reached the river, and turned to walk along the

row of shacks where the river people lived. He recalled that the last patient he had seen before the plague had been the tinker's little girl, and he remembered that he had seen her body buried in one of the first plague pits to be dug. The last house in the row belonged to the tinker, but only one child stood outside to greet him this time.

Entering the single room, he walked over to the pile of rags in one corner that served as a bed, and crouched down to look at the person huddled there. He was pleasantly surprised to see a healthy woman lying on the bed.

She appeared startled to see him, and exchanged a puzzled glance with the child who had followed him in.

'You sent for me,' said Bartholomew, kneeling on the earth floor. 'What can I do?'

The woman exchanged another look with the child, who shook her head. 'I would not send for you for this, Doctor,' the woman said. 'My baby is coming. The midwife is dead, and I had to send my lad to fetch a woman to help me. I do not need a physician.'

Bartholomew returned her puzzled look. 'But you sent me a note . . .'

He stopped as the woman tensed with a wave of contractions. When she relaxed again, she blurted out, 'I did no such thing. I cannot write, and nor can my children. I do not need a physician.'

And could not pay for one was the unspoken addendum. Bartholomew shrugged. 'But since I am here, and since your time is close, perhaps I can help. And I will require no payment,' he added quickly, seeing concern flitting across the woman's face.

Bartholomew sent the child to fetch some water and cloths, and not a minute too soon, for the top of the baby's head was already showing. Between gasps, the tinker's wife told him how the other women who lived nearby were either dead or had the pestilence, and she had sent her son to fetch her sister from Haslingfield. But since that was several miles, she had known help might come too late. Physicians usually left childbirth to the midwives, and Bartholomew was only ever called if there was a serious problem, usually when it was far too late for him to do much about it. He was not surprised to find that he was enjoying doing something other than dealing with plague victims. When the baby finally slid into his hands all slippery and bawling healthily, he was more enthusiastic over it than were the exhausted mother and her wide-eyed daughter.

'It is a beautiful girl,' he said, giving the baby to the mother to nurse, 'perfectly formed and very healthy.' He pulled back the cloth so he could look at her face, and exchanged grins with the mother. He took one of the tiny hands in his. 'Look at her fingernails!' he exclaimed.

The tinker's wife began to laugh. 'Why, Doctor, anyone would think a newborn baby was something special to hear you going on!' she said. 'You would not be like this if it was your ninth in twelve years!'

Bartholomew laughed with her. 'I would be happy to help with any more babies you might have, Mistress Tinker,' he said, 'and would consider it a privilege to be asked.'

Bartholomew left the house feeling happier than he had since the plague had started. He made his way back along the river, whistling softly to himself. As he turned the corner to go back to College, a figure stepped out of the shadows in front of him, wielding what looked to be a heavy stick.

Bartholomew stopped in his tracks and glanced behind him, cursing himself for his foolishness. Another two shadowy forms stood there similarly armed. The note! It had been a trap! He swallowed hard, a vision of Augustus's mutilated body coming to mind. His stomach was a cold knot of fear. He had a small knife that he used for medical purposes, but it would be useless against three men armed with staves. He twisted the strap of his bag around his hand, and suddenly raced forward, swinging the bag at the figure in front of him as he did so. He felt it hit the man, and heard him grunt as he fell. Bartholomew kept going, hearing the footsteps of the two behind him following.

He fell heavily to the ground as a fourth figure shot out of some bushes in the lane and crashed into him. He twisted round, and saw one of the men who had followed raise his stick high into the air for a blow that would smash his head like an egg. He kicked out at the man's legs, and saw him lose his balance. Bartholomew tried to scramble to his feet, but someone else had grabbed him by his cloak and was trying to pull it tight around his throat. Bartholomew struggled furiously, lashing out with fists and feet, and hearing from the obscenities and yelps that a good many of his blows were true.

He brought his knee up sharply into the groin of one man, but he could not hold out for ever against four. He looked up, and saw for the second time an upraised stick silhouetted against the dark sky, but now he was pinned down and unable to struggle free. He closed his eyes, waiting for the blow that he was certain would be the last thing he would know.

The blow never came. Instead, the man toppled onto him clutching his chest, and Bartholomew felt a warm spurt of blood gush over him. He squirmed out from underneath the inert body, and made a grab for the cloak of one of his attackers who was now trying to run away. The man kicked backwards viciously, and Bartholomew was forced to let go. He heard their footsteps growing fainter as they ran up the lane, while others came closer.

He drew his knife, knowing that he did not have the strength to run a second time, and prepared to sell his life dearly should he be attacked again. He squinted as a lamp was thrust into his face.

'Matt!' Bartholomew felt himself hauled to his feet, and looked into the anxious face of Oswald Stanmore.

'Matt!' Stanmore repeated, looking down the lane after Bartholomew's attackers. 'What happened? Who is this?' He pushed at the body of the man who had fallen with his foot.

Bartholomew saw that Stanmore's steward, Hugh, was with him, armed with a crossbow. Stanmore kept looking around, as if he expected the attackers to come again.

'I was sent a note to see a patient by the river,' Bartholomew said, still trying to recover his breath, 'and these men attacked me.'

'You should know better than to go to the river after dark,' said Stanmore. 'The Sheriff caught three of the robbers that have been menacing the town there only last week. Doubtless these are more of the same.' He glanced around. 'Who sent you the note? Surely you can tie note and attackers together?'

Bartholomew showed him the now-crumpled message. 'The tinker did not write this,' he said.

Stanmore took it from him and peered at it. 'The tinker most certainly did not,' he said, 'for he died last month. I heard that only two of his children live, and his wife is expecting her ninth, poor woman.'

Bartholomew bent to look at the man on the ground. He was dead, the crossbow bolt embedded deeply in his chest. Bartholomew rifled hurriedly through his clothes, hoping for something that would identify him. There was a plain purse, filled with silver coins, but nothing else.

Bartholomew shook the purse at Stanmore. 'He was paid this money to attack me,' he said. He thought about the tinker's baby: it would make a fine gift for her baptism.

Stanmore began to lead the way cautiously up the lane towards Michaelhouse. Bartholomew caught his sleeve as they walked. 'What were you doing here?' he asked, keeping a wary eye on the trees at the sides of the lane.

Stanmore raised the lamp to look into some deep shadows near the back of Michaelhouse. 'A barge came in today,' he said, 'and I have been sitting with the captain negotiating the price of the next shipment.' He nodded at his steward. 'When I am at the wharf after dark, I always tell Hugh to bring his crossbow. You never know who you might meet around here.'

Bartholomew clapped Stanmore on the shoulder. 'I did not say thank you,' he said. 'Had you been a second later, you would have been rescuing a corpse!'

They reached Michaelhouse, and Stanmore joined Bartholomew for a cup of spiced wine in the hall, while Hugh was despatched to take the news to the Sheriff.

Father William was there too, trying to read by the light from the candles, and several students talked in low voices in another corner.

Stanmore stretched out his legs in front of the small fire. 'These robbers are getting bold,' he said. 'They have only picked on the dead and dying up until now. This is the first time I have heard them attacking the healthy.'

Bartholomew put the purse on the table. He quickly told Stanmore about the blacksmith, and how he had been paid to do Bartholomew harm during the riot. Stanmore listened, his mouth agape in horror.

'For the love of God, Matt! What have you got yourself mixed up in? First this blacksmith business, then Philippa, and now this!'

Bartholomew could only look as mystified as his brother-in-law.

When Hugh returned, Stanmore rose to leave, declining Bartholomew's offer of a bed for the night. 'No thank you, Matt!' he said, looking round at the College. 'Why should I spend a night in this cold and wretched place when I can have roaring fires and bright, candle-lit rooms with Stephen?'

Bartholomew went back to his own room, and undressed ready for bed. He had to wash and hang up his clothes in the dark, because scholars were not usually given candles for their rooms. It was considered wasteful, when they could use the communal ones in the hall, or, more usually, the conclave. He tidied the room as best he could, and lay on the creaking bed, rubbing his feet together hard in a vain attempt to warm them up. Stanmore was right: Michaelhouse was cold and gloomy. He tried to get comfortable, wincing as the wooden board dug into a place where one of his attackers had kicked him.

So, who had tried to kill him? Both the blacksmith and the dead man had been paid about five marks in silver in leather purses. Were they connected? They had to be: surely there was not more than one group of people who would pay to have him killed! Bartholomew shifted uncomfortably. He could hear Michael's Benedictine room-mates chanting a psalm in the room above. Then, somewhere in the lane outside, a dog barked twice. A gust of wind rattled the shutters, and rain pattered against them. He curled up in a ball, and attempted to wrap the bedclothes round his frozen feet. He tried to concentrate, but his thoughts kept running together. Next he knew, it was morning.

It was overcast and wet. Bartholomew went to the church for mass, where he was the only one present other than Father William. The Franciscan babbled the Latin at such high speed that Bartholomew barely heard most of it. He wondered whether William could really be sincere at such a pace, or whether he believed God liked His masses fast so He could get on with other things. Bartholomew would have asked him had he not been reluctant to be drawn into a protracted debate.

Remembering his obligation to Wilson, Bartholomew went to look at the spot the lawyer had chosen for his glorious tomb. Bartholomew had already asked one of the Castle stonemasons to order a slab of black marble, although he wondered when he would be able to hire someone to carve it. The Master Mason had died of the plague, and the surviving masons were overwhelmed by the repair work necessary to maintain the Castle. As he gazed at Wilson's niche, he thought it unfair that good men like Augustus and Nicholas should lie in a mass grave, while Wilson should have a grand tomb to commemorate him.

Bartholomew left the church and stepped into the street, closing the door behind him. He pulled his hood up against the rain, and set off to check the plague pits. On his way, he met Burwell, who greeted him with a smile and told him that there had been no new cases of plague in Bene't Hostel for two days.

As they talked, a beggar with dreadful sores on his face approached, pleading for alms. Bartholomew knew the beggar prepared his 'sores' every morning with a mixture of chalk, mud, and pig's blood. The beggar suddenly recognised Bartholomew under his hood, and backed off in dismay, as Bartholomew grasped Burwell's hand to prevent him from giving his money away.

As Bartholomew turned to explain to Burwell, he saw the purse in the hand he held. It was made of fine leather, and had 'BH' embellished on it in gold thread. Bartholomew had one just like it in his pocket. He felt his stomach turn over, although there was no reason why the Sub-Principal of Bene't Hostel should not have one of its purses. Burwell looked at him curiously. 'Doctor?' he said.

'Sores painted on fresh every day,' mumbled Bartholomew, hoping Burwell had not noticed his reaction, and if he had, did not guess why.

Burwell looked up at the sky as the church bell rang out the hour, and drew his hood over his head. 'Well, I must be about my business, and I know you must be busy.' He started to walk away, and then stopped.

'When you next see that rascal, Samuel Gray, could you tell him that he still owes us money for his fees last term?'

Bartholomew was a little angry at Gray. He should have cleared his debts with the hostel before changing to a new teacher. It was just another example of the double life the student seemed to lead. Bartholomew wondered what else he kept hidden. Since he was passing, Bartholomew went into St Botolph's Church to look for Colet. The Physician sat in his usual place, staring at the candles and twisting the golden lion round his fingers again and again.

When Bartholomew tried to talk to him, Colet fixed him with a vacant stare, and Bartholomew was in no doubt that Colet no longer knew who he was. His beard was encrusted with dried saliva, and his clothes were filthy. Bartholomew wondered if he should try to do something for him, but Colet did not seem to be in any discomfort. He decided to wait for a day or so and reconsider it then.

He left the church and continued along the High Street. As he passed the King's Head, Henry Oliver emerged and gave him such a look of undisguised enmity that Bartholomew stopped dead in his tracks. Oliver began to walk towards him. Bartholomew waited, taking the small knife out of his bag and keeping it hidden under his cloak so that Oliver would not see it.

'Found your lady yet, Doctor?' he said, his voice little more than a hiss.

Bartholomew wanted to push him into the stone trough that was full of water for horses, just behind him. 'Why do you ask?' he said, his voice betraying none of the anger that welled up inside him.

Oliver shrugged nonchalantly and gave a cold little smile. 'Just curious to know whether she continues to hide from you.'

Bartholomew smiled back. 'She still hides from me,' he said, wondering what Oliver thought he was going to gain from this cat-and-mouse game. 'Now, if you will excuse me, pleasant though it is to talk with you, the plague pit calls.'

He walked away, wondering what on earth could be the matter with the young man, and decided to speak to Swynford about it when he returned to College. The unpleasantness had gone on quite long enough.

As he approached the plague pit, an urchin darted up to him and mumbled something before turning to race away. Bartholomew, quick as lightning, grabbed him and held him as he struggled frantically, kicking at Bartholomew with his small bare feet. Bartholomew waited until the child's frenzy was spent and spoke gently.

'I did not hear what you said. Say it again.'

'A well-wisher has sommat to tell you if you come here at ten tonight,' he stammered, looking up at Bartholomew with big frightened eyes. 'But you got to come alone.'

Bartholomew stared at him. Was this another ploy to get him into a place where he could be dispatched as he almost had been the night before?

'Who told you to tell me this?'

The brat struggled again. 'I don't know. It was a man all wrapped up. He asked if I knew you – you came to my ma when she was sick – so I said yes, and he told me to tell you that message and to run away after. He gave me a penny.' He thrust out his hand to show it. Bartholomew let the child go and watched him scamper down the muddy street.

Now what? he thought. As if the plague, the College and Philippa were not enough to worry about!

The rain had eased off during the day, and, as night fell, patches of blue began to appear in the sky. But by the time Bartholomew returned to Michaelhouse after attending his patients, it was so late that most of the scholars were already in bed.

He went to the kitchen where Cynric dozed in front of the dying fire, and rummaged in the pantry until he found the remains of a loaf of bread and some hard cheese. While he ate, Cynric stoked up the fire, and set some wine to mull for them both. Bartholomew considered whether he should go to meet his 'well-wisher' at the plague pit. It seemed an odd choice for a rendezvous, but it would certainly be private, for no one in his right mind would frequent that place of desolation and despair in the dead of night. He glanced at the hour candle. He would need to make up his mind fairly quickly, for the meeting was in less than an hour.

Perhaps the mysterious sender really did wish him well, and would have information about Philippa. He tried to consider it logically. The people who attacked him would hardly expect that he would accept a second invitation to meet an unknown person in the dark in some god-forsaken spot after what had happened to him the previous night. Therefore, his 'well-wisher' must be someone who did not know about the attack. Of course, his attackers might use the same line of reasoning as he had just done. He stared into the fire and tapped his fingers on the table as his mind wrestled with the problem.

Abruptly, he stood. He was going. He would arm himself this time, and would be alert to the possibility of danger, unlike the previous night. He had spent hours in taverns and hostels trying to learn something about the disappearance of Giles and Philippa: it was possible that his well-wisher might have the information he wanted, and he did not wish to miss out on such an opportunity by being overly cautious.

Cynric looked at him sleepily. 'You going out again?' he asked. His eyes snapped open as Bartholomew took a large double-edged butchery knife from its hook on the wall and slipped it under his cloak.

'Now what are you going to do with that?' he said. He sat up straight in Agatha's fireside chair, his interest quickened. 'Not roistering about the town?'

'I have a meeting,' said Bartholomew. He saw no reason why he should not tell Cynric where he was going. At least then, if he were attacked, Cynric could tell the Sheriff it had been planned, and was not some random skirmish by the robbers as Stanmore plainly believed had happened the previous evening.

Cynric grabbed his cloak from where it lay in a bundle on the floor. 'At this time of night? After what happened to you yesterday? I had better come too, to keep you from mischief.'

'No,' said Bartholomew, thinking about the message. It told him to come alone, and he did not want to run the risk of frightening off a potential informant.

Cynric threw his cloak around his shoulders, and stood next to Bartholomew. 'We have known each other for a long time,' he said quietly, 'and I have seen that there has been something amiss with you since Sir John died. Perhaps I can help. I know you are anxious about the Lady Philippa. Is that what this meeting is about?'

Bartholomew gave a reluctant smile. He had forgotten how astute the small Welshman could be. He nodded and said, 'But I have been told to come alone.'

Cynric dismissed this with a wave of his hand. 'The day someone sees Cynric ap Huwydd when he does not want to be seen will be the day he dies. Do not worry, boy, I will be there, but none will know it other than you. Now, where are we going?'

Bartholomew relented. He was nervous about the meeting, and it would be reassuring to have Cynric nearby. If nothing else, at least he could run for help if things took a nasty turn. 'But you must be cautious,' he said. 'I have no idea who we are meeting, or what they want. If there is trouble, run for help. Do not come yourself or you may get hurt.'

Cynric shot him a disbelieving look. 'What do you take me for, boy? You should know me better than that. I learned something of ambush tactics in the Welsh mountains, you know.'

'I am sorry. It is just that so many people have met untimely deaths in the College and I do not want to lose anyone else.'

'Like Augustus, Paul and Montfitchet, you mean?' asked Cynric. Bartholomew looked at him askance.

'Just because I have no degree, like you scholars, does not mean I have no sense,' said Cynric. 'I know they were murdered, despite the lies that fat Wilson put about. I will keep my mouth shut,' he added quickly, seeing Bartholomew's expression of concern. 'I have done until now. But you should know that you are not alone in this.'

It was a long speech for Cynric, who indicated that the subject was closed by pinching out the candles and selecting a knife of his own.

Bartholomew slipped out of the kitchen door and across the courtyard. He walked briskly up St Michael's Lane and turned into the High Street. It was not easy to walk in the dark. The night had turned foggy, blocking out any light the moon might have given, and it was almost impossible to see the pot-holes and rubbish until he had stepped into them. At one point, he stumbled into a hole full of stinking water that reached his knees. Grimacing with distaste at the smell of urine and offal that came from it, he picked himself up and continued. From Cynric there was not a sound, but Bartholomew knew he was there.

At last he reached the field where the plague pits had been dug. A crude wooden fence had been erected around the field to prevent dogs from entering and digging up the victims. Bartholomew climbed over it and looked around. The mounds from the two full pits rose from the trampled grass like ancient pagan barrows. The other pit gaped like a great black mouth, and Bartholomew could make out the paler layer at the bottom where the lime had been spread over the last bodies to be laid there.

He tried to detect whether there was anyone hiding in the hedges at the sides of the field, but he could see nothing moving. A sound behind him made him spin round and almost lose his balance. His heart beat wildly and he felt his knees turn to jelly. He grabbed at the fence with one hand, while the other groped for the long knife that he had tucked into his belt.

A figure stood outside the fence, heavily cloaked and hooded. It made no attempt to climb over, and when Bartholomew took a step forward, it held up its hand.

'Stay!'

It was a woman's voice. Bartholomew's heart leapt.

'Philippa!' he exclaimed.

The figure was still for a moment, and then shook her head. 'Not Philippa. I am sorry.'

Bartholomew's hopes sank. It was not Philippa's voice: it was deeper, older, and with an accent that suggested the speaker came from the Fens rather than the town.

The woman looked around her quickly. 'I am glad you came, but it is not safe for us to meet like this.'

She glanced around again, and leaned over the fence so she would not have to speak so loudly. 'There is a meeting tomorrow at Bene't Hostel. I cannot say what it is about, but you should try to find out because I think it will affect you. The best way would be for you to go to the back of the house and climb to the window in the room they use for the hall. There is a deep sill there, and you will be able to hear what is being said through the shutters. You must take utmost care, for these are dangerous men. But I think you will be safer knowing than not knowing what they say.'

Bartholomew was totally confused. 'Is this about Philippa?' he asked.

The figure took a step away. 'I cannot say. You will have to listen and work it out for yourself.'

'But who are you?' Bartholomew asked.

The woman took another step away. 'Please! I will

lose everything if anyone finds out I met with you tonight. Now I must go. Please do not follow me. I ask you this because I took a risk for you tonight.'

Bartholomew assented. 'Is there anything I can do for you?'

The woman stopped and he could feel her looking at him from the depths of her hood. 'You have done enough,' she said softly, and slipped away into the mist.

Bartholomew looked after her, totally mystified. What kind of meeting held at Bene't Hostel could possibly have any relevance to him? And how was he supposed to climb up the back of the building and eavesdrop like some spy? Was this a ploy to discredit him, to get him into some dreadfully compromising position so that he could be dismissed from the University? Were there Oxford scholars plotting against him? Wilson and Aelfrith would probably think so, but there was something about the Oxford plot that Bartholomew could not accept. He understood why Wilson and Aelfrith had believed in it, but he still felt that the entire business was far more important to Cambridge than Oxford, and that Oxford would not waste time on it.

Cynric materialised in front of him, making him jump almost as much as he had when the woman had appeared. Cynric put his hand on his shoulder.

'Easy, boy! Not so jumpy. Shall I follow her?'

Bartholomew dug his nails into the fence, taking deep breaths to calm himself down. The woman had taken a risk to give him information she considered to be important to him, and had asked him not to put her in further danger by following her home.

'No, Cynric,' he said. 'Let her go.'

'Who was it?' Cynric asked, sounding disappointed. Bartholomew had the feeling his book-bearer was enjoying this nocturnal escapade.

'I do not know, but I think she means us no harm,' he said, climbing slowly over the fence.

'What did she want?'

Bartholomew was silent for a moment before telling Cynric what she had said.

Cynric rubbed his hands together gleefully. 'Should not be too difficult to do,' he said. He screwed up his eyes as he thought. 'Yes. It is possible to climb up the back of Bene't Hostel. It is all covered with ivy that they have never bothered to cut. They throw their rubbish in the back yard, and one of the garderobe chutes empties there. No one bothers to go there because it is so filthy, so I think we should have no problems.'

'We?' queried Bartholomew nervously. 'I cannot drag you into this . . .'

'You cannot keep me out of it! And anyway, I am much better at this sort of thing than you are.'

Bartholomew had to acknowledge that he was right, but he did not feel comfortable with the notion of dragging Cynric into anything unsavoury or dangerous. He stared out into the mist in the direction in which the woman had gone. The fog thinned slightly for a few moments, and Bartholomew could see the King's Head opposite.

As he watched, a figure emerged. Bartholomew tensed. It looked like Oswald Stanmore. He blinked, and the figure had gone. He shook himself. He was imagining things. Stanmore would be tucked up safe and warm in his bed in Trumpington by now, and would never be seen frequenting a disreputable place like the King's Head. Bartholomew was obviously tired and prone to an overactive imagination. He took hold of Cynric's sleeve and tugged, indicating the way back down the High Street towards home.

Cynric was already making plans for entering Bene't's yard the next night, and Bartholomew, seeing his eyes gleam with excitement, did not have the heart to tell him he could not go. He was not even sure whether he wanted to go himself. The mist clung to their clothes as they walked, and seemed to muffle the usual sounds of the night. Distantly, Bartholomew heard wailing. Another plague death? Or a cat hunting among the piles of rubbish? He was glad when the walls of Michaelhouse loomed up out of the fog, and too tired to speculate any further on his well-wisher's intentions. He fell asleep in his clothes listening to the regular breathing of Gray in the other bed.

Early the next day, Bartholomew received a message from the barber-surgeon Robin of Grantchester saying that he had convened a meeting with representatives from the town to discuss what they were going to do about the settlement near All Saints-next-the-Castle, where all had lain dead for many weeks. Rumours abounded that the dead walked down into Cambridge at night, and were spreading the pestilence. The meeting was acrimonious, and the real issue about what should be done about the community beyond the Castle was sidestepped until Bartholomew rapped on the table with the hilt of Stanmore's dagger to make the voices subside.

'Everyone who lived in settlement beyond the Castle is either dead or has left,' he said. 'I have seen that there are bodies rotting in virtually every house. While I do not believe they walk in the town at night, the area should be cleared in the interests of health. I propose we burn it down.'

Horrified faces stared at him, open-mouthed.

'With the bodies still inside?' whispered Stephen Stanmore.

'Unless you would like to go and fetch them out,' said Bartholomew.

'But that is sacrilege!' said Father William, aghast. 'Those people must be buried decently.'

'So fetch them, and then we will burn the houses.'

There was a silence, and then mutterings of reluctant assent. Clerics and medics alike accepted that there was no other safe way to deal with the problem, but no one had wanted to be the one to suggest such an unpopular solution.

Bartholomew had a hasty meal with William, and set off for the settlement. Two lay-brothers had volunteered to help, and people came out of their houses to watch them pass. The burning did not take long: the houses were flimsy and, despite the rain that had drenched them during the past few weeks, fired easily.

When the flames died down, Bartholomew found he was shaking, and wondered if he had really condemned the spirits of the people to walk in perpetual torment as the rector of St Clement's had claimed. William scattered holy water about, and Bartholomew watched it hiss and evaporate as it touched the still-hot embers of the houses. Bartholomew knew he would never want to visit this part of the town again.

'That was a foul day's work,' William remarked as they returned to Michaelhouse. 'But it had to be done. The rector was wrong: the souls of those people will go wherever they were destined to be, and nothing you have done today will change that. Put it from your mind, and think of other things.'

Bartholomew smiled gratefully. William was most certainly not a person to give false assurances; if anything, he tended the other way, and his words made Bartholomew's mind easier.

'I heard you helped Mistress Tinker to give birth to another child,' said William.

Bartholomew thought back to his delight at seeing the baby born and remembered the purse he had taken to give her. He asked William if he would give it to the mother when he baptised the child the following day. William raised his eyebrows.

'Not your own child, is it?' he asked.

Bartholomew was taken aback. What twisted minds these University people had! What made them read sinister motives into even the most innocent of acts? William caught his look and changed the subject. 'Have you seen Brother Michael today?'

Bartholomew had not seen Brother Michael for some days and was growing anxious. He had even looked up in the attic that morning, to satisfy himself that the murderer had not been at work again. He was about to voice his concerns to William, when he saw Colet being escorted out of St Botolph's Church by two monks. Colet was laughing uncontrollably, and drooling even more than usual. His eyes, instead of being blank, were wild and starting from his head.

'What has happened?' Bartholomew watched in pity as Colet cackled to himself.

'He acts so around this time of day,' one of the monks said, 'and we have to take him home.

His mind has gone. There is nothing you can do, Doctor.'

Agatha would not let Bartholomew into the kitchen, saying he smelled of the 'fires of death'. She took his clothes away to be laundered, and made him wash thoroughly in water she had liberally peppered with herbs to take away the smell. Although the water was cold, Bartholomew felt better when the smell of burning had gone. He sat shivering next to the kitchen fire, eating stale marchpanes.

Cynric drew a stool up next to him. He glanced around to make sure Agatha could not hear, but she was busy trying to persuade William to go through the same process as Bartholomew, and was unlikely to be distracted from her purpose until William had bent to her will.

'I have been out and about,' he said in a low voice. 'The steward at Bene't's has been given the night off tonight, and told he can visit his mother. They are also short of candles, and the Sub-Principal has suggested that all lights be extinguished at eight o'clock until they can replenish their stocks. You know what all this means?'

Bartholomew could guess. The steward was being invited to leave the premises overnight, and the students, deprived of light, would probably go to bed early since there was little they could do in the dark. All this suggested that his well-wisher was right, and that there would be a clandestine meeting at Bene't Hostel that night. He had not given the matter much thought during the day since he had had so much else to think about, but now he needed to come to a decision.

He slipped out through the back of the kitchen and

made his way to the orchard, remembering that the last time he had done this was when Aelfrith had spoken to him. Now, it was bitterly cold, and the branches of the trees were grey-brown and bare. He sat for a while with his eyes closed, trying to concentrate on the silence of the orchard and not the roaring in his head from the fires. He began to think about whether he should go to Bene't Hostel to spy. Was it safe, or was it a trap? Who was this woman who claimed to wish him well? He rubbed a hand through his hair, and stood, hugging his arms around his body to keep warm. But when he thought about Philippa, he knew he would eavesdrop on the meeting. After all, Cynric would be there, and if anyone could enter and leave places unseen it was Cynric. He began to walk slowly back through the College heading for his room, but was intercepted by a breathless Cynric.

'There you are!' he said, his tone slightly accusatory. 'You had better come quick. Henry Oliver is here, and he is terrible sick of the plague.'

X

AS BARTHOLOMEW AND CYNRIC HURRIED through the College, they could hear Henry Oliver's enraged yells coming from the commoners' room. Cynric told Bartholomew that two students had found him lying outside the King's Head tavern, and had brought him back so he could be cared for in the plague ward. Oliver, it seemed, had other ideas, and had kicked and struggled as much as his weakened body would allow, demanding to be taken to his own room.

The Benedictines were having a difficult time trying to quieten him down, and his shouts and curses were disturbing the other patients. One of the monks was almost lying on top of him to keep him in the bed. When Oliver saw Bartholomew standing in the doorway, his struggles increased.

'Keep him away from me,' he screamed. 'He will kill me!'

Slowly Bartholomew approached the bed, and laid his hand gently on the sick student's head. Oliver shrank away, pushing himself as far back against the wall as he could.

'Come, now, Henry,' Bartholomew said softly. 'No

one is going to hurt you. You are ill and need help, and this is the best place for you to get it.'

'No!' Oliver yelled, his eyes darting frantically round the room. 'You will kill me here!'

'Now why would I do that?' asked Bartholomew, reaching out to turn Oliver's head gently, so he could inspect the swellings in his neck.

Oliver's breath came in short agonised gasps. 'The Master told me,' he whispered, flashing a terrified glance at Bartholomew.

'Swynford?' asked Bartholomew, astonished. 'Swynford told you I would kill you?'

Oliver shook his head. 'Master Wilson. Wilson said you would kill him. And you did!' He sank back against the wall, exhausted. Bartholomew looked at him thunderstruck, while the monk knelt to begin taking off Oliver's wet clothes.

The Benedictine smiled briefly at Bartholomew. 'Delirious,' he said. 'They claim all sorts of things, you know. Poor Jerome over there keeps saying he was responsible for the murder of Montfitchet!'

Bartholomew groaned. It was all happening too fast. Did this mean that Jerome, in his feverish delirium, was declaring that he was the murderer? And why had Wilson told Oliver that Bartholomew was going to kill him?

His energy spent, Oliver was unresisting while the monk and Bartholomew put him to bed. He began to squirm and struggle again when Bartholomew examined him, but not with the same intensity as before. The swellings were as soft as rotten apples in his armpits and groin, and Bartholomew knew that lancing them would bring no relief. While the monks tended to the other patients, Bartholomew tried to make Oliver drink some water.

Oliver spat the water from his mouth, and twisted away from Bartholomew.

'Poison!' he hissed, his eyes bright with fever.

Bartholomew took a sip from the water cup himself, and offered it again to Oliver, who took it reluctantly, but drank thirstily.

'Now,' said Bartholomew. 'You must rest.'

He stood to leave, but Oliver caught at the edge of his sleeve. 'Master Wilson said he was in fear of his life from you, Physician,' he said. 'My aunt believes you killed him.'

Bartholomew had had enough of Oliver and his unpleasant accusations. 'Well, she is wrong,' he said. 'And how would she know anyway, since Wilson never left his room to talk to anyone, and your aunt never leaves her Priory?'

Oliver sneered and spat onto the floor. '*He* went to see *her*,' he said.

'Wilson visited your aunt?'

'Of course!' Oliver said, his voice dripping contempt. 'Most days, between Compline and Matins.'

'In the middle of the night?' said Bartholomew, amazed. 'Wilson visited your aunt in the middle of the night?'

'They were lovers,' said Oliver, 'although what she ever saw in that fat pig I will never know.'

'He was going to take major orders,' said Bartholomew, bemused, 'vowing to abstain from physical relationships with women.'

Oliver gave a short bark of laughter. 'My aunt had already taken such a vow,' he said, 'but what did that matter?'

Bartholomew stared at the student. Oliver glowered

back at him spitefully, and once again, Bartholomew wondered what he had done to earn himself such an intense dislike. Oliver, however, was growing exhausted, and Bartholomew did not want to tire him further with more questions. He went to sit with Jerome, who was still fighting his illness with a spirit of defiance that Bartholomew never guessed he had. Jerome's skeletal hand gripped his.

'I did it,' he muttered. 'I killed Montfitchet. I made him drink the wine when he said he had already had enough. Jocelyn and I made him drink the Master's health, and he died. His death is on my head.'

'Did you know the wine was drugged?' asked Bartholomew.

The old man shook his head slowly, his eyes filling with tears. 'No, I did not. But that does not absolve me,' he whispered.

Bartholomew rose to leave. 'Father William will come to you,' he said. 'He will absolve you.' He felt a sudden urge just to leave Michaelhouse and Cambridge and go to York or Lincoln where he could practise medicine in peace, and escape from the vile intrigues and affairs of the University. Even Father Jerome, who had probably never harmed anyone in his life, had been drawn into its murky depths, and would die believing he had committed a crime in which he had played no knowing part.

As he left the commoners' room and made his way back to the kitchen, he thought about Oliver's words. Oliver had said that Wilson had left the College almost every night to visit his mistress, the Abbess. That certainly explained how he might have caught the plague when, in everyone's eyes, he had isolated himself from the outside world. Bartholomew and Cynric had slipped unnoticed in and out of College the night before, so there was no reason why Wilson could not have done the same.

But it still made no sense. Bartholomew had already established that Wilson could not have been the murderer, because Augustus's body had been dumped in the stables after Wilson had been buried. Did Wilson believe Bartholomew was the murderer? Did he talk to him on his deathbed so that Bartholomew would fall into some kind of trap and be exposed? But that made no sense either, because if Wilson believed Bartholomew to be capable of committing so grave a sin as murder, why did he ask him to ensure that his tomb was built? Why not Michael, or William?

He went to huddle near the kitchen fire, elbowing Cynric to one side so that they could share the warmth. They could not risk going too early in case they were seen, so Bartholomew dozed until Cynric announced it was time to leave. The Welshman made Bartholomew change his white shirt and dispensed with cloaks and scholar's robes because they were difficult in which to climb. Both wore two pairs of woollen leggings and two dark tunics to protect them against the cold. When he was satisfied that they were well prepared for a long chilly wait on a narrow window-sill, Cynric led the way out of the College.

Bartholomew was amazed at the way the nimble Welshman could blend into the shadows, and felt clumsy and graceless by comparison. When they reached Bene't Hostel, it was in total darkness, but Cynric insisted on waiting and watching for a long time before he decided it was safe. He slipped down a narrow passageway like a cat, Bartholomew following as quietly as he could. The passageway had originally led to the yard at the back of the hostel, but had been blocked off by a wall when the yard had become more of a refuse pit.

The wall had not been built of the best materials, and Bartholomew found it easy to gain hand- and footholds in the crumbling mortar, and climb to the top. Cynric pressed him back into the shadows, where they waited yet again to ensure it was safe to continue. At last Cynric motioned that they could drop over the wall into the yard below. Bartholomew was used to foul smells, but the stench that rose from the deep layer of slime on the floor of the yard made his eyes water. Cynric quickly led the way to a row of straggly shrubs that grew against the wall of the hostel.

Bartholomew cursed under his breath as he skidded on something slippery and almost fell. Cynric grabbed at his arm, and they waited in tense silence until they were certain that no one had heard. They reached the bushes where they could hide from anyone looking out of the windows, and Bartholomew smothered an exclamation of disgust as his outstretched hand touched a rotten slab of meat that had been thrown there.

Cynric pushed his way through the bushes until he reached the ivy that climbed the wall of the house. It was ancient and sturdy, and Bartholomew nodded that he could climb up it without difficulty. They had agreed that Bartholomew would climb to the window-sill, while Cynric would keep watch down the passageway from the top of the wall for any indication that the well-wisher had led them into a trap. If that were the case, they would effect an escape by climbing up the ivy, and over the roofs.

Gingerly, Bartholomew set his foot on the vine,

and began to climb. The slop drain was apparently directly above, for the ivy was treacherously slick, and all manner of kitchen waste was caught on its branches. Bartholomew tried not to think about it, and continued upwards. Glancing down, he could not see Cynric. He must already have slid into his vantage point in the shadows at the top of the wall.

The sound of soft singing came through the slop drain. Bartholomew prayed that it was not a scullery boy who would throw the kitchen waste down on his head. Cautiously, he climbed a little further, noting that the singer's words were slurred and his notes false. One of the scholars, objecting to an early night, must have slipped down to the pantry to avail himself of the wine and ale stored there. From his voice, it would take a thunderbolt to disturb him, not someone climbing stealthily outside.

He climbed higher, until he saw the lancet windows of the hall just above him. For an awful moment, he thought the woman had misinformed him, for there was no deep window-sill on which he could wait and listen, but then he realised that he was too far to one side, and needed to move to his right. This proved more difficult than he had anticipated, and he had to climb down past the kitchen drain before he could find a stem of the ivy large enough to bear his weight.

At last he saw the window-sill above him, and he was able to grasp its edge with both hands and haul himself up. The shutters were firmly closed, but he could just see the merest flicker of light underneath them, suggesting that someone was there. He almost fell when a branch he had been holding snapped sharply in his hand. He held his breath and waited for the shutters to be flung open and his hiding place discovered, but there was no sound from within, and gradually he relaxed.

He eased himself to one side of the sill, his back propped up against the carved stone window-frame. He learned that, by huddling down a little, he could see a fraction of the main table in the large hall through a split in the wood of the shutter. But, although one of the Sub-Principal's precious candles burned, there seemed to be no one there to appreciate it. The meeting was evidently not due to start for a while. Bartholomew tried to make himself more comfortable. A chill wind was beginning to blow, and, although the sky was clear and it seemed unlikely to rain, he knew that, despite Cynric's precautions, he was going to be very cold before he could go home.

He heard the church clock strike the hour twice before anything happened. He was beginning to wonder whether he had been sent on a wild-goose chase, and was considering giving up. It was freezing on the window-sill, and the bitter wind cut right through his clothes. He felt that if he did not climb down the vine soon, he would be too cold to do so at all.

Suddenly, he became aware that something was happening. Huddling down to peer through the split wood, he saw Master Burwell pacing around the hall, and heard him giving orders to Jacob Yaxley, who had been ousted from his room to make way for the plague ward. Yaxley was lighting more candles and sweeping the remains of the scholars' evening meal off the table onto the rushes. Burwell walked across Bartholomew's line of vision and seemed to be talking to someone else. The wind rattled one of the shutters, and Bartholomew swore softly. If this happened, he would not be able to

hear what was going on in the meeting. Carefully, he
broke off a piece of vine, and jammed it under the
loose wood. The wind gusted again, and Bartholomew
saw with satisfaction that he seemed to have solved that
problem at least.

The clock struck the hour again, and the activity
in the hall increased dramatically. There was a growing
murmur of voices, and Bartholomew could see a number
of people filing into the hall. He was surprised: he had
been expecting a small gathering of perhaps four or
five people, but there were at least fifteen men, with a
promise of more to come.

He heard someone banging softly on the table to
bring the meeting to order.

'Gentlemen. I would not have called you here in this
manner unless there was an important reason,' Burwell
began. 'I am afraid that our cause has suffered a grave
setback.'

There was a mumble of concerned voices, and
Burwell waited for them to die down before continuing.

'We have heard that the Acting Master of
Michaelhouse has established contact with Oxford.'

The voices this time were louder, and held
questions.

Burwell raised his hand. 'I do not need to spell
out the implications of this to you, gentlemen. We have
been uncertain of Master Alcote's loyalties, and this
proves we were correct. Our spies have intercepted
messages from him telling which hostels were the
weakest and most likely to flounder under pressure.
Oxford will now see that pressure will be brought to
bear against these places, and the University will be
undermined as they fall.'

The room erupted into confusion again, and Burwell had to bang on the table to bring the meeting back under control.

'What do you suggest we do?' asked one man. Although he had his back to Bartholomew, he recognised the wiry black hair as belonging to the Principal of Mary's Hostel, Neville Stayne.

Burwell sighed. 'We could take Alcote from the equation,' he said. Bartholomew saw Stayne nod his head in approval, but there were voices of dissent.

'Who would succeed him? We might end up in a worse state,' asked another voice that Bartholomew did not recognise.

'It is most likely that Swynford would return,' Burwell said. 'He is an unknown quantity to us: we do not know where his loyalties lie, but since he is not obviously for Oxford, like Alcote, it might be possible to talk to him and put forward our point of view.'

Bartholomew could see Stayne nodding again.

'But how would we rid ourselves of Alcote's mastership?' another person asked.

Burwell spread his hands. 'There are ways and means,' he said simply.

'I am concerned about the physician,' said Stayne, abruptly changing the subject. 'He has been asking questions at Mary's about Abigny.'

'We agreed that he would be left alone,' someone said firmly. Bartholomew felt physically sick as he recognised the voice of his brother-in-law, Oswald Stanmore. He struggled to get a better view of the men seated at the table, and saw the blue sleeve embroidered in silver thread that was unmistakably Stanmore's. Bartholomew's shock made him clumsy, and he fell back harder against the window-frame than he had intended.

'What was that?' said Stayne, coming to his feet and looking towards the window suspiciously. Burwell joined him, and together they approached the window. Bartholomew could see them standing only inches from it. He held his breath. Stanmore, too, came over, and to Bartholomew's horror, began to open the shutters. Now he would be discovered! He heard Stanmore swear as the shutter jammed. Bartholomew glanced down and saw that the twig of ivy he had used to stop the shutter from rattling was preventing Stanmore from opening the window.

'It is stuck,' Bartholomew heard him mutter. A sudden gust of wind rattled the other shutter.

'It is only the wind,' Burwell said, relief in his voice. 'We are all so nervous we are even afraid of the wind. Come and sit down again.'

Bartholomew saw him put a hand on Stanmore's shoulder to lead him back to his seat. He let out a shuddering breath, and tried to concentrate on what was being said.

'No harm comes to Bartholomew,' said Stanmore firmly, 'or we are out of this. Your University can go to the Devil.'

'Hush, hush,' said Burwell placatingly. 'We will leave it to you to keep him out of our way. But you must understand that we cannot allow him to jeopardise the social stability of this country, which is what his meddling might bring about if he exposes some of our actions and the University falls.'

'I will talk to him,' mumbled Stanmore. 'I can ask him to join us.'

Stayne tutted angrily. 'He will not! I believe he holds us responsible for the death of Babington. He will not join us, and even if he did, I would not trust him.'

'Let us not leap to conclusions,' said Burwell, intervening smoothly. 'Let Stanmore talk to Bartholomew, and we will leave it at that. For now,' he added ominously.

Bartholomew felt as though he was listening to arrangements for his own death and, despite the cold, felt beads of sweat break out on his face and prickling at the small of his back. Was it Burwell's group who had paid the blacksmith and the men in the lane to kill him? How had Stanmore become involved in all this? He had nothing to do with the University. Bartholomew fought to quell the cold, sick feeling in his stomach, and concentrate on the meeting.

'Bartholomew is not the main problem,' Burwell continued. 'Michaelhouse is. Something is afoot at Michaelhouse of which we know nothing. I heard that Wilson never left his room, so how did the plague take him? How was it that the Michaelhouse Fellows arranged for him to be buried in the churchyard, and not in the plague pit? What of the rumours about the commoners that died that were so firmly quashed last summer? And finally,' he said, 'I still do not accept that Babington killed himself. Neither did Father Aelfrith or Master Wilson when I questioned them. I think Michaelhouse is a rotten apple, and the quicker it folds in on itself and collapses, the better for us all.'

There were mutters of assent, and the meeting went on to discuss various scraps of information that had been gleaned via the spy networks: there had been a convening of anti-Cambridge scholars at Bernard Hall in Oxford; one of Cambridge's spies had been killed in a town brawl; and two new halls had been established in Oxford, but none in Cambridge.

'We must not allow them to become too much bigger than us,' said Yaxley. 'The bigger they become, the easier they will be able to crush us.'

'We are putting pressure on that widow who lives in the house near St Nicholas's Church to bequeath it to us,' said Burwell. 'That will become St Nicholas Hostel, and we are in the process of altering the house by Trumpington Gate. It should be ready for new scholars in a matter of weeks.'

Heads nodded, and murmurs of approval were given. Bartholomew saw Stayne glance at the hour candle. 'It is growing late,' he said, 'and we must end this meeting. So, we are all to keep a keen ear for potential houses that can be converted into hostels; Stanmore is to deal with his brother-in-law; and as for Michaelhouse, do we act, or let it drown in its own corruption?'

'I do not see what else we can do but watch,' said Burwell. 'We know Father William sympathises with us generally, and we know that Alcote and Bartholomew do not. We do not know where Swynford or the Benedictine stand, and that flighty boy – Abigny – has apparently vanished. I suggest we wait and watch. We especially watch Alcote and his dealings. I would like everyone here to make that a priority.'

The meeting began to break up. Bartholomew saw Stanmore clearly through the crack in the shutter, and watched him leave the hall, followed by Richard and Stephen. Stephen looked unhappy and fiddled with the silver clamp on the cloak Stanmore had lent him when Abigny had stolen his. Richard looked solemn, but Bartholomew could see the excitement in his eyes at being included in such a meeting.

Bartholomew closed his eyes in despair. He had battled to keep his problems from Stanmore and his family in the belief that it would keep them from harm, despite his increasing loneliness and desperation to talk to someone. Now it seemed he had made the right decision, but for entirely the wrong reasons. Everyone was involved, even his young nephew.

He watched Yaxley and Burwell through the crack in the shutter as they fussed about the hall hiding evidence that the meeting had taken place. The rushes were stamped down, furniture moved back into place, and wax from the candles scraped away. Eventually, they were satisfied, and went to their beds, leaving the hall in darkness. Bartholomew sighed in relief, and began to flex his frozen limbs. He was so cold and stiff, he wondered whether he would be able to climb down the ivy and back up over the wall without falling and giving himself away. He rubbed his arms and legs vigorously for a few moments to try to warm them, and then began his descent. He almost slipped twice, and discovered that it was much easier climbing up slime-covered vines than down them. He really did lose his footing when he was near the bottom, and landed with a crackle of dead, broken branches in the bushes.

Cynric was there to help him up. 'You will wake the dead!' he whispered irritably. 'Try to be quieter.'

Bartholomew followed him across the disgusting yard, even more slippery now that some of the filth had turned to ice in the night air. Getting over the wall proved difficult, for Bartholomew could not feel his cold fingers sufficiently to find handholds in the stones. They managed eventually, and Cynric retraced his silent steps back through the shadows into Michaelhouse. The front gates were closed, but Cynric, showing characteristic foresight, had left the back gate unlocked, and they made their way through the College vegetable gardens, past the laundry, and into the College itself. It occurred to Bartholomew that Wilson must have made the same journey when he returned from seeing his lover, the Abbess.

Bartholomew sank gratefully into Agatha's chair. His knees were still trembling from the shock of hearing that his family was involved in the University's business, and that there were people who obviously wanted him out of the way. How had he managed to manoeuver himself into the position where he stood virtually alone against his family and friends? He had no wish to see the country short of trained clergy and educated men who would be able to serve their people, and he had no wish to see the social order of England crumble because there was only one University from which these men could graduate. It was probably fair to say that he actually approved of the aims of this clandestine group. But there remained something odd about the whole business, a sinister edge to it that Bartholomew could not define.

Cynric began to prod some life into the embers, and they both stretched cold hands towards the meagre flames. Bartholomew went into a storeroom and emerged with one of Wilson's bottles of wine. Cynric took the bottle and pulled the cork out with his teeth. He took a hearty swig, and passed it to Bartholomew.

Bartholomew followed suit, grimacing at the strength of the wine. Cynric grinned at him, and took the bottle again. 'This was the one Gilbert said was the best,' he said, peering at the label in the firelight. 'This single bottle cost six marks; Wilson was saving it for when the Bishop came.'

Bartholomew took the bottle and studied it. The parchment wrapped round it said it came from the French Mediterranean, and so would be more expensive than English wine, or wine from the north of France. He took another sip. It had a tarry flavour that Bartholomew was already beginning to like. He took a third swallow and passed it back to Cynric, who raised it into the air in a salute.

'To Master Wilson, for leaving us his wine. And for leaving us.' He gave a short laugh, and drank. 'Now,' he said, 'what did you learn?'

Bartholomew began to relate what he had learned, embarrassed that his voice cracked when he mentioned the involvement of his family. Cynric sat quietly, not inter-rupting. Eventually, Bartholomew faltered and stopped. What more could he say? He started to tell Cynric that he would talk to Stanmore, and reason with him about the University business, but got no further than the first few words. Would Stanmore then be forced to kill him, as Sir John and Aelfrith had been killed because they had been in the way? Or would it be Stephen or Richard who would perform that duty?

He rubbed his eyes hard, feeling an aching tiredness underneath that made them burn. He was at his wits' end, and knew no more what to do than would the great rat that sat boldly washing its whiskers in the middle of the kitchen floor. He watched as it snapped into alertness, standing on hind legs and sniffing the air, before scampering away to disappear down a hole in the corner. At the same time, there was a chill draught as the door was opened.

'Matt?' said Philippa softly, walking towards him and dropping to her knees by his chair. She took one of his hands in hers. 'You look tired and miserable. Tell me what is wrong.'

Bartholomew looked in astonishment over her fair head to Abigny, who stood in the doorway.

'The last time we met, you were wearing a dress,' Bartholomew said coldly, trying to control the sick, churning feeling in his stomach.

'I was a damn fine woman!' Abigny said proudly. 'Fooled your family for almost four days. Would have done for longer if you had not been so ungentlemanly as to burst into a woman's boudoir unannounced.'

Bartholomew half rose, pulling his hand away from Philippa, but then sat back down again, uncertain what he had been intending to do. Abigny settled himself comfortably on one of the benches.

'We owe you an explanation,' he said.

Bartholomew looked at him warily. 'I should say you do,' he said, trying to keep his voice from wavering. When he dared to glance at Philippa again, she smiled at him lovingly, but without remorse. Chilled, he moved away so that no part of her touched him.

'Oh, Matt!' she said, giving him a playful push. 'Do not sulk! You knew why I went!'

'I know nothing!' he said with a sudden intensity. 'I left you with Edith, then there was some peculiar story about you refusing to see me, then Giles pretended to be you for God knows how long, and then you both disappeared!'

'What?' she said, her small face puckered. 'No! Giles explained it all to you. You know I would never give you cause for concern!' She turned to her brother. 'You did tell him. You told me you did!' Her voice was accusing, and Abigny stood and backed away, his hands raised in front of him in a placatory gesture.

'I decided against it. I thought it was best. You do not know him like I do; he would have tried to see you, and then you both would have been in danger! I did what I thought was right.'

Philippa stopped from where she had been advancing on her brother, and looked back at Bartholomew with a curious mixture of shame and resignation. 'Well, then,' she said in a small voice. 'You do owe Matt an explanation.'

Cautiously, alert to every movement his sister made, Abigny perched on the edge of the table. Philippa stayed where she was, at a distance from either of them. Abigny took a deep breath, and began to speak.

'In order that you understand what I did, and why, I must start at the beginning. When Philippa was still a baby, she was married. The marriage was legal, although it was of course never consummated. Her husband died shortly after, and Philippa inherited a considerable amount of property in Lincoln. Before our father died, he arranged for Philippa to stay at St Radegund's until she chose either to marry, or to take the veil. The Abbess, of course, was keen that Philippa should take the veil, because then all her property would go to the convent.'

He shuffled on the table, while Philippa watched him, her face pale.

'The fact that you were paying her obvious attention was not likely to encourage her to a life of chastity, so the Abbess, God rot her soul, decided she would remove you: if you could be persuaded to give up your courting, she imagined that Philippa, in paroxysms of grief, would become a nun, and all her worldly wealth would go to the convent. Her plan was that her dreadful nephews, the Olivers, were to start a riot and the blacksmith was paid to deliver a warning – "stay away". It seems the warning was too obtuse for you, because you continued to visit Philippa. The blacksmith swore he had given you the message when pressed by the Olivers. Then the plague came, and the Abbess was able to imprison Philippa in the convent under her policy of isolation.

'Anyway, to take things in order, I managed to work out what the Abbess had done by listening at doors and chatting to the nuns, who told me that the Abbess was bringing great pressure on Philippa to take her vows.'

Philippa nodded her agreement. 'She told me it was my duty to take the veil because so many clerics were dying of the plague. She said there were not enough left to say masses for the dead, and that I could not, in all conscience, refuse to commit myself to a monastic life when there were the souls of so many at stake.'

Abigny watched her for a moment before continuing. 'I became afraid that the Abbess might use the Death to her own advantage, and that she might kill Philippa for the property and blame it on the plague. I decided I had to take Philippa away from her. So I sent you a message with that cocky medical student, and his cousin, Sister Emelda, agreed to pass a note to Philippa. You were supposed to meet each other in the shed, fall into each other's arms, marry, and live happily ever after. But poor Sister Clement chose that shed in which to die, and you, of course,' he said, bowing to Bartholomew, 'began to suspect all sorts of foul play, and took Philippa to your sister's home.'

He stopped for a minute, and chewed on one of

his nails. 'Philippa could not be safe there. The Abbess would work out where she was and take her back. And this time, I was certain she would kill Philippa. You had upset my plans horribly. Instead of taking her to the safety of matrimony, you took her to the very unsafety of Trumpington – and on top of that, she got the plague. I was furious with you,' he said to Bartholomew with a flash of defiance.

Bartholomew interrupted him, piecing together Abigny's story with what he had learned himself. 'So you hung around Trumpington until she began to recover, seen by the Gilbertine friar and the barmaid from the Laughing Pig,' he said, his voice hard. 'Then you stayed with Philippa for a few days, pretending Philippa was distressed because of her scars, so that poor Edith would not know there were two of you.'

The barmaid had told him Abigny seemed terrified of something. Could it have been the Abbess? Or was Abigny afraid of a more sinister foe – the Oxford scholars, or even the Cambridge men?

'More or less,' said Abigny, unperturbed by Bartholomew's hostility. He glanced at Philippa who stood motionless near the door. He continued. 'I took her to Hugh Stapleton's house in Fen Ditton, where she would be safe, and I took Philippa's place in Edith's house, waiting with my crossbow to see whether the Oliver brothers would come. It was a tense wait, I can tell you. I was almost relieved when you came and uncovered my disguise in that dramatic way, and I could get away from such a nerve-racking situation. We have both been at Fen Ditton ever since.'

'You used my sister!' said Bartholomew, his voice dangerously quiet. He stood abruptly and swung round to face Abigny, who blanched, but did not flinch. 'How did you know the Abbess or the Olivers would not harm her while you skulked in her house?'

'I reasoned it out. I made sure that news of my escape was common gossip. The Abbess would hardly go there if she knew Philippa was gone.'

'But you were there for almost a week!' exploded Bartholomew. 'They might have come then.'

'And who took Philippa there in the first place?' yelled Abigny, his temper snapping. 'If anything, this was all your fault!'

Cynric, anticipating violence, uncoiled himself from the fire and moved between them, but Philippa was there before him.

'Please,' she said. 'Hear Giles out.'

Abigny mastered his temper with an effort, and resumed his explanation. Bartholomew listened, his face white with fury. 'I assumed that the Abbess would not harm you. With Philippa gone, what possible importance could you be to her? Well, I misread her. She held you responsible for Philippa's flight, while Wilson, her lover, claimed that you meant him harm. Within days, Wilson lay dead, burned to death in his own room with you conveniently first at the scene. Sister Emelda told me that she had overheard the Abbess and Henry Oliver discussing how they sent hired thugs to kill you. The Abbess was furious that your brother-in-law made a timely intervention. Not only that, but the money she paid to the thug that was killed was stolen! She sent Elias Oliver to retrieve it from the body: he found the body but the purse had gone.'

Bartholomew gritted his teeth, trying to master the fury, mingled with relief, that welled up inside him. If the blacksmith had been given a clearer message to deliver, perhaps some of this might not have happened. Philippa came to stand next to him. 'Hugh Stapleton's son came a few hours ago to tell us that the Abbess was dead,' she said. 'Apparently Henry Oliver became ill in the convent, and passed the sickness to her. We went immediately to hear the truth from Sister Emelda. And the next thing we did was to come see you.'

Bartholomew let out a huge sigh and stared up at the ceiling, feeling the energy drain out of him. He flopped back into the chair, trying to make sense of what he had heard. He looked at Philippa, her face ashen, and at Abigny, eyeing him expectantly. Could he believe their story? It was certainly true that Henry Oliver had the plague, and may well have passed it to his beloved aunt. Henry had said that Wilson believed Bartholomew meant to kill him. And the essence of the story fitted in with the facts as he knew them. But was there something more? Could he trust Abigny's explanation? How could he be certain that they were not somehow tied up with the University business and the murder of his friends? It seemed pertinent to Bartholomew that Abigny fled to the house owned by Hugh Stapleton – the dead Principal of Bene't's Hostel – where he had so recently heard his death discussed by his own family.

Outside, the first streaks of dawn were lightening the sky. Philippa rose to leave.

'It seems there have been misunderstandings,' she said coolly, her gaze moving from Bartholomew to Abigny, 'and I am sorry that people have been hurt. But I am not sorry to be alive, and I doubt that I would be had not Giles acted as he did.' She turned to Abigny. 'I will never forgive you for lying to me, although I appreciate you felt it was in my best interests.'

She swept from the kitchen before Bartholomew could respond. Abigny darted after her, and Bartholomew heard the philosopher's voice echoing across the yard as he tried to reason with her. Bartholomew was overwhelmed with a barrage of emotions – anger, grief, hurt, relief. The whole business had gone far enough. He had spent weeks agonising over Philippa's safety, and had undergone all kinds of mental torment because he did not want to run the risk of endangering his family when he had been desperate to confide in someone. Now, within a few hours, his trust in his family and in Philippa had been shattered. Gradually, as he considered what he had learned, his confusion hardened into cold anger. He stood up abruptly and reached for his cloak. Cynric looked at him in alarm.

'I am going to see Oswald,' he said. 'Perhaps then I might learn the truth.'

'No!' exclaimed Cynric, starting forward. 'Do not act foolishly because a woman has upset you. You know Sir Oswald is involved in all this. What can be gained by a confrontation?'

Bartholomew's face lit in a savage smile that made Cynric step back. 'A confrontation is the only way I will gain any peace. This wretched business has taken my friends, my family, and now it seems it will destroy all I had with Philippa.'

He turned on his heel and stalked out, leaving Cynric uncertain as to what to do.

The gates to Stanmore's business premises were just being opened by a yawning apprentice. He told

Bartholomew no one else was awake, and suggested he wait in the kitchen. Bartholomew ignored him and made for the solar. This large room leading off the hall on the first floor served as Stanmore's office, and contained all his records of sale and purchase, as well as the petty cash. As Bartholomew expected, the door was locked, but he knew the spare key was kept in a hidden pocket in one of the tapestries that lined the wall of the hall. He found it, unlocked the door and entered.

Stanmore was meticulous in his business dealings, and records of all the transactions he had undertaken were stored neatly in numbered scrolls on the shelves. Bartholomew began to sort through them, knocking some onto the floor and piling others onto the table. He was not sure exactly what he was looking for, but he knew Stanmore well enough to know that if he had done business with the University men, there would be a record of it.

'Matt! What are you doing?' Stephen Stanmore stood in the doorway, still wearing his night clothes. Perhaps the apprentice had woken him up and told him Bartholomew was waiting. Bartholomew ignored him, and continued his search. He saw that, two years before, Bene't Hostel had bought a consignment of blankets from Stanmore, who had been paid handsomely. Stephen watched him for a few moments, and then disappeared. When he came back, Oswald Stanmore was with him, followed by a sleepy-eyed Richard, whose drowsiness disappeared in an instant when he saw his uncle ransacking his father's office. They must have declined to make the journey back to Trumpington in the dark and stayed the night with Stephen.

'Matt?' said Stanmore, watching Bartholomew in

bewilderment. 'What do you want? Perhaps I can find it for you?'

Bartholomew waved the document at him. 'I am looking for transactions you have had with the men of Bene't Hostel,' he said tightly. 'I am looking for evidence that shows that you were involved in the murders of my friends and colleagues.'

Bartholomew saw Stephen turn white, while Richard's mouth dropped open. Stanmore took a step towards him. 'Matt! What are you talking about?'

Bartholomew's eyes blazed. 'Enough lies! Where are they, Oswald? Where are the documents that show how much it cost to buy you?'

Stanmore froze in his tracks, and looked unsteadily at Bartholomew as realisation began to dawn on his face. 'I do not know what you mean,' he said, but his voice lacked conviction.

Bartholomew advanced towards him menacingly. 'I thought your rescue was timely two nights ago. You knew, because your Bene't Hostel associates planned it with the Abbess of St Radegund's! Why did you bother, Oswald? Or does your conscience balk at the murder of relatives?'

The door was flung open, and Hugh stood there, brandishing his crossbow. He saw Bartholomew moving threateningly towards Stanmore, saw his face dark with anger, and fired without a moment's hesitation. Simultaneously, Richard screamed and Stanmore lunged forward and knocked into Hugh so that the bolt thudded harmlessly into the ceiling. Hugh started to reload while Bartholomew gazed open-mouthed in shock. He had known Hugh since he was a child, and yet Hugh had not given a second thought to shooting him. Had the plague and the University business changed their lives so much?

'This is not necessary, Hugh,' said Stanmore in an attempt to sound in control. 'Please leave us.'

Hugh looked as if to demur, but Stephen took him roughly by the shoulder and pushed him from the room, closing the door behind him. Richard stared at the quarrel that was embedded, still quivering, in the wooden ceiling. Stanmore lost his usual, confident bearing, and slumped into a chair, where Richard and Stephen came to stand behind him. Bartholomew suddenly noticed the similarity between the three of them. Oswald and Stephen had always been alike, and Richard was beginning to look like a younger version, without the silver beard.

Bartholomew eyed Stanmore sitting in his chair with his head bowed, and moved cautiously to the other side of the room, where he could see all three of them at once.

It was Richard who broke the silence.

'You are wrong,' he said, his voice unsteady. 'My father would never let them harm you. He always made sure they understood that.'

Stanmore seemed to pull himself together. He gestured that Bartholomew should sit next to him. Bartholomew declined, and stood waiting, tense and wary. Stanmore took a deep breath and began to speak, his voice sometimes so low that Bartholomew had to strain to hear it.

'It started about a year ago,' he said. 'You know I maintain my own network of informants about the town? Well, word came to me that there were moves by Oxford scholars to try to undermine the University here, but I assumed that it was merely overpaid scholars with too much time on their hands playing games. Perhaps it started like that, but last year the business seemed to escalate. There were all sorts of rumours of spies, secret messages, and the like. Then people began to die: there were the two lads who had eaten bad oysters, and the Master of King's Hall, to name but three. Anyway, it became clear that there was a plot afoot to strike at the University through some of its most powerful members – the Fellows and Masters of the Colleges.'

He paused and studied his fingernails. Bartholomew waited impatiently.

'Last spring, Burwell came to me and told me that the hostels had set up a secret committee to look into the matter. Deaths were occurring in the Colleges, and there was speculation by the hostels that the Colleges were riddled with spies from Oxford. The hostel group believed that Oxford, by striking at the Colleges, might force prospective benefactors like the Bishop of Norwich and Edmund Gonville to withhold money from Cambridge, because the Colleges appeared to be rank with corruption. The hostel group did not include anyone from the Colleges because they could not be sure who was honest and who was a spy. Are you following me?'

Bartholomew nodded restlessly.

'The hostel group also decided to include some trustworthy citizens from the town. The hostels are poor, unlike the Colleges that have their endowments and support from the King, and it takes money to set up a system of spies. They included me and five others because we conduct a lot of business with the University, and it is in our interests to ensure that the University does not flounder. So, we provided them with money, and they ensured that we had custom. A harmless relationship.'

'It was not harmless for Augustus, Sir John, or Aelfrith,' said Bartholomew coldly.

Stanmore looked up sharply. 'Father Aelfrith? He died of the plague.'

'He was poisoned,' said Bartholomew bluntly.

Stanmore stared at Bartholomew in disbelief. 'I did not know,' he said eventually. 'But I have not finished, Matt. For a while, it seemed as if the hostels' system of spies was having some success, for the deaths ceased. Then, without warning, they started again. Two Fellows from the Hall of Valence Marie died, Sir John committed suicide, and then there were all those rumours about the commoners being killed for his seal. We have been meeting regularly and secretly to try to find out what is happening. In the last few months, most of the trouble has been at Michaelhouse. There is something going on there that none of us understand. Perhaps the entire conspiracy against the University is coming from Michaelhouse.'

He glanced up at Stephen, who nodded agreement. Bartholomew kept his expression neutral, although his mind was teeming. Aelfrith had told him that there were deaths at King's Hall, Clare, and Peterhouse, and then a long gap before those at Valence Marie and Michaelhouse. Bartholomew wondered, since Stanmore's information coincided with Aelfrith's, if Stanmore's motives were pure after all.

'The University buys cloth from me rather than from other merchants,' Stanmore continued. 'In turn, I give them money to help them maintain their network of informants. But I have most certainly not been involved in murder, and I have never done anything that would harm you. That was one of the conditions on which I joined the hostels' group – that if there was anything that would affect you, I would be told first so that I could keep you out of it.'

'And what about the plan to dispose of Alcote?' asked Bartholomew.

Stanmore looked at him in shock. 'How do you know about that?' He put his head back in his hands again. 'Oh, God, no! We have a spy in our midst, too! Do not tell me our group is known of in Michaelhouse. If that is so,' he said, looking up at Bartholomew, 'then all our lives could be in danger.' He turned to Richard. 'Why did I involve you in this?' he cried, suddenly desolate.

Richard met his eyes with a level stare. 'You did not, Father. I was approached independently of you.' He looked at Bartholomew. 'At Oxford, I can listen and learn, and I, too, can send back information that may help to put an end to this silly plot.'

Bartholomew ignored him. 'You did not answer my question,' he said to Stanmore. 'What about the plan ... how was it put? ... to take Alcote out of the equation?'

'It was you!' said Stephen suddenly. 'That noise we heard outside the window. It was you listening!'

Bartholomew continued to hold Stanmore's eyes. 'Well?' he said.

'Not what you think,' he said wearily. 'Our group does not condone murder. There are other ways. A word to the Chancellor to say that women have been seen coming out of his room early in the morning. Or even boys. A rumour that he has been drinking too much, or that his College has become riotous. It is not necessary to kill to remove a man from office. And if Alcote is a spy for Oxford, as our intelligence suggests, then he should not be in a position to run your College anyway, would you not agree?'

'But who are you to judge?' Bartholomew said quietly. He glanced round at the three men, and was suddenly sick of it all. He wanted to make for the door. Richard barred his way. Bartholomew did not want to manhandle him and stopped in his tracks.

'We have done nothing wrong,' Richard said with dignity, 'except to try to sort out this mess, to stop more people from dying. I would do the same again. And I also want you to know that Father has been using the hostels' spies to try to find out about Philippa for you. He has paid a good deal of money and spent a lot of his time following false leads and asking questions on your behalf. We all have. Father and I spent all of the night before last in that seedy King's Head because someone had told us that a traveller would be there who may have seen Abigny on the London Road.'

A memory flashed into Bartholomew's mind. He had thought he had seen Stanmore coming out of the King's Head after he had met his well-wisher by the plague pit. So, his eyes had not deceived him after all.

'I am sorry,' Stanmore said. 'We found the traveller, but he could tell us nothing about Abigny.'

Bartholomew suddenly felt ashamed and bewildered. He had become so confused by all the lies and deceit, and so accustomed to suspecting his colleagues of intrigues, that he had applied the same rules to his family. Perhaps he had also misjudged Philippa and Abigny. Stanmore's neat office was in total disarray, with scrolls scattered everywhere and a crossbow quarrel in the ceiling. Bartholomew sank down onto a stool, uncertain whether his weariness came from the fact that his family's apparent involvement appeared to be harmless after all, or from the battering his senses had taken in the past few hours.

In an unsteady voice, Stanmore said, 'I dread to think what Edith will say if she ever learns that her beloved brother was shot at in her husband's office.'

'Your steward seems somewhat trigger-happy,' said Bartholomew, also shakily, when he recalled how Stanmore's quick reaction had saved his life. 'Remind me never to haggle over cloth prices in your office.'

'It is a dangerous game we play, Matt,' Stanmore said. 'You were attacked by the river; Giles Abigny pursues some strange business of his own under my very roof; and Richard and I were ambushed by footpads the other night. Hugh saved our lives, as he saved yours down by the river, and doubtless the responsibility is beginning to tell on him. He had never, in thirty years of service, been called upon to use his crossbow, and then, in a matter of days, he is required to use it three times.'

Bartholomew looked from Richard to Stanmore, bewildered. 'Ambushed?'

Richard nodded vigorously. 'When we left the King's Head. Four men ambushed us just outside the gates here. Hugh shot one of them and captured another.'

'They were farmers from out Shelford way,' said Stanmore. 'They heard how easy it was to steal in Cambridge with so many dead of the plague, and thought to try it for themselves. Of course, it is easy to steal from the dead and dying, but these four fellows felt that was unethical, and decided to steal from the living instead.'

'The Sheriff should shoot anyone seen out after the curfew,' said Stephen. 'His laxity is the cause of all this villainy.'

'And what if he had seen you out last night as you returned from Bene't's?' retorted Bartholomew. 'I am often called out to patients at night, and would not relish being shot at before I had a chance to explain myself.'

'We would not have been able to explain our business last night, Stephen,' Stanmore agreed. 'We swore an oath of secrecy, and we could hardly tell the watch where we had been and what we had been discussing.'

Stephen acquiesced with a sideways tilt of his head, and there was silence. As if it were a magnet, the gaze of all four lit upon the crossbow bolt.

'What will mother say?' Richard said, echoing his father's words.

'Why would she find out?' asked Bartholomew with a weak smile.

'Well, thank the Lord we have resolved all that!' said Richard heartily, his natural cheerfulness bubbling to the surface again. 'I hated having secrets from you, Uncle Matt. We all wanted to tell you, but we were afraid it might put you in danger, being at Michaelhouse and all. We have tried hard to keep you away from it as much as we could, but I suppose it is your home.'

Bartholomew smiled at him. Richard was at an age where he could make astonishingly adult observations, but could still make things childishly simple. Bartholomew could see that Richard considered that no lasting damage had been done by the scene in his father's study, and was quite happy to continue his life in exactly the same way as before.

'I will tell the cook to make us some breakfast,' he said, marching out of the room.

'You really let him spy in Oxford?' asked Bartholomew, after he had gone.

Stanmore looked askance at him. 'Of course not, Matt. What do you think I am? He is a bright boy, and he is good at listening, but the information he sends us is nothing. It pleases him to think he is helping, and I would not hurt his feelings by telling him otherwise.'

'I believe I owe you an apology,' said Bartholomew.

'And we owe you one. We should have told you. We wanted to, but we honestly believed you would be safer not knowing. I had decided I would tell you everything if you ever asked, but you never mentioned anything to me. I also did not want to distress you by telling you I thought Sir John had been murdered. Especially since there was nothing you could have done, and I was afraid you would start on some investigation of your own that might lead you into danger.'

He laughed softly. 'We involve a child like Richard, and we keep you in the dark. How stupid we must seem to you!'

'I am sorry,' said Bartholomew. He rubbed his hand over his eyes. 'All this intrigue, with the plague on top of it, must be addling my mind, like Colet. I misjudged you.'

The Stanmores dismissed his words with impatient shakes of their heads. Stephen suddenly gave him a hard poke in the chest. 'You lose my best horse, and now you tear our offices apart. Just stay away from my hounds and my falcons,' he said, feigning severity. Bartholomew smiled and followed Stephen down the stairs, where Richard was shouting that breakfast was ready. Hugh slouched in the inglenook in the fireplace, and looked uneasily at Bartholomew. Stanmore whispered in his ear, and he gave Bartholomew a grin before leaving the room.

'What did you say to him?' Bartholomew asked.

'Oh, I just told him you had spent the night sampling Master Wilson's best wine,' said Stanmore.

'You told him I was drunk?' asked Bartholomew incredulously.

Stanmore nodded casually. 'He loathed Wilson, and it will give him great pleasure to think you have been drinking his wine. His collection of fine wines is quite the envy of the town, you know.'

Bartholomew did not, and sat for a while, talking to the Stanmores before they were obliged to attend to their business. Bartholomew fell asleep in the parlour, and only awoke when a clatter of horses' hooves echoed in the yard. He sat up and stretched, scrubbing at his face with his hands, and thinking about what he should do that day. He glanced out of the window, and stared morosely at the raindrops that pattered in the mud. He wondered why he felt so gloomy when Philippa was safe, and his family had exonerated themselves from the evil doings of the University.

But the University was still at the heart of the matter. Despite all that he had learned over the last few hours, there were questions that remained unanswered. Such as who had killed Sir John. He knew why, but he was no further forward in discovering who. Did the same person murder Sir John, poison Aelfrith, and take Augustus's body? Bartholomew rubbed his chin. Whoever killed Sir John for the seal must also have killed Augustus and desecrated his body – also for the seal. But why had Aelfrith spoken Wilson's name on his deathbed? Bartholomew knew that Wilson had not killed Augustus, and if not Augustus, then probably not Sir John.

Could it have been Alcote? He was the spy in their midst, according to the hostels' information. Was he also the murderer? Wilson had said that Alcote had been so drunk that he had not known when Wilson had left their room to search Augustus's room for the seal. But supposing Alcote had not been drunk, and had been pretending? Then he too could have been up and sneaking around the College. But Wilson had said that Augustus had already gone from the room when he got there, and Wilson and Alcote had been together until then.

Of course, Bartholomew thought, all this was assuming everyone was telling the truth. Alcote and Wilson may have been in this together, each lying to protect the other. Bartholomew wondered if Alcote knew of Wilson's nocturnal visits to the Abbess, and whether he approved. He wondered whether he should warn Alcote that his information had been intercepted. Bartholomew had no doubt that the Stanmores believed that Alcote would merely be discredited to remove him from his position of power, but Bartholomew thought of Sir John, Augustus, Paul, Montfitchet, and Aelfrith, and was not so sure.

He thought of Alcote – small, fussy, and petty. Could he have had the strength to drive the knife so deeply into Paul's body? Could he have overpowered Sir John? Bartholomew thought of Wilson hauling himself through the trap-door, and of Michael's strong arm in hauling him to his feet once. Perhaps he spent too much time with the weak and dying, and no longer appreciated the strength of the healthy, strength that could be magnified by fear or desperation.

The more he thought about it, the less he understood. Despite all that he had learned from eavesdropping, Philippa and Abigny, and his confrontation with the Stanmores, he was as much in the dark as ever. Far from easing his mind, his conversation had made him even more concerned for the safety of his family. Abigny had thought nothing of endangering Edith when he was trying to help Philippa. Bartholomew thought about what Stanmore had told him of the Oxford plot, and wondered whether the survival of the University was enough of a reason for men like Yaxley, Stayne, and Burwell to become involved. Stanmore claimed he knew nothing of murder, and Bartholomew believed him. But Yaxley, Burwell, and Stayne might. So was the University's survival sufficient reason for which to commit murder? Wilson intimated on his deathbed that there were those who cared passionately about it, and might give their lives for it. Would they also take lives?

And so he came back to the same question yet again: who was the murderer in Michaelhouse? All the Fellows had alibis for Augustus's death, so was the killer an outsider after all? And where was Michael? Had he fled Cambridge to escape the plague like so many others, or was he, too, lying dead somewhere? Bartholomew stood watching the rain for a while longer, but his thoughts began to repeat themselves. He wondered what he should do next. He was too battered emotionally for a confrontation with Philippa, Abigny, or one of the hostel men, but he still had patients to see. Reluctantly, he left the warmth of Stephen's house, and prepared to trudge back to Michaelhouse.

XI

BARTHOLOMEW HAD BARELY RETURNED TO Michaelhouse when a messenger arrived with a note from Edith saying that she had hurt her arm. She said it was very painful, and asked that he come to tend it as soon as possible. A shout from the commoners' window made him look up.

'Father Jerome is dying,' the Benedictine called, 'and he is asking for you.'

Bartholomew was torn with indecision. Should he go to the dying man or his sister? As if in answer to his prayers, Gray came sauntering through the gates. Bartholomew strode over to him in relief. Gray could go to Edith; a sore arm did not sound too serious.

Gray listened attentively to Bartholomew's instructions, secretly gratified that Bartholomew was allowing him to attend his sister: he was not to try to set the arm if it was broken; he was to make sure that if there was a wound, it was clean before he bound it; he was only to use water that had been taken fresh from the spring; he was to check carefully for other injuries and fever; and he was to give her one measure only – and here Gray was subjected to a stern look from his teacher – of a sleeping draught if she complained of too much pain.

Proudly carrying Bartholomew's bag of medicines, Gray set off at a jaunty pace towards the High Street, while Bartholomew hurried back to the commoners' room.

Father Jerome was indeed dying. He had already been anointed, and his breath was little more than a reedy whisper. Bartholomew was surprised that, after his long and spirited struggle, his end should come so fast. Almost as fast as that of Henry Oliver, who had died several hours before.

William came and Jerome confessed to enticing Montfitchet to drink the wine that had been left in the commoners' room the night of Augustus's murder, even though Monfitchet had said he had drunk enough already. Without Jerome's encouragement to drink, Montfitchet might still be alive. Bartholomew thought it was more likely that Montfitchet would have been dispatched in the same way as Brother Paul, but held his silence. Finally, Jerome laid back, his face serene, and waited for death. He asked if Bartholomew would stay with him until he died. Bartholomew agreed, hoping that Edith was not seriously hurt, and that Gray would not attempt anything beyond his capabilities.

In less than two hours, it was over, and Bartholomew helped the monks to stitch Jerome into a blanket. Bartholomew was torn between grief and impotent anger that he had not been able to do anything other than sit at the sick man's bedside. He laid Jerome gently in the stable next to Henry Oliver, and stalked out of the College towards the church. Everything seemed grey to Bartholomew. The sky was a solid iron-colour, even though it was not raining, and the houses and streets seemed drab and shabby. The town stank, and the mud that formed the street was impregnated with bits of rotting food and human waste. He made his way through it to St Michael's, where he paced around the church for a while, trying to bring his emotions under control.

After a while, he grew calmer and began to think about Philippa. She was safe – something for which he had been hoping desperately ever since Abigny had fled from Edith's house. He wondered again whether he had perhaps been over-hasty the previous night, and whether he should have shown more understanding for Abigny's point of view. But he had been exhausted by his eavesdropping excursion in the cold, and still shocked to learn that the Stanmores had been involved. He wondered where Philippa had gone, and felt a sudden urge to talk with her, and to resolve the questions about her disappearance that still jangled in his mind. The best way to find her would be through her brother, who would be most likely to seek a temporary bed at Bene't's until he deemed it safe to return to his own room.

Bartholomew set off down the High Street, his mind filled with unanswered questions. As he approached Bene't's, he shuddered, thinking about the hours he had spent perched on the window-sill above the filthy yard. He had scarcely finished knocking on the door when it was answered by a student with greasy red hair. The student said that Abigny was out and he did not know when he was likely to return, but offered to let Bartholomew wait. Bartholomew assented reluctantly, not wanting to be inside Bene't's, but his desire to see Philippa was strong. He expected to be shown into the hall, but a glimpse through the half-closed door indicated that the students were engaged in an illicit game of dice, and would not want him peering over their shoulders. He was shown into a small, chilly room on an upper floor, and abandoned with cheerful assurances that Abigny would not be long.

He was beginning to consider leaving Abigny a note asking him to go to Michaelhouse, when he heard the door open and close again. He hurried from the chamber and peered down the stairwell.

But it was not Abigny climbing the stairs, it was Stephen, preceded by Burwell. Bartholomew was on the verge of announcing himself when he heard his name mentioned. He froze, leaning across the handrail, his whole body suddenly inexplicably tense.

'. . . he is too near the truth now,' Stephen was saying, 'and he does not believe in the Oxford plot. I could see in his face he was doubtful.'

'Damn,' said Burwell, pausing to look back at Stephen. 'Now what do we do?'

'Kill him,' came a third voice, oddly familiar to Bartholomew. 'It will not be difficult. Send him another note purporting to be from Edith and have him ambushed on the Trumpington road.'

Heart thumping, Bartholomew ducked back into his chilly chamber as Burwell reached the top of the stairs. There would be no need for an ambush: they could kill him now, in Bene't Hostel. Bartholomew felt his stomach churn and his hands were clammy with sweat as he stood in the semi-darkness. To his infinite relief, the three men entered the room next to his, closing the door firmly behind them. Leaning his sweat-drenched forehead on the cold wall for a moment to calm himself, Bartholomew eased out of his chamber, and slipped along the hallway to listen outside the other door. It was old and sturdily built, and he had to strain to hear what was being said.

'Another death at Michaelhouse might look suspicious,' Stephen was saying.

'On the contrary,' came the voice of the third man, smooth and convincing. 'It might improve our cause immeasurably. We have sown the seeds of an idea into the minds of these gullible people – that Michaelhouse is a rotten apple. What better way to have that idea confirmed than yet another untimely death there? What families will send their sons to Michaelhouse where the Fellows die with such appalling regularity? And then our Oxford plot will seem all the more real, and all the more terrifying.'

Bartholomew fought to control the weak feeling in his knees and tried to bring his jumbled thoughts into order. Had he been right all along in his uncertainty about the Oxford plot? He had never accepted the concept fully, as Aelfrith, Wilson, and even Sir John had done. Could there be a plot within a plot? The group of hostel men who had gone to Stanmore had fed him lies about a plan by Oxford scholars to bring down Cambridge. Or had they? What was Stephen doing there? And who was the third man whose voice was so familiar? It was not Stanmore or Richard. Was it a Fellow from Michaelhouse? He racked his brain, trying to identify the smooth intonation, but it eluded him.

'What about Oswald?' Stephen was saying.

'Now there is a real problem,' came the familiar voice. 'Neville Stayne was foolish to have mentioned Bartholomew in front of Oswald. Now if anything happens to him, it will immediately arouse his suspicions, and all we have worked for will have been for nothing.'

'We cannot allow that, not after all we have done!' Stephen said emphatically. 'Five Michaelhouse men have died for this, and we have carefully nurtured so many rumours. We have invested months in this!'

'Easy,' came the reassuring tones of Burwell. 'We will not allow your brother and his tenacious in-law to interfere in our business. Too much is at stake.'

Stephen appeared to have accepted Burwell's assurance, for he made no further comment. The third man continued to speak, outlining a plot that would have Bartholomew and Stanmore ambushed together. Bartholomew clenched his fists, his instincts screaming at him to throw open the door and choke the life from Stephen's miserable, lying throat. But that would serve no purpose other than to allow Burwell and the third man to kill Bartholomew. And then they would be able to slay Stanmore.

Bartholomew was so preoccupied with his feelings of loathing for Stephen that he almost missed the sound of footsteps coming towards the door. Startled, he bolted back into the other room, wincing as his haste made him careless and he knocked a candle from its holder. The three men did not hear, however, and stood in the doorway conversing in low tones.

'Tonight it is, then,' came the familiar voice. Bartholomew risked opening the door a crack to see his face, but he had already started off down the stairs, and all Bartholomew saw was the hem of a cloak.

Bartholomew itched to be away to warn Stanmore of the impending threat on their lives, but Stephen and Burwell lingered at the top of the stairs, discussing the possibility of increasing hostel rents. Bartholomew silently urged them to conclude their tedious conversation so that he could leave. A dreadful thought occurred to him. Supposing Abigny arrived and found him? Then his death would be immediate, for how could they let him go after what he had heard? And, Bartholomew thought, Abigny must be 'involved, for how could he spend so much time at Bene't's and be unaware of what was happening?

'Here.' Bartholomew heard the tinkle of coins as money was passed from Burwell to Stephen, followed by the rustle of cloth as Stephen secreted them in his cloak.

'This is important to you,' said Burwell suddenly. 'More than just wealth.'

Bartholomew risked looking at them through the crack in the door. He saw Stephen shrug, but noted that he was unable to meet Burwell's eyes. 'I have worked for my brother all my life,' he said, 'but it will not be me who will inherit the business when he dies. It will be Richard. And what then? What of my children? The Death has made it necessary for me to consider alternative sources of income.'

Burwell looked surprised. 'But I understand that young Richard is anxious to follow in his uncle's footsteps and become a leech.'

Stephen faltered for a moment. 'People change,' he said. 'And I do not, cannot, rely on my nephew's charity for the rest of my life. What if I were to be taken by the pestilence? I must leave some funds to safeguard my children. It is no longer viable to rely on relationships and friendships to secure a future. Only this works.' He held a gold coin between his thumb and forefinger and raised it for Burwell to see.

'And you would sacrifice your brother for this?' mused Burwell. In the shadows of his chamber,

Bartholomew closed his eyes and rested his head against the wall.

'Yes,' said Stephen softly, 'because by this time tomorrow I might be in the death pits. What if Oswald and I were to die, and Richard? How could the womenfolk maintain the business? Even if they were allowed to try, and that in itself is unlikely because the Guilds would not permit it, they would be easy prey for all manner of rogues. They would be gutter fodder within the month.' He turned to face Burwell. 'I do not relish what I am about to do, but my future and the future of my children is more important than Oswald.'

Bartholomew listened as their voices faded down the stairs. He was almost beside himself with anxiety. Where had the third man gone while Stephen and Burwell chattered? Was Oswald already in danger? The two men stopped to talk again by the front door before finally taking their leave of each other. Bartholomew forced himself to wait several moments before hurrying down the stairs. Looking down the High Street, he saw Abigny walking towards him. Bartholomew ignored him, and fled in the opposite direction towards Stanmore's shop.

He raced through the gates into Stanmore's yard, his feet skidding as he fought to keep his balance on the slippery mud. He was about to go into the house to seek Stanmore out when he saw him entering the stable with a tall figure that looked very familiar. It was Robert Swynford.

Bartholomew was relieved beyond measure. Good. Now Swynford was back, he could take over the College, and Alcote would be spared being discredited, or worse, at the hands of the hostels. Breathlessly, Bartholomew ran over to the stable, pushed the door open and staggered inside. Stanmore stood just inside the door with his back to Bartholomew, but turned when he crashed in. Bartholomew's stomach flipped over when he saw it was not Stanmore at all, but Stephen. Bartholomew cursed himself for a fool as he realised Stephen was still wearing Oswald's cloak. Stephen and Swynford seemed as disconcerted to see him as Bartholomew was to see Stephen, but Swynford recovered almost immediately and shook Bartholomew by the hand, saying how pleased he was to be back in the town and asking how the College was faring.

Bartholomew, smiling politely, began to back out of the stable, but Stephen was quicker. He made a sudden movement with his hand, and Bartholomew found a long-bladed dagger pointing at him. Bartholomew gazed in panic before trying to bluff it out: Stephen did not know Bartholomew had heard him speaking with Burwell and the other man at Bene't's. 'What are you doing? Where is Oswald?'

'At Trumpington seeing to Edith. Which is where you were supposed to be,' Stephen said coldly. 'Why did you not go?'

'I had to stay with Father Jerome. I sent Gray,' Bartholomew replied, bewildered.

Stephen laughed without humour. 'You have been a problem to us almost every step of the way. I tried hard to keep you out of all this, but you have been remarkably uncooperative!'

Bartholomew tried to move away as the knife waved menacingly close, but he was hemmed in by walls on one side, and Stephen and Swynford on the other.

'I thought we had agreed to be honest with each

other this morning,' Bartholomew said, looking from Swynford to Stephen.

The knife waved again, and Bartholomew felt it catch on his robe. He gazed at Stephen in horror.

'Was it you?' he whispered. 'Was it you who killed Sir John and the others?'

Stephen grinned nastily and looked at Swynford, who eyed Bartholomew impassively.

'We cannot allow him to interfere any more than he has already,' Swynford said. 'There is too much to lose.' Stephen nodded, and Bartholomew wondered whether they meant to kill him there and then in the stable. Stephen obviously thought so, for he took a step towards Bartholomew, tightening his grip on the knife.

'Not here!' snapped Swynford. 'What will your brother say if he finds blood in his stable and the physician missing? Put him downstairs.'

'Downstairs?' said Stephen, lunging at Bartholomew, who had made a slight move to one side. 'Are you serious?'

'There are rooms with stout doors,' said Swynford. 'We must plan his death carefully or the Bishop might discover some streak of courage in his yellow belly and order some kind of enquiry.'

Bartholomew was lost. Swynford the murderer? He looked desperately towards the stable door, but Stephen guessed what was in his mind, and prodded him hard with the knife. 'You should have gone to see Edith,' he said, edging Bartholomew towards the end of the stable. 'Oswald and Richard went, and they will be safely out of the way until our meeting has finished.'

Stephen shoved Bartholomew against the back wall, while Swynford cleared some straw from the floor, and indicated that Bartholomew should pull up the trap-door he had uncovered. Bartholomew did not move. Stephen moved towards him, brandishing the knife threateningly, but Bartholomew still did not move.

'Open it,' said Swynford impatiently.

'Open it yourself,' said Bartholomew. If they did not want Oswald Stanmore to find blood on his stable floor, what did he have to fear from Stephen's knife?

'I do not want to kill you here,' Swynford said, as his cold, hard eyes flashed, 'but I will if necessary. Blood can be cleaned away, and a knife wound can always be hidden with other injuries, as you have probably guessed was the case with Sir John. Now, unless you wish your death to be long and painful, open the door.'

Bartholomew slowly bent to pull open the trap-door. Stanmore had shown him the small storerooms and passages under the stables when he had been a boy. They had been built by a previous merchant to hide goods from the King's tax-collectors. As far as Bartholomew knew, Stanmore had never used the underground rooms, and they had lain empty for years.

The door was made of stone, and was heavy. Bartholomew hauled at it and stood back as he let it fall backwards with a crash that echoed all over the yard. Stephen and Swynford looked at each other.

'That was rash,' said Swynford. 'One more trick like that and I will kill you myself.'

Swynford took a lamp from a shelf, and lit it. He held out a hand for Bartholomew to precede him down the wooden stairs that disappeared into the darkness below. Bartholomew climbed down cautiously, wondering if this were to be his last journey. Swynford followed him, and Stephen brought up the rear.

Bartholomew was prodded along one of the musty corridors and told to open the door to the largest chamber. To his surprise, it was already lit with candles and filled with people. A hard shove in the small of his back sent him stumbling into the middle of the room.

'We have something of a problem, gentlemen,' said Swynford calmly.

'Why did you bring him here?' It was no surprise to Bartholomew to see Burwell and Yaxley there, standing shoulder to shoulder with Neville Stayne from Mary's Hostel. Jocelyn of Ripon, too, was present, his face creased into its perpetual scowl.

'What did you expect us to do?' snapped Stephen. 'Send him home? We did our best to make sure he was out of the way. It is not our fault he failed to answer a call of mercy from his own sister!'

'What do we do with him now?' asked Burwell.

'We will keep him here until I think of a way to get rid of him that cannot be traced back to us,' said Swynford. 'We have done it before, and we can do it again.'

'Then it was you who killed Sir John and poisoned Aelfrith!' exclaimed Bartholomew.

'No. That was me.' It was the voice he had heard at Bene't's but could not identify. Bartholomew spun round and looked into the face of Gregory Colet.

Bartholomew was rendered speechless, and could only gaze dumbly as Colet sauntered round the room and perched himself on the edge of the table. He saw Bartholomew's expression of disbelief, and laughed.

'I was convincing as the drooling fool, wasn't I?' he said, crossing his legs and looking at Bartholomew. 'You were quite a nuisance, though. You would insist on visiting me when I had a great many other things to do. And I had to keep wearing these,' he said, pulling distastefully at his filthy clothes. 'You were supposed to have given up on me and left me to my own devices.'

'Why?' whispered Bartholomew, looking at his friend. 'What brought you to this?'

Swynford snapped his fingers impatiently. 'Enough of this! We have better things to do than to satisfy the curiosity of this meddling fool.'

Bartholomew was bundled out of the room and into a long chamber down the corridor by Yaxley, Jocelyn, and a man he had seen at Garret Hostel. They made him sit down on the floor at the far end and backed out of the room, slamming the door behind them. Bartholomew heard bolts shooting across on the other side. He sat in the darkness trying to comprehend what had happened to him. Stephen and Colet, whom he had believed to be friends, were so deeply embroiled in whatever foul plans were afoot, that they were prepared to kill him for them. And Colet had killed Sir John and Aelfrith!

He leaned his head back against the wall, and tried to think rationally. But it would do him no good to speculate. What he needed to do was to think of a way out. There was no window in the chamber and it was pitch black. Bartholomew felt his way along the walls, searching for other possible exits or even a weapon. There was nothing. He discovered there were several large crates in the room, but other than that the room was empty. He pushed against the door with all his strength, but it was made of thick oak bound with iron, and he knew from his childhood visits to the cellars that there were two huge bolts and a stout bar on the outside.

He sat down again despondently. Unbidden, an image of Philippa came into his mind. Was she involved too? Would she be the one to offer to make his death look like an accident? He leaned back against the wall again and closed his eyes. He could hear raised voices from the room down the corridor. He was glad they were arguing with each other: such an unholy alliance should not be free from dissent and strife. The meeting did not last long, and it was no more than half an hour later when it finished and he could hear people leaving.

The heavy stone trap-door was dropped into place with a hollow thump, and Bartholomew's prison was as dark and silent as the grave. He found it strange at first, and then disconcerting. Michaelhouse was usually noisy during the day, with scholars coming and going, and at night there was always some sound – students debating in low voices, someone's snoring through open window shutters, or footsteps on cobbled paths leading to the kitchens or the latrines. Bartholomew was aware that he could not even hear the bells that called parishioners to church or scholars to lectures and meals. In a sudden panic, he crashed towards the door and hammered on it until his fists were bruised and his voice was hoarse from yelling.

He forced himself to pace out the room in an effort to calm himself, counting the number of steps, and then exploring every unevenness in the earthen walls. In one of the crates he found some bales of cloth and wrapped them round him against the chill of the room. When he felt as though he had mastered his panic, he perched on a chest, tucked his feet up underneath him, and began to review what he had learned. At least he would not go to his death confused and demanding answers.

He knew the men involved: Colet, Burwell, Yaxley, Stayne, Jocelyn, the man from Garret Hostel, Stephen, and Swynford. Swynford was clearly in charge: even Colet had obeyed his instructions. Jocelyn obviously had no intention of founding a grammar school in Ripon, but had been imported by his kinsman into Michaelhouse to help him in his plotting. Stephen's role was probably to encourage Stanmore and the other merchants to maintain their support of the bogus hostels group, while the money they invested was pocketed by Swynford. With a start he remembered Burwell telling him that he had heard of Philippa's flight from Stephen, although there was no reason why they should have known each other well enough to exchange gossip. And Colet? Colet, by his own admission, had been the one to murder Sir John and Aelfrith. Did he also kill Paul and Augustus, and drug the commoners? And how far was the Abbess of St Radegund's involved? While Abigny's story had a ring of truth to it, the blacksmith had been paid to warn Bartholomew in a purse from Bene't Hostel.

Bartholomew wrapped his arms around his body more tightly for warmth, and pressed on with his reasoning. It would probably have been easy to kill Sir John. Cynric had seen him leaving the College after he had eaten dinner with Aelfrith and Bartholomew, probably called to a meeting connected with the alleged Oxford plot. Bartholomew and Stanmore had received false messages from Swynford and his clan, and Colet had probably sent a similar one to Sir John. Sir John had suspected something was amiss, however, because he had taken the precaution of leaving the seal behind. He had gone to the meeting by the mill, a place where few went after dark, where he was murdered by Colet. Swynford had indicated that the fatal wound had been hidden by the injuries sustained when Sir John was crushed by the water-wheel. Colet had been unable to find the seal, and so had exchanged Sir John's clothes for another set – probably the ones he had worn himself as a disguise when he went to meet Sir John with the intention of killing him.

But if the Oxford plot was a sham, why did Colet want the seal? Bartholomew rubbed his arms hard, trying to force some warmth into them. He supposed it was to add credence to the Oxford plot, to show that the business was worth killing over. He wondered what the Oxford scholars thought about the business. He had no doubt that the rumours had reached them, and that they must be as mystified by the whole affair as were the Cambridge men. Perhaps they had even initiated their own investigation, word of which would filter back to Cambridge, where it would be used by Swynford to underline further still that something untoward was happening.

So when did it all start? Bartholomew thought back to what Aelfrith had told him about the uncannily high number of deaths of Fellows in the Colleges last year: Aelfrith's friend who had drowned in the Peterhouse fish-ponds, supposedly in his cups; the Master of King's Hall who was said to have fallen down the stairs; two deaths from food poisoning; and four cases of summer ague. So Aelfrith's assumptions had been correct, and the Fellows had been murdered by Swynford and his associates so they could start a rumour discrediting the Colleges and blaming Oxford for the deaths. Aelfrith's friend had been drowned, the Master of King's Hall hanged, and the others probably poisoned. He thought of the two young men he had attended as they lay dying from bad oysters. He closed his eyes in the darkness as he recalled who had been with him. Colet. Colet had been dining at Clare that night, and it had been Colet who had called Bartholomew so it would seem that he had made every effort to save their lives. Clever Colet, using Bartholomew as a shield so no blame for the deaths should ever fall on him. And of course, who better to have access to subtle poisons, and to know how to use them, than a physician?

These deaths, it seemed, had been sufficient to force the merchants into action. When the so-called hostels group was formed, Stanmore had said that the deaths had stopped. The merchants must have felt that their financial contributions were doing some good. But why kill Sir John and the others if the merchants had fallen for the ploy and were paying their money? Bartholomew rolled the possibilities through his mind. The merchants must have grown complacent, secure in the knowledge that they had done their bit for the town. Perhaps news of the plague took their minds away from the University. The deaths at Michaelhouse would serve to show them that the business was far from over.

But what of Augustus? Who had killed him? It was obvious why: Wilson had told him that Sir John had visited Augustus before attending the fatal meeting that Bartholomew now knew was with Colet, and half the world suspected that the seal had been hidden in his room. The first attempt on Augustus's life had failed, and the killer had returned three nights later. Bartholomew supposed that Augustus's room could hardly be searched with Augustus in it, and he had been murdered to secure his silence. Poor Augustus had given the killer reason to believe he had swallowed the seal. The killer must have hidden in the attic when Alexander came to bring Paul and Augustus some wine. He must have been watching Bartholomew from his hiding place, wondering what he had been doing when he examined Augustus's body and looked under the bed. When Aelfrith had come to keep vigil, it had been an easy thing to knock him on the head and drag Augustus into the attic. Wilson had come then to begin his own search for the seal, and he too had fled to the attic when disturbed, first knocking Bartholomew down the stairs. How crowded the attic had been at that point: the killer, Wilson, and Augustus's body.

But who had actually killed Augustus? And how? There had been no signs of poisoning or violence, but the expression of abject terror on his dead face confirmed that his death had not been natural. All the Fellows and commoners had alibis for the time Augustus had died, so it must have been an outsider. Could it have been Colet again? Bartholomew thought about it, and decided there was no other plausible possibility. Whoever had sliced Augustus apart to investigate his innards had possessed some degree of surgical skill. The incision was crude and brutal, but it would take a physician's knowledge to search the inside of a corpse, and perhaps a physician's nerve and stomach.

So Colet must have determined, with the help of Swynford and perhaps Jocelyn, to search Augustus's room for the elusive seal while Michaelhouse scholars were at Wilson's feast. Poor Brother Paul was too ill to attend, something that Colet had probably not anticipated. So, Paul was dispatched as a precaution against him crying out. Bartholomew screwed up his eyes in thought. When he had gone to check Augustus, he had heard Paul cough, but now he could not be sure that it had not been Colet, standing next to Paul's bed, and imitating the hack of an old man to prevent Bartholomew from checking on him too. But even if Bartholomew had looked at Paul, what then? He would have seen exactly what he had seen the following morning – Paul with his blanket tightly tucked around him hiding his face, the spilled blood, and the knife in his stomach.

Drugged wine was left in the commoners' room, lest they returned from the feast too early. And Jocelyn had told Bartholomew that it had been his idea to drink Wilson's health with the wine he had found on the table. He must have known it was drugged, and also that the others were too drunk to question how the wine had come to be there so conveniently. How Jocelyn must have gloated at the ease with which that part of the plan had gone. Montfitchet did not want to drink because he felt ill, but, luckily for Jocelyn, Father Jerome persuaded him, unwittingly bringing about his death. D'Evéne, who had a bad reaction to wine, had also been persuaded to drink.

Bartholomew stood and began jumping up and down on the spot, trying to force some warmth into his legs. As he considered the information he had, it was easy to see what Colet had done. He must have hidden in Swynford's room. Swynford was the only Fellow to have a room to himself, so no one would have seen Colet once he had slipped into the College in the commotion before the feast. He could then have used the second trap-door in the hallway outside Swynford's room to gain access to the attic, and gone from there to Augustus's room.

But how did Colet know about the doors to the attic? Wilson had said they were a secret passed from Master to Master. Wilson himself did not know about them until he read about them in the box from the Chancellor.

Try as he might, Bartholomew could come up with no reason why Swynford or Colet should know, and he felt his carefully constructed argument begin to crumble. He could not imagine that Sir John would have broken trust by telling Swynford, and Swynford had not been at Michaelhouse long enough to have known the previous Master. Exhausted by his thinking and the events of the day, Bartholomew finally slipped into a restless doze huddled in a corner.

Bartholomew lost track of the time he was kept in his underground tomb. Once the door opened briefly and some bread, salted beef, and watered ale were shoved inside, but it occurred so quickly that by the time Bartholomew realised what had happened, the door had been closed and he was alone again. He sniffed at the food suspiciously, wondering if Colet meant to poison him, but he was hungry and thirsty enough to throw caution to the wind.

He thought about what his death might mean. Colet had said in Bene't Hostel that it would fit nicely into their plan, and would reinforce the notion that something was sadly amiss at Michaelhouse. What of Stanmore then? He would never accept Bartholomew's murder, no matter how cunningly disguised. He would try to seek out Bartholomew's killer, would confront members of the hostel committee, and generally make problems until he, too, was dispatched. And then Richard would guess something untoward had happened, and perhaps start an inexperienced, clumsy investigation of his own. Where would it all end? Would Stanmore's colleagues be suspicious of three accidental deaths in one family? Would they, too, start to look into matters?

Bartholomew recalled with a pang why he had been captured in the first place – trying to warn Stanmore that Stephen and Burwell planned to kill him. He cursed himself again for his ineptitude. He had seen Stephen wearing that cloak before. But the more he thought about it, the more he came to believe that Stanmore would be safe until his own body was found. Stanmore had no reason to be suspicious of Bartholomew's disappearance – since the plague had come he had kept such irregular hours that no one knew for certain where he was – and the hostel group was unlikely to cut off a source of funding in Stanmore before it became absolutely necessary.

He was dozing in the corner when the room was suddenly filled with light that hurt his eyes. There was noise too – shouting and arguing. Through painfully narrowed eyes, Bartholomew saw Swynford outlined in the doorway, flanked by a burly porter from Rudde's Hostel who was armed with a loaded crossbow. Irrelevantly, Bartholomew remembered Colet telling him that the porter was a veteran of the King's wars in France before exchanging a soldier's career for a more sedentary life keeping law and order in one of the University's rowdier establishments.

Swynford held up the torch and the light fell on Bartholomew. Bartholomew squinted, wondering if they had come to murder him. He struggled to his feet, dazed and clumsy, but prepared to sell his life dearly. Swynford glanced at Bartholomew disinterestedly, and gestured to someone outside. Bartholomew had a fleeting glimpse of Brother Michael, firmly in the grasp of Jocelyn and Colet, before he was hurled into the room.

'Company for you, Physician,' said Swynford. 'Now you have someone with whom you can discuss what you think you know of us.' He turned to leave. Bartholomew, savouring the sound of voices after so long alone, was strangely reluctant to let them go. He thought quickly, wondering how he might detain them.

'Gregory!' he called, trying to disentangle himself from Michael who had stumbled into him. 'Did you kill Augustus and Paul?'

'Yes and no,' replied Colet smoothly, ignoring Swynford's look of disapproval. 'I killed Paul. He kept calling out for someone to bring him water. He was a nuisance, and had to be silenced. But I did not kill Augustus, he killed himself.'

'What do you mean?' said Bartholomew. 'There were no marks of violence on him.'

'So that was what you were doing with his body,' said Colet. 'I wondered what you were up to. I had planned to kill the old fool, and had my knife ready to slip between his ribs as he slept. But he was awake when I entered his room, and I saw him swallow something. I was wearing a black cloak and hood, and I really think he believed I was Death coming for him. He just keeled over and died of fright.'

Bartholomew remembered Wilson's dismissive words when Bartholomew told him he had been trying to discover the cause of Augustus's death. 'He probably frightened himself to death with his imagination,' Wilson had said, and he had been exactly right. But, even if no weapon were used, it was still murder to frighten an old man so much that his heart stopped. Colet seemed about to continue, and Bartholomew could tell from the tone of his voice that he was only too happy to talk about the deeds he had done and boast of his own cleverness in evading detection, but Swynford took him roughly by the arm and pulled him away. The door was slammed shut and firmly bolted and barred again from the outside. Once more the room was plunged into pitch blackness. Bartholomew heard Michael groping around in the darkness, and moved across to him. The fat monk was damp with sweat and trembling violently.

'How do you come to be here, Brother?' Bartholomew asked, leading him to a crate, the position of which he knew so well from his wanderings in the dark.

'How do you?' retorted Michael angrily, pulling away from Bartholomew and stumbling against the chest. 'The word is that you have gone to Peterborough on a mercy call from your old mentor the Abbott.'

Bartholomew immediately appreciated that it was a clever ploy on the part of Swynford to say that he had gone to Peterborough. It was very plausible that Bartholomew might answer a call of distress from the monks at the abbey where he had gone to school, and at any time other than while the plague raged in Cambridge, Bartholomew would have gone without hesitation. But Colet and Swynford did not know him as well as they thought.

'I would not leave,' said Bartholomew, 'when there is only me and Robin of Grantchester to help the sick. And the Abbott would know I would not desert my patients, and would never ask me to go.'

Michael gave a grunt. 'I suppose that seems reasonable. But you still have not explained how you come to be here.'

'Oswald!' said Bartholomew suddenly. 'How is he?'

'He was hale and hearty when I saw him this morning. Why do you ask?'

Bartholomew sagged in relief. His reasoning had been correct, and Stanmore was still safe. 'I overheard Colet plotting to kill him,' he said. 'I was coming to warn Oswald when I very stupidly ran into Stephen and Swynford, and I have been here since Wednesday.'

'Which was when you were said to have left for Peterborough,' said Michael. Bartholomew heard a metallic sound as Michael struck a flint, and helped him smash one of the crates so that they could kindle a splinter of wood. The light was feeble, and it gave off eye-watering smoke, but Bartholomew was grateful to be able to see, if only dimly.

Michael put the burning stick near Bartholomew's face and peered at him closely. 'Oh lord, Matt! You look terrible. You should never have involved yourself in all this. I warned you against it.'

'The same could be said for you,' retorted Bartholomew, 'for we both seem to be in the same predicament, regardless of our respective motives.'

'Never mind that,' said Michael. 'We need to get out. Come and help me look.'

'There is no way out,' said Bartholomew. 'Believe me, I have checked.'

He watched as Michael went through the same process that he had; how long before had it been? The monk hammered and heaved at the door, he banged at the ceiling with a stick, and he prodded at the walls. Finally, defeated, he came to sit next to Bartholomew again.

'I have been in Ely with my lord the Bishop,' Michael said. 'We have been going over all the information he has been sent during the past few months about the Oxford plot.'

Bartholomew shook his head. 'There is no plot,' he said.

Michael looked at him curiously. 'We also came to that conclusion,' he said. 'Is there anything to eat here? I missed dinner.'

Bartholomew indicated a few crusts of bread that he had been saving, and a dribble of water in the pitcher. Michael looked at them and shuddered. He continued with his story.

'I arrived back last night,' he said, 'and it is now Friday evening. You probably have no idea of time in this wretched hole.'

'Have you seen Philippa?' Bartholomew interrupted, thinking of the reason he had gone to Bene't's in the first place.

'No,' said Michael, 'but I have seen Giles Abigny, and he told me his tale. He is not mixed up in all this, you know. I imagine that while you were ferreting around for information about Philippa you inadvertently picked up clues about this Oxford business. But I can tell you with absolute certainty that the Abignys are wholly unconnected with it all.'

'Really? Do you not think it a coincidence that all this should happen at the same time, and that Bene't Hostel figures in the Oxford business and is also Giles's second home? And that the Principal of Bene't's – before he died – was Hugh Stapleton, in whose house Giles and Philippa hid?'

'No, I do not,' said Michael. 'I can see why you are suspicious, but the Oxford business has been rolling on for more than a year now. Philippa and Giles only executed their little plot over the past few weeks. And I would be as suspicious of Giles as you are, if I were not sure that Hugh and Cedric Stapleton were also innocent in all this. Hugh suspected something was fermenting in his hostel and contacted the Bishop about it. He sent reports on various comings and goings, and Cedric continued them after Hugh's death. Hugh and Cedric were fickle, frivolous men, like Giles, and quite the wrong kind of people to be recruited by Swynford. They were not even recruited for the bogus hostel group that your brother-in-law was mixed up with.'

'You know about that?' said Bartholomew, startled. 'What else do you know?'

'I was telling you,' said Michael with a superior expression, 'but you interrupted me with your question about Philippa. And while we are on that subject, she has taken your supposed journey to Peterborough very personally. Abigny tells me she fluctuates between anger and sorrow, and will think of nothing else. How can you doubt her, Matt?'

Bartholomew shook his head. So he had been wrong, and Philippa and Abigny were innocent after all. If Philippa were acting as Michael described, then she could not know that he was being kept prisoner in Stephen's dungeon. But it would not matter soon anyway if Swynford's plans came to fruition. Bartholomew's greatest regret would be that he would never have the opportunity to tell Philippa he was sorry, and she might hate him for it.

Michael kindled another piece of wood, coughing as it released a choking grey smoke. 'As I said before, I have been sifting through reports the Bishop has received during the last year in an attempt to understand this, and I believe I now know the truth.'

'Then how did you come to be taken by Swynford?' asked Bartholomew.

'I was rash,' said Michael. 'I reported my findings to the Bishop, and he told me to return to Michaelhouse and do nothing. But there were gaps in my knowledge, and I could not resist trying to fill them in. I undertook to question Burwell, and then Stayne. They obviously grew suspicious, and I received a message from Stanmore asking me to visit him. I went, and found not Stanmore, but his younger brother. I brazened it out, asking guileless questions and pretending to be convinced of the reality of the Oxford plot, but it was all to no avail. Colet and Swynford appeared out of nowhere, and I was hauled down here.'

'A note,' said Bartholomew, bitterly. 'How many times have Colet and Swynford used that device? They sent such a note to Sir John, enticing him to the meeting at which he was killed; they sent one to me saying I was needed by a patient, after which I was attacked; and they sent one to Oswald and me purporting to be from Edith, intending to get us out of the way so Swynford could have his meeting here.'

'It seems we are in a fix, Matt,' said Michael, his flabby face serious. 'Will they kill us?'

'They will try,' Bartholomew replied.

Michael gave him a weak smile. 'It will do them no good. The Bishop knows everything I do, except your role in all this, and Abigny's innocence, of which I have only recently learned.'

'What of rescue?' asked Bartholomew hopefully. 'Did you tell anyone where you were going?'

Michael smiled ruefully. 'The note purporting to be from Oswald asked me to keep our meeting a secret.'

'But what of the Bishop? Will he not grow suspicious of your disappearance?'

'Undoubtedly. But unless one of the hostel cabal reveals where we are, he is unlikely to stumble on us by accident.'

Bartholomew thought about the cunningly concealed entrance in the stable and concurred. Stanmore and Richard knew about the chambers, but they would never imagine that Stephen had used them to imprison him. They might not visit the underground storerooms for years to come.

'What about you?' asked Michael. 'Will Cynric wonder about your sudden disappearance?'

'I think I would have been rescued by now if he had,' said Bartholomew. 'And he probably thinks I have gone to Peterborough, as you did. Even if he is suspicious, he will blame Oswald, not Stephen.'

They were silent for a while, each wrapped in his own thoughts. Michael's piece of wood crackled and the flame went out.

'I thought you were involved in all this,' said Michael distantly, kindling another piece of wood. 'You talked to Aelfrith in the orchard, but would not tell me what you had discussed. You spent ages with Augustus after he died, and I thought you were looking for the seal. Wilson singled you out to talk to on his deathbed. You had no alibi for when Augustus and Paul were murdered. And how was I to know that you had not hurled yourself down the stairs that night to confound us? You also searched my room, and I found you reading my note to the Bishop.'

'The Bishop!' said Bartholomew. So that was to

whom Michael was writing. He reached forward to grab Michael's arm. 'I did not search your room. The note just fell on the floor when I opened the door to look for you.'

'Well,' said Michael, 'there were occasions when I was convinced you were the killer, while other times I was uncertain. I took a terrible risk for you when I agreed not to tell anyone you had read my note. I suppose I could not bring myself to think that you would harm Augustus and Paul, and I also believe you are a good physician and would not make mistakes about the quantity of whatever foul potion was used to drug the commoners. But even more, I know how close a friend Sir John was to you, and could not suppose that you would ever have done anything to harm him.'

'When I read the note I thought you might be the murderer,' said Bartholomew.

'Me?' said Michael aghast. 'On what grounds? I have never done anything the least bit suspicious!'

'You were one of the first to arrive when the initial attempt was made on Augustus's life. Aelfrith, who was poisoned, died in your room. And you acted most strangely over Augustus's corpse. You refused even to look at it.'

'Ah, yes,' said Michael, struggling to light another piece of wood. 'Augustus.' He shook his head sadly. Bartholomew waited for him to continue.

'He was murdered, you know, for Sir John's seal. You know about the seal?' Bartholomew nodded, and Michael continued. 'Before he died, Augustus claimed that devils were in his room. Remember? Well, before all that happened, he had told me that someone would try to kill him. He kept me up a long time that night with his rantings. I thought I had calmed him down, and went off to the kitchen for something to eat. Within a few minutes, he started screaming again. I ran to his room where you and I broke the door down together. It was full of smoke, and he was insane with fear. I realised that I was not the only person to have worked out that Augustus's room was the only place Sir John could have hidden the seal before he died. You arrived just after me.'

Bartholomew remembered well. He had wondered at the time how Michael had managed to reach Augustus's room before him. That he had been raiding the kitchen made perfect sense.

'You offered to stay with Augustus for the rest of the night, and so I knew he would be safe if anyone really had been trying to kill him in order to search for the seal. I kept a close eye on him for the next couple of days, and went to check on him before Wilson's installation dinner. I was absolutely horrified when I heard he had been killed during the feast, especially after one attempt on the poor man had already been made. Anyway, I had never seen a murdered man before, and I am afraid it unnerved me more than I would have thought. I was afraid to look into his face, because I have heard that a picture of the murderer is always burned into the victim's eyes. I have also heard that a victim's body bleeds in the presence of his murderer, and I felt that Augustus might bleed for me because I was unable to save him when I knew his life was in danger.'

He stopped, and looked at Bartholomew with a weak smile. 'All silly nonsense, of course, and I would not usually stoop to such superstition. But the whole of that day was unreal – Wilson's endless ceremonies, all that wine, town people in the College, the riot, the

Oliver brothers trying to lock you out, and then Augustus dead. It was all too much. I was deeply shocked, because I had seen him alive such a short time before. Does this explain my behaviour to you?'

Bartholomew shrugged. 'I suppose so, but you do not usually panic so easily.'

'Well, there was one other thing too,' he said. 'The Bishop spoke to me that day, and said that he wanted me to act as his agent in Michaelhouse. He told me about the deaths of Fellows in other Colleges, and said that Aelfrith was already acting as his spy. He said he wanted me to act totally independently of Aelfrith, so that if one line of communication were to fail, the other would remain intact. He gave me until the following day to decide whether I would take on the task. When Augustus died, I realised exactly what he was asking me to embroil myself in, and, frankly, it terrified me. But the next day, I spoke to the Bishop, and told him I would do it – for the College and for the University.'

He paused again. 'I have been acting on behalf of the Bishop ever since. I tried to warn you to keep out of it, Matt. I thought you did not realise what you might get into, and Augustus's murder showed me that it was no longer a silly game played by bored scholars with active minds and too much free time, but something far more deadly.'

Michael's lighted stick crackled and popped, and Bartholomew realised again how wrong he had been. He stood up, and stretched carefully. He sat again, and made up his mind. He began to tell Michael everything he knew and had surmised.

XII

ICHAEL GAVE UP LIGHTING HIS FRAG-
ments of wood, and most of Bartholomew's
tale was delivered in darkness. That he had
been alone and in darkness for so long occasionally made
him wonder whether Michael was really there at all, and
several times he reached out to touch him, or asked
him a needless question just to hear his voice. Michael
added scraps of his own evidence here and there, and by
the time he had finished, Bartholomew felt at last that
he understood most of what had happened. He heard
Michael give a sigh as his narrative was completed.

'The Colleges will be powerful forces in the University, Matt. There are five of them now, and there
are plans to found another two next year. That will
mean there will be seven institutions with Fellows and
their own property. The Fellows will be more secure in
their futures than the teachers in the hostels, and the
longer they remain at the Colleges, the more power
they will accrue. The hostels own no property, and are
therefore inherently unstable, and, in time, the Colleges
will take their power. As it is, the most powerful men in
the University now are Fellows of the Colleges, not men
from the hostels. Swynford must have determined that

the advance of the Colleges had to be stopped, because in time, they will become so powerful that they will become independent of the University, and they will crush the hostels.'

'But why?' said Bartholomew. 'Swynford is a Fellow with a powerful voice in the University, and he is now the Master of Michaelhouse.'

'The Bishop's records show that he owns many of the buildings that are used as hostels,' said Michael. 'The rents he charges have made him a rich man. He would not wish to lose this source of income.'

'Is that it?' asked Bartholomew incredulously. 'Is it about money? Like Stephen?'

Bartholomew heard Michael laugh softly in the dark. 'Matt! Have you spent your life asleep? Do you not know that nearly all crime in this country is committed with the intention to increase personal wealth? Of course, there is good old-fashioned lust, too; that often plays a part. But the overriding human emotion is greed.'

They sat in silence for a while, before Bartholomew started talking again, more to hear Michael's voice than to resume their discussion. 'I wonder why Swynford wants so much money. It is almost as if he is aiming for something specific.'

'Perhaps he is,' said Michael. 'Another hostel perhaps? A position?'

'A position?' queried Bartholomew. 'What sort of position would he need to buy?'

Michael shrugged. 'I do not know. Mayor? A position at court? A See?'

'A See?' exclaimed Bartholomew. 'You cannot pay to become a bishop!'

'Oh, but you can, Matt. Not direct payment perhaps,

but a sum of money forwarded to the King's coffers might ensure a position of some kind.' He suddenly slammed his first into his open palm. 'Of course! That is it! The Bishop of Lincoln grows old, and Swynford asked our Bishop about who might be next in line to succeed him at Wilson's feast. I heard him! Swynford was saving to become a bishop! And what a bishop he would make: he is learned, of noble birth, and highly respectable.'

'Respectable indeed,' said Bartholomew. 'Murder, corruption, fraud. All highly respectable talents.'

Michael said nothing, but Bartholomew could hear him shifting around, trying to get comfortable on his crate.

'So, let us summarise what we have reasoned,' said Michael. 'About a year ago Swynford decided to crush the Colleges to strengthen the hostels. He, and a band of selected helpers, put about rumours to blame it all on Oxford, and even killed Fellows in King's Hall, Peterhouse, and Clare to make it appear serious. Merchants were persuaded to give money on the grounds that were the University to collapse, they would lose a good deal of trade. Sir John unwittingly aided them in this because they took advantage of a spy system that had nothing to do with the Universities, but one in which Sir John played a minor role for the King. When Sir John became suspicious, he was murdered, and his death was made to look like suicide. Michaelhouse was discredited because his body was discovered . . . not wearing his own clothes.'

'Shortly afterwards, Colet and Swynford decided to add credence to the plot by undertaking to look for Sir John's seal. They killed Augustus and Paul, and Montfitchet died too. They failed to find the seal, even after tearing out Augustus's entrails. Wilson sneaked off into the night to search for it too, acting on behalf of the Chancellor, but he also failed. The damage was done to Michaelhouse, even though the seal remained hidden. The Bishop, realising that there was more at stake than Michaelhouse's reputation, forced the Fellows to deny the truth. Perhaps Colet and his friends realised they had gone far enough, or perhaps they were more concerned with the approaching Death, for they made no further attempts to find the seal. They poisoned Aelfrith when his enquiries brought him too close to the truth.'

'Of course!' exclaimed Bartholomew, leaping to his feet and pacing in the darkness. 'William, without knowing what he said, told me why Aelfrith was killed a long time ago, but I did not see it. He told me that before his death Aelfrith had seemed depressed because he had heard the deathbed confession of the Principal of All Saints' Hostel. That Principal must have been involved too! News must have got out that he had made a confession, and Aelfrith was killed in case he had been told something sensitive.'

'Aelfrith believed in the seal of confession,' said Michael. 'Even if the dying Principal had told him everything, Aelfrith would never have revealed it to another.'

'Stephen is prepared to kill his own brother for this,' said Bartholomew, 'and the others seem equally fanatical. Killing a friar as a safeguard would be nothing to them.'

'Sadly, I suspect you are right,' said Michael. 'But, to continue. Wilson told you about the attic, perhaps so that you might try to see justice done for the poor victims whose deaths he and the Bishop had ensured went unavenged. It was no secret Wilson spoke to you at length on his deathbed, and it would not take a genius to suppose that Wilson might have told you of the attic, where Augustus's body still lay. I imagine either Colet or Jocelyn carried the body to the stables, hoping that it would be taken away unnoticed by the plague cart.'

He paused again and sniffed. 'Lord, it is as cold as the grave in here.'

'Apt description,' muttered Bartholomew, his mind still on the web of intrigue he and Michael were unravelling.

Michael continued. 'The pestilence must have brought about the deaths of some of those involved in this affair – like the Principal of All Saints'. I suppose now is a good time to strike more blows at the Colleges, while we are weakened and unsuspecting. They have made moves against Alcote, an attack on whom will not reflect badly on Swynford, and might even enhance his reputation – he will be seen now as an honourable man returning from protecting his female kinsfolk in a vain, but noble attempt to save the College from corruption. You and I will also provide them with a godsent opportunity to kill us in a way that will bring Michaelhouse into further disrepute. What a fool I was to try to question them!'

'Do you think all the hostels are involved in this?' Bartholomew asked after a pause.

Michael sucked in his breath. 'I doubt they could have operated so efficiently and secretly for such a long time if all the hostels were implicated. The Bishop's records indicate that certain people are definitely involved: John Rede, Principal of Tunstede Hostel, but he is dead of the plague; Jocelyn and Swynford from Michaelhouse; Burwell and Yaxley from Bene't's; Stayne from Mary's; the Principals of Martin's and All Saints' Hostels, although the plague took them, too; Colet from Rudde's; and Caxton and Greene from Garret Hostel, but Greene is dead.'

Bartholomew leaned against the damp wall and folded his arms. 'And do you know which of the merchants were involved?'

'None,' said Michael. 'Only hostel men were allowed in on the real plot. But the merchants were an essential component in Swynford's plan. It would not have worked without them. He would not wish to spend his own money, nor that of his colleagues, on fighting the Colleges. The merchants contributed generously, thinking that they were saving the University from being crushed by Oxford, when the reality was that their money was used to undermine the Colleges.'

Lies, counter-lies, and more lies, thought Bartholomew. Good men had lost their lives because of this wretched business.

'What about the need to protect both Universities so that there will be two places in which to train new priests and clerics when we recover from the effects of the plague?' he asked.

'I am sure they endorse it fully. The more priests and clerics that can be encouraged to come to the University the better. They will live in the hostels Swynford owns, and their rents will swell his coffers. The Bishop believes that half our clergy will perish from the Death, and that the country will desperately need to train more if we are to retain our social order. Without priests among the people, there will soon be insurrection and bloodshed. Swynford's hostels will be offering England a vital service.'

At least Stanmore's money had not totally been squandered, thought Bartholomew, if it could help to achieve some degree of social stability once the plague had burned itself out.

'Why do you think Colet became involved?' asked Michael. 'I always understood he had a glorious future as a physician – far more so than you because he is less controversial.'

'I do not know. Perhaps because of the pestilence? First, a good many of his wealthy patients were likely to die, thus reducing his income. Second, the plague is not a good disease for physicians: the risk of infection is great, and the chances of success are low. We discussed it *ad nauseam* before it came, and he knew as well as I that physicians were likely to become social outcasts – shunned by people who were uninfected, and treated with scorn by those that were because we would be unable to cure them. His leeching for toothaches and hangovers would not stand him in good stead with the Death. He was probably taking precautions against an uncertain future, like Stephen.'

Bartholomew gazed into the darkness and thought about Colet. He had stopped treating his patients when Bartholomew became ill and Roper had died. But about the same time, the wealthy merchant Per Goldam had died, and he had been Colet's richest patient. Colet must have decided that helping Bartholomew in the slums and with the plague pits was not for him. What better way to escape from constant demands from people for help than to feign madness? In the church, he would be relatively safe from plague-bearing people, and would be in a place where his associates could easily drop in to see him. His ramblings around the churches and his trips for blackberries were merely excuses to go about his business.

Bartholomew was overcome with disgust. He had liked Colet. What an appalling judge of character he must be to misjudge Philippa, Stanmore, and Michael, and not to suspect Colet. There was nothing more to be said, and each became engrossed in his own thoughts.

Although time dragged in the dark room, it did not seem long before they heard the sound of the trap-door being opened again. Bartholomew heard Michael draw in his breath sharply, thinking, like himself, that their executioners might be coming. There was a crash as Michael, backing away, knocked a chest over. Bartholomew stationed himself near the door. The bolts were drawn back with agonising slowness, and Bartholomew felt sweat breaking out at the base of his neck.

The door swung open slowly, and light slanted into the room, dazzling him.

'Stand back,' said Colet. 'Master Jocelyn carries his crossbow and will not hesitate to use it if you attempt anything foolish.'

Slowly Bartholomew backed away, his eyes narrowed against what seemed like blinding light. He saw Jocelyn standing beyond the door, his crossbow aimed at Bartholomew's chest. The Rudde's porter was there too, holding a drawn sword. Colet was obviously taking no chances with his two prisoners.

'What do you want?' said Bartholomew with more bravado than he felt.

'You are an ingrate, Matt,' said Colet, and Bartholomew wondered why he had never detected the unpleasant smoothness in his friend's voice before. 'I have come to bring you food and wine. I thought you must be hungry by now, and your fat friend is always ravenous.'

He nodded his head, and the porter slid a tray into the room with his foot. On it there was bread, wizened apples, and something covered with a cloth. Red wine sloshed over the rim of the jug as the tray moved.

'So,' said Colet. 'You two must have had quite a conversation down here.'

When Bartholomew and Michael did not answer, Colet continued, his voice gloating, goading. 'So now you understand everything? What we have been doing, and why?'

Again, Bartholomew and Michael did not reply, and Colet's composure slipped a little. 'What? No questions? Surely we have not been so careless as to leave nothing that you have been unable to work out?'

Michael affected a nonchalant pose on the crate he had knocked over. 'Doctor Bartholomew lost his taste for questions when the answers proved so unpleasant,' he said. 'But I confess there are two things that puzzle me still. First, how did you kill Aelfrith? We know why and that you used poison. But we remain uncertain as to how you made him believe it was Wilson.'

'I do not wish to know,' said Bartholomew in disgust. 'That you murdered a good man, and that you used so low a weapon as poison to do it is more than enough for me.'

'Oh, surely not?' said Colet, laughing. 'What happened to your spirit of learning and discovery? I never thought that you, of all people, would refuse to learn after all our debates and experiments together.'

'We were different men then,' said Bartholomew, with undisguised loathing.

'Perhaps,' mused Colet. 'But Brother Michael asked me a question, and I feel duty-bound to answer it. Aelfrith was coming too close to the truth. I heard from the monks in St Botolph's that Aelfrith heard Wilson's confession every Friday. So, I sent Aelfrith a small bottle of mead with a signed message from Wilson saying he appreciated Aelfrith's understanding, and he should drink the mead to help him relax after his hard work in the town. The message, of course, was written by me, and the mead was poisoned. I retrieved the rest of the bottle the night he died, lest you should find it.'

He smiled absently. 'I was almost caught. The poison was slower-acting than I had imagined, and Aelfrith was still alive and staggering around when I came for the bottle. You, Brother, tried to take him back to his room, and I only just managed to lock the door before you came. You took Aelfrith elsewhere to die, but it was a narrow escape for me.'

Bartholomew remembered Michael telling him that Aelfrith's door had been locked, and recalled assuming Aelfrith's room-mates had shut it because they did not want a plague victim in the chamber with them. But Colet had been hiding there, with the murder weapon in his hands.

'So you kill by stealth,' said Bartholomew bitterly. 'As I am sure you did with Sir John, for you would never have overpowered him in a fair fight.'

'True enough,' said Colet, 'and I most certainly was not prepared to try. I had help that night. Masters Yaxley and Burwell accompanied me.'

'Why did you go to so much trouble for the seal?'

asked Michael. 'It would have been no use to you at all after the death of Sir John.'

'You are right, the seal is nothing,' said Colet. 'Once it was known by the King's spies that Sir John was dead, there would have been no value in his seal, and it could never have been used for the same purpose again. But it suited our plans to make believe that there were men desperate to retrieve the seal. If people thought the seal was important enough to kill for, they would also think that the information Sir John received from his spy – our messages – was of great significance.'

'Was it you or Swynford that tried to burn poor, sick Augustus in the middle of the night?' asked Michael.

'Neither, actually. We did not want to set Augustus's room on fire or burn him in his bed. That would have drawn attention to the room we were trying to search. Our notion was to make the fire smoke to asphyxiate him.'

'I see,' said Bartholomew sarcastically. 'And how could you possibly have made such a mess of this simple operation?'

Colet eyed Bartholomew malevolently for a moment. 'Jocelyn thought the fire was taking too long, and lit another under the bed to speed the process along. Instead of smoke, there were flames and the old man woke.' He looked in disgust at Jocelyn, who curled his lip in disdain at Colet. 'Fortunately he was too confused to identify Jocelyn, who managed to put out the fire and escape by the trap-door before you two came and broke down the door. When I returned to make amends for his bungling the night of the feast, I was careful to remove all evidence that there was ever a fire.'

Bartholomew recalled the cinders that had clung to his gown when he lay on the floor to retrieve the lid of

SUSANNA GREGORY

the bottle Michael dropped. When he had looked for
them the morning after, they had gone.

'You disgust me, Colet,' said Bartholomew softly.
'You are a physician, sworn to heal. Even if you did not
use a weapon, it is still murder to frighten an old man
to death.'

'You almost caught me, actually,' said Colet, and
Bartholomew could see that the entire affair was little
more than an intellectual game for him. 'I let myself out
of the other trap-door and hid in Swynford's room, since
I was uncertain whether you would know about the one
in Augustus's room, and you might have come looking
for me in the attic. But you did not and so I climbed
back into the attic ready to continue my search.'

Bartholomew had a sudden, sharp memory of the
shadow flitting across the door as he walked down the
stairs after he had examined Augustus's body. If only he
had looked harder, this whole thing may have ended
there and then.

Colet smiled. 'It was no simple matter lifting a body
through the trap-door. But even so, I had an easier time
of it than when that fat slug Wilson tried to heave his
bulk into the attic. You must have rattled him when
you found him prising up Augustus's floorboards, Matt,
because had he been himself, he would certainly have
spotted the blood on the floor and one of Augustus's
legs sticking out of the passageway. But he did not, and
we both escaped.'

'Not only did you break your oath to heal, but you desecrated the dead too,' Bartholomew said accusingly.

'That was most disagreeable,' Colet agreed, 'but it
had to be done. I was never as adept at surgery as you,
Matt, and I am afraid I made rather a poor job of it. I

told you I saw Augustus swallow something. What else could it have been but the seal? After I had completed my inspection of his innards, I wrapped him up and hid him in the blocked-off passageway.'

'I take it you found nothing,' said Bartholomew.

'On the contrary,' said Colet. 'I found this.' He held up an object for Bartholomew to see. There, glittering in the light from the candle was Colet's golden lion. Bartholomew felt sick. Colet must be an ill man indeed to have ripped out a man's entrails and to have kept a pathetic ornament he had discovered there.

'And this brings me to the second point I do not understand,' said Michael. 'How did you know about the trap-doors? They were meant to be a secret passed from Master to Master.'

'Poor, sick Augustus told Swynford about them. Augustus was Master of Michaelhouse once, if you remember,' said Colet. 'They made things easier, but we would have managed without them. We would have just planned differently.' He took the golden lion from his pocket and began to twist it through his fingers. He started suddenly as voices could be heard down the hallway. Swynford. Bartholomew recalled his disapproval of Colet speaking to him before, and was not surprised when Colet left abruptly.

In the darkness, Bartholomew heard Michael move towards the food that Colet had brought. 'I wonder what poison they have used,' he mused, smiling grimly as he heard Michael drop the plate.

'Damn you, Matt,' Michael grumbled. 'Do we starve here or die of poison?'

'The choice is probably yours, Brother,' replied Bartholomew.

SUSANNA GREGORY

Once again, time began to drag. Bartholomew and
Michael talked more about what Colet had told them,
but he had revealed little they did not already know,
merely answering how Aelfrith had come to believe
Wilson had killed him, and how Swynford had known
about the trap-door in Augustus's room. Bartholomew
presumed that Stanmore's underground rooms were
used for secret meetings only at night, when Oswald
Stanmore went home to Trumpington, and Stephen
had the premises to himself.

When he heard the scratching noise outside the
door, he first assumed it was his imagination, or Michael
fidgeting in the darkness. But the sound persisted, and
Bartholomew thought he could see the merest glimmer
of light under the door. So, this is it, he thought. Swynford
had conceived another diabolical plan, and he and
Michael would be murdered just like the others who
had threatened his objectives. He shook Michael awake,
cautioning him to silence with a hand over his mouth.

The door swung open very slowly, and two figures
slipped in, one shielding the light from the stub of a
candle with his hand. The other closed the door behind
them and they stood peering into the gloom.

'Michael! Matt!' came an urgent whisper.

Bartholomew was bracing himself to jump at one of
the figures to see if he could overpower him when the
candle flared and he found himself looking at Abigny,
his youthful face tense and anxious.

'Thank God! You are unharmed!' he whispered,
breaking into a smile, and clapping Bartholomew on
the back.

'Giles!' exclaimed Bartholomew in amazement.
'How . . .?'

380

'Questions later,' said the philosopher. 'Come.'

The other figure at the door gestured urgently, and Abigny led the way out of the chamber and along the passageway. They quickly climbed the wooden stairs and Abignyclosedthetrap-doorcarefully,coveringitwithstraw. The other person snuffed out the candle, leaving them in darkness and together they set off for the door at the far end of the stables.

They froze at the sound of someone in the yard. Hastily, Abigny bundled them into a stall with an ancient piebald nag, hoping that it would not give them away. Bartholomew saw Stephen come into the stable with a lamp, while outside, they could hear some of the men who worked for him chattering and laughing. Stephen set the lamp down, and went to a splendid black gelding, which he patted and caressed lovingly. Oswald had bought Stephen the horse to compensate for the one Abigny had stolen.

Bartholomew's legs were like jelly and, judging from Michael's shaking next to him, the fat monk felt the same. To his horror, Michael give a muffled sneeze. The straw! Michael frequently complained that straw made him cough. Bartholomew pinched Michael's nose to stop him from sneezing again. Stephen ceased crooning to the horse, and looked up.

'Who is there?' he asked. He picked up the lamp and shone it down the building. Next to them, the piebald horse stirred restlessly, its hooves rustling in the dry straw. Stephen tutted as he heard it, and went back to the black horse. He gave it one last pat on the nose, and left, carefully shutting the stable door behind him. Bartholomew heard the voices of Stephen and his men recede as they crossed the yard to the house.

'We must leave here as soon as we can,' said Abigny. 'Cynric is keeping watch outside.'

He opened the door a crack and peered out. 'They have gone into the house,' he whispered, 'and the candles are out. Come on.'

The night was clear, and the yard was lit brightly by the moon. Bartholomew hoped Stephen's dogs would not begin to bark, for anyone looking out of the windows of the house would surely see them in the yard. Cynric appeared out of nothing, and beckoned them to follow, moving like a cat through the shadows. To Bartholomew, he, Abigny, and Michael sounded like a herd of stampeding pigs compared to Cynric, and he kept glancing at the house, certain that he would see someone looking out because of the noise.

Finally, they reached the huge gates, where the smaller person stepped forward with a key to unlock the wicket gate. Cynric pushed it open, and all five of them slipped outside.

In the moonlight, Bartholomew saw the face of the small person as she turned to go back inside.

'Rachel Atkin!' he said in surprise.

'Shhh!' she said, glancing fearfully about her. 'Go now, quickly. I must get back to bed before anyone realises I am missing.'

'You were my well-wisher!' he said, light dawning suddenly. 'You must have overheard Stephen talking . . .'

She put her hand over his mouth. 'Go,' she said again. 'Master Abigny will explain.'

Before he could say anything else, she had slipped back through the wicket gate, and they could hear it being locked from the inside.

Cynric led the way through the dark streets and

into Michaelhouse, where Bartholomew sank gratefully into Agatha's chair.

Michael sat heavily on a stool next to him, wiping the sweat from his eyes, and snatched the bottle that Cynric was handing to Bartholomew.

'My need is greater than yours, Physician,' he said, downing a good quarter of the bottle in the first gulp.

Bartholomew sat back in the chair and asked Cynric for some water. Although he wanted to drain it in a single draught, he sipped it slowly, because he knew that the cold water would be likely to give him stomach cramps after so long without drinking.

He leaned forward and touched Abigny on the hand. 'Thank you,' he said. 'And Cynric, too. How did you know?'

Cynric closed the shutters on the windows, and sat near Bartholomew so he could poke at the fire. Michael took another hearty swig from his bottle – another of Master Wilson's, Bartholomew noted.

'Your friend told us,' said Abigny. 'Rachel.'

Bartholomew was amazed. Once he had arranged for Rachel to work for Stephen, he had not given her another thought. He had seen her around Stephen's house several times, and had been told that she was settling in well, but that was all.

Cynric took up the tale. 'She was grateful for what you did for her when her son was killed – she could not have paid for a decent funeral for him, and you saw to it, as well as finding her work and a place to live. She is a silent sort, who people come not to notice after a while.' Cynric paused, and Bartholomew wondered whether Cynric saw some of himself in Rachel Atkin.

'She overheard conversations between the Stanmores

organising a secret meeting, and she knew you were seeking information about Philippa. She heard them mention your name and so thought you might learn something to your advantage if you eavesdropped. She knew what the back of Bene't Hostel looked like because she and her son were sometimes hired to clean the yard when the smell got too unbearable. You know the rest: we met her by the plague pits and we listened in on the meeting.'

Abigny continued. 'Cynric grew worried about you when you did not return Wednesday night. He was still concerned that the Stanmores might be involved and felt that, in the light of what he had been through with you the night before, you would not have gone to Peterborough without telling him. He did the only thing he could think of and waylaid Mistress Atkin on her way to the market. She already knew that meetings took place in the rooms under the stables when Oswald was away, and so they considered it a possibility that you were being kept there.'

Cynric interrupted. 'I also saw Michael given a note on Thursday, and I followed him to Stanmore's business premises. He also did not return.'

'Cynric, in the absence of anyone else he could trust, asked me to help,' concluded Abigny.

'How long were we in that wretched place anyway?' said Bartholomew, leaning down to rub some warmth into his cold feet.

'It is now almost Saturday morning. When Gray came back with your brother-in-law and said that they had been sent on a wild goose chase regarding Edith's supposed sore arm, Cynric guessed that the hostel men had been up to something.'

Abigny was full of questions, and despite his tiredness, Bartholomew felt that he and Cynric were owed answers. Michael began the long, elaborate explanation that had Bartholomew dozing in the warmth of the fire, and Abigny and Cynric mesmerised. Eventually, Michael rose, and Bartholomew started awake.

'I am afraid we are going to have to go through all this again,' he said. 'The Bishop will arrive this morning.'

Bartholomew groaned. 'We have been talking for days.'

Michael waved a fat white finger at him. 'Which is far preferable to what Swynford and Colet had in mind for you.'

There was no disputing that Michael was right. They stood outside the kitchen for a while, Bartholomew enjoying the clear, crisp smell of night, and looking at the sky he had thought he might never see again.

Cynric yawned hugely. 'I had better get some sleep. The University Debate is due to start in a couple of hours, and I have been invited to earn a shilling by being a deputy beadle and keeping an eye out for pickpockets in the crowd. That is, unless you want me to stay with you,' he added suddenly, looking at Bartholomew anxiously.

Bartholomew smiled and shook his head. 'You will enjoy yourself at the Debate, so go,' he said. He looked up at the sky, and a thought occurred to him. 'I thought the Debate had been cancelled because of the plague.'

Michael sniffed. 'It is an important occasion with people coming for miles to listen. Why would the town cancel an event from which it can make money? What is the containment of the Death when there are goods to be sold, beds to be rented, and deals to be made?'

*   *   *

Bartholomew woke to darkness. At first he thought he was still in the cellar, but he was warm and comfortable and knew he was in his bed in Michaelhouse. He remembered leaving the window shutters open when he went to sleep – he had been in darkness so long that he felt shutting out any daylight would be a terrible sin. But the shutters were closed now. He snuggled further down under the bedclothes. Perhaps Abigny had closed them after he had gone to sleep; perhaps he had slept right through the day, and it was now night again.

He tensed suddenly. Someone was in the room with him.

'Giles? Michael?' he said, raising himself on one elbow.

There was a scraping noise, and a shutter was thrown open. Bartholomew gazed in horror at the victorious smiles of Swynford and Stephen, each holding an unsheathed sword.

'We have come for you,' said Swynford sweetly. 'We have decided upon the plan for your death and we have come to carry it out. Your escaping and returning here was no great problem, since we had decided to kill you here anyway. You merely saved us the bother of bringing you here ourselves.'

Bartholomew listened intently. It was daytime, but the College was strangely quiet. He could hear shouting, carried distantly on the wind. Swynford heard it, too, and cocked his head to one side.

'The University Debate at St Mary's Church,' he said. 'Always a lively affair. The entire College is there as usual, including your faithful Welsh servant. Giles Abigny is one of the leading participants this year – quite an honour for Michaelhouse; do you not think? Meanwhile, Brother

Michael has had a message asking him to meet the Bishop at the Carmelite Friary in Newnham, and, like a good lackey, he has gone scurrying off. When he arrives, he will find Master Yaxley waiting with a surprise for him. I had already suggested to Alcote that the servants be given the day off. After all, the scholars will be at the Debate, so why would servants be needed?'

Bartholomew was, once again, dazzled by the ruthless efficiency of these men.

'All the scholars and servants have gone,' said Swynford, re-emphasising his point. 'Except you, and the man who will kill you. The Bishop will arrive just in time to try to cover it all up with another tissue of lies. Of course, it will be much more difficult a second time, and questions will be asked in all kinds of circles.'

Bartholomew stared at him uncomprehendingly. 'Alcote!' said Swynford impatiently. 'Who has still not left his room, even though he is Acting Master. Two birds with one stone. A petty quarrel between two Fellows that erupts into a fight with knives. In the struggle, a lamp will be knocked over, and Michaelhouse will burn. Wilson gave me the idea for this,' he added conversationally. 'You and Alcote will die in the fire, as well as your patients in the plague ward and the monks caring for them.'

Bartholomew pushed the blankets back and climbed out of bed, keeping a wary eye on Swynford and Stephen.

'It is no good expecting a second rescue,' said Swynford. 'Jocelyn, out of kindness, took your patients a large jug of wine a while ago. He will ensure that they all drink some, including the Benedictines who are with them. By now, they should all be sleeping peacefully. It worked so well last time that we could not resist trying it again. In case they wake, he has locked the door of the room to make sure that none will come to cause us trouble.'

Bartholomew looked at them in disgust and reached for his gown. Swynford poked at his hand with the sword. 'You will not be needing that,' he said. 'Shirt and leggings are good enough.' He gave Bartholomew a sharp prod to make him leave the room and walk across the courtyard. Swynford was right. It was deserted.

Stephen took a grip on his arm to stop him from running away, and jabbed the point of the short sword into his side. 'I will use this willingly if you make more trouble,' he hissed. 'You have hindered our cause too much already.'

Bartholomew was marched across the yard and up the stairs to the hall. Colet was there already, pointing a crossbow at the petrified Alcote. A pathetic look of relief came over Alcote's face when he saw Swynford.

'This mad physician brought me here,' he began, and stopped short when he saw the sword Swynford held, and how it was pointed at Bartholomew. He put his hands over his face, and began to weep silently.

'It was Robert,' Bartholomew could hear him moan. 'Robert killed them all.'

Swynford set about preparing the room to make a convincing show of a struggle. He knocked benches over, threw plates and cups onto the floor, and ripped one or two wall-hangings down. When he was satisfied, he turned to his victims.

'Right,' he said, rubbing his hands together. 'Let me think.'

'Your plan is fatally flawed,' said Bartholomew.

The hand-rubbing stopped. 'Nonsense,' Swynford said, but there was hesitation in his voice.

'Alcote would never consider taking me on in a fight! Look at him! No one would believe that he would fight me.'

'True,' Swynford said. 'It would be an uneven match. He probably wounded you with a crossbow first,' he said, nodding to Colet, who raised the instrument and pointed it at Bartholomew.

'Even worse,' said Bartholomew. 'Everyone knows that Alcote cannot tell one end of such a weapon from another, and certainly would not be able to wind it and loose a quarrel at me before I could overpower him.'

'Well, perhaps he dashed your brains out with a heavy instrument,' said Swynford, growing exasperated.

'Like what?' said Bartholomew, gesturing round. 'A pewter cup? A piece of fish?'

'It really does not matter, Rob,' said Colet. 'So what if this all looks like the elaborate plot it is? Anyone working out what really happened will believe what we tell them – that the Oxford men are becoming bold again. What a formidable force they must be to sneak into the heart of a College and murder two of its Fellows in broad daylight.'

Swynford's face slowly broke into a smile, and he nodded.

'Come on, let us get it done so we can leave,' said Colet. He took a lamp from a table, lit it, and dashed it onto the floor. The rushes immediately caught fire, and Alcote screamed as the flames danced towards him. Bartholomew twisted suddenly and drove his elbow into Stephen's stomach with all his strength. Stephen gasped and dropped to his knees. Bartholomew kicked the sword away from him and leapt onto a table to escape a lunge from Swynford. Colet swung round and aimed the crossbow. Running along the table, Bartholomew felt the missile pluck at his shirt as it sped harmlessly by.

Colet began to reload, and Bartholomew dodged Swynford's sword, picked up one of Agatha's iron loaves of bread and hurled it as hard as he could at Colet. It hit him on the side of the head, stunning him sufficiently to make him drop the crossbow. Swynford stabbed at him again, entangling his sword in Bartholomew's legs.

Bartholomew, balance gone, toppled from the table, and landed heavily on the other side. Swynford leapt over the table and threw himself at Bartholomew, flailing wildly with the sword. The flames in the rushes licked nearer, but Swynford seemed to see nothing but Bartholomew. Bartholomew jerked his head away as the sword plunged down and heard the metal blade screech against the stone floor. He struggled violently, tipping Swynford off balance, and scrambled away under the table. He felt his leg gripped as Swynford seized him, and his fingernails scrabbled on the floor as he felt himself being dragged backwards.

Bartholomew twisted again and kicked backwards. Swynford's grip lessened for an instant, and Bartholomew scrambled under the table, clambering to his feet on the other side before Alcote crashed into him, knocking him down.

'What the hell are you doing?' he gasped, and then stopped as he saw Swynford totter forward holding his stomach.

'Damn!' Colet was already reloading the crossbow, ignoring Swynford's increasing bellows of pain as he concentrated on his task.

At the same moment, Stephen, seeing Swynford shot by Colet, bolted across the burning rushes towards the door. Right into the arms of Brother Michael.

'Watch Colet,' Bartholomew yelled. Colet had seen the flicker of movement out of the corner of his eye, and had heard Stephen's dismayed yell. He whipped round and pointed the crossbow at Michael. Bartholomew scrambled over Alcote and threw himself at Colet's legs. Colet toppled, and the crossbow fell to the ground. Colet desperately tried to reach it as Bartholomew fought to get a better grip on him.

Suddenly, Colet had a knife in his hand, and Bartholomew let him go as it swung down in a savage arc that would have pierced his eye had he not wrenched his head backwards. Colet shot away from Bartholomew and ran towards the servery door. Bartholomew raced after him, dimly aware that there were others entering the hall through the main entrance. Colet spun round, his face a mask of fury, and flung the knife at Bartholomew. It was a move born of desperation, and was nowhere near its mark. Bartholomew sprang at Colet, forcing him to the ground.

Almost immediately, he felt himself hauled up, and, thinking it was Swynford, lashed out with his fists as hard as he could.

'Easy! Easy!' Bartholomew became aware of his surroundings, and his intense anger faded as quickly as it had come. Colet, already in the custody of two burly beadles, looked fearfully at Bartholomew, his face battered and bleeding. Bartholomew was held in a similar grip by Michael and one of the Benedictines.

A loud snap dragged their attention away from Colet and Bartholomew.

'The fire!' yelled Michael, releasing Bartholomew's arm. 'Stop the fire!'

The flames had secured a good hold on the rushes on the floor and were licking up the wall-hangings. Bartholomew raced to drag them down before the flames reached the wooden ceiling. Outside, someone had started to ring the bell, and the hall filled with scholars using their black gowns to beat out the flames.

One of the students gave a shout, and, with a groan, the carved wooden screen behind the servery gave way, crashing onto the floor in an explosion of flames and sparks. More scholars poured into the hall, some from Michaelhouse, but many from other Colleges and hostels. Bartholomew and Michael quickly organised them into a human chain passing all manner of receptacles brimming with water from the well.

Bartholomew yelled to Alcote, flapping uselessly at some burning rushes with his gown, to evacuate the sick from the commoners' room. Bartholomew knew that once the fire reached the wooden ceiling of the hall it would quickly spread to the wings. Thick smoke billowed everywhere, and Bartholomew saw one student drop to the floor clutching at his throat. He hauled him down the stairs and out into the yard where he coughed and spluttered. Bartholomew glanced up. Flames leapt out of the windows and thick, black smoke drifted across the yard.

The plague victims were brought to lie near the stable where they were tended by Michael's Benedictine room-mates, one still reeling from the effects of the drugged wine. Alcote hauled on the College bell, and scholars and passers-by ran in to help.

Bartholomew darted back up the stairs to the hall.

William and Michael had affixed ropes to the wooden gallery and rows of people were hauling on them to pull it over. Bartholomew understood their plan. If the gallery were down, the fire would be less likely to reach the wooden ceiling and might yet be brought under control. He took an empty place on one of the ropes and heaved with the others.

The gallery, wrenched from the walls, tipped forward with a screech of tearing wood and smashed onto the stone floor of the hall. Men and women dashed forwards and began to beat out the flames. The hot wood hissed under a deluge of water, and gradually the crackle of flames began to relent. Eventually, all was silent, and the men and women who had answered the bell surveyed the mess.

'It was about time the rushes on the floor were changed anyway,' said Bartholomew. He had intended his remark for Michael's ears only, but in the silence of the hall it carried. The tense atmosphere evaporated, and people laughed. Disaster had been averted.

Agatha, who had worked as hard as anyone, sent people here and there with brushes, and ordered that burned rushes, tables, benches, and tapestries be thrown out of the windows. At Bartholomew's suggestion, Cynric fetched all that remained of Wilson's fine collection of wine, and scholars and townspeople alike fortified themselves for their work with wines that cost more money than most of them would earn in a year.

In the panic to control the fire, Bartholomew had almost forgotten Colet, Stephen, and Swynford. He made his way over to a small group of people who stood around a figure lying on the floor. William was kneeling next to Swynford anointing him with oil, and muttering the words of the absolution. Swynford's eyes were closed, and blood bubbled through his blue lips.

He opened his eyes when William's mutterings finished. 'The third Master to die in less than a year,' he said in a whisper. He looked around the group of people until he found Bartholomew.

'You are still alive,' he said. 'I was not sure whether Colet would get you. You have really confounded my plans this time. Another few months, and I would have been Bishop, and I would never have needed to step in this accursed town again.'

He closed his eyes then, and did not open them again.

Colet and Stephen had already been hustled away to the Castle when Oswald Stanmore, his face white with strain, sought out Bartholomew.

'Oh, God, Matt,' he said. 'What happened?'

Bartholomew could think of nothing to say, and made him sit on one of the benches that was not too singed and drink a cup of wine. Richard sat next to him, his face tear-streaked.

Stanmore sipped at the wine and then cradled the cup in shaking hands. 'He played me like a fool, Matt,' he said. 'He took my money, made me believe all Swynford's lies, and then tried to kill you. My own brother!'

Bartholomew rested his hand on his shoulder. 'What will happen to his wife and children?'

'Stephen and his wife had not been close for some time,' Stanmore said. 'She had been complaining about his absences during the night. I should have listened to her. Richard has offered to stay with her for a while at the house on Milne Street. There is plenty of room, so there is no reason she and the children should not stay. Also, Edith will help them as much as she can.'

'I will help, too,' said Bartholomew.

Stanmore nodded. 'I know you will. What will happen to him, Matt?'

Bartholomew did not know. He imagined there would be a trial, and there was enough evidence to hang them all. Michael told him that Stephen had started to confess everything before he was even out of the College gates, despite dire threats from Colet. On his evidence, the Sheriff and the Proctor would round up the others who had been involved.

'I am sorry, Matt,' sighed Stanmore. 'What a vile mess.'

'It is over now,' said Bartholomew. 'We both need to put it behind us and look to the future.'

'Yes, I suppose so,' Stanmore replied. Accompanied by Richard, he left to tend to his affairs. He was still not out of the woods, and there would be many questions to be answered and accounts to be examined before this business was over.

Brother Michael had been engaged in deep conversation with the Bishop in the solar. As Stanmore left, Michael poked his head round the door and beckoned Bartholomew over. The Bishop was wearing a plain brown robe, a far cry from his finery of the previous visit. He looked at Bartholomew's bruised hands. 'I hear you tried to give Master Colet his just deserts,' he said.

Bartholomew looked at Michael. 'I was stopped before I had really started.'

'Just as well,' said the Bishop. 'There has been enough murder in this College to last a century.'

'What happened?' Bartholomew asked Michael.

'How did you manage to arrive in the nick of time? How did you escape Yaxley?'

'I was sent a message, supposedly from the Bishop,' said Michael, 'asking me to meet him at the Carmelite Friary at Newnham. I saw nothing odd in this and assumed my lord the Bishop merely wanted me to provide him with the details of what I had learned before he arrived at Michaelhouse. As I walked, I heard St Mary's bell in the distance calling scholars to the Debate in the church and I suddenly realised I had made a dreadful mistake. We had already discussed Swynford's love of false messages, but I never thought he would dare to send me another.

'It became horribly clear. Me out of the way, perhaps heading into a trap, and all the scholars at the Debate. You are a heavy sleeper at the best of times, and I knew the bell would not wake you. Colet, who knows you well enough, would also guess you would sleep through the bell. I knew he was going to come for you, Matt, as you slept alone in the College. I ran back as fast as I could, stopping at St Mary's to raise the alarm on the way.'

'The Chancellor was none too pleased at being interrupted mid-argument by my yelling, but your Gray got the students mustered. When we came near the College, I saw smoke coming from one of the windows. I thought perhaps we were too late, and rushed up the stairs. I saw Colet kill Swynford by mistake, and then try to shoot me.'

He poked Bartholomew with his elbow. 'I saw what you did,' he said.

'What do you mean?' asked Bartholomew wearily.

'You saved me from Colet's crossbow. He could not have missed me from that range. I saw you knock him over.'

Bartholomew gave a soft laugh. 'Alcote did the same for me. The bolt that killed Swynford was meant for me, and he pushed me out of the way.'

The Bishop spread his hands. 'So, Michaelhouse Fellows risk their lives to save each other,' he said. 'Not all that has come of this is bad, and now you know whom you can trust.'

At last, thought Bartholomew, looking out of the window at the bright blue sky.

The Bishop stood to leave. 'These men have committed treason, and they will be taken to the Tower to stand trial. Stephen's willingness to confess in a vain attempt to save himself will ensure that they are all caught, and then the University – both hostels and Colleges – can begin again. I believe the Chancellor will need to make a visit to Oxford to explain what has happened, and to offer his abject apologies for blaming her for crimes of which she was wholly innocent.' He put his hand on Bartholomew's head. 'No secrets this time,' he said softly. 'Everything will be made known, from the murder of the Master of King's Hall fifteen months ago right up until the evil-doings of today.'

He went to the door, and then turned. 'Sir John Babington,' he said. 'He was no suicide, and can rightly be buried in the church. Shall I arrange that?'

Bartholomew thought about the revolting black effigy he had promised to have made for Wilson and shook his head. 'Sir John would prefer to be where he is, among the oak trees, and as far away from Wilson's glorious tomb as possible.'

The Bishop smiled. 'I believe you are right,' he said, and left.

Bartholomew and Michael sat in companionable

silence for a while, each rethinking the events of the past few days.

Michael went to look out of the window. 'The Death is still out there,' he said softly. 'Despite all that has happened, it is still there.'

Bartholomew stood next to him. 'And I still do not understand it,' he said. 'I still do not know why some live while others die, and I have no more idea how it spreads now than I did when it first came.'

'Perhaps there is nothing to understand,' said Michael, watching the Proctor organising his beadles in the yard for the arrest of the hostel men. 'Perhaps we are all doomed.'

'No, Brother. There are those that have remained healthy, like you and Agatha, and there are those who have recovered. We will survive it.' He shivered, and wondered whether he should ask Cynric to build a fire. He glanced through the open door where Gray and a few other industrious students were clearing the floor of debris, and decided that he had had enough of fires for one day.

'Matt!' Philippa exploded into the solar, followed more sedately by Abigny. 'Thank God you are safe! We saw the smoke coming from Michaelhouse, and I thought . . .'

Bartholomew rubbed his hands over his face, leaving smears of black. 'I owe you and Giles an apology,' he said. 'I misjudged you both, and Giles has saved my life.'

'Yes. I was there when Cynric came to him with his dilemma, and I told them the answer was quite simple,' said Philippa. 'I told them to enlist the help of Rachel Atkin and to go to see whether you and Michael were being held prisoner under Stephen's stables as she surmised. They were considering leaving it until tonight, but I said to go there and then. I would have gone myself, but I am not so foolish as to risk the success of such a mission merely to satisfy my own curiosity.'

Bartholomew stared at her wonderingly, and then hugged her, first gently, then harder. He could feel her laughing as she tried to catch her breath, and was reminded of how carefree they had been in the summer.

Abigny and Michael watched with obvious delight, and Bartholomew became embarrassed. Still with an arm across her shoulders, he spoke to Abigny.

'Thank you again for last night,' he said.

'Think nothing of it,' said Abigny cheerfully. 'All in a day's work for a philosopher.' He became serious again. 'I spoke to Elias Oliver on our way here. He is grief-stricken at the loss of his brother and aunt, and more than prepared to spill his heart. He says it was Henry who organised the riot, and Henry who tried to kill you in the lane. He also told me that both Wilson and Master Yaxley of Bene't Hostel were seeing the Abbess, although neither knew of the other.'

'Really?' said Brother Michael with gleeful fascination. 'Whatever next!'

So that explains how the blacksmith came to be paid with money in a Bene't Hostel purse, thought Bartholomew. It must have been Yaxley's, although it had been rash of Henry to pay the blacksmith with a marked purse. Perhaps he disapproved of his aunt's illicit relationships, and was hoping that Bartholomew would begin to suspect Yaxley. He remembered the blacksmith bearing down on Elias Oliver during the riot, and almost stabbing him in the process. No wonder the Olivers had glowered so, when they were almost victims of their own plotting.

'Elias also said that Wilson had been in quite a panic one night, saying that he feared the physician,' said Abigny. 'The Abbess and her two dear nephews thought he meant you, and that you were going to kill him. But by "the physician" Wilson must have meant Colet, not you at all.'

'And you had nothing to do with this University business?' asked Bartholomew.

Abigny looked at him as though he were mad. 'Me? Get mixed up with that crowd of calculating, power-hungry maniacs?' he said in disbelief. 'No fear! I have more sense, and frankly, Matt, I would have thought you had, too. I am appalled that you allowed yourself to become embroiled in such filthy matters.'

'One of the keys to the whole affair was the presence of the trap-door. If you think back to when we found Paul's body, it was you who suggested that there might be a secret door . . .'

Abigny laughed. 'That just goes to show, Physician, that you need a philosopher to sort out all your mysteries! So, I immediately lit upon the essence of the problem, did I? What an amazing mind I have.' He preened for a while. 'I do not even remember saying it,' he admitted. 'I was just throwing out ideas and trying to think through the thing logically. I had no idea the College was furnished with such devices, and if I did mention it, it was purely owing to my sense of logic.'

Bartholomew sighed. At last. All the loose ends had come together. One stupid error in all this was his assumption that Philippa's disappearance was connected to the University business, whereas the reality was that they were totally unrelated. There were tenuous links – Wilson and Yaxley sharing the Abbess's favours, Abigny's frequenting of Bene't Hostel – but that was all.

He held out his hand to Philippa, who took it and pressed it to her lips. He smiled at the black smudges that his hand left on her white skin, and tried to wipe them off. He only made them worse. Philippa began to giggle, and out of the corner of his eye, Bartholomew saw Abigny bundle a goggle-eyed Michael out of the room and close the door, leaving him alone with Philippa.

'Why did you not tell me you had been married as a child?' he said, recalling what Abigny had told him – some days ago, now.

'I thought you might not marry me if you thought I were a rich widow,' she said.

Bartholomew stared at her. 'Are you serious?'

She nodded. 'You told me so many times you did not want to treat rich patients for the money that I thought you might prefer a poor wife. The irony of all this silly mess was that I was thinking I would give all the property to the convent anyway,' she said. 'To please you.'

Bartholomew groaned. 'You will never believe the problems caused by my failing to understand what money means to people,' he said.

Philippa squeezed next to him on the window seat. 'So tell me,' she said.

EPILOGUE

I T WAS MARCH, AND ALTHOUGH THE PLAGUE STILL raged, and reports of enormous numbers of deaths remained common, Bartholomew felt that it was beginning to relinquish its hold on Cambridge. The death toll was lower than it had been in January and February, and, with the coming of spring, many felt a new hope.

Colet, Stephen, Jocelyn, Yaxley, Burwell, Stayne, and five others were taken for trial at the Tower of London. They were accused of treason for attempting to undermine the University, particularly King's Hall, which was endowed with royal money. All were executed at Smithfield, although the news of their deaths did not reach Cambridge until three weeks later. Oswald Stanmore was at London for the trial, and told Bartholomew that Stephen was fully repentant for his wrongdoings. Colet was less so, and sent Bartholomew a package. Inside was the golden lion. When Bartholomew explained its significance to Philippa, she dropped it in disgust, and walked away. Bartholomew looked at it for a moment and then followed her. The small child that found it lying in the mud in the High Street sold it to a passing traveller for a penny later that day.

The University began to settle back into the business of teaching. Although officially closed because of the plague, there were still students who wanted to learn, and scholars who wanted to teach. Bartholomew was as busy as ever, teaching, seeing his patients, trying to control Gray, and visiting Philippa, now living with Stephen's wife in Milne Street.

One bright day when the air was filled with the fresh smells of spring, masking even the stench of the river, Bartholomew and Michael walked to Newnham, Bartholomew to see to a wheezing cough, and Michael to persuade children to join his depleted choir. The sun shone, and the first lambs of the year gambolled about the fields. Michael and Bartholomew completed their business, and turned homeward. They walked in silence, enjoying the clean air and the feel of the sun through their clothes.

When they reached the small footbridge, Bartholomew stopped and looked down into the swirling waters underneath. Michael stood next to him, leaning his ample forearms on the handrail.

'Sir John's seal caused a lot of deaths, and it was basically worthless,' said Bartholomew.

Michael looked at him askance. 'What brought that up?' he said. After a while, watching Bartholomew drop blades of grass onto the water he said, 'The seal was nothing. It could only be used by Sir John for the King's business, and as soon as he was dead, the seal was defunct. It was given unwarranted significance by evil men for evil reasons. Sir John would have been horrified if he knew what trouble it would cause.'

Bartholomew reached into his pocket and handed something to Michael, whose eyes widened in shock.

'Where did you get this?' he asked in wonder, turning Sir John's intricate seal to the sun so he could look at it closely.

'Sir John gave it to me on the night he died,' said Bartholomew, 'although I did not realise it at the time.'

Michael gazed at Bartholomew in stupefaction. 'How?' he managed to ask.

'He must have slipped it into the sleeve of my gown,' said Bartholomew. 'You know how those sleeves are for us non-clerics? They are sewn up at the bottom, with slits for the arms half-way up. The ring was there for quite a while before I thought to look.'

'But what made you look?'

Bartholomew gazed over the meadows, edged with the pale yellow of primrose. 'Sir John did not leave it with Augustus, and it was not found on his body when he was killed. It *was* with him when we had dinner. I saw it on the cord around his neck. The only logical conclusion was that he must have given it to Swynford or Aelfrith when we parted after dinner. Sir John would not have given it to Aelfrith because Aelfrith was already involved and would be an obvious target, and I know he was always a little wary of Swynford. He often wondered why a man with Swynford's connections and wealth should deign to become a poor University teacher. Then I wondered whether Sir John had passed the seal to me. I searched through all my clothes, and there it was, lying in a corner at the bottom of my sleeve.'

'And Wilson accused you of being a poor logician!' said Michael, shaking his head and smiling. 'Now I think about it, it is the only obvious answer. Sir John trusted you above all the other Fellows, and would have been far more likely to give you the seal than anyone else. Thank God no one else thought the same, or you may have gone the same way as Augustus!'

'Sir John must have had some misgivings about his meeting that night, and decided to leave the seal behind.'

'Unfortunately, his misgivings were not strong enough,' said Michael sadly. 'If they were, he would never have gone to the meeting, and he most certainly would not have put you at risk by hiding the seal with you. And he would never have visited Augustus if he could have foreseen the consequences. I suppose he intended to recover it from you when he returned.'

Bartholomew scuffed some small stones from the bridge into the water with the toe of his boot and watched as they disappeared with tiny splashes. 'I think Sir John may have believed that the purpose of the meeting that night was to entice him out of the College so that his room could be searched, not so that he could be murdered. I think he knew that the person he was meeting would guess he would not wear the seal as usual because of the unusual circumstances of the rendezvous – during the night in a remote place. I expect he thought he would be able to retrieve it from my sleeve himself before anyone else had had the time to reason where he may have hidden it.'

'When did you work all this out?' asked Michael.

'When Wilson told me to find it,' said Bartholomew. 'I told no one, because I did not know whom I could trust, and I did not want anyone else to die for it. So, I kept my silence.'

Michael started to laugh, looking at the seal in wonder. 'You are a dark horse, Matt! So many people looked for this wretched thing, and all the time it was with you! Why have you chosen now to tell me about it?'

Bartholomew shrugged, watching the sunlight dance on the river. 'I have told no one else, not even Philippa.' He turned to Michael. 'I suppose I thought you would like to know.'

Michael held the ring between his thumb and forefinger and looked at it intently. 'Who would think that such a tiny thing would cause so much harm?'

'No,' said Bartholomew, 'the ring did not do the harm. The people who used it did.'

Michael was silent for a while, still looking at the small gold ring with its intricate knots and ties. 'So what are you going to do with it?' he asked.

Bartholomew sighed and turned his face up to the sun, his eyes closed. 'Give it to you, for your Bishop.'

'To me?' exclaimed Michael. He looked at it a little longer, then shook Bartholomew's arm to make him open his eyes.

'Watch,' he said. He pulled back his arm, and flung the ring as far as he could down the fast-flowing river. They saw it flash once in the sunlight before it dropped soundlessly midstream, and was gone from sight. They stood for a while, looking at the place where it had fallen, thinking about the people whose lives it had affected. Bartholomew gave another huge sigh and looked at Michael. Michael gazed back, the beginnings of a smile twitching the corners of his mouth and twinkling in his eyes.

'Come on, old friend,' he said, tugging Bartholomew's sleeve to make him move, 'or you will make me miss my dinner.'